NAMELESS

Jessie Keane was born rich. Then the family business
went bust and she was left poor and struggling in dead-
end jobs, so she knows both ends of the spectrum and
tells it straight. Her fascination with London and the
underworld led her to write the No.1 Heatseeker *Dirty
Game*, followed by bestsellers *Black Widow*, *Scarlet
Women*, *Jail Bird*, *The Make* and *Playing Dead*. She now
lives in Hampshire. You can reach Jessie via her website
www.jessiekeane.com.

JESSIE KEANE

NAMELESS

PAN BOOKS

First published 2012 by Pan Books
an imprint of Pan Macmillan, a division of Macmillan Publishers Limited
Pan Macmillan, 20 New Wharf Road, London N1 9RR
Basingstoke and Oxford
Associated companies throughout the world
www.panmacmillan.com

ISBN 978-0-330-53862-6

1 3 5 7 9 8 6 4 2

A CIP catalogue record for this book is available from
the British Library.

Typeset by Ellipsis Digital Limited, Glasgow
Printed and bound by CPI Group (UK) Ltd, Croydon, CR0 4YY

To Cliff
With all my love

ACKNOWLEDGEMENTS

There are so many people and sources that have assisted and/or supported me in the writing of *Nameless*. Thanks to Louise, to Judith, to Wayne, to Paul Norman at *Books Monthly*, to Lynne and Steve, to Karen and Paul.

Thanks too to Donald Thomas who wrote *Villains' Paradise: Britain's Underworld from the Spivs to the Krays*, and *An Underworld at War*, and to Helen Chislett for her *Marks in Time*, and to Fiona MacCarthy for *Last Curtsey*.

Thanks to all my fabulous Facebook and Twitter (find me on Twitter at realjessiekeane) friends and fans, who lift my spirits every single day. And thanks too to all the newsletter enthusiasts and the visitors to my website at jessiekeane.com. Thanks, guys!

Onward and upward!

PROLOGUE

1974

Ruby Darke found out the hard way that when you are about to die, your past life really does flash by in front of your eyes. She was working late in her office at her flagship store near Marble Arch in London. Her assistant Jane, who had been with her since almost the beginning of the Darkes department store phenomenon, had gone off at five with a cheery 'See you tomorrow'. Not realizing, of course, that she wouldn't be seeing Ruby tomorrow at all.

All afternoon, with total concentration, Ruby had been mapping out her ideas for the expansion of the childrenswear departments throughout the chain. She wanted to include more daywear. A fuller range of gorgeous party frocks. To call in a new designer for some fresh ideas to zap up the baby range, where sales were flat. And schoolwear. Why had Darkes never thought to do schoolwear?

Now it was getting late. Finally, Ruby stretched, stood up, locked her papers away. She gathered up her black cashmere coat and stepped outside. Rob looked up expectantly from his chair. Rob was her minder. Courtesy of Michael Ward, who was her lover and – not to put too fine a point on it – a big-time crook. She liked Rob, and found the young man's big, solid presence reassuring – but she hated the necessity of having him with her. Rob was in his mid-thirties. He had the muscled bulk of a rugby centre forward. Treacle-blond crew-cut hair. Watchful khaki-green eyes. And a minimal line in chat.

'Ready then?' she asked, forcing a smile. It wasn't *Rob's* fault she'd been threatened, after all.

He nodded and stood up, and together they went down in the lift and through the long corridor to the staff exit at the back of the store. They passed the night security guard, just coming on duty. Rob swung open the heavy fire door, and Ruby stepped outside ahead of him while he paused for a word with the guard. Slowly, the door swung closed and she was standing outside alone.

Ruby inhaled deeply, glancing around, blinking, trying to acclimatize her vision as she'd come from strip lighting to almost total darkness. The night was frosty, the air bitingly cold.

There was a motor running somewhere out here in the back alley; her car, with her chauffeur at the wheel.

It wasn't glamorous out here. Front of Darkes department store was immaculate, chic, polished and brightly enticing. She often paused outside the frontage of one or another of her stores to cast a fiercely proprietorial eye over the window displays to make sure that they were perfect. The staff quivered with nerves whenever she did this, or when she stalked in unannounced, as she liked to do. Service and quality had to be just so. She wasn't called the Ice Queen of Retail for nothing.

But here was the belly, the bowels of the store. Packing crates. Bins. Not much lighting. Big sliding warehouse doors for goods inwards and out.

Ruby shivered a little. The motor she could hear had been idling, but now – suddenly – it roared. Ruby glanced around, trying to locate the car she could hear. Ben, her driver, never drove like that. Her car was a sleek purring Mercedes, and Ben was old. Too old for boy-racer stunts.

'What the . . . ?' she wondered aloud, and then a set of headlights blazed on, blinding her with their glare.

The engine screamed.

The car was coming straight at her.

The noise was deafening, a high, shrieking whine. For a moment she stood there, frozen in place, disbelieving. When the car was nearly on top of her, she got her legs to move. She threw herself to one side. Felt herself being jolted and scraped as she hit the cobbles and rolled. She connected painfully, full-speed, with the back wall of the store, knocking all the breath from her body.

She crawled to her knees, dazed, disbelieving, and stared after the car that had – Jesus, so nearly! – mown her down. Its red tailgate lights were lit up like the eyes of a demon. It screeched to a halt twenty yards away.

Then white lights came on.

Reversing lights.

She saw a faint shadowy figure behind the wheel move, look back.

Heard the hurried crunch of gears.

The car shot back towards her, its exhaust steaming in the cold night air.

She was rigid with fear, unable to get to her feet. Her eyes were glued to the car that was going to crush the life out of her. And as she stared at it, the past unravelled in her head – a blurring kaleidoscope of love and loss, hope and death.

Rob wasn't there.

It had all been for nothing. She was never going to find the answers to it all.

She was going to die.

BOOK ONE

1

1941

Ruby Darke was eighteen the first time her dad's belt drew blood. It was a Sunday and as usual Ted Darke was maudlin and moody after a heavy Saturday night's boozing. Also as usual, he had been to church, clutching a tatty little bouquet of wild flowers to lay upon his wife's grave in the church cemetery.

Since his wife's death, all Ted wanted to do was pray to God and drink himself into a stupor. It didn't seem to occur to him that the benefits of one might cancel out the other. Ruby's eldest brother Charlie had gone to church with him, as always. They were mates together, Dad and Charlie, although Charlie wasn't really much interested in any sort of gospel – except the gospel according to Charlie Darke.

Dad and Charlie drank together, and held more or less the same views: that God helped those who helped themselves, and that the powers that be had never done them any favours – so they lived by their own rules and to hell with anyone else's.

Her other brother Joe was twenty-three, and he was different to Ted and Charlie. Big, quiet, strong as a bull. He had none of Charlie's fire and aggression. None of Dad's bone-deep belligerence.

Today when Dad and Charlie came back from the church it was obvious they'd stopped off at the pub on the way home. Their rolling gait and their loud-mouthed utterances made Ruby step very carefully around the place. She made the tea, keeping her head down.

She wished they'd stop going to the bloody church. Even more, she wished they wouldn't visit Mum's grave afterwards. It seemed like something Ted Darke felt he was duty-bound to do, but it depressed him; then he would stop at the Rag and Staff and get plastered. And come home and cuff Joe, big as he was, round the ear, and then lay into Ruby.

Ruby, most of all.

And of course she deserved it.

Didn't she?

After all, it was through her birth that Ted Darke had lost his wife Alicia, and his children their mother. He said so often enough, mostly while he rained blows down upon his daughter's cringing head.

'Why did the good Lord inflict you on me?' he'd wheeze, hobbling on his bad foot. 'God curse you!'

Ruby had asked once if she could go and visit the grave too. Dad had reacted with fury.

'You don't go near there, you bitch!' he'd yelled, and slapped her.

Because he was right, wasn't he? It *was* all her fault.

If she hadn't been born, her mother wouldn't have been lost.

She never asked again.

'Little black *cow*,' he spat at her.

Then he'd get tearful and ramble on, addressing Ruby sometimes and at others his dead wife. 'Why'd you do it, girl, eh? My lovely Alicia. You loved me once, I know you did . . .'

Not even Joe, big amiable Joe, dared intervene. And Charlie just sat there and sneered.

Sometimes Ruby stood in front of the mould-spotted mirror in her bedroom and repeated her father's words back to herself.

Little black cow.

But she wasn't black. Not really. The mirror told her that she was the colour of pale milky coffee, and her features weren't like those of what everyone around the East End of London called *coloured folk,* the ones who were fresh off the boat from warmer climes. Were those people mad? Given the choice, she'd have stopped in Jamaica – stuff this place. What with Hitler raining bombs down on their heads every night and the English weather, it was weird to consider that some people actually came here by choice.

No, she wasn't black. Her reflection told her that her nose was straight and almost delicate. Her lips were full, her eyes were dark but glowing with warm chestnut flecks. Her hair was wavy, but not tightly curled. She *wasn't* black. Not *full* black, anyway. In fact, she had heard really black people passing in the street, pointing her out, whispering she was 'high yellow' – whatever that meant. She was tall and well proportioned. She was *attractive*. But no one ever told her so. To her family, to all the people who lived around here, she was a curiosity; a misfit. The whites looked down on her, and the few blacks she'd come across eyed her with suspicion.

She wanted to shout back at her father, but the habits of the beaten and abused were too deeply instilled in her. So she took the beatings, the endless beatings, suffered the bruises – always on the body, rarely on the face; he wasn't a complete drunken fool, even though he behaved like one.

And she deserved it. Didn't she?

Because she was half-caste. *And* she'd killed her mother

by being born to her. She wasn't the same colour as Charlie and Joe. Not at all. They were white as pints of milk, both of them. She tried to work it all out, to make sense of it. But she couldn't.

There were no pictures of their mother anywhere in the house, not a single one. No one would explain to Ruby why she was dark and the rest of her family was pale-skinned. Not even Joe, who never treated her badly, who was out in the yard, in the privy when *it* happened. No one would say they had different mothers, or that the mother who had given birth to two handsome white boys had later indulged in some sort of dalliance that had resulted in a tar-brush 'mixture' like Ruby.

'Cross between a bull bitch and a window shutter,' her dad said of her, eyeing her with disgust.

But he'd kept her. Put a roof over her head, seen that she was fed and clothed.

Yeah, because I'm his burden, thought Ruby. *I'm the cross he has to bear, to make himself look good among those holier-than-thou old farts down the church.*

The whole thing boiling and fulminating in her mind, she kept her head down as always. Quiet, timid little Ruby. Tomorrow she would be in Dad's corner shop, helping out like she always did. Charlie and Joe never helped in the shop. She knew damned well they should have been signed up and over in France by now, doing their bit for King and country, but they weren't.

'It's the land of the greased palm,' Charlie would say with a grin. 'Pay a wedge and people soon look the other way.'

It seemed to be true. Charlie and Joe and the gang of hoodlums who had trailed around after them ever since school stripped lead and iron from emergency homes. They stole hurricane lamps used in the blackout to mark obstructions. They insinuated themselves into workplaces and then pilfered food and cigarettes from the canteens and sold them on to hotels at a profit.

Dad was unbothered by all this ungodly activity going on right under his nose. Charlie could do no wrong in Dad's eyes. But Ruby always felt uneasy at what Charlie and his gang got up to – it was always Charlie who was the instigator, never Joe – but you didn't snitch, you never did that. You couldn't grass up your family, not even if you despised them. It just wasn't done.

So Charlie, Joe and their boys ducked and dived, dodged around streets looting bombed-out buildings and flogging the proceeds far and wide. While she, the hated one, worked her arse off in Dad's corner shop, weighing out rations to moaning housewives.

She poured the tea – and then it happened.

The pot dripped from the spout. It always did, it was an old enamel pot and heavy; her arm trembled when she had to lift it. The scalding liquid fell on her father's leg, staining his best suit trousers, burning through to his skin.

'You stupid *bitch!*' He shot up off his seat, swatting at the wet place, his whole face suffused with redness as temper grabbed hold of him.

'Sorry! Sorry, Dad,' Ruby said hurriedly, putting the pot down. 'I'll get a cloth . . .'

'You've burned me, you silly mare,' he roared.

'Sorry! I'm sorry, Dad, really,' Ruby gabbled.

'You fucking well *will* be,' he said, pulling his belt from around his waist. Despite his bad foot, he could move horrifyingly fast. He lunged forward and whacked the strip of leather around her bare legs.

'No!' Ruby screamed. All the time she was aware of Charlie sitting there, grinning. Finding it funny that his sister was being beaten. Tears of humiliation and pain started to course down her cheeks. 'No!'

The belt was drawn back and whipped around her arms. The buckle caught her, tearing her flesh.

'What's going . . .' asked Joe, coming through from the privy, buttoning his fly. He saw what was happening and turned on his heel. He went back out into the yard. Ruby would always remember that.

The belt struck again, again, again.

Ruby cringed, saying, *Sorry, sorry, I didn't mean to do it,* and still the belt kept lashing her. The pain was awful, and blood was spattering down on her Sunday-best dress, the cornflower-blue one she loved so much. It would be ruined.

'Stupid little *whore*,' spat Ted, and then he was gone, lurching away from her, reeling out into the pantry to get to the sink and get the stain out of his trousers before it set.

In the sitting room, the only sound was Ruby sobbing.

Charlie stood up.

'Ah, shut yer yap,' he said, and slapped her, hard, across the face.

2

If Sunday had been bad, Monday was even worse. Ruby's arm was painfully sore when she dressed for work next day. She'd got the stain out of her favourite dress; that was the main thing. She couldn't ask Dad for a new one. Do *that,* and she'd get another hiding.

After she had made the breakfast and cleaned up the house, her and Dad walked around the corner to the family shop, her dad limping and using his stick today because his ulcerated foot was playing him up.

He'd had surgery for an ingrown toenail two years ago, and somehow it had gone wrong. Now he wore a slipper on his right foot, with the middle slit open to accommodate the swelling, and Ruby had to change the putrid dressings on it every couple of days. As they walked, she hoped that it hurt him a lot – as much as he'd hurt her.

The new emerald-green sign Dad had installed just a couple of weeks ago was there above the door. *Darke & Sons* was picked out in luxurious Gothic gold lettering.

Joe and even Charlie had laughed to see it.

'Jesus, Dad! A fucking bomb could gut the place any day,' Charlie chuckled.

'Sod Hitler,' grumbled Ted, affronted that his grand gesture had met not with praise but derision. 'You have to have confidence in this world, son. Believe that one day things'll get better.'

But Ruby couldn't even raise a smile. Charlie took the Lord's name in vain and never got a single word said back to him from Dad. And that damned sign: *Darke & Sons*. Not Darke and daughter. It was her, his daughter, who worked all hours in the bloody shop; the boys weren't expected to. They didn't show the slightest interest in its running. And she didn't believe that things would get better – what was Dad talking about? This was her life: the beatings, the feeling that she didn't measure up, that she would always disappoint and fail to fit in, fail to be what was expected of her.

'Caught one over in Brooke Road last night,' said her father as they walked.

Ruby shuddered. The sun was out, but the mention of the bombing raids that seemed to go on every night now made her feel chilled. Last night they'd had to hurry down into the Anderson shelter at the bottom of the garden when the siren sounded. The all-clear had come after an hour or so, and they had returned to their beds.

But this morning there was the scent of fire in the air, the smell of destruction. A pall of smoke lingered in the streets, mingling with threads of London smog. Ruby hadn't been able to get back to sleep after last night's raid; she'd lain awake listening to the fire engines racing around, imagining people blown apart, crushed, killed. The Darkes had survived, but some had not been so fortunate.

As they crossed the road to the corner shop, they could see all the way down to Brooke Road.

'Oh God,' said Ruby, staring.

Smack!

Ruby recoiled. Ted had cuffed her hard around the ear.

'You *don't* take the Lord's name in vain,' he snarled.

'Sorry, Dad, sorry,' she said, her head ringing from the force of the blow.

But her eyes were fastened on the scene down there. There were still-smouldering fires from the incendiary bombs. There was a crater where once a house had been. Rubble was piled up – chairs, fragments of beds, bricks with scraps of gaily coloured wallpaper still clinging on, drawers, broken bookshelves.

People were picking over the remains. An ambulance driver wearing a tin hat with a white-painted A on the front was pulling something out of a tangle of cables and dirt. It was a young woman's body, mangled and bloodstained. Two watching women, older women, set up a wailing and shrieking as they saw the body emerge.

'What the—' said her father suddenly.

Ruby jumped, flinching. She froze to the pavement. *What had she done?*

But her father wasn't raising his fist. He was running forward with his faltering gait, heading for the shop.

Ruby's heart was thwacking hard against her chest wall. For an instant, she'd been not only sick to see such horrors, but terrified. Anything made her jump, she was such a coward. A loud noise. The bombs falling. A dog barking, a sudden movement, a sudden sound. *Anything.*

Dad was limping full speed to the door of the shop and now she ran after him. The door was hanging open. She could see the wood had splintered away from the lock. Ted Darke fell inside and so did Ruby. He stopped dead in the centre of his small empire, and Ruby only just managed to avoid cannoning into his back and getting another thick ear for her trouble.

Ted was staring around. Sacks of flour had been kicked all over the floor. All the containers and bags of loose tea were gone. The two precious hams, which had hung so enticingly at the back of the shop above the till, were missing. So was the till itself. Piles of eggs had been upturned and smashed, making a sticky mess all over the floor. Most of the stock had been taken, but some of it had just been vandalized.

On the far wall someone had smeared in black paint: SHOULD HAVE PAID UP.

'What . . . ?' Ruby stared at the message. She looked at her father. 'What does that mean – *Should have paid up*? What for? Who to?'

Ted was breathing hard, red-faced. He turned, nearly knocking her flat as he went back outside the shop. Bill Harris, the insurance clerk who rented the flat over the shop from Ted, was coming out of the side door on his way to work. Ted caught his arm.

'D'you know anything about this?' he demanded.

Bill looked first annoyed and then scared. Ted was a big man, intimidating despite his disability. He looked furious, as if about to inflict damage. The little clerk's eyes flickered to the smashed door, the wrecked interior.

'No, Mr Darke. Not a thing.'

But he must have heard something, thought Ruby. She looked back at the wreckage of her father's shop. No one could do this much damage and not make a noise.

Ted released the man with a flick of the wrist. 'Is that so?' he asked, his mouth twisted in a sneer.

'Yes. Now if you'll excuse me . . .' The man hurried away.

'Don't want to get involved,' grunted Ted. 'Little *fucker*.'

'What does that mean, Dad?' asked Ruby. 'What they wrote on the wall? Paid up what? To who?'

'Will you *shut up* for a minute?' Ted shouted.

Ruby subsided. People were passing in the street, staring at them.

'This is that bastard Tranter's doing,' said her father.

Ruby's attention sharpened. She knew Tranter. Tranter

was a spiv, selling things on the black market and running a gang of boys who struck fear into many of the traders. He was a very influential man in the area.

'Did he ask you to pay protection money?' she asked.

Ted's big beery face came right up to hers and he bawled: *'Will you shut your filthy black mouth for one second, you cow?'*

Ruby cringed. People stepped around them. No one tried to intervene. No one ever did. She stared at the ruined interior of the shop, and could have cried. She'd stacked those shelves, lined up all the products so neatly, made everything shining and clean to tempt the customers. Now all her orderly efforts had been trashed overnight. Tranter had asked Dad for money and he had refused to pay it. And this was the result.

3

'You should have told me sooner,' said Charlie that evening, when he got home and Ted poured out the whole woeful tale.

This had been boiling up for a long time. Ted Darke had been leaned on – him and many, many others – to pay Micky Tranter money out of the till.

Ted shook his head, feeling sick with impotent rage. He'd wanted to deal with this himself, but he could see now that it was beyond him. He hated the thought of Tranter having a touch on his living. His own father had started the shop, and he'd carried it on. Times had been hard but he'd kept it going, long after his dad had bought it with a cripplingly hefty loan from the bank; now Ted's boys were grown up and he felt things ought to be getting easier.

He was hurt by their disinterest in his business. All he had was the girl, and she was nothing, an embarrassment; a painful reminder of life gone wrong. And now Tranter and his mob wanted a cut of his blood, sweat and tears.

Ted despised Tranter; most people did, even though they feared him. Greasy, smarmy bastard, oozing his way about the place with his fedora pulled low over his eyes and his swish camel-hair coat draped over his shoulders, smiling and patting people on the shoulder while his heavies followed him around ready to dole out punishment to anyone who failed to see things his way.

'I thought he'd leave it,' said Ted shakily. 'I refused to pay. I thought he'd back down.'

'Tranter?' Charlie shook his head. 'Not him. Thinks he's fucking invincible, he does.'

'He's wrecked my bloody shop. It'll be weeks before I can get it open again.'

Charlie stood up and paced around the room. Joe and Ted watched him from the kitchen table. Ruby was upstairs.

'I ain't having this,' said Charlie, and left the room. Joe snatched up his jacket and quickly followed him.

Charlie found Tranter and his boys in the Rag and Staff, and walked straight up to him. Without pausing in his stride, Charlie walloped the spiv straight round the chops.

Tranter's boys grabbed him instantly. The barman leaned over, anxious, and the punters scattered.

'Not in here, boys,' said the barman. 'Come on. Please.'

Joe stood there, a heaving mound of muscle, and thought that his brother had gone crazy. But he'd back him, because he always did. He pushed forward. Some of Tranter's boys grabbed him too, and held him still.

'Go on then, but why not act the big man proper, if that's what you are?' Charlie demanded of Tranter. 'Easy, picking on old men, ain't it? You did my dad's shop over, and I'm not having that.'

Micky clutched at his bleeding lip. Blood had splashed down his thirty-shilling Savile Row suit and he looked down at it in disbelief and distaste. Then he looked back at Charlie.

'You got nerve, doing this,' he said, very low, his eyes cold. 'You're the Darke boy, ain't you? Ted's kid?'

Charlie was struggling against the men who held him. 'You know who I am.'

'I know you been doing things on my patch without my permission,' said Tranter.

'Permission? I don't need your permission for fuck-all,' returned Charlie. 'Listen, you cunt, why not sort this out? Your boys and mine, back of the Palais tomorrow night. Let's see who's the real big man, shall we?'

Tranter stared at Charlie, veiling his surprise. So the kid had balls. He'd be wearing them for a neck ornament shortly, but you had to admire his gumption.

'Let him go,' he said to his heavies.

They let Charlie go. He stood there, panting, wondering what next. A knife in the guts? He didn't know. He was a marked man now, he knew *that*. Curiously, that didn't make him afraid – all he felt now was excitement. He was fired up, ready for a ruck. Joe was still being restrained, but he was watching, ready to wrestle himself free if he could, and jump whichever way was necessary.

'Back of the Palais?' Tranter was smiling a little through the blood. It gave him a shark-like look. He couldn't believe a small-time chancer like Charlie Darke had been foolish enough to cross him.

Charlie couldn't believe it himself. The impulse had just come over him and *whoosh*, there he was, up to his arse in it. As per usual.

'Back of the Palais it is,' said Tranter.

4

The following evening, Charlie Darke was out the back of the Palais with his mates and they were ready. Tranter always came here with his hangers-on and his muscle, Charlie knew it. He'd been watching the cunt and he had been brooding over what his dad had told him. He'd seen Tranter about, the smooth bastard, touching people for money because they were scared of him. Well, Charlie wasn't scared. And tonight he was going to prove it.

'All right, Joe?' he asked his younger brother, who was very quiet – quieter than normal, and that was saying something.

'Yeah. Still think this is fucking stupid though.'

Charlie gave his brother a half-smile. Joe would always err on the side of caution; his first reaction to any new experience was 'no' rather than 'yes'. Really, they couldn't be less alike. Charlie was impulsive and fiery, Joe so relaxed he was practically horizontal.

They didn't even *look* alike. Charlie was tall, thin, quicksilver in his movements and very good-looking with his dark curly hair and arresting blue eyes. Joe was blockish, square, slow-moving, a little dull with his brown eyes and straight dark hair – but he had a certain sensual charm.

'Shit, here we go,' muttered Charlie, seeing other shapes coming out now from the back of the big, quiet building.

The clear moonlight glinted on all the bike chains, cudgels and flick knives.

Charlie's boys formed up closer, Joe and Charlie at the centre front. Charlie's eyes were searching for Micky Tranter in his expensive hat and coat, but of course he wasn't there; Tranter rarely did his own dirty work, he was big enough now to pay others to do it for him.

He was making a point, deliberately insulting Charlie. Suddenly, Charlie felt like the small fry he was, kicking against the big boys.

And now here they were, all Tranter's toughs and the Darke mob, the same mob – Chewy, Ben, Stevie and all the others – who had been following Charlie and his little brother Joe around since their schooldays. The Darke boys were hard nuts, everyone knew that. All through school they had ruled the roost, Charlie flying into rages and cracking heads, Joe giving solid backup. Separately, they were safe, but together they were bloody dangerous, a lethal team. Charlie might be impulsive to the point of actual craziness, but Joe's more thoughtful demeanour usually kept both of them out of the worst scrapes.

It wasn't going to keep them out of this one.

Joe didn't know which way this was going to go. The numbers were fairly even – there were about twenty on each side. But Tranter's boys were experienced fighters. And although the Darke boys had youth on their side, Joe thought that experience could probably outweigh that.

Suddenly Charlie let out a bellow and all the boys surged forward. Joe followed. There were shouts, yells and a crashing impact as the two gangs converged. Chains swung and knives zipped through the air. Joe pummelled his way through the worst of it, swinging left and right with knuckledusters on one hand and a hammer in the other. There were bodies piling up. He was tripping over one bloke with his head stove in and falling forward, slipping on blood and *shit,* that was someone's ear, laid out like a wet fungus right there on the cobbles.

He righted himself, half-charged again, hit some cunt in the stomach and took him out. He'd lost sight of Charlie, but he was there somewhere, Joe could hear him screeching swear words at the top of his voice. Christ, sometimes Charlie even frightened *him*.

Now the brawl was thinning out. He looked around again for Charlie and he was there, leaping over fallen bodies and barging into the back door of the Palais. Joe followed, quick as he could. He knew Charlie was after Tranter himself, not this lot.

Joe felt a sharp stab of misgiving hit his guts. Charlie wasn't going to stop now, he was going to *have* that bastard Tranter. Joe followed, pushing past people who shouted things in his face, he didn't know what; his blood was up.

He charged into the bar area, and there they were: Tranter and Charlie, facing each other down. Now Tranter didn't look quite so cocky. He was cringing against the bar, watching Charlie as Charlie advanced on him, an old officer's dress sword from the Boer shindig held in his right hand.

'Now hold on,' Tranter was saying, his face white. There was no greasy shit-eating smile in evidence any more.

Take no prisoners, thought Joe. But Charlie wasn't really going to do it. Was he?

Joe looked around; there was no one about. No witnesses.

He turned back as the sword swooshed through the air, his mouth opening to say, Hold on, don't, come on, we've won, what's it matter whether he's still breathing?

Tranter's mouth opened too, on a hideous scream. The sword bit into his neck and a pulsing gout of blood sprayed. The silence was sudden as Tranter's head rolled from his body and fell onto the bar. There it sat, the eyes wide open as if surprised, the severed neck leaking dark blood onto the beer mats.

'*Shit*,' said Joe loudly.

Charlie just stood there, breathing hard, the headless corpse lying at his feet.

Joe forced himself to move. He grabbed Charlie's arm, grabbed the sword off him, tucked it under his coat. 'We got to get rid of all this,' said Joe.

'Yeah.' Charlie was staring at the corpse as if hypnotized.

It was Joe who moved first. 'Come on,' he said, and bent over the body.

5

'Sod *that* for a game,' said Betsy, throwing the sheet of paper irritably aside.

'Sod what?' Ruby asked vaguely.

'Working in a flaming shell-filling factory to help the war effort. Bevin wants volunteers. One pound eighteen shillings a week for a trainee. No thank you.'

It was late evening. The daylight was sneaking off to the west, and Venus the evening star was winking into life above them. Soon the raids would start again, and terror would descend. Searchlights would strafe the night sky as the anti-aircraft guns sought their targets, and the bombs would fall. With any luck they'd live through it, but they might not.

All this played on Ruby's mind a lot, since she'd seen the carnage in the next street. Dad was already in bed asleep, apparently unworried. But *she* worried, she really did. Tomorrow they might awake to see daylight once again, and see the big dome of St Paul's still looming over the smoking city like an unsinkable leviathan; or it might be destroyed, and them with it.

Something had changed in Ruby when she'd seen that young woman being pulled dead from the wreckage of her home. She'd felt all of a sudden that she was older, stronger – strong enough to see Dad for the pitiful wreck he really was. Day by day, a steel-hard core was growing in her. A determination that this would *not* be her life. It *couldn't* be. If she lived through all this, then one day she was going to break free. She just couldn't think *how*.

The two young women were sitting out in the backyard of Ruby's dad's little two-up-two-down in the East End, its windows taped up in case of bomb blasts. They were kicking their heels against the wall and discussing their prospective futures. They'd been doing this since they were ten years old in school together, and their ambitions still amounted to the same thing: get married. Have a big wedding. Start a family.

Ruby took a glance at the leaflet Betsy had discarded. A smiling woman was depicted there, arms raised against an orange sky, factory chimneys behind her, planes flying over-head. *Women of Britain,* it said at the bottom of the sheet, *Come into the factories.*

She could feel her heart sink just looking at it. Fucking Hitler. Life had seemed almost bearable once, but now look – most of the young men had gone off to fight, so that knocked the marriage bit on the head. And the big wedding? Might as well forget *that*. It would be a dress fashioned from parachute silk and a cake made out of cardboard – if you were lucky.

Still . . . one pound eighteen shillings was far more than she ever got in Dad's corner shop. There she doled out minuscule rations of butter, bacon and flour to bad-tempered housewives who sneered at her because of the colour of her skin. There she was groped by delivery drivers who thought she would be easy meat because of it. And now there was this *new* trouble.

That creep Micky Tranter had been demanding money off Dad. He'd trashed the shop. She'd cleaned the mess up and Dad had restocked as best he could. She didn't know what was going to happen. Would Dad pay up? Would Tranter back off? She hoped that Dad hadn't told Charlie about it all, because he'd flip and do something stupid, she just knew it.

She looked at the leaflet again. 'Pay's good, though,' she said to Betsy.

'Vi can earn five times that in an evening, not a sodding week,' said Betsy with a sigh.

Ruby was careful to keep her gob shut about that. Betsy's big sister Vi was, as some of the women around here whispered, 'no better than she should be'. She'd only met Vi a couple of times when she'd gone round Betsy's parents' house, and she'd been too shy to talk to her, but the memory had lingered.

To Ruby, Vi had seemed as exotic as a butterfly, sashaying nonchalantly around her and Betsy's shared bedroom in a peach-coloured silk robe, with her glossy dark-red dyed hair cut in a stylish short bob and her lips painted carmine red. Her eyes were the clearest, most luminous emerald green, shockingly intense. Ruby was fascinated by her, and that fascination was all wrapped up with unease because she knew what the people around here thought of Vi, she knew that Vi was *bad* – but she thought she was wonderful.

'You're not thinking of doing it, are you?' demanded Betsy, seeing her mate's distracted look. That was gentle, quiet Ruby: always dreaming, always with her head stuck in the clouds.

Ruby handed the sheet back with a shrug.

'You could do what Vi does down that theatre place,' said Betsy. 'You've got the looks.'

'Dad'd skin me alive.' Ruby looked Betsy square in the eye. 'Why don't you do it?'

'Ain't got the legs, have I?' Betsy pouted down at her short but attractive pins.

Ruby looked at Betsy. Her friend was pretty, with her kittenish heart-shaped face, pale green eyes and thick wavy strawberry-blonde hair. Ruby often thought that Betsy was like a watered-down version of Vi. And she wished she could be small and dainty like both Vi and Betsy were, instead of long-legged, big-breasted and dark-haired – and with an arse you could balance a pint of beer on.

'Josephine Baker danced in Paris in nothing but a skirt made out of a bunch of bananas,' said Betsy.

Ruby frowned. She was very sensitive about her colour, and Josephine Baker was black. 'So what? You think I'd want to do the same?'

'No, of course not. But just think about it. You got options in your life. Me, I couldn't do it. You, you could. You don't have to go on working in a corner shop all your life; I ain't got much choice.' Betsy stared morosely at the sheet of paper again. 'I might do this,' she sighed.

'Yeah, or you might not,' said Ruby. Betsy was always getting 'inspirations', and trying – and failing – to whip Ruby up into a frenzy over them. Work in an explosives factory. Become a land girl and dig turnips all day. Go dancing at the Windmill, for God's sake! The list went on and on.

Betsy grinned at her mate and flung the paper into the air. The strengthening breeze caught it and whipped it away, out into the alley. At the same moment the back gate was thrown open, and Charlie and Joe fell through it, covered in blood.

'You don't tell no one about this,' said Charlie.

Ruby nodded dumbly. It had been a hell of a shock, seeing them like that. Both girls had shrieked in surprise as the boys tumbled through the gate, and Joe had quickly told them to shut up, daft cows, the blood wasn't *theirs*.

'Then who the hell's is it?' asked Betsy, watching Charlie as he stripped off his coat and his jacket and then his shirt beside the yard tap. There was blood all over his arms and chest, but it was true what Joe had said, it wasn't his own.

Charlie was scrubbing himself, splashing the water over his torso. Pink water was running off him onto the yard. The metallic scent of blood was strong in the air and his chest and arms rippled with hard muscle.

He glanced up at Betsy and she blushed. Betsy had never said as much, but Ruby knew she'd had a terrible crush on Charlie for years. Charlie was always polite to her, but – until now – dismissive. She was his kid sister's pal, little more than a kid herself.

But now Ruby saw something pass between her big brother and her friend. Ruby went into the lean-to and came out with a towel. Charlie stood drying his chest and arms with it, while Joe started stripping off. Charlie's eyes were on Betsy and he was smiling faintly.

'Nobody gets to hear about this,' he said again, staring straight into her eyes.

'No! 'Course not,' she said, staring back as if hypnotized.

Joe went over to the privy and put something inside the door. Then he came back to the tap, and started sluicing the remnants of the evening's entertainments off himself. Ruby and Betsy sat silent now, their heads full of questions they would never ask. But Ruby remembered the scene later, and thought: *Yeah, that was when it all started to happen.* That was just about the time that Micky Tranter turned up dead on a bombsite. That was when the Darke boys became a force in the East End.

6

In the midst of war, the police didn't seem to care much about the disappearance of a rat like Tranter. There had been another gang fight. More casualties. So what? A few days later, Tranter himself was found under a pile of bricks on a bomb site far from where the fight took place, his head severed from his body, maybe by a pane of glass. The rozzers had no reason and little time to question it. They had enough on their plates without getting into all *that*.

Tranter's funeral was low-key. He left a wife, who everyone knew he duffed over on a regular basis, so she must have thought all her Christmases had come at once now she was rid of the bastard. She was childless, but not exactly penniless, although word on the grapevine was that she was pretty near it. Tranter had pissed all his money up against a wall, indulged himself, he hadn't been saving for his old age. And just as bloody well, Charlie joked on the day they buried him, because look what happened!

The remnants of Tranter's boys had scattered. Now it was the Darke brothers who took charge of the bomb-ridden streets, and Charlie saw it as his first solemn duty to visit the grieving widow, bung her a few quid and reassure her that she would be looked after.

'Gang money?' she asked him, looking him over and clearly finding him wanting.

Charlie was a handsome man. Dressed in a black over-coat with a Homburg hat in his leather-gloved hand and his curly hair slicked into submission by Brylcreem, he looked the part of the boss now.

'I don't want your dirty money,' she said, but she left it there on the table where he had placed it and went to put the kettle on. Out in the scullery, she ran the water into the kettle and came back into the kitchen to place it on the gas. Then she looked at him. 'I suppose it was you?'

'Me? Me what?' asked Charlie, but he knew.

'You killed him?'

Charlie shrugged, said nothing.

A wry smile twisted her face. She was around thirty-five, not exactly ugly but no beauty either; she looked forty if she was a day. Only her ginger-brown eyes retained any vestige of spirit. The years of marriage to Tranter had taken their toll.

'Not saying much, are you? Well, if it *was* you, all I can say is thanks. You did me one fucking big favour,' she said. She glanced down at the money on the table. Then her eyes met Charlie's again. 'Don't get like him,' she said. 'Don't ever get like him.'

'I won't.'

'Yeah, you say that. Fat chance. It changes a person, you know. People creeping around frightened of you, it twists you after a bit. Makes you feel the power you got. Then you abuse it. And then *it* abuses *you*.'

After he'd visited the widow Tranter, Charlie met up with Betsy in the street.

'Oh – hello,' she said, colouring up like she always did when she saw him.

'Hello,' said Charlie with a smile, thinking that she was sweet, and tiny, with her Betty Grable pinned-up curls and the lines drawn up the backs of her shapely little legs with gravy browning to make it look like she had stockings on. He'd bung her a few pairs, he could lay his hands on just about anything. She'd love that. He liked her smallness. Made him come over all protective. He thought briefly of Mrs Tranter. She was a *dog*, compared to Betsy. 'Glad I caught you. I wanted to talk to you.'

'Me?' She was looking at him as if he was God Almighty. And he liked that too.

'Yeah, in private.'

'What?'

'Over here,' he said, and guided her into an alley.

'What about?' Her cheeks were flushed bright red now.

'This,' said Charlie, and kissed her. His tongue went into her mouth and Betsy let out a strangled squawk of surprise.

Charlie drew back. The Tranter woman was, annoyingly, there in his head again. What was he thinking about that tired old mare for, when he had *this* on offer?

'Come on, you can't say you haven't been expecting this?' he smiled.

'Well, yes. No. I didn't. You just . . . startled me,' said Betsy, but she was smiling back at him. This was great. This was *Charlie Darke*, and he was a big noise around here now, everyone knew it. And he was kissing her!

'Come on then,' said Charlie, and kissed her again, and his hands were quickly inside her blouse and then inside her bra, touching her nipples, teasing them into hard little points. Hot bolts of sensation were shooting down from her breasts to her groin, and she moaned at the sweetness of it. It felt so nice, but when his hands roamed lower, she stiffened in shock. She wasn't *that* sort of girl; did he think she was?

'Charlie . . .' she struggled to say, but his tongue was in her mouth again and now he was tugging her panties down.

'You want it,' he gasped. He'd felt worked up ever since that run-in with Tranter, he needed this. 'Don't you? I know you've always fancied me. And don't be afraid, I'll look after you.'

'You mean get married, be together?' she said, her eyes frantic and feverish on his.

'Yeah,' said Charlie, pushing his fingers between her legs. That felt good too, so good Betsy could hardly bear it.

Then he was unbuckling his belt, unzipping, his cock springing out. Betsy glanced down and was shocked by the size of it. She'd never seen an erection before.

Jesus, I'm going to be Mrs Charlie Darke, she thought.

He was lifting her up, her thighs clamping onto his waist as he guided his penis into her wet opening. He brought her down onto it, sliding in deep, and Betsy let out a small cry.

'OK?' Charlie panted, already thrusting.

'Yeah,' said Betsy, and let him do it. Somewhere in the back of her mind she thought, *This ain't romance, is it? Is this what it comes down to, him rutting at me down a bloody alley, like a dog covering a bitch?*

But if it meant being Mrs Charlie Darke, she would tolerate it. Men were beasts, her mum had always told her that, and here was the proof. But it seemed, after all, to be making him happy. She just hoped he wouldn't take too long over it.

7

On the same day that Joe took the sword that had been the death of Tranter and threw it in the canal, Ruby was at Betsy's house, up in Betsy's bedroom, the room she shared with Vi. Betsy's side of the room was girlish. She still had her teddy bears and old dolls propped up on the bed.

But Vi's side . . . well, Ruby just loved wandering over there, looking at all the powders and perfumes Vi had on her dressing table. There was a copy of *London Life* there too, with three flimsily clad Windmill beauties on the front cover wearing gas masks to encourage ARP drill.

'The one in the middle's Vi. And don't touch anything,' said Betsy, who was reclining on her little bed by the wall, watching Ruby with a smile.

'What?' Ruby turned round with a guilty start.

'Vi thinks she's the queen or something. She don't like people touching her stuff.'

Ruby nodded and moved away from the heady environs of Vi's territory.

'Don't your mum and dad mind, Vi working at the Windmill, showing her bits . . . ?' asked Ruby, curious.

Betsy gave a derisive grunt.

'Vi calls it "art". And you know Dad's always at work in the docks. He don't take no notice of nothing. Mum don't tell him what Vi's up to. She's got no say in it anyway. Vi does what she pleases, she always has. Rules apply to other people, not her. Mum's a bit of a mouse, you know. And Vi's a bloody tiger.'

Even if Vi seemed terrifying, Ruby envied Betsy, having a sister – and such an exotic one too. Being the only sister of two older brothers wasn't any fun at all. In fact – what with Dad being ill with his foot and bad-tempered all the time and Charlie kicking off at her – it was a pain in the arse. And Charlie and Joe's behaviour frightened her lately.

It seemed to Ruby that her brothers had changed in the months since they'd run into the backyard soaked in someone else's blood. Before that, they had been, well, just Charlie and Joe, dead-legging about the place, dodging the draft – Charlie with an imaginary 'heart murmur', Joe with 'flat feet' – and doing a few iffy deals.

Now, they had acquired a new aura; people – even their own father – spoke to them more respectfully. They dressed immaculately now, and expensively. It was wartime, for God's sake, everyone was skint; but Charlie and Joe Darke had an air of prosperity about them.

It worried Ruby. She had strong memories of Tranter oiling his way around the bomb-damaged streets, doling out smiles and smacks. Something in the way Charlie and Joe conducted themselves now reminded her of him.

Still, it wasn't her business. Best to keep her nose out and her head down.

'What you two doing up here?' asked a purring female voice, startling Ruby out of her thoughts.

She turned – and there was Vi. She was struck anew by how stunning, how *distinctive*, Vi's style was. She was dressed in a well-cut dark-green coat, which she now pulled off and tossed casually aside to reveal a chic, cleverly cut grey dress that wouldn't have looked out of place on a twenties flapper.

Vi just *oozed* charisma.

'I live here,' said Betsy chirpily. 'And Ruby's visiting. You not working today?'

'Not today. Tomorrow. Unlike you, I *do* work. I do my bit for the war effort.'

'Prancing around on a stage ain't work,' scoffed Betsy.

'Try it,' advised Vi, sitting down at her dressing table, taking up a hairbrush and applying it to her shiny dark-red bob. 'It's work, all right, I promise you. Van Damm's a slave driver.'

'I thought that place might close down, with the war,' said Betsy, watching her sister with a sour little smile as Vi pouted and preened in the mirror.

'We never close,' said Vi.

'It can't help the war effort, doing what you do.'

Vi turned her head and sent Betsy a pitying smile. 'Don't be daft, 'course it does. Keeps the boys cheerful, don't it?'

'Cheerful? That ain't what *I'd* call it.'

'As if you'd know,' sighed Vi, turning her head this way and that, picking up a lipstick, touching it briefly to her lips.

'Oh, I know *plenty*,' said Betsy.

Ruby was watching Vi, too fascinated to look away. Vi was so beautiful, she even *smelled* beautiful, of sweet Devon Violets. There was a little round bottle on her dressing table, containing liquid of a brilliant acid-green and with a tiny violet silk bow tied around its stubby neck. According to Betsy, she never wore any other perfume.

Vi's brilliant up-slanted eyes met Ruby's in the mirror. Then they moved down, over her body. Vi put the lipstick down and turned to eye Ruby assessingly.

'Can you dance?' she asked.

'Well, I . . .' Ruby was caught off guard. 'A bit.'

Vi's eyes were still on her. 'You look . . .'

Ruby froze. She knew what was coming.

'Well . . . dark, maybe. Just a bit. You've got that big arse, and your lips . . . you got a touch of the tar brush, baby?'

'Vi! You can't ask her that,' Betsy intervened, her eyes moving between her sister and her friend. 'Look, she had lessons before the war, before the old dance hall got bombed out. We both did,' said Betsy. 'You remember.'

Vi might not have remembered her sister and her little mate going for ballroom dancing lessons, but Ruby certainly did. She'd pleaded to be allowed to go, and Dad had finally let her. Ruby remembered the embarrassment of realizing the neat little sailor-suit ensemble she had stored up especially for the lessons made her look like a gink, and oh, the crucifying humiliation of discovering that she was taller than every single boy in the class. Some of them had called her *Darkie* – such a witty play on her name – and she had cried and thrown up in a hedge on the way home.

'Well, the dancing don't matter much. They're always looking for new girls, girls with that certain something . . .' Vi hesitated, then turned away, back to the mirror . . . 'You're a looker, all right. But maybe you haven't got it. Think about it, though. We could all be dead tomorrow. Bombed to fuck.'

''Course she's got it. Look at her, she's *gorgeous*,' piped up Betsy.

Shut *up*, Ruby mouthed at her.

'Well, you can come along with me tomorrow,' said Vi. Her eyes met Ruby's again. 'That's if you're interested . . . ?'

Betsy was silent.

'But the shop . . . What'll I tell Dad . . . ?'

'Tell him you're volunteering or something.' Vi shrugged.

'I can do a turn in your dad's shop, stand in for you,' piped up Betsy. Anything that brought her closer to Charlie's orbit was absolutely fine with her.

Ruby hardly dared even consider it. She had seen the WVS ladies about in the bombed-out streets, proudly wearing their green uniforms and their silver-and-red lapel badges bearing the legend WVS above the words 'Civil Defence'. They provided food, blankets and clothing for homeless families, and worked all hours running the local salvage centre, all instigated by Lord Beaverbrook.

'I . . . suppose I could say I was doing salvage voluntary work at the centre, it's just down the road,' said Ruby.

The thought of going anywhere with the fabulous Vi was daunting, but my God! What would Dad and Charlie and Joe think if they ever found out the truth? They'd hit the roof.

'Your dad would like you volunteering,' said Vi. 'He's a churchgoer, isn't he? He'd think of it as an act of Christian charity.'

Ruby considered this. It was true, what Vi was saying. And there was less chance of him pounding her if she could keep out of his way during the day.

'Think of that bleeding shell factory,' said Betsy. 'Would you rather be doing something like *that*?'

'I don't know . . .' Ruby didn't relish the prospect of change the way Betsy did; she never had. But she was bored, and unhappy, and Vi was right: they could all be dead tomorrow. Probably *would* be, the way things were going.

'Well, make your mind up, girl,' said Vi. 'What's it to be, yes or no?'

Ruby looked at Vi. Thought of her boring, routine life and had a whiff – just the tiniest whiff – of the life she *could* be leading. If she dared.

'I don't know . . .' said Ruby.

'Jesus, you're wet,' said Vi with a sharp sigh. 'Think it over. We'll meet up outside the Windy. Monday at ten. That'll give you time to get your story straight. If you're not there, I'll know you're not interested.'

8

After Ruby left Betsy's she had an hour or two to spare before she had to get the tea on, so she wandered down to the church. There were a lot of new graves there, casualties of the war, with soil piled up on them. The misty rain was spoiling the petals on the floral offerings, smudging the ink on the small poignant cards left on the new graves by loved ones.

Ruby walked around the graves, looking at the headstones. She didn't know exactly where Mum's grave was. She had never been privileged with that information. Only Charlie and Dad and occasionally Joe ever came here; she was never invited.

She ended up at the cluster of older graves, right over in the far corner, shaded by ancient yews. It was cold here, and the grass was spongy with moss. She looked around nervously; she didn't want anyone spotting her. She didn't want word getting back to Dad or Charlie that she'd been here looking for the grave. But there wasn't another soul around.

And . . . there it was. The wording on the headstone seemed to leap out at her.

Here lies Alicia Darke
Beloved wife and mother
Sadly missed

There was nothing else, except the date of Alicia's birth, and the date of her death, which was the twenty-ninth of July 1923 – the day after Ruby's birth. She stood there staring at the headstone and felt tears spill over. In giving life to her, Alicia had forfeited her own. And for what? So that her daughter could live caged in by fear and guilt?

Ruby couldn't believe her mother would have wanted that for her. She thought of Vi, and the Windmill. Of what it must be like: the excitement of theatre life, the bright lights and the gaiety of it. Her own world was dull and troubled by comparison. She had never been inside a theatre, or even a cinema. There had never been culture, or even much laughter, in the Darke household.

But she couldn't do it . . . could she?

No. She couldn't.

She couldn't lie to her father; that wouldn't be a Christian thing to do, would it? But then . . . was his treatment of her all that Christian? She didn't think so. It wasn't *her* fault her mother had died, it wasn't something she could have prevented, any more than she could change the not-quite-acceptable colour of her skin.

Ruby turned away from her mother's grave; far from being comforted by coming here, she felt sadder and even more bewildered than she had before. She walked home in the gently falling rain. Nearly time to get the tea on.

Joe was cleaning his shoes in shirtsleeves and braces at the kitchen table when she got back home. Flanagan and Allen were singing 'Underneath the Arches' on the radio and Joe was whistling along to the tune.

'Where's Dad?' asked Ruby, coming in and taking off her coat. This was always her first question. She wanted to know where Dad was, know where any new threat was going to come from.

Joe stopped whistling and looked at her. 'Went up to bed early. You'll have to take him up his tea on a tray. Foot's playing him up.'

'And Charlie?'

'Out. Tea in the pot, if you want it.'

Ruby sat down and poured herself a cup. She sat there, looking at Joe.

'What is it?' he asked, glancing at her, buffing the black leather to a high shine.

Joe wasn't a bad sort, not really. Ruby had always believed him to be a cut above her dad and Charlie. He'd never laid a finger on her, there was that to say in his favour. Even if he never intervened, at least he never *participated*, unlike Charlie.

Still, Ruby had to force the words out of her mouth. 'About Mum . . .' she said.

Joe looked taken aback. Then he spat on his shoe and went on rubbing at the leather.

'What about her?' he asked, not looking at her face.

'Do you remember her at all?'

Joe's big stubby hand stopped rubbing. He looked up at her. 'No,' he said. 'I don't.'

'Only,' Ruby went on in a rush, before her nerve failed her, 'you were five when I was born. I just thought . . . if you remembered anything, I'd like to know.'

'I don't remember a thing,' said Joe, his jaw set. 'Drop it, will you?'

'But Joe . . .'

'I said *drop* it,' he snapped, his eyes suddenly fierce. 'Didn't you hear me? And don't ever be daft enough to ask Dad or Charlie about it, or you'll get a right hiding.'

Ruby was going to bed that night when Joe stopped her on the landing.

He hesitated, glanced left and right, then spoke. 'She had

37

a gramophone. A Maxitone Dad bought her. It had an oak case,' he said. 'She used to play jazz music on it. Jelly Roll Morton, you heard of him? And Fats Waller. *Nigger* music, Dad called it. And she was pretty. Blonde. I remember that.' He paused. 'Dad smashed the Maxitone. I remember that, too. Now get off to bed.'

9

1922

Alicia Darke was crossing the road to the corner shop when she saw him for the first time. He was young – younger than her, she thought – and very black, with the loosely muscular way of standing his kind so often displayed. He was outside the shop talking to two other black men, and all three turned and looked as she passed by.

Alicia was a little surprised to see them there. All around these streets, the hotels and guest houses displayed signs in their windows that said No Irish, No Coloureds. *They weren't welcome here, they were viewed with suspicion.*

She kept her head down, but she heard one of them say: 'Hey, sweetness,' and she glanced up, ready with a sharp retort.

She looked up, straight into his face. His skin had the grain and polish of finest ebony, his nostrils were flaring, his eyes dark as night, his mouth broad and very sensual. When he smiled at her – he was smiling now – his whole face seemed to light from within.

Alicia felt herself blushing. She was a married woman, wed seven years to Ted Darke. He was much older than her, but her mum and dad had been impressed by his prospects; Ted had his own shop, inherited from his parents. He was a man of substance. And Ted had been kind to her, attentive – at first. Now she worked day in, day out in the corner shop, lugging stuff up from the cellar to line the shelves – and then at home, scrubbing and polishing, white-leading the doorstep, polishing the brass, while their kids – little Charlie and Joe – went to school, and Ted sat back, counted the takings, and did fuck-all.

But still, whoever said marriage was going to be perfect? She was a married woman – and this stranger was black. *She didn't answer him. She hurried on into the shop.*

He was there again the next day when she went to open up, on his own this time. She saw him loitering by the shopfront as she crossed the road, fumbling for the keys.

'Hi,' he said.

Alicia looked at him nervously. 'Hello,' she said, fiddling with the keys, getting the damned thing into the lock with fingers that suddenly felt stiff.

'How are you?' he asked, turning towards her.

'Fine.' The key wasn't working. She'd put it in upside down. She righted it, feeling hectic colour rising in her cheeks. 'Where are your friends?' she asked, for something to say.

'Working.'

Alicia was still having trouble with the lock. Working? According to Ted, black men were lazy scroungers, they didn't work. But then Ted had strong opinions on nearly everything, and she'd more or less stopped listening to them now. Ted wasn't exactly the fastest things on two legs, himself.

'What do they do?' she asked, not wanting to be rude by ignoring him. At last, the door swung open.

'A little jammin', you know.'

Jammin'?

'What's that?' she asked, curious, looking at him fully for the first time.

He was very elegant, wearing the new fashion in trousers – Oxford bags, they were called – and a brown jacket. He was *holding a black bowler hat in his hand; he'd removed it as she drew near. She noticed that his shoes were snazzy two-tone brogues.*

'We're musicians,' he smiled. 'We're renting a place just over there.' He pointed across the street. 'We hang out, we jam, you know.'

Alicia didn't know. She was just amazed that someone around here had let rooms to three black men. They must be really strapped for cash, whoever they were. And what he'd just described sounded like . . . like fun, and she had very little experience of fun in her life.

'What do you play then?' she asked.

'Trumpet,' he said. 'You ought to come over and hear us play.'

'I have to go,' she said, and yanked the key out of the lock and went on into the shop.

'I'm Leroy,' he said, and held out a white-palmed hand. 'What's your name?'

Alicia looked at his hand and, not wishing to be rude, she shook it reluctantly. 'I'm Mrs Ted Darke,' she said.

'No – I mean your name.'

'Alicia,' she said, and went inside and closed the door.

10

It was nothing fancy. That was Ruby's first thought as she stood outside on Monday at ten in the morning and waited for Vi to show up. The Windmill Theatre stood on a corner of a block of buildings where Archer Street joined Great Windmill Street, just off Shaftesbury Avenue, and it was very plain, nothing to write home about.

'You came then,' said Vi with a slight smile as she joined Ruby by the front steps.

'Yeah,' said Ruby, her mouth dry with apprehension.

She'd lied to Dad, told the absolute whopper that she was starting work in the salvage centre. And he'd swallowed it, to her surprise. It was for charity, and as a churchgoer he had time for that.

'It ain't the Moulin Rouge, is it?' she said.

Vi led the way around the side of the building to the stage door. 'You ever *seen* the Rouge?' she asked.

'Well, no . . .'

'Well no. Thought not. Let me tell you it's every bit as good as the Rouge. We have *tableaux vivants* and everything.'

Tableaux vivants?

Vi caught her puzzled look and gave a quick, feline smile. 'You'll see.'

Ruby wasn't even sure she wanted to. But she'd agreed to this, God help her. She'd *lied* to be here. She hurried after

42

Vi and they stepped inside into chaos – or that's how it seemed to Ruby.

'Hello, Gord,' Vi said to a man behind a counter just inside the stage door.

He nodded.

Vi hurried on, past surging hordes of people in glitter, in feathers. There were pretty girls, tall boys with painted eyes. Ruby stared around, open-mouthed. Vi's Mary-Jane shoes beat out a tattoo on the wooden floorboards as she surged ahead. She shot down a set of stairs with Ruby trailing behind.

'We're open from midday to ten fifty at night. Continuous performances, five or six a day, one right after the other,' Vi threw back over her shoulder.

'Apart from during raids,' said Ruby.

'No, we don't close. Fuck Hitler. We *never* close. Below street level, see. Safe as houses.' She came to a halt. Ruby could hear a girl singing 'We'll Gather Lilacs', and an accompanying piano. Vi shushed her, putting one manicured finger to her lips, and they edged forward until they were standing in the wings.

'Look,' Vi whispered in her ear.

Ruby looked. The lights out on the stage were dazzling. There was a dark-haired girl in a pink satin evening gown lounging against a grand piano, singing her heart out. In the background there were massive empty gold-filigreed frames, four of them, each one in darkness. And then the lights changed.

'Oh!' burst out Ruby.

'Shhh!'

One by one the frames were illuminated, revealing the 'tableaux' within – four bare-breasted beauties depicted as Britannia, Liberty, Hope and Glory.

'They mustn't move,' hissed Vi to Ruby. 'That's the only thing. Not a muscle. Or Lord Cromer goes straight off his head.'

Ruby was dumbstruck with shock. Surely Vi didn't expect her to do *that*?

Finally she found her voice. 'But you said *dancing*.'

Vi turned her head and looked at her. 'We do have dancers. But be honest – you that good a dancer?'

Ruby wasn't. She shook her head miserably.

'Sing?'

Again the headshake.

'There you go. But you've got a bloody good body, and Liberty there – that's Jenny – she's going off to marry her forces sweetheart soon, so there'll be a vacancy. Ah!' Vi was staring across the stage towards the wings on the other side. 'There's Mr Van Damm now, he's the manager – you'll love him. Mrs Henderson's the owner, she's here all the time, you'll love her too. It's like one big happy family. We'll go round the back and I'll introduce you.'

Oh Jesus, thought Ruby.

But she was doing it, wasn't she? She was breaking free, breaking *out*. And right now, stupidly, she couldn't help wondering what her mother would have made of it all.

11

'What the fucking hell . . . ?' asked Ted.

Ted and Alicia were sitting by the empty hearth. It was a warm summer's night. Too hot to go to bed yet, although it was late. The kids were asleep upstairs, the day's exhausting shop-work done. It was nice to just sit, and rest.

Only . . . there was this noise going on out in the street.

'Where's that coming from?' asked Ted, getting to his feet.

Alicia stood up too, feeling a prickle on the hairs at the back of her neck. Together, they walked through the house and out onto the front step. The street was dark, no one about: out here, the sound was much louder.

The shimmering notes of the trumpet seemed to twine like golden ribbons around the still evening air.

'Coming from over there,' said Ted, pointing to the bed and breakfast opposite.

Alicia shivered. She was entranced by the sound. It was him, she reckoned. Leroy. Playing his songs to the night. She could see an open window on the first floor of the house. The room beyond was in darkness. But she knew it was him.

She glanced at Ted. He hated music, although he had indulged her by buying the gramophone for her birthday. He didn't indulge her much. Sometimes she played her records on it, just things *like Richard Tauber, serious stuff, nothing like* this. *Ted always moaned about the noise and she always, in the end, switched it off.*

That was marriage, her old ma had told her: give and take. But Ted seemed to do most of the taking, and she all the giving. Since the kids had come along, he never bothered to paw over her any more, and that was a relief in a way. But it still left her feeling rejected, less than a woman. It was like she was a slave, a nothing, kept to do the housework, raise the kids, run the shop . . .

'You want to stop that bloody racket!' *bellowed Ted suddenly, making her jump.*

The music stopped.

The spell was broken.

'Let's get off to bed,' *said Ted irritably.*

Alicia followed him indoors. She only glanced back once.

12

When Betsy next met up with Charlie she didn't tell him about what Vi and Ruby were up to. Friends were friends, she wasn't going to drop Ruby in it. And anyway, she didn't want to say a single thing that would upset Charlie or make him mad at her. She was already beginning to realize that Charlie could get mad at the drop of a hat.

She and Ruby had been friends all through school and beyond. They met frequently and sewed and made cakes together when they could get the rations to do it. It was Betsy who had explained to a panicking Ruby that she wasn't dying when she got her first period at the age of twelve, that it would only last for a week and then she'd be fine again. It had been Betsy who explained the facts of life to Ruby – that the man put his thing inside the lady and then they had a baby. Ruby hadn't believed her, she said the whole thing sounded crazy.

Betsy felt sorry for Ruby, in a superior sort of way. Ruby couldn't help the fact that she had no mother, that she was . . . well, *coloured*. Although how that could be, given the whiteness of Ted, Charlie and Joe, she couldn't even guess. But Ruby couldn't help it that her father was a drunk and a religious nutter. She couldn't help it if people talked about her brothers because they'd avoided the draft and were into all sorts of dodgy dealings. She couldn't *help* coming from a bad family.

Betsy was magnanimously determined to help Ruby, to continue to be her friend forever, and it galled her – just a little – to see how star-struck Ruby was becoming around the older and more glamorous Vi. *She* was Ruby's best friend in all the world. But the way Ruby was starting to hang around with Vi, you wouldn't think it.

If Ruby was giving Betsy cause for concern, at least Charlie was not. She loved being out with Charlie. People had begun to defer to him, tipping their hats. He would shake their hand, pat their shoulder, and she was impressed. He was a big man in the neighbourhood, and she was his girl.

Betsy loved Charlie. Every time she saw him her heart nearly stopped in her chest, she was so stricken with love for him. And she knew he felt the same about her. She was the luckiest girl in the world. Soon they would get engaged, then married; Charlie would look after her and there would be babies, loads of them, dark-haired little boys like Charlie and pretty little blonde girls like her. She was so happy she could burst.

Charlie had acquired a flashy motor, something a bit similar to the one Tranter used to roar around the bomb-battered streets in. Betsy wondered if it actually *was* Tranter's old motor; Charlie seemed to have taken over everything else that had belonged to him.

One night he drove them down to the Mildmay Tavern in the Balls Pond Road at Dalston. Charlie said he had a bit of business to do there, which was fine with her. She liked to see him doing well, being the big man; he was soon to be her fiancé. She was proud of him.

When Joe and one of the other toughs who always seemed to be hanging around the Darke boys got in the back though, she pouted a bit.

'But, Charlie, I thought it was just going to be you and me . . .' She hadn't expected a mob-handed outing.

'Shut up, darlin',' said Charlie, and it was said fondly – but in such a way that she thought she better had.

The pub was busy, people out trying their best to enjoy themselves even though Hitler was giving them all a bit of a bashing one way or another. They all lived in fear these days: of being bombed to death in their beds, or of getting one of those much-dreaded telegrams telling them a loved one had been killed in action.

'Mr Darke,' said the landlord, then he lowered his voice and tipped his head towards the half-open door of the snug: 'He's in.'

'Is he, by God?' Charlie's eyes followed the landlord's.

So did Betsy's. She could see a thin, semi-bald bloke in there, laughing uproariously with a gang of his mates.

'How's Carol?'

'Shattered, poor bint. Shook her up something rotten. Since Mr Tranter stopped drinking in here, it's been bloody bedlam.'

'Well, we can't have that,' said Charlie with a smile. 'Can we?' He looked at Betsy. 'You stay here, darlin', OK?'

And what if it ain't? wondered Betsy. But she nodded. When they were actually engaged to be married, she'd start to stamp her authority on the situation a bit more firmly; but for now, she wanted to be seen as the sweet little girlfriend, eager to please. Even if she wasn't.

'Come on,' said Charlie, and together with Joe and the other man he pushed into the snug. Betsy stood at the bar, and the landlord put a sweet sherry down in front of her. She watched Charlie, his broad back, his casual elegance, through the open door of the snug. He was much more attractive than Joe, who was so bulky, so slow. And Charlie was the boss. She liked that.

'You Bill Read?' asked Charlie of a skinny balding man in there.

'Who wants to know?'

And then she *saw* it. A switchblade razor seemed to jump into Charlie's hand and he lunged forward. Yelling and screaming and cursing started up in the snug and in horror she saw the dark spurt of blood just as Joe put his back to the door from the other side, cutting off the smaller room from view.

People out in the main bar exchanged looks as the shouts and screams went on. The landlord continued pulling pints like nothing was happening.

Suddenly, everything went quiet.

Joe came out, closing the door swiftly behind him. There wasn't a spot on him, not a mark. 'You got the key to that other door in the snug?' he asked the landlord.

The man nodded and quickly fetched the key from a hook behind the bar. He came round the counter and went into the snug with Joe.

Betsy thought she heard groaning when the door opened briefly. But then Joe closed it again, put his back against it. She could hear her own heart beating hard, and the sip of sherry she'd taken was starting to come back up in a sticky-sweet surge of vomit.

Everyone was chatting and laughing now in the bar, as if nothing had happened.

But something had.

Charlie and Joe were gone for over an hour while the landlord kept supplying her with glass after glass of sherry. She drank a bit, forced the sickly stuff down, and noticed that no one came near her, not a soul. She was a pretty girl, surely some bloke would sidle up and chance his arm? They always had before. Betsy with her flirty eyes and her pert little figure always drew the men in.

But no. She was stepped around like she was an invisible

obstruction, like people would instinctively avoid a cold spot where a ghost hovered.

She was a ghost.

She was Charlie Darke's girl.

She was, quite suddenly, afraid.

13

The legend of the Darke boys grew fast and furious after they did Bill Read over the Blind Carol incident. Where once Tranter had ruled the streets, now that task fell to the Darkes, and they relished it.

'What was it about?' Betsy asked Charlie one day.

'What?' He looked absent, as if his mind was elsewhere.

That annoyed her. He rarely paid her proper attention, unless he was trying to get her legs open. And she'd said no more of *that*, after that first time. He'd taken her unawares, surprised her. That wasn't going to happen again. Fortunately there hadn't been any repercussions, she wasn't up the duff. If she was going to get him up the aisle, she knew she was going to have to call a halt to the sex stuff. He was moody over it, of course; all men were like that. Take their toys away and they turned from charming to nasty in an instant.

'This "Blind Carol" business,' said Betsy.

Charlie shrugged, looking unconcerned. 'Well, she ain't exactly blind, but she's so short-sighted she might as well be. She worked in one of the Dean Street clip joints Tranter used to police with his boys, as a hostess, stinging the customers for cash – you know what, the silly sods could pay up to five hundred quid for a bottle of watered-down Scotch!'

Charlie sneered at the thought of such foolishness. With

Charlie, everything was about what a thing cost. What was that old saying? *He knows the cost of everything, and the value of nothing.*

'All on the promise of a quick bunk-up with a tart like that. Anyway, Bill Read went in there one night and, when he realized the Scotch was diluted, he worked her over. Right there in the club. The cheeky little fucker wouldn't have had the nerve to do it if he hadn't known Tranter was off the scene. He must have heard we were taking over the area, but he thought he'd chance his arm, see? He's pushed us once or twice before, but this time he was throwing down the gauntlet good and proper, really taking the piss. He scared her witless, ruined her looks. We couldn't have that.'

Betsy nodded. It had been less about the damage to this poor Carol and more about Charlie's offended pride. But she supposed it was nice, the way he stepped in to protect the girl, whatever his motives. Betsy felt a fuzzy feeling of warmth at his valour. She hugged his arm against the side of her body as they crossed the street. She'd felt put out lately, what with Ruby being so often in a huddle with Vi; she felt hurt and rejected, and in need of company. But at least she had Charlie.

'We ought to be looking at rings, soon,' she said shyly, smiling hopefully up at his face. 'D'you think it's time you talked to Dad?'

Charlie nodded. Yeah, he'd get her an engagement ring, but after that she'd better start putting out again. And he'd talk to her father if it meant keeping her sweet – not that he needed to. Charlie Darke didn't need anyone's permission to do anything. He could do whatever he fucking well liked.

He called on the widow Tranter that afternoon – he dropped in most weeks, gave her a wedge, had a cup of tea. It was nice, sitting at the table with her, eating scones she'd baked because she didn't have to worry about rationing, everything was available on the black market to those in the know, and Charlie Darke was in the know all right.

Charlie Darke was a big man now and he felt that respect was due to him. So it irked him that Mrs Tranter accepted his dosh, entertained him politely, but seemed in no way impressed by him.

'You miss him?' he asked her, as they sat at the table.

'What? Micky?' Her mouth tilted up in a sour smile. 'Why would I?'

Charlie shrugged. 'He put bread on the table.'

'You're right,' she agreed. 'He did.'

'You don't seem heartbroken he's gone.'

She shrugged. There was something so casual, so accepting and yet so *closed off* about her that it was really starting to annoy him.

'People lose loved ones all the time in a war. That's what happened to me. The fool was out and about doing deals and a bomb fell on his head. So what?'

With that she took the teapot out to the scullery for a refill. He watched her go. She was stocky, robust; no hot little sylph like Betsy. Her hair was mousy brown and pulled back into a bun like someone's granny would wear it. Why didn't she take more care of her appearance, for the love of God?

After a while she came back with the refill, placed the pot on the table, pulled the little hand-knitted cosy over it. Her steady ginger-toned eyes met his.

'At least,' she said, 'that's the tale. Ain't it?'

'Hm?'

'That the Luftwaffe got him. Bomb blast took his head clean off his shoulders. Of course, there are *other* tales . . .'

'Like what?'

'Like you wanted to take over his pitch and you did it and made it *look* like just another wartime casualty.'

Their eyes locked. Hers were steady and questioning. Charlie's were blank, devoid of guilt.

'And if it was . . . ?' he asked.

'Then I'd have to say . . .' she started to smile '. . . what do I care? He's dead. But don't think I can't read between the lines, Mr Darke, because, as I've told you before, I can. More tea?'

Charlie smiled and nodded.

She might be a bit of a dog, but he liked Mrs Tranter.

'What's your name?' he asked, as she poured.

'What?'

'Your *name*. You know. Mine's Charlie.'

She sat down and looked him straight in the eye. 'I know that. And Mrs Tranter will do for now,' she said.

He looked at her. The cheeky mare had some front, talking to *him*, Charlie Darke, like that.

He stood up. 'You know, I don't *have* to act the gent with you. I could do anything I damned well like here. You do know that, don't you?'

Her eyes held his. She didn't flinch and she didn't look afraid. She had balls, this one.

'I know,' she said. Not a tremor in her voice.

Balls *and* class. Shame she was such a plain Jane.

'Only you act like you don't.'

A thin smile twisted her lips. 'Mr Darke, I've had everything done to me already. You want to try and shock me? Go ahead. Be my guest.'

Charlie shook his head, smiling, amazed at her audacity. He picked up his hat and went to the door. Paused there. 'This ain't over,' he said, looking back at her.

She shrugged, and turned away.

14

'Seashells,' said Mr Van Damm. 'Conch, starfish, coral, fish, eels, the lot. And you girls as mermaids. I can picture it now. We'll get new costumes made. It's going to be wonderful.'

Ruby exchanged a look with Vi, who raised a wry eyebrow in return. They were backstage in the big communal dressing room all the girls used between performances to rest, dress, relax, gossip, and knit mufflers for the troops.

Ruby had been in the employ of the Windmill Theatre for three months and already she had portrayed in *tableaux* an Egyptian queen, a cowgirl and a pirate. It was like dressing-up for adults, all powered along by Vivian Van Damm's manic enthusiasm. He was a funny little man, quick-moving and with beady eyes under huge dense eyebrows. You could hear him coming a mile off; he jingled the change in his pockets all the time – he was full of restless energy.

Ruby was actually beginning to enjoy herself. Of course, the first time had been awful. Vi had told her it would be; it always was.

'But it's like swimming or riding a bike. Once you get the knack, you're off.'

And she was right. That first night, Ruby had stood there in the darkness, frozen in fear, and then the lights had flashed on and the crowd had roared. So many people, all staring at her standing there dressed like Cleopatra in black wig, filmy long harem pants and a heavy gold necklace – nothing else. Then the other *tableaux* had one by one been revealed, and the crowd cheered and clapped and stamped and the attention was now focused on the other girls too, which made her feel a little less . . . *conspicuous.*

'All right there, sweetheart?' Mr Van Damm asked her as he went to leave the room. 'Settling in?'

'Yes. Thanks,' she said.

'She's a real trooper,' said Deena, a stunning blonde, putting an arm round Ruby's shoulders in happy camaraderie.

They were on in ten minutes, her and Vi, Deena and Joan, and now they were all scrabbling to put the finishing touches to their Red Indian squaw outfits, checking their headbands and feathers were straight, their tiny tasselled waistcoats *(very* tiny) were pushed well back from their breasts, their long fringed fake buckskin skirts were decently buttoned.

They went out onto the stage – the curtains were still closed – and positioned themselves behind the big frames, ready to hold their poses, ready to be lit, to be admired. As Vi scampered by wearing a long blonde wig she hissed to Ruby: 'Got to talk to you after.'

Ruby shot her a questioning look. 'What . . . ?'

'After,' said Vi firmly, and dropped her peignoir and took up her pose: an alabaster-skinned Apache maid posing on a rocky desert outcrop to lure Red Indian warriors.

'Go on then, tell me,' said Ruby.

Vi took a long pull on her cigarette and said, 'How do you feel about a private party?'

'A what?'

'Private party. I've been approached by a gentleman – very respectable – with a request that two of us should perform privately, for a select group. What do you think?'

Ruby thought she wasn't very keen on the idea. There were always crowds of men, soldiers on leave, civilians, outside the stage door, waiting to see this or that girl, to get their programme signed by these mortal goddesses they saw in the glittering, unreal setting of the vividly lit stage. Usually Ruby hustled past them, ignoring the outstretched hands, the pleading eyes. They made her feel uncomfortable. But Vi always accepted their worship as if it was her due.

'What, one of the stage-door johnnies?' she asked.

Vi was watching her assessingly. She shook her head and blew out a plume of smoke.

'Nah. Not one of them. This one's a gent. A real toff.'

'Where then? Here? In the Windy?' There was a small room they used for staff parties.

'Not here, dopey. At a proper gentlemen's club in the City. All fares paid, all expenses covered.'

'I don't know.'

A quick look of irritation crossed Vi's face. 'Cash in hand,' she added with a sigh.

That was the thing Ruby would remember later, that moment when Vi looked annoyed with her and said *cash in hand*. She knew Vi thought she was limp. That she had no spirit.

But hadn't she already proved her wrong? She'd lied to get here. God hadn't yet struck her dead for her audacity. Dad hadn't raised so much as a murmur. He really believed she was working day in, day out at the salvage depot. And Betsy was covering the lie, standing in sometimes at the shop. Everything – to Ruby's amazement – seemed to be working out. She was gaining in confidence, pushing the boundaries.

'All right,' she said at last. 'I'll do it.'

'Good girl!' said Vi with a smile.

Ruby felt sure her mum would have been proud of her. Wouldn't she?

15

Leroy was outside the shop again when Alicia opened up the following morning, leaning against the doorway.

'Was that you?' asked Alicia.

'Huh?' He was smiling at her, thinking that she was beautiful.

'Last night. We heard someone playing the trumpet.'

'Yeah. That was me.'

'You play so well.' Alicia paused. 'I'm sorry about Ted shouting like that,' she said, getting the key out and flushing with embarrassment at the memory of Ted's crassness.

She was sure that Ted would be over there, complaining to Leroy's landlord today. And then probably Leroy and his friends would be thrown out, and she would never hear that bewitching, sultry sound again.

'He the man? The one that shouted? That your husband?'

'You heard him?' Alicia felt hot with shame.

'He don't like music?'

Alicia opened the door and paused to remove the key. She didn't know what to say. Ted would tolerate Ivor Novello or Caruso. But what he called nigger music, he hated. And she couldn't tell Leroy that.

'He don't like it very much,' she said.

'You do, though?' Leroy was staring into her eyes.

'Yes, I like it,' she said, flustered by the intensity of his gaze.

'You want to come to my room sometime?' he asked softly. 'Hear me play?'

'No,' she said, feeling a distant, warm clenching of excitement in the pit of her stomach. 'No, I don't.'

With that, she walked on into the shop.

16

The Darke firm was branching out, spreading its tentacles throughout London. Charlie had some of his boys get taken on as porters at a new frozen-food depot. They turned up for the job in hats, gloves, donkey jackets, thick trousers and steel-capped boots and proceeded to rob half the stock.

It was lucrative; everyone was scrabbling on the black market because of rationing, so Charlie's boys made a mint. If there was trouble in the workforce – and there often was – the manager called on Charlie's mob to sort it out, so they made a profit there too. The money was rolling in.

Then one of the drivers asked if they were organized.

'Organized?' Charlie's boy asked.

'In the Union.'

They weren't in the Union, and the management weren't keen for them to *get* in the fucking Union. As it was, they could hire and fire at will, and pay as low a wage as they liked. They didn't want the Union in like it was over at Smithfield, arsing things up. But there was a prize involved, and that was a Meat Market ticket, which meant a job for life – and access to a lot of stuff going begging.

Once it was established that over half the workforce (Charlie had been careful to get plenty of his boys in there) were coming out on strike, picket lines were formed.

The manager stuck to his guns. He didn't want the Union

in, and his boys – all four of them – were standing firm. At least they *were*, until Charlie and his lot got two of them in the cold store and beat the crap out of them.

And then there were two. Charlie confronted them as they left work – a joke, there was no work going on, no lorries coming through, nothing. The firm was dead, the bosses just weren't bright enough to see it yet.

'Hiya, boys,' he said warmly.

They eyed him warily and drew closer together. They knew about Charlie Darke, everyone did. They looked around nervously, but it seemed he was alone.

They mumbled a hello.

'Enjoying the job still?' asked Charlie with a smile.

'We don't want no trouble,' said one, a bald burly man with bad teeth.

'You don't *want* trouble?' Now Charlie's expression was puzzled.

'No. We don't,' said the man's mate, who was shorter, but still squat, still strong; the job required muscle, and these boys had it. But now, standing here in front of Charlie Darke with his bright smiling stare, they felt unsure.

'Then why you behaving like this?' asked Charlie.

'We're just doing the job we're paid for,' said the bald one, who was right in the manager's pocket, right up the manager's *arse*, Charlie had heard. He was so tight in with the bosses it was a wonder he wasn't to be found hanging out the back of one of them.

Charlie shook his head. 'Now don't be silly,' he said gently. 'Pay'll improve once the Union's in, and we'll see you right on other matters.'

'We're happy with the way things are.'

Charlie stepped forward. The two men stepped back.

'Now listen,' said Charlie. 'You two cunts listen good.

You're standing in the way of progress here. Progress happens and those that don't accept it can come to grief.'

'You threatening us?' asked the smaller of the two.

'Yeah. He is,' said Joe, appearing from the darkness and coming to stand at his brother's shoulder.

The men were starting to get nervous. It was dark, and cold, and they were alone here with these two and they *knew* what they were capable of. They'd heard all about the rackets they were into, and how they used force to get what they wanted – and look what happened to Micky Tranter. A bomb had got him? *Yeah,* they thought. *My arse.*

'You're starting to get right up my nose,' said Charlie. 'Clinging on to the old ways ain't sensible. Getting in my *way* ain't sensible. I'm beginning to think you pair don't have a fucking brain between you. And you know what? I might just decide to *test* that theory by booting both your heads around on these cobbles until they leak out your ears. You think I won't?'

They both shook their heads.

'Now you're not wanted around here any more. You're leaving your job, getting another somewhere else. That clear?'

They both nodded.

'See?' A smile broke out on Charlie's face again; it was like the sun appearing through storm clouds. 'Was that so hard, us doing a bit of business together? Thanks for your cooperation, boys. You shouldn't have messed us about, you know.'

Charlie was slipping on his brass knuckledusters.

'Now wait . . .' said the smaller one, backing away until he hit the wall.

'People get to hear about me being made to look a cunt because two little wankers won't stand aside when they're told? Sorry, boys. I don't think so.'

Charlie piled in, and Joe followed.

★

A week later, Charlie was taking tea round at Betsy's place. He was feeling very pleased with himself. The last two anti-Union boys had obligingly disappeared the day after their little meeting with Charlie and Joe, and after that the management caved in at last. The Union was in, and Charlie was rewarded with tickets to Smithfield; he got five of his boys in there straight away, and soon that would pay dividends.

And now . . . now he had to charm Betsy's mum and dad, Mr and Mrs Porter, which was a piece of piss. He had been very relieved when she'd told him there was no sprog in the offing after their little tumble in the alley, and even if she let him within a mile of her again he told himself that he was going to have to take more care. If he hadn't been so worked up after offing Tranter, he wouldn't have taken such a chance with her.

He was stringing her along at the moment, not quite sure which way to jump. She wanted marriage, of course she did – didn't they all? – but did he? When he thought of married life, he thought of a curtailment of his freedom, answering to a nag who wanted to know where you were day and night.

He also thought of kids, and of course he wanted that; he wanted boys, like him, little bruisers to play with and get started in the business. Sure, he was fond of Betsy. She was impetuous and pretty. But there were so many women in the world.

When Vi joined the little family gathering his doubts increased. Vi was a hot number, smoother than her sister, regal in her bearing and mannerisms, more *impressive*. Her parents didn't seem to know quite what to make of her. Charlie didn't either, but he reached the firm conclusion that she probably fucked like a stoat.

His thoughts turned to Mrs Tranter, so calm, so composed in the face of adversity, in the face of a husband who abused her, in the face of anything Hitler or even Charlie Darke threw at her. Then Mrs Porter cut him another slice of fruit-cake and said, 'More tea?'

He nodded. For now, he was going to keep his options open. Betsy's dad was in a reserved occupation in the docks, and jobs in there were always passed from father to son or even *sons-in-law* – or pals, for a price – and someone in the docks was always a useful contact to have.

17

They were masters of the universe. That's what Ruby thought, when she first peeped out from behind the curtain and saw them.

'God alive,' she said out loud.

'What?' asked Vi, busy powdering her nose.

'They're a bit . . . *loud*,' said Ruby, closing the curtain quickly.

What she had seen was a group of young men, about twenty of them, all rigged out in black frock coats, red bow ties, matching silk waistcoats and white shirts with stiff starched collars. They were laughing in that haw-haw way the upper classes had, chucking hunks of bread roll at each other and downing enough wine to sink a battleship.

Actually what she felt was frightened. 'D'you think . . .' She hated to say it; she knew Violet thought she was a bit limp. 'D'you think it's safe?'

Vi stopped powdering and gave her a startled look.

'Don't be daft, Rubes, these are *gentlemen*. It's like I told you. They all belong to this old boys university drinking club and they have these parties, these *exclusive* parties. They're paying us a mint for this.' Vi joined her and tweaked back the curtain. 'See that one there?' She pointed to a skinny, effete-looking individual. 'That's Perry Maltzer, heir to a dukedom. There's Frederick Holmes, he's the son of the

Shadow Chancellor. Nigel Farraday, his dad's the British Ambassador to America. All officer material, but the cunning bastards know how to dodge the draft if they want to, you can bet your life on that. Their families wouldn't have them put at risk, and they can pull all sorts of strings. They own the earth, this bloody lot; do precisely whatever the fuck they like. And that one, what the hell's his name . . . ? Never mind. Can't remember, but his dad owns a bank.'

'Who's he then?' asked Ruby. 'The blond one.'

'Oh, him. That's Cornelius, son of the late Sir Hilary Bray, KBE. He was president of the Students Union once. Cornelius was an MP too, before the war, but there was some sort of trouble over undeclared interests, so he went to the back-benches. Then he joined the War Office, I think. You needn't worry about *that* one sinking without trace; he's got plenty to say for himself. None of his posh mates would let him down. He'll go on to great things, you mark my words.'

Ruby stared at the blond one. He had the brightest blue eyes she had ever seen, this big unruly thatch of very light – almost white – blond hair, a grin that seemed to illuminate the room. He was well built, tall but muscular too, powerful; and yes, Vi was right, he was a noisy bastard. He was cavorting around the room with his pals, bellowing and lobbing bread rolls, having a thoroughly good time.

Vi had turned her attention from the roomful of young men to the girl at her side. She smiled and pulled Ruby's chin round so that their eyes met.

'Don't go getting a crush on any of this lot,' she said.

Ruby was glad when Vi turned away and started hunting for her lippy. She took one more peek at the blond one. Vi was right. It would be stupid to want someone like that. He was *way* out of her league. But oh God, he looked good.

*

The men settled down to eat eventually. Staff served them starters, mains, pudding, cheese, and a wine for every course then port to follow. Ruby kept checking on the room, feeling increasingly nervous as the evening wore on. And then the blond one stood up and tapped his glass with a knife, calling for silence.

'And now – my friends . . .' he grinned at his audience and there was a roar of approval. 'Pray welcome for the ladies from the world-famous Windmill Theatre.'

It was all going well, Vi and Ruby were posing up on the stage in their little Red Indian tableau, a picture of beauty; the men stomped and cheered to see them standing there in buckskin skirts, their long black wigs tumbling down over their torsos and modestly concealing their breasts.

Then one of the revellers, drunker than most of them, reached up and grabbed Ruby's ankle in a crushing grip. It hurt, and Ruby let out an undignified yelp.

The blond one was there in an instant, catching his friend's arm.

'Steady,' he said.

'Just larking about, old boy,' said the drunk.

'Then don't,' said Cornelius, and suddenly he wasn't the big laughing buffoon any more, his eyes were very serious as they held the drunk's. 'Let go of the lady, Bertie. Right now.'

'Just a joke,' slurred the drunk.

'Let go.'

The drunk stared hard at the blond one's face for a long moment; then slowly he released Ruby's ankle.

'Thanks,' said Ruby when the drunk staggered off and flopped back into his seat. Her ankle throbbed. There'd be a bruise. She was given full voltage from the bright blue eyes, the dazzling smile as Cornelius Bray looked up at her.

'Are you all right?' he asked.

Ruby raised a smile. 'Yeah. Thanks.'

She felt a little breathless. Not just from the fright the drunken toff had given her, but from the waves of charm Cornelius seemed to give off, like heat from a fire. For a moment their eyes locked and held.

'I do apologize. Just high spirits,' he said, and walked off.

Ruby resumed her pose. But her eyes followed him.

18

Charlie and Joe had high hopes of the Post Office. They had their boys out robbing meat trucks up and down the highways, but now they'd found bigger fish to fry. One night Charlie walked into a pub near the Angel with Joe at his side to have a chat with a Post Office driver. After *that*, he got a few of the boys drafted in as drivers and sorters.

'Money comes up from the West to be returned to London by registered post,' the man was telling Charlie and Joe over a pint.

Joe was watching him suspiciously. He was an iffy-looking geezer, all skinny drinker's sunken cheeks and furtive eyes; he'd done some time once, they knew that – that's why they were talking to him. He'd been inside, he knew the score. It held no fear for him.

'Some of it goes for pulping at the Bank of England, but most of it goes to the big banks in the City. Comes into Paddington in the small hours, then it gets driven over by Post Office van to the East Central branch at St Martin's le Grand.'

'What, a single van?' asked Joe, sipping his pint.

'Yeah, with just the driver, a postman and a guard. Not armed.'

'They got an alarm or something on board?' asked Charlie, intrigued.

'There's a button for the siren.'

'How'd you stop it?'

'You can't. Once it's on, it's on.'

'Fuck off.'

'Serious.'

'That's bad news,' said Joe.

'Maybe,' said Charlie. 'You got what I asked for? That other thing?'

'Yeah,' said the man, and handed it over.

After their meeting, Joe went on home but Charlie went round to the Tranter house and knocked on the door.

Silence. Then a light went on and she said: 'Who is it?'

'Charlie,' he called back.

'Who?'

Oh, she was *really* pushing her luck. He found himself grinning, genuinely amused.

'Charlie Darke,' he said.

She opened the door. He stepped inside, closing it behind him.

'I was just going to bed,' she said, an edge of complaint in her voice.

'I said this ain't over,' said Charlie, taking off his hat. 'And it ain't.' He pulled out the gun, the neat little .22 the man had given him in the pub, and rested the muzzle against her forehead.

She froze. 'What the . . .'

'Shocked yet? Scared yet?'

She said nothing, just stared at him.

'Now, what's your name? And if you say Mrs Tranter again, watch out.'

'Why do you even want to know it?' she asked, and he saw her swallow hard.

So she *was* human after all.

'Humour me.'

'It's Rachel.'

It suited her. It was dignified and solid, it had endurance, that name; just like her.

'Well, Rachel, let your hair down.'

'What the . . .'

'Don't even start. Just do it.'

She reached back and loosened the bun, shook her mid-brown hair out. It was long, falling almost to her hips. It made her look gentler, sweeter. She stared at him. She was almost pretty, with her hair down.

Charlie kept the pistol levelled on her forehead.

'Now – upstairs, I think. Don't you?'

'No. I don't.'

Charlie laughed. Jesus, she was annoying! 'Mrs Tranter, I'm holding a loaded gun to your head.'

It wasn't loaded, but she wasn't to know that. Most women would have been gibbering and pleading by now, but not her. She was staring him out, the audacious cow.

'So you are. And if I thought you were actually going to use it, I might be more inclined to go along with you. But you're not. Are you?'

She was calling his bluff.

Their eyes locked.

Charlie lifted the pistol away from her head, slipped it back into his pocket.

'You know what?' he asked.

'What?'

'This *still* ain't over.' And with that, he opened the door and was gone.

19

Life went on at the Windy, and Ruby loved it. After the private booking, her and Vi became close, a double-act; and one night they were leaving the theatre when she spied, among the soldiers on leave and the crush of civilians, a blond head above the others.

Her heart leapt into her throat. 'Oh God,' she said, clutching Vi's arm.

'What?' Vi was autographing programmes; she glanced up at Ruby's face, saw what she was staring at. Vi's face took on a knowing look. 'Well, I saw *that* coming a mile off,' she said.

'You didn't.'

'I bloody did. You've been mooning around ever since that night. You've fallen prey to the Eton wall of charm, that's what it is.'

'The *what?*'

'They're taught to be charming. They *drip* charm.' Vi looked at Ruby's crestfallen face and added: 'But I could see he was really taken with you. So go on then.' She shook her arm loose of Ruby's grip, shooed her in his direction. 'Might as well talk to him, now he's here.'

He was easing his way through the crowds, coming towards her, that full-beam smile on his face. Other women were looking at him, she noticed.

'Hello,' he said when he reached her side. 'How are you?'

'Fine. Thank you.' Suddenly she felt tongue-tied. Didn't know what to say or how to act. He was so far above her, so much her social superior, that she felt humbled and inadequate.

'How's the ankle?' His smile widened to a grin. 'No bruises?'

She shook her head. There *had* been a bruise, but she had almost welcomed it. If not for that drunken fool, *he* wouldn't have spoken to her that night; she had hugged that memory to her, thinking that was all she would ever have, just that one brief encounter. She'd thought she would never see him again. But now he was here, talking to her – so why couldn't she be like Vi and think of witty things to say?

Vi was standing yards away, surrounded by a host of admirers, tossing her head, laughing, acting the star. And here was Ruby, tongue-tied and with her head bowed because Cornelius Bray was here with her.

'How about dinner?' he said.

Ruby looked up at his face briefly. She had thought he must be joking, teasing her, but she could see he was serious. She looked quickly away, dazzled. She felt like a flighty female Icarus in one of Mr Van Damm's tableaux, flying too close to the sun and doomed to crash to earth. She felt she'd be burned, blinded, if she looked at him too long. But she *wanted* to look.

'Dinner?' he asked again, smiling, when she said nothing.

Finally Ruby nodded. 'OK,' she said.

'Come on. Let's get a taxi . . .'

And he tucked her hand over his arm and led her away from the crowds at the stage door. Ruby looked back. Vi was gazing across at her. As their eyes met, Vi gave her a long, knowing wink.

20

1922

Leroy wasn't there when Alicia opened up the shop next morning, and she felt a twinge of disappointment. She went through the motions of serving customers. Then she locked up to get home to make Ted's dinner at one. She came back at two, opened up . . . Still no Leroy.

Feeling glum, she worked on and was glad when it was time to shut up shop. The kids were at her mum's today, she didn't have them to worry about. As she locked the door, Leroy appeared at her side.

'Hiya, sweetness,' he said with a grin.

'Oh! Hello.' Alicia pocketed the key and looked at him. He was so exotic, so beautiful. She knew she was staring.

A silence fell between them.

'You got to get on home right now?' he asked at last, very softly.

Alicia glanced at her watch. She didn't, not really. Ted would be dozing, and he wouldn't want his tea for at least another hour. 'Well, I should . . .' she started.

'Half an hour?' he asked.

'Half an hour for what?' asked Alicia.

His eyes were playing with hers. 'For whatever you want, sweetness. Up there in my room. Some music, maybe . . . ?'

Ted would be asleep. The kids were with Mum. She could say – if anyone asked – that she'd been reorganizing the stock or something, couldn't she?

'I loved your music,' she said.

'Then come with me,' he said, his voice like honey.

Alicia hesitated. 'Someone might see. I'm a married woman . . .'

'I'll go first. You follow.' And he turned and went back across the quiet street.

Alicia stood there looking after him, her heart in her throat, her pulses racing.

She was only going over there to listen to music, wasn't she? No. She knew that wasn't it. Not at all.

She shouldn't do this. But she looked left and right. There was no one she knew about, not right now. She quickly crossed the street and went through the door he'd left open, closing it softly behind her.

She was standing in a dingy hallway. He was at the top of the stairs, gesturing her to follow. She hurried up, afraid that at any moment his landlord was going to appear and ask what the hell was going on.

By the time she reached the top of the stairs she was laughing and breathless at her own daring. He led the way along the landing, unlocked a door, slipped inside. She followed, and he locked it behind them. They fell against the door, both laughing now, and suddenly he was kissing her, and the laughter stopped.

'Oh, my sweetness, my Alicia,' he murmured against her mouth. 'You're so beautiful.'

She thought that he was, too. She put her arms around his neck and pulled his mouth back to hers, thinking of Ted, of her mum with the kids, of her grinding, lonely life with nothing to look forward to but middle age, old age, death.

But here was life. Here was Leroy, so strange to her, so wonderful, bursting with life.

This was a gift from the gods, it had to be.

Now they were tearing at each other's clothes, giggling like children, pulling at fastenings, popping buttons, and finally they fell naked, laughing, onto the crumby little bed in the corner of this horrible room.

'So beautiful,' he said, marvelling as the daylight from the grimy window fell on her skin.

Alicia squirmed and tried to hide her body. She had huge purple stretch marks on her stomach from having the kids. Her breasts had drooped from feeding them.

'Oh God, don't look at me,' she said, embarrassed.

'You're perfect,' said Leroy in those velvety tones.

'No – you are.' She gazed at him. He looked like an African carving, so smooth and muscular, his skin as fine as dark polished leather. 'We shouldn't be doing this,' she said fretfully.

But it was thrilling, arousing; she'd never felt so alive. When he caressed her, when he pushed inside her, she knew – at last! – the meaning of total bliss.

Leroy had to cover her mouth with his hand to stifle her cries; his own were muffled against the silky white curve of her shoulder.

'This is wrong,' said Alicia afterwards, when they lay quietly together. But she no longer cared about her stretch marks or her saggy breasts: he thought she was beautiful, and so she was.

'How can it be?' he asked, and kissed her again.

21

Joe and Charlie realized that they were going to have to hit the mail van in a way that was more subtle than they would have liked. They would have to hijack the whole thing, take it off somewhere quiet.

They started checking timings, rehearsing the robbery repeatedly. On little-used country roads they worked out exactly what they would do, time after time; and on the third rehearsal, to their absolute shock, a copper cycled past and asked what they were doing.

But Charlie was quick thinking. While the others, Joe included, stood there dumbfounded, he said cheerily: 'We're going to be shooting a film here soon for the war effort. We've got to make sure it's all perfect for the next take.'

To the group's amazement, the copper then went happily on his way, saving them the trouble of having to do something drastic to him.

They followed the Post Office van discreetly and recorded journey and location times; Charlie had his boys check parked cars along the quieter parts of the route so that they knew which ones they would nick on the night when the robbery went ahead. They had an electrician fix the traffic lights in the street selected for the hit. It was north of Oxford Street, running parallel to it.

The traffic lights were under the gang's control. There

were roadworks in the street, which was all to the good; it would slow the van even more.

Finally, all was as perfect as it could be; they were ready.

'Bloody traffic lights. Day or night, the damned things stop you,' said the driver of the mail van.

The postman was sitting beside him, yawning. He hated night work, but what could you do? The lights were red. The street was silent, a few parked cars about, nobody walking around. It was four o'clock in the morning, who but a nutter or a night worker would be abroad at this hour?

The guard leaned over from the back and said: 'Gawd, won't I be glad to get home to the missus. What's the lights red for at this time of the night? Not a damned thing happening.'

Suddenly a black Riley parked to the left of the stationary van screeched out from the curb and blocked the van's way forward.

'Oh, *shit*,' said the driver, and threw the van into reverse. In his rear-view mirror he saw a Vauxhall saloon draw up close behind. '*Shit!*' he yelled.

Men in gloves and masks were tumbling out of the two cars. The driver pressed the siren button just as the door on his side was yanked open and he was jerked out of his seat and thrown into the road. He lay there, winded, as the postman was hauled out, and thought, *What's wrong with the bloody siren?*

It didn't make a sound.

Charlie's knack of always having boys on the inside was paying dividends yet again. The siren had been disabled.

The driver fought back instinctively, but he was punched, kicked, coshed into submission. Finally he just lay there, dazed and bruised, while they piled the postman and the guard alongside him. They looked like a pile of meat on a slab, there was blood everywhere.

'Silly buggers, it's not *your* money,' said Joe in disgust. 'Fucking well lie there, will you?'

It took just eight minutes. One man got in the Riley, another in the Vauxhall. The rest of them piled into the van. All three vehicles roared away into the night, and the driver, the postman and the guard lay there, groaning on the street, until they were found by an early worker passing by at half past six; then the police were called.

They dumped the two stolen cars at Covent Garden market, which was already busy with deliveries of fruit, vegetables and flowers being made; no one would notice the cars parked there until much later.

Then they all took off in the van. And everything was going fine, they were roaring with laughter, excited after the tension of the heist . . .

That's when they hit the bloody dog.

It was just a mutt, white with black patches here and there. A mongrel – big and bony and plug-ugly. And it ran straight out in front of the van. Chewy, who was at the wheel, braked hard, but they all felt the bump as the thing was struck.

'Fuck!' said Chewy.

'Drive on,' said Joe.

Charlie looked around. All was quiet. 'Hold on. I'll take a look.'

The poor damned thing was lying there with its back leg jammed half under the front wheel on the passenger's side. It was alive, but there was a lot of blood. It was whining.

'Back up a bit,' Charlie called to Chewy.

The dog's whining changed into a howl as the van backed up, off its leg. Fucking thing. He couldn't leave it lying there in agony. He pulled the cosh out and took aim at the dog's head: give it a good hard whack and send it on its way. But then he hesitated, staring down at the dog's pleading eyes. They were somehow full of hope, full of expectation that he, Charlie, would help. The stump of a tail twitched in a pitiful wag.

'*Fuck!*' said Charlie with feeling, and he put the cosh away and gathered the dog up in his arms, went round to the back of the van and slung the thing in on top of the money bags. It stopped whimpering. Maybe it had slipped away, died. He hoped it had, poor bastard.

'Shit, you're having a laugh! What we supposed to do with that?' demanded Joe.

The knock on the door was loud and insistent and went on and on. The widow Tranter tumbled from bed, knocking into the side table in her alarm and haste.

What the hell?

She switched on the little lamp beside her bed and looked at the time. It was five thirty in the morning, not even light yet. She pulled on her robe and hurried down the stairs, crossing to the door. She halted there. The knocking had stopped. Now it started again.

'Come *on*,' she heard from the other side.

'Who is it?' she called.

'Who do you *think*, Father fucking Christmas? Open the bloody door.'

She opened it. Charlie was standing there and he was holding a bundle of tattered black and white fur in his arms. The light from her living room glinted on wetness, redness; blood. She shrank back. What the hell now?

Charlie stepped forward and dumped the whole revolting mess into her arms. She felt blood seep straight through her robe and stick clammily to her skin. There was a big ugly head, a wet black nose nudging at her. The thing whined. She looked at it in complete disgust and disbelief. Her eyes lifted and she stared, thunderstruck, at Charlie.

'*What . . . ?*' she started.

'Look after it, will you?' he said, and he turned on his heel.

'You're not *seriously* . . .'

'Things to do,' he said, walking away.

'Wait a minute,' she snapped.

'Quiet, don't want to wake the neighbours,' he warned, looking back at her, holding a finger to his lips.

'Charlie *fucking* Darke, come back here!' she hissed.

But he was gone.

After they'd dumped the dog at the widow Tranter's, they drove the van off to the yard in Camden Town. It was all prearranged, carefully thought through by Charlie. Another van was waiting there, and this one was second-hand. It had false plates, and a new coat of navy-blue paint. Charlie had had partitions built into the thing so that the banknotes would be stashed in there, invisible.

By eight o'clock Charlie and Joe and their accomplices had stuffed the van full of notes. Charlie had doled out three thousand pounds each to Chewy, Ben and Stevie on the spot.

'You get the rest in six months, that way no slip-ups,' said Charlie as he handed over their wedge. His own much bigger share would be stashed where only he could find it. The same went for Joe's. They'd already agreed that neither of them should know the whereabouts of the other's loot. It was safer.

The boys didn't have to count it. They'd been Charlie Darke's gang since schooldays, they trusted him implicitly.

Then Charlie and Joe jumped up into the cab, the gates were opened, and they drove the haul away.

'Piece of piss,' said Charlie, grinning as they headed off to Essex.

22

Ruby had succumbed to temptation. She was in bed with Cornelius when he broke the bad news to her.

'I'm married,' he said.

She'd been lying there in his arms and she had never been so happy in her entire life. Her mind had started skipping forward, dreaming of courtship, marriage, babies . . . impossible, stupid dreams, she knew that. She also knew that she shouldn't have slept with him, not yet, but these were desperate times, *terrible* times, weren't they. Vi was *so* right. They *could* all be dead tomorrow. You had to grab life whenever you could. And she had. She was in love. She loved him.

But *what* was he saying? Married? Well, Vi had warned her. But still, she felt as if her entire world had caved in.

'I'm sorry, darling. I know it must come as a shock.'

'Well, I . . .' Ruby didn't know what to say.

A shock? Yeah. It was certainly that.

'How long . . . ?' she asked, because she couldn't think of anything else to say. She should be angry. She knew that. But all she felt was *crushed*.

'Five years.'

Now she felt the anger building, taking hold. She glared at him. Her big golden beautiful man. Three dinners and then *straight* into bed at his house in one of the city's more select squares. She preferred being here, in bed, to the expensive restaurants he took her to. In company, she was all too aware that other women wanted him. They probably threw themselves at him all the time. Here, in his house, they were alone, and that was better: she felt more secure.

Only – she wasn't secure at all. He was *married*.

She had a sudden appalling thought. 'My God. Is she here . . . ?'

He was shaking his head. 'She lives in the country. We have a small manor house.'

A small manor house.

Ruby had never felt more conscious of who she was, where she had come from. Her dad ran a corner shop. She was nothing special. Oh, she was good-looking. People stared at her in the street, with her long legs and her olive-skinned beauty, her long fall of lusciously wavy black hair. But she was nothing, she had come from *nothing*. While he . . . from birth, he'd been blessed with wealth. He was easy with it, and now he was telling her, oh so casually, that he was *married*, and that his wife lived in a manor house in the country.

'You *bastard*,' she burst out.

He looked dismayed.

Ruby started hitting him, hardly knowing what she was doing, only that she was gutted, she was completely *destroyed*, and he was lying there as if surprised at her reaction. He caught her wrists, held her still.

'Don't,' he said.

'Bastard,' she said again, trying to get free and failing.

'I suppose now you won't want to see me any more.'

Ruby stared at his face. She was panting with fury. But then she remembered the other thing that Vi had told her about men like him. That they owned the world, that they were taught from birth that they could have anything: the chairmanship of the company, the house in the country, the swanky place in town, the tolerant wife, the accommodating bits of fluff on the side.

Except, Ruby wasn't feeling very accommodating. She jumped out of the bed and started flinging on her clothes. She glared at him as she did so.

'Fucking well *right* I don't,' she said. 'What do you take me for?'

He shrugged. He looked unhappy, but he didn't look *that* cut up about her reaction.

'Look, I didn't lie to you,' he said.

'You didn't tell me the *truth*, either.'

'I know. But this has been so marvellous. I suppose I simply put off the evil hour.'

'Because you knew how I'd react.'

'I thought you'd be angry.'

'I *am* angry.'

'I'm sorry. I hoped you might have understood.' His head went down. 'My wife and I, we . . .'

'Oh, for God's sake don't start giving me *that*.' Fully dressed, Ruby snatched up her bag. 'Spare me the "my wife don't understand me" bollocks.'

'Ruby . . .'

'Goodbye, Cornelius.'

She left, before she started to cry.

23

1922

After the first time, Alicia met with Leroy often over the following weeks. They fell joyously into bed together, then lay there sated, listening to his jazz records. He gave her a 78 rpm by Jelly Roll Morton, and she sneaked home with it, played it on the Maxitone when Ted was out down the Legion.

For a while, life was blissful.

Until she found out she was pregnant.

Alicia knew that Leroy would look after her: he had told her so.

'It's yours of course,' she said, as they lay in bed together. 'I haven't slept with Ted since I got up the duff with Joe. He wasn't interested after that.'

But Leroy was unfazed by her expectant state. She had been frightened of telling him, of breaking their perfect little dream in two, but she needn't have worried.

'I'll take care of you,' he said.

They lay there and planned their future together, somewhere far away from here. She would take the boys, of course – she couldn't leave her kids. But they would have to get away. She couldn't pass the newborn off as Ted's. That was impossible.

'It'll be fine,' he assured her, enfolding her in his arms. 'We'll go away. We'll work things out.'

She didn't see him next day outside the shop, or the next. She started to worry. Was he ill? The day after that, taking the Jelly Roll Morton record he'd lent her as an excuse, she went and knocked at the door over the road. An old woman with a whiskery chin answered, scowling out at her.

Alicia swallowed nervously. 'Um . . . Mr Bird lent me this record; I'm just returning it to him.'

'Ain't you Ted Darke's wife?' she asked.

'That's right.' Alicia's palms felt wet.

'Seen you in the shop,' said the woman.

'Can I . . . is Mr Bird in?'

'Him and his mates moved out yesterday,' said the woman. 'Said they were going to try their luck in Manchester or somewhere like that. Sorry.'

The woman shut the door.

Alicia staggered blindly back home, clutching the record. Ted was out. The boys were with Mum. She went up to the bedroom and with shaking hands put Leroy's record on the gramophone. Then, crying as she listened to Jelly Roll singing about love, she started planning how she was going to get rid of Leroy's baby.

24

'They're saying they think US Army deserters carried it out,' said Dad over breakfast as he read the paper.

Charlie was staring disapprovingly at Ruby, who was off her grub, probably fallen out with some boy or other. 'Eat that up, Rube, for God's sake. There's people starving and you're pushing that damned egg round the plate – it's driving me mad.'

Charlie and Joe, seated on either side of the breakfast table, had not even exchanged a look when Ted spoke. Both kept their heads down, mopping up egg with thick slices of bread.

'This mail van robbery,' their dad went on. 'Would you bloody believe it? Look at this. The Postmaster General said the system had been in place for thirty years and had worked fine. Well, it ain't working *now*, is it? Two hundred thousand pounds gone, and no one knows where.'

Neither Charlie nor Joe looked up. Ted glanced at them both. He knew they were into all sorts. But this?

He wondered.

A month later, two boys were playing on the edge of the flooded sandpit near their home in Dagenham. It was a brilliant summer's day, the sun glinting dazzlingly off the water so that at first little Toby doubted the evidence of his eyes.

He had to blink, and look twice. There *was* something floating in the water. He yanked a branch down off a tree, and belted his mate Dan with it as he passed by.

'Oi!' shouted Dan, laughing.

But Toby had moved on; he was down at the water's edge, using the branch to haul in the bits of dark cloth he'd spied there. He pulled them out one by one, dripping, from the water.

'What are they?' asked Dan curiously, peering over Toby's shoulder.

There were six of them in total.

Toby's dad was a postal worker; Toby knew exactly what they were.

'They're mail bags,' he told Dan. 'You don't think . . . ?'

Everyone had heard about the mail van robbery, it had been plastered all over the papers and Toby's dad had joked that he wished he'd thought of it first, he'd have done it himself.

'There's a reward for information,' said Dan excitedly. 'Thousands of pounds!'

'I'm gonna take these home and tell Dad,' said Toby.

Toby's dad took the mail bags to the police, and when he got back home Toby asked him about the reward. His dad told him that the police would be coming round tomorrow to speak to him about the find. Toby could hardly contain himself, the reward was a *fortune*.

'But don't go getting your hopes up,' said his dad, settling down with pipe and slippers for the evening. 'If it leads to an arrest, they might pay out. If not, there's no chance.'

25

'So how's the mutt?' asked Charlie when he went round to the widow Tranter's house.

Rachel Tranter looked him straight in the eye.

'You haven't been near in over a month. He could be dead and gone, what do you care?'

Charlie was smiling, but underneath he was anxious. This last month since the job had played hell with him. Friends had been hauled in for questioning, and a couple of his boys had been found with a few stolen notes, but the most the Old Bill could get them for was possession. They had been acquitted as receivers. Which came as no surprise to Charlie, because he'd gotten into the jury and made sure of the verdict.

But the police weren't about to let it go. Charlie had got a bit too lively with a steel pipe and, although the postman was out of hospital now, the driver and the guard were still in a very bad way.

Charlie sensed the Old Bill were still snooping around his territory, trying to see if they could pin this on him. But they couldn't and he knew it. He was home free. So was Joe and so were the rest of the boys. Nevertheless, these were worrying times. He had to keep his head down.

'What, you been counting the days, have you? You've missed me?' he asked her.

Rachel didn't even dignify that with a reply. She led the

way into the lean-to, and there the dog was, in a box lined with a tatty old red tartan blanket. When Rachel came in it stared up at her, its big threatening jaws open in a grin, and its stumpy tail started to wag. Then it saw Charlie and emitted a low growl.

'Well, he's a good judge of character, I'll say that for him,' said Rachel.

'Ungrateful little sod! I saved the bastard's neck and this is how he repays me.' Charlie reached down to pat the dog's head, and it snapped with its teeth. Charlie fell back. 'Good God.'

The dog jumped to his feet. He had a peculiar gait, with his left back leg hanging an inch or two in thin air, unused. But he shambled forward three-legged and was eyeing up Charlie in a very unfriendly manner. Rachel grabbed his collar and held him still.

'I cleaned him up after you brought him round, stitched up the wound with thread and bound it up,' said Rachel, patting the dog's head while he strained and snarled at Charlie. 'I thought I'd come out here one day and find him dead, but he slept for a day or two and then started to want food, and after that he mended. The leg'll never be right, but it don't seem to bother him much.'

'Well, I couldn't leave the poor bastard just lying in the road, could I?' But looking at the snarling dog, Charlie now wished he'd done exactly that. Little fucker didn't know the meaning of the word gratitude.

'I couldn't help wondering what you were doing at that hour of the morning, roaring about the roads in a van and running down dogs.'

'Oh, just this and that.'

'That was the night that mail van was robbed.'

'Was it?'

'Yes, it was.' As the dog lunged forward again, Rachel said

a sharp word and it subsided. She nodded to Charlie. 'We'd best go back indoors; he's taken a dislike to you.'

They went back into the house, closing the door on the dog. He scraped at it and whined, but subsided after a little while.

'Tea?' offered the widow Tranter.

Charlie looked at her. You couldn't throw this woman. Hold a gun to her head, chuck a bloody wreck of an animal into her arms . . . she'd take anything and come up smiling and serene. He thought of Betsy with her silly grin and her flighty charm. Then he stared at *this* one, and thought: *One's a girl, the other's a woman. That's the difference.*

'Nah. I want more than tea.'

Suddenly the atmosphere was charged, full of tension.

'I've already told you, Mr Darke . . .' she started.

'Shut up and come here.'

She didn't move. Not that he'd expected her to, anyway. Charlie moved forward until they were nose to nose.

'All right,' he muttered under his breath. 'I'll come to you, then. OK?' And he kissed her.

'Charlie . . .' She was pushing him away, or trying to.

'What?' he asked against her mouth.

'This is no good.'

'Feels good to me,' he said, and it did. He'd wanted this from the first moment he'd set eyes on her, and now here she was, in his arms.

'You only want this because I was his wife,' she said, her ginger-brown eyes hard as they held his.

'No. That ain't true. All right, it might have been. At first. But not now.'

He was telling the truth. He'd been covetous at first, wanting to possess the woman that Tranter had possessed. To the victor, the spoils. That's what he'd thought, then. But he'd got to know her, to admire the strength of her. And now

. . . now he seriously wanted her. Not in the way he wanted Betsy, to cool off after he'd been doing business, to just let off some steam; he wanted Rachel Tranter in a way he'd never wanted a woman before. He wanted to *know* her, to feel her lying skin-to-skin with him, to break down that reserve of hers and find out what went on inside her head. He'd never felt that with a woman before, and it startled him.

'So let your hair down, Rachel Tranter, let me see you,' he murmured against her lips, touching them with his own, feeling her breath coming a little faster, seeing her pupils dilate with the beginnings of passion.

'What, no gun this time?' she asked, with a tiny smile.

'Do I *need* it?'

Rachel's eyes held his. She reached back, unpinned the bun, shook out her hair.

'No. You don't,' she said, and her arms went around his neck as she kissed him back, properly, for the very first time.

'I suppose you'll agree to marry me now?' asked Charlie.

They were lying in her bed upstairs an hour later, naked and twined together like snakes. Rachel propped herself up on Charlie's chest and stared down at his face.

'No, I bloody well won't,' she said.

'*What?*' Charlie sat up abruptly, dislodging her. He looked back at her with disbelief. He was pretty surprised that had popped out of his mouth at all. He hadn't *intended* it to. He'd shocked himself. Didn't he have Betsy lined up for all that, Betsy with her handy dad in the docks where he wanted to get some of his boys placed, Betsy who was young and fit and likely to churn him out plenty of strong sprogs – unlike Rachel Tranter, who was already thirty if she was a day, well past the kids stage, surely?

Yes. He did.

Yet he'd just said, right off the top of his head, that he

wanted Rachel Tranter to become Mrs Charlie Darke. But . . . *did* he? Did he really?

He stared at her. White silken skin over hot womanly curves, the veil of her hair half-concealing her body, the body he'd got to know with extreme intimacy over the past sixty minutes. Her serious ginger-flecked eyes in her sweet smooth oval face, her mouth kissed into pinkness by his own.

Shit. Yeah, he did.

But . . . she'd reacted like he'd offered her poison. And that hurt.

'Well, you don't have to say it like *that*,' he shot back.

Rachel lay back and looked at his angry face.

'I've *had* all that,' she told him. 'I'm like that bloody dog downstairs – too old to learn new tricks. I had the marriage things before, remember? Cleaning up after Micky day and night, washing his dirty pants? And then nothing but a fucking beating for my troubles. Listen, Charlie – I *like* being here on my own. I don't want kids and I'm too long in the tooth for all that anyway. OK?'

Charlie said nothing.

'And all the dodgy business. Being afraid of the Bill coming knocking day and night, having to lie through my teeth to cover for him. It'd be the same with you, no good saying it wouldn't, because it would. And, Charlie . . .' Her eyes were grave as they held his. Grave and sad. 'You know how it ended for him? Well, it's going to end the same for you. And you know what? Call me a coward, if you like, but when it *does*, I don't want to be there to see it.'

Charlie flung back the bedclothes.

'Then I suppose I'd better just go,' he said, grabbing his long johns and pulling them on with quick, angry movements.

There was nothing more to say.

Charlie left; and he was so angry, so bloody *hurt*, and he

never thought any woman would have the power to hurt him as Rachel Tranter had just done. Out in the street he walked away, head down, uncaring and unseeing, scalded by her rejection and wondering if he was going mad, proposing marriage to a dried-up old stick like her. Just as well she'd turned him down flat. He'd had a lucky escape.

26

'Joe, can I ask you something?' asked Betsy.

She'd been very careful to find Joe when he was on his own. She wanted to talk to him about this; she didn't want to ask Charlie, she didn't want Charlie thinking she didn't trust him and getting all indignant about it. There was of course some completely innocent reason for him going round to the widow Tranter's as much as he did.

Innocent or not, though, Betsy didn't like it. People had begun to *talk*. Her mother had mentioned to her that the gossips were saying there was something going on there.

Of course there *wasn't*, and Betsy had told her mother so straight away. The widow Tranter was ancient. Charlie wouldn't bother with her. He had Betsy. But . . . it niggled at her. After all, Betsy herself hadn't put out since that first time, that one and only time, in the alley. And she knew men had needs, overpowering needs, her mother had told her that. But he *couldn't* be doing anything like that with Mrs Tranter. Well, just look at her. Not only *old*, but ugly.

No, Charlie wouldn't do anything like that, so there had to be a simple explanation and now, thank goodness, she had tracked down Joe. At last, she could stop her head spinning, stop coming to all sorts of frankly *crazy* conclusions.

'You can ask me anything you like,' said Joe.

Betsy liked Joe; she liked his air of stability. If anything was troubling you, you could go to Joe. Charlie . . . well, Charlie was *Charlie*. Hotter than Joe, more likely to fly off into a rage. But Charlie was the boss, he was the number one man, and she liked that.

She was already smarting over Ruby, who didn't seem interested in spending time with her any more. Now Ruby was in tight with Vi, Betsy hardly ever saw her. But she was looking forward to this weekend, when Ruby had – at last – agreed to meet up.

'I didn't want to ask Charlie about this,' she told Joe.

'About what?'

'I'm not sure I should even ask you.'

Joe looked at Betsy with a frown. This was – from what Charlie had hinted at in the past – his future sister-in-law. She was a pretty little thing; the sort he would almost have gone for himself. But Charlie had got there first. Charlie always did.

'Come on, spit it out,' he said. 'You might as well, now you've started, or I'll be wondering all day what this is about.'

Betsy paused. Then she blurted: 'It's about the widow Tranter.'

'What about her?'

'There's been talk.'

'Talk? What sort of talk?'

'About Charlie always being round there.'

So far as Joe knew, Charlie went round to Tranter's widow to pay her a wedge now and then, that was all. And he'd dumped the injured dog there on the night of the mail van robbery. Which suggested . . . well, all it suggested was that Charlie wasn't as big a bastard as everyone thought he was. He'd wanted to help the poor suffering animal. It *also* suggested that he trusted Mrs Tranter to care for it.

'He looks after her,' said Joe. 'Pays her a wedge.'

'Yeah, but is that all there is to it?'

'*What?*' Now Joe was laughing. 'What, that old bird, and Charlie? You serious?'

'She's not *that* old,' said Betsy, embarrassed that Joe thought she was blowing all this up out of nothing. Well, maybe she was. But there was no need for him to laugh at her fears.

'No, but look at the face on her! Serious, Betsy, what are you worrying about? Don't be daft. And as for the talk, there's *always* talk. People got nothing better to do than stand around flapping the lip about other people's private business. Just ignore it.'

So she was supposed to be reassured. But she wasn't, not really.

And as Joe walked away from her, he was thinking *Jesus! The widow Tranter and Charlie? Was that possible?*

That night Charlie and Joe were at the pub drinking beer and waiting to meet one of their many contacts who had a load of forged petrol coupons going cheap, along with a truckload of black market nylons and eighteen thousand tins of fruit that had come his way. Stan was a 'larker'; he'd been to the National Assistance office after nineteen raids claiming he'd been bombed out. Charlie and Joe were taking bets on whether he'd be banged up when he got to twenty, but it was a poor bet.

The city was in chaos, officials were overwhelmed, they couldn't check everything. Some of them were busy lining their own pockets, making out blank billeting forms and filling them in so they could draw allowances for non-existent people without having to suffer a real live lodger – someone made homeless by the Blitz, or a serviceman – on the premises. Mostly the councils paid out, and shut up.

'We'll offload the fruit at one of the wholesale firms,' said Charlie. 'Right?'

'Fine. I had to have a word with Ben.'

'Oh?' Charlie glanced at him. Ben was one of his most trusted boys: sound as a pound, he'd always thought.

'He's been splashing his cash around. Bought his old lady a fucking fur coat.'

'He *what*?'

'Been looking over new motors too, the tit.'

'What about Chewy and Stevie?'

'They're OK. Keeping their heads down.'

'You sorted Ben out, though?'

'It's sorted.' Joe sipped his pint. He'd given Ben a good going-over about this. Silly cunt.

Charlie nodded, satisfied. "The nylons can go door-to-door.'

'Fine. So what you been up to at the widow Tranter's, then?'

Charlie choked on a mouthful of best bitter.

'You *what*?' he spluttered.

'You heard. People are talking.' He didn't mention Betsy, he didn't want to land her in a screaming match with Charlie. He knew his brother well. Accuse him of anything, and he'd kick off like a mad bastard.

'Who?' asked Charlie, slapping his pint back down onto the mat.

'No one in particular,' shrugged Joe. 'There anything going on then? Anything I should know about?'

'What, you think I'm *poking* the old biddy?' Charlie was half-laughing, but in his heart he was hating himself for it. It diminished everything that had passed between him and Rachel, cheapened it.

'She's not *that* old,' said Joe, in a perfect echo of Betsy's words.

Charlie picked up his pint and looked his brother square in the eye.

'There's nothing going on, bruv. Nothing at all.'

27

Cornelius was outside the Windmill the following week, waiting to see her again, beautifully turned out as always, devastatingly handsome, wearing his blue-striped Old Etonian tie.

'Oh, for fuck's *sake*,' said Ruby angrily.

'What's up, kid?' asked Vi, signing busily, smiling, being her charming, infinitely desirable self while Ruby stood there, her heart in her mouth at the sight of him, feeling like a moody, truculent child.

'He's married, Vi. *That's* what's up.'

Vi stopped signing and stared at her friend. Then her mouth tilted up in a smile.

'Ruby,' she said. 'He's in his thirties. He's rich. He's good-looking. Can you really say you were surprised?'

'Well, no. Not really. I suppose,' said Ruby unhappily. 'I just hoped . . .'

'Hoped what? That he was going to fall on his knees and propose marriage to *you*?' Vi snorted and carried on signing programmes for the adoring stage-door johnnies clustered all around her. 'Honey – it's just fun. That's what you should treat it as.'

Fun.

But it wasn't fun to Ruby. She'd fallen for the bastard.

'And listen,' said Vi, lowering her voice, 'if you want them to marry you, here's what you do. Choose an ugly one, not a looker. Keep your legs together. Act the nervous virgin and you might, just *might*, get one of the really big boys up the aisle.'

Cornelius came over. He was holding a programme. 'I don't suppose you'd sign this for me?' he asked Ruby in his beautiful, cut-glass voice. His blue eyes looked slightly wary.

'I ought to tell you to roll it up and stuff it straight up your arse,' she returned.

'I'm sorry if I hurt you. I was trying to be honest. I want to see you again.'

Ruby said nothing for a long moment. Then she said: 'What's her name, your wife?'

'Ruby – darling . . .'

'Don't "darling" me. Tell me her name.'

'Vanessa.'

'And what's she look like?'

'Nothing like you.'

'It was a shock, you know.'

'I know. I'm sorry.'

'This can't go anywhere.'

'I know. Still, I want to see you again.'

'No,' she said. 'Fuck off.' And walked away.

He was back the night after that, and the night after that, and again on Saturday, drawing the eyes of every woman around him like he always did.

'You may as well talk to him,' said Vi. 'You've had a miserable face on ever since you threw him over. What's the sense in making yourself sad like this?'

'But he's *married*.'

'So what?' Vi shrugged. 'Some of mine have been married too. They don't expect too much and they treat you like royalty. You get all the good stuff, the gifts and the fun, while poor bloody wifey gets the dirty socks and the bad moods.'

Ruby thought about that. She'd take bets that Vanessa didn't wash socks, but she understood what Vi was saying and it even made sense. She should treat the whole thing lightly, not behave like a love-struck schoolgirl. Vi did well with furs and jewels from her married admirers; enjoyed the fun, left the rest of it to the wife. And maybe Vi had it right.

'Am I forgiven yet?' he asked, coming back again with the programme to sign. She took out a pencil and scrawled her name across the front cover. Then she smiled. All right, he was a practised charmer. Probably a philanderer, too. But she could play this game. It might even be fun, just like Vi said it was.

'I'll never ask anything about your wife again,' she said. 'Not ever. OK?'

'OK,' he said, and she put her hand on his arm and he led her away to the waiting taxi. Ruby forgot all about her promised meeting with Betsy.

Betsy was at home, upstairs, that same evening. She and Mum had made fairy cakes, and Betsy had taken a plateful of the delicacies upstairs and placed them on her bedside table with a warm pot of tea and two of Mum's best china cups, all ready for nine o'clock when Ruby was going to call round.

She sat there, buffing her nails, until nine thirty. She ate one of the fairy cakes at a quarter to ten. At ten o'clock her mum poked her head round the door.

'Ruby not coming?' she asked.

Betsy shrugged like it was of no importance at all, but hurt and resentment and jealousy burned in her like hot, acidic bile. Ruby would be with Vi, of course, laughing, drinking, living the high life while she, Betsy, sat here like a fool, patiently waiting.

'It doesn't look like it,' she said, slipping a hand under the cosy to feel the pot. It was stone-cold.

'She must have forgotten,' said Mum, coming in and sitting on the bed.

How could she have forgotten? This was *important*. Betsy had been looking forward to this for *days*. She had baked the cakes especially. And to think she had been *covering* for Ruby in her lies to her family, supporting her in the fiction that she was doing volunteer work at the salvage centre. If Ruby's lot *really* knew what was going on, they'd be livid. And Ruby's preoccupation with Vi and the Windmill would be over.

Over.

The word clanged around Betsy's head. She had only to say the word, and Ruby's attention would be focused on her once more, not Vi. They would be close again, like they were before.

'Don't worry about it,' said Mrs Porter, seeing how dismal Betsy looked. 'I'm sure she's just mixed the days up or something.'

'Yeah,' said Betsy. 'Probably.'

But she was thinking that really, Ruby had just better watch her step.

28

The whole thing about the Post Office van robbery had died down and might have been filed as a dead case, if elderly Bob Julius hadn't been on his way to the shop one day and seen Rachel Tranter walking the same way with a dog, *his* dog, on a length of rope hobbling beside her.

'Hey!' he called out, crossing the road and planting himself in front of Rachel.

The dog knew him. It wagged its stumpy tail, and its big ugly mug split open in a grin.

Rachel stopped walking and stared at this grey-haired wheezy little man with his watery blue eyes, heavy jowls and cod-like mouth.

'That's my dog,' he said indignantly.

'What?' Rachel was eyeing him in confusion.

'It's my dog. Bruiser. Here, boy.'

Bruiser surged forward. Rachel pulled him back.

'What's happened to him? He's limping.'

Shit, thought Rachel. 'It isn't your dog. You've made a mistake. It's *my* dog.'

'You think I don't know my own dog? I brought Bruiser up from a pup. He went missing months ago.'

'I told you. You've made a mistake. This is my dog,' said Rachel, and now she could see a part-time War Reserve policeman coming towards them from the direction of the shop.

Shit, shit, shit.

It was Alvin Paisley, the bank teller. She knew him, they nodded if they passed in the street. He was a prissy self-important idiot, always immaculately dressed, with a stupid little Hitler moustache and beady eyes, and she knew he looked down on her because she'd been married to dodgy, conniving Micky Tranter.

He was neat as always, in grey twills and a dark blazer, wearing his helmet with POLICE written large upon it, and his panniers and gas mask, and a whistle.

She stepped around the old man and hurried on. But the dog was yanking her back, craning towards him.

'Come *on*,' said Rachel, yanking the dog's rope, starting to panic.

Then the old chap saw the teller with his police helmet on.

'Help!' he shouted. 'Police! Help!'

Ah, *fuck*, thought Rachel, and Alvin Paisley hurried forward.

'What's the trouble here?' he asked. He nodded to Rachel, his lip curling slightly.

Oh yes, they knew each other. She knew he was a skinny buttoned-up little prude who only ever used his hands to get his dick out for a piss. And he knew that she had been married to Micky Tranter, whose gang of thugs had run the streets around here.

'It's my dog,' said the old man quickly, not wanting Rachel to get in first. 'He went missing and now here he is, this woman's got him. I've raised him since he was a pup – haven't I, Bruiser?'

And the fucking dog wagged its tail.

Is that all I get for bringing you back to life, you stupid mutt? wondered Rachel.

'Well, he does seem to know you,' said Alvin.

'He's friendly to everyone,' said Rachel. 'He looks fierce, but he isn't.'

'I let him out the front to do his business,' the old man went on. 'There was a commotion outside, a car or something. Then we heard brakes, and a thump and a shout. We ran out, we thought he must have been hit. It was blackout, accidents can happen. But Bruiser wasn't there. Neither was the car.'

Rachel was thinking fast. Now she didn't dare agree with the old fart, say that the dog had only been dumped on her months back; she didn't want in any way, shape or form to incriminate Charlie. She *had* to stick to her story.

'You're imagining things, old man,' she said to the dog's owner. She sent a look at Alvin, and her look said, *Senile, poor old bugger.*

'What's the dog's name?' asked Alvin, watching her with suspicion in his beady little eyes.

'Bruiser,' snapped the old man.

'Mitch,' said Rachel, plucking a name from thin air. She had never named the dog. It was just a *dog*, and it had never been her intention to own one. The thing had been foisted upon her as an act of revenge by Charlie. If she ever thought of the mutt at all, it was as *that damned dog*. She had nursed it back to health; she didn't like to see anything suffer. But she didn't *love* the sodding thing. And it was obvious that this poor old chap did.

But she mustn't let sentiment stand in her way. Her heart was galloping along in her chest. Her mouth was dry as ashes.

'He's my dog,' she insisted, swallowing nervously. 'I've had him for years.'

'Let go the rope,' said Alvin.

'What?'

'Let go of the rope. Let's see who the dog goes to.'

'This is stupid, I want to get to the shop before it closes
. . .' Rachel was stepping forward, dragging the dog after
her.

Alvin stepped in front of her, blocking her path.

'Let go of the rope, Mrs Tranter,' he said sternly. 'The
dog'll show the truth of it, one way or the other.'

Rachel eyed the two men in exasperation.

Shit, what now?

'This is ridiculous,' she said flatly, and made to push her
way past Alvin.

He grabbed her arm. His eyes were sharp as they rested
on her flushed face. And now Rachel could see to her horror
that there was another policeman, a *real* policeman, not a
reservist, on the other side of the road, and he was staring
across and now *oh shit oh no* he was hurrying over to the
little group, wondering what was going on.

'Come on, Mrs Tranter, don't be difficult, just let go of
the rope,' Alvin was saying.

'What's going on here?' the big burly policeman asked.

'Mrs Tranter says this dog belongs to her. This old
gentleman says it's his.'

'It *is* mine,' said the old chap, and there were tears, real
tears in his eyes as he stared at his long-lost pet. 'Aren't you,
Bruiser?'

The dog wagged its tail again, and strained towards the
old man.

'Let go of the rope,' said the policeman, eyeing Rachel
with hard eyes. *Tranter.* He knew that lot. Villains, thugs,
spivs.

Rachel looked around at them all. This was getting
dangerous.

She threw down the rope. The dog went to the old man, and jumped up and licked his face.

'All right,' she said. 'Truth is, it just turned up injured on my doorstep and I nursed it better.'

'When was that?' asked the policeman.

'God, I don't know. Months back.' Rachel looked at the old man. 'Have the bloody thing. I'm not bothered. In fact, I'll be glad to be shot of it.'

And she turned towards home, and walked quickly away.

29

Astorre Danieri was a major face in the East End. He was an Italian immigrant, a big solid man who'd fought his way up from a Naples gutter. He had a shock of wiry black hair and dark eyes that bulged from his deeply tanned head whenever he got excited – which was often.

'I'm Italian,' he would say with a shrug. 'What can you do?'

Astorre had his fingers in a lot of pies. He had a flotilla of informants on the streets, listening out for snippets of gossip that Astorre might find useful. A whisper came back to him that the Darke mob had been involved in the mail van robbery.

'Ben Morrison's been spending like a mad man,' one contact told him.

'Oh? On what?'

'His missus. Big fat blonde, tits out to here. Strolling about in a mink. And he's been in the car showrooms. Not the cheap end of the market, either.'

'Really.'

Astorre considered this. He knew of the Darke mob, run by Charlie and his brother Joe. Ben Morrison was one of their closest cohorts, along with two others – Malcolm 'Chewy' Carson and Stevie Boyd.

'What about Charlie and Joe – they been spending?'

Two hundred thou had been snatched off that mail van. Astorre could feel his mouth watering at the thought of it.

His contact shook his head. 'Nah. They're not stupid.'

'But they got friends who are.' Astorre gave a twinkling smile. 'Let's have a word with these friends of theirs, shall we?'

30

Ruby knew she was in love. This was first-time, head-over-heels love, and she was sure – despite the fact that he was tied to his wife – that Cornelius loved her too. He took her to dinner in fancy restaurants, then home to his London house where they whiled away the hours in bed. Her life became a whirl of enjoyment; working at the Windy, being met at the stage door by him, then being whisked away to this or that elegant, expensive destination.

She loved him.

And Vi was right: what was the point of being miserable because he was married? It was a fact of his life. This was wartime. The normal rules no longer applied. She had to just get over it. Besides, he told her that it wasn't much of a marriage anyway. He said this as they lay in bed together, naked, upstairs in his lovely Georgian town house.

Ruby thought of her self-imposed rule: *I won't ever talk about your wife again.*

But it was him who had raised the subject, not her.

She propped herself up on her elbow and looked at him. Her big golden-haired god, she loved him so much. His skin was much lighter than hers. It amused her, to lay one of her arms against his, to see the difference in the colours of their skin. His was milk-white. Hers was toffee-brown.

'What do you mean, not much of a marriage?' she asked. Thinking, *I swore to myself I wouldn't do this.*

But the lure of it was irresistible. She was curious about Vanessa, his wife. She couldn't help it.

'She hates . . . this.'

'What?'

'Sex. Making love. She hates it. She tries to pretend she doesn't, but she does. I feel sorry for her most of the time, having to do it.'

Ruby thought about that. 'Well, she doesn't *have* to.'

He turned his head. The blue eyes held hers.

'Yes, she does. She wants children. Well, we both do. Desperately. Of course we do.'

At least he's not telling me they don't share a bed any more, thought Ruby. *At least he's not lying to me.* But her chest tightened with pain, as if a blow had been inflicted.

'But you've been married five years, isn't that right?'

'Yes. Five years.'

'And she's not . . . ?'

'She had a miscarriage in the first year,' he said. 'After that? Nothing.'

Ruby swallowed hard past a lump in her throat. This was horrible, painful, talking about Vanessa having sex with him. But it was like a scab – she just had to pick at it.

'She's small,' he said.

'What?'

'Vanessa,' he said. 'She's too small, it hurts her. She complains I'm too big.'

He *was* big. But too big? No. She didn't think so. When he was in bed with her, they seemed perfectly matched in every way.

'But she's so desperate to have a child,' he sighed. 'Well, we both are.'

'So she keeps on with it, even though it hurts?' Now Ruby was feeling sorry for Vanessa too.

He nodded.

'That's awful.'

'I know. She does it because she sees it as her duty. But every time, I see the pain in her eyes, and she denies it when I ask her. I say, "Do you want me to stop?" But she never says yes. Sometimes I can't even do it at all with her, I can't bear to have a woman who's so obviously doing it against her will.'

'You poor thing,' said Ruby. It was tragic.

'That's why I'm so lucky to have you, my darling,' he said, turning to her, running his big hands down over her hips. 'You make up for all of it.'

He buried his blond head between her breasts. Ruby stared into space, thinking about Vanessa, desperate to have a child yet hating the very act that could create one. No wonder he needed the release of this, no wonder he needed to be with a woman who enjoyed bed, not dreaded it. But she felt a twinge of unease as she lay there, just the tiniest sliver of foreboding.

31

1922

When she was alone in the shop, Alicia put up the CLOSED sign, then went behind the counter and opened the trapdoor into the cellar where she kept the surplus stock. She switched on the light down there, illuminating the chilly gloom of it. Dense shadows bloomed along the side of the steeply slanting staircase.

Alicia gulped. She was nearly three months gone now and soon she'd really start to show. Sick with fear, she took a step forward. Hesitated. Then she flung herself down the cellar steps.

She was bruised, sore all over and stunned by the impact of falling. Sobbing, she clawed herself onto the bottom step and sat there. She couldn't believe Leroy had abandoned her like he had. But now it would all be as it was before he came. Now the baby would come away.

When it didn't, she threw herself down the stairs again.

The baby seemed to be refusing to give up its life. After those two hideous, painful, terrifying times, she couldn't summon the nerve to do the steps again, she couldn't bear the pain of more scrapes and bruises. If she wasn't careful, she'd break her bloody neck and that would be the end of that. Her boys would be motherless.

She thought of knitting needles, metal coat hangers to claw the baby out of her. She sat one day with them in her shaking hands before dropping them with a shudder.

Instead, she tried gin, lots *of gin to deaden the pain of Leroy's betrayal and the fear of what would become of her. Time and again she took the scalding-hot baths that should have made Leroy's baby perish and abort.*

It was on her fifth attempt at this, when she'd just stepped from the tin bath in front of the kitchen fire, her skin lobster-red from the nearly intolerable heat of the water, that Ted came home early. He stepped through the back door into the scullery, then into the kitchen where she stood exposed.

Alicia lunged for the towel, but not quickly enough. Ted stood there staring at her nakedness, at the full round belly, the distended breasts.

'What the fuck's this?*' he said, stunned.*

'Ted . . .' She didn't know what to say.

Ted seemed to gather himself.

Suddenly his face twisted and reddened. He yelled: 'What the fuck you been doin', girl?'

Then he was across the room, grabbing her arm, his fist coming up and whacking her around the face.

What followed that day was worse than the cellar steps. Much, much worse. But still, the child held on. Ted smashed the Jelly Roll Morton record, and the Maxitone.

'Nigger music!' he bellowed in fury.

As Alicia lay crying and broken-hearted in bed that night, her husband rigid with disgust beside her, she knew that this was her destiny. She would carry Leroy's child to full term. And then, probably, Ted would kill it – and her.

32

Vanessa Bray was first made aware that her husband had taken a mistress by her sister-in-law, Julianna, who came over to take tea with her at Brayfield in the deep wilds of Hampshire.

Vanessa didn't much like Julianna. She was big, robust and blonde, just like her brother, Cornelius, with flaring blue eyes that widened and leapt with fire and fury as she spoke forcibly about this issue or that.

Julianna was so unlike Vanessa that she could have been a separate species. Vanessa was a tiny woman, delicately boned and quietly spoken. She found Julianna, with her passionate rantings, more than a little wearing.

Vanessa was the well-bred and beautifully schooled daughter of a blustering major general in the British Army. She had long ago learned to just nod and smile, like her mother did. Also like her mother, she took refuge in her garden, and tried to ignore the chaotic state of the outside world.

She saw the planes go over – *Nazi* planes – and heard their horrible deathly drone. She knew they were bombing Southampton to get the Spitfire factory, knew they were going to London to bomb the docks, knock out the gasworks, bring the city to its knees. She worried about Cornelius being there, going about his War Office business amid the catastrophic impact of the Blitzkrieg.

She tried not to think about it. Her nerves were delicate, her mother's had been too. She couldn't allow herself to become upset. She had been trying so hard for a baby, they had *both* been trying. She did her duty with absolute forbearance. Every time Cornelius penetrated her, she flinched and tightened, it was agony and all she wanted was for it to stop. She thought he sensed it, although she was always careful not to let her anguish show.

She shuddered even to think of it, him undressing and then approaching her with his naked penis rearing up like a one-eyed snake. Pushing her back onto the bed, finding the place, pushing it inside her, panting and pawing at her breasts, bruising her in the throes of his passion, until he cried out and released his seed into her sore, waiting body.

But now – at last! – she had been to the doctor and he had confirmed it: she was pregnant. The end result was worth all the discomfort; she would have a child, she *longed* for a child, to prove that she was worthy, not the disappointment that her witch of a mother-in-law so clearly believed her to be.

Then she thought of that awful day when she had bled uncontrollably, the baby she had miscarried in their first year of marriage. She had lost one baby already. She couldn't bear to lose another, she knew she'd fall apart.

And now here was Julianna, intruding on her fragile peace, forcing her to confront things she would far rather be in ignorance of.

'I just thought you should know, that's all,' said Julianna bracingly. 'No good burying one's head in the sand, is it? He's got this girl, up in town.'

'Girl?' Vanessa didn't want to hear this. But Julianna was relentless in her honesty, bludgeoning Vanessa's fragile tranquillity with her careless words.

'Don't fret about it for a moment,' said Julianna. 'They

all do it, don't they? Terence has had a few dalliances, they mean nothing really.'

'Who is this . . . girl?' Vanessa was pouring tea with only a slightly shaking hand. She wanted to throw the pot at Julianna, to stop that busily working mouth and its careless outpourings.

She'd known from early on in the marriage that Cornelius was what people called a *player*. There had been tearful phone calls from dejected floozies, receipts for gifts he'd been too careless to hide. She didn't want to *hear* about it – couldn't Julianna see that?

'She's a tart, darling, nothing to worry about.' Julianna was slathering butter onto a scone. 'Works at that dreadful theatre place where they all stand around nearly naked. Can you believe that? It's a complete scandal. I just think it's unfair how people collude to keep such things from us. A wife should at least *know*.'

'Is she . . .' Vanessa put down the teacup before she gave in to temptation and lobbed it straight at Julianna's bright blonde head. 'Is she pretty?'

'Pretty?' Julianna spoke through a mouthful of scone. 'Well, yes, I suppose so. Very *dark*. I saw them at the Ritz. She's tall with black hair. Attractive, I suppose. You know Cornelius – he never could resist dipping his hand in the honeypot. It'll blow over soon. These things always do.'

When they next met, Ruby could see straight away that something was different. Cornelius was jittery, on edge. Usually he chatted easily to her, telling her a little – only a little, because careless talk really could cost lives – about his War Office work, about Churchill and what a great man he was, and about the newly proposed Consultative Assembly of the Council of Europe, which would be formed when the war was over.

'Will it *ever* be over?' asked Ruby gloomily when he spoke so confidently about it.

'Yes, it will – and of course we'll win,' he always said. 'I shall become a British delegate.'

But tonight there was little conversation. And finally, at the end of the evening, after they'd made love, he spilled the beans.

'She's pregnant,' he blurted out. 'Vanessa. She's pregnant.'

So this was his great, exciting secret. Ruby just lay there, thinking, *What am I supposed to say now? That I'm happy? That I'm sad?*

Truthfully, she didn't know *how* she felt about it. Clearly, he was delighted. Vanessa must be over the moon. But her . . . Where did this leave her? Would he forget her now, become wrapped up in family life? She didn't think so. He needed the release of sex, and in Ruby's limited experience, having kids made a bad sex life worse, not better. But . . . she couldn't be sure. She could never be sure of anything, because she was just the bit on the side. He was always careful not to impregnate *her*.

But Vanessa was his *wife*.

'Well . . . say something,' he said, watching her anxiously.

'I'm pleased for both of you,' said Ruby.

'Really?' He was staring at her in disbelief. 'I thought you'd be mad as hell about it.'

Ruby shrugged. She was wounded to the heart, but she kept her face clear of all emotion.

'What would be the point of that? I knew you were still sleeping with her. I know that's what you both want, so it's good news. Isn't it?'

'Darling, you're a marvel,' he said, and kissed her.

But something inside Ruby had shrivelled up and died. Her place in the pecking order was *way* down the line. This just confirmed it.

33

Alicia Darke gave birth to her baby on a black rainy night. When the little girl emerged into the world, Ted was there in the room, pacing around. Waiting. There was no midwife with her; Ted wouldn't even allow Alicia's mother to attend.

When he saw the child, his lip curled in disgust.

'It's black,' he said, eyeing his wife accusingly. 'Fuck you to hell and eternity, Alicia. It's a little black bastard.'

Exhausted and ashamed, Alicia could only stare at the little girl. She wasn't black. She was a beautiful caramel-coloured child. Ted himself cut the cord and tied it, and took the baby and bathed it.

Alicia was afraid, watching him handle the little girl. She had chosen a name already.

Rupert for a boy. Ruby for a girl. She held her breath as she watched Ted holding the child at arm's length, like she was something loathsome, distasteful. When he placed Ruby back in her mother's arms, Alicia breathed out at last, relieved he hadn't harmed her.

'You're still bleeding,' said Ted, seeing the blood pooling on the sheets.

'That'll stop,' said Alicia. She had bled a fair bit with Charlie and Joe too. It was nothing new.

But it didn't.

By morning, she was unconscious.

By midday, Ted panicked and called the doctor. But it was too late. Alicia was dead.

'Haemorrhage,' said the doctor, snapping his bag shut. 'Should have called me sooner.'

Ted stared down at his dead wife and at the tar-brush baby in the crib.

This was God's work.

Alicia had paid for her evil ways. Now he would have to raise the child, and his two poor boys, alone. He didn't shed a tear for his wife, the treacherous mare. Let her burn in hell for her sins.

34

Something was niggling at PC Churcher. It had been a silly little incident, the old man and the woman scrapping over the ugliest dog he had ever clapped eyes on. And Alvin the reservist, what a twat he was, playing at coppers on his evenings off. You heard such bloody stupid things. The ARP wardens, trying to get people charged for lighting a fucking candle or puffing too brightly on a cigarette. A lot of these part-timers were *loonies*, in his opinion, finally getting some power in their drab little lives and instantly getting drunk on it.

PC Churcher was an ambitious man. He wanted to make his mark, to step up the ladder of promotion in the force. He was always on the lookout for the possibility of advancement. And something about the dog incident set his copper's nose twitching.

The old man, Bob Julius, had gabbled on to Alvin and him after the Tranter woman had departed, giving them chapter and verse about the night when his dog vanished, and neither of them had really been listening. He had his dog back; end of story.

But something penetrated. PC Churcher heard him talking about blood in the road next morning. His ears perked up.

'There's never many cars or vans about in the night, petrol rationing's seen to *that*,' said the old chap. 'But when I went out in daylight to look for Bruiser, there was blood on the road.'

'So you think the dog must have been knocked down?' Now PC Tranter was staring at the dog, with its crooked hind leg lifted an inch or two off the ground.

'Must have been. Look at his poor bloody leg.'

'Give me your address, sir.'

Bob Julius gave it, while busily patting the dog's head and grinning with delight at finding Bruiser again.

'Well, that's odd,' said PC Churcher.

'What is?' asked Alvin.

'It looks like the dog was run over by a car or a van . . .'

'I think it *was* a van, I heard an engine and it sounded too loud for a car,' chipped in Julius. 'And there was something else. I didn't think nothing of it at the time. I heard a bloke shout: "Back up a bit!"'

PC Churcher was writing all this down in his notebook. 'Like he – no, like someone else with him in the van maybe – had run over the dog, it was lying under the wheels, and he had to back up to release the injured animal?'

'Like that I suppose. Yeah,' said Julius.

'That's odd,' repeated PC Churcher.

'*What's* odd?' asked Alvin impatiently.

'Well, that was the widow Tranter, who lives two streets down from here. While Mr Julius here lives half a mile away. So how did the dog get from outside Mr Julius's house to Mrs Tranter's?'

They all three looked at each other. If injured but able to walk, the dog would have surely gone back indoors, to his home. But if the injuries had been severe . . .

'In the van,' said Alvin and Bob Julius, at the same time.

'It's likely,' agreed PC Churcher.

It was interesting, but it was nothing of any real importance. Except that the widow Tranter's husband had been

Micky Tranter, local gangster, so she couldn't be all that straight herself, surely?

But so what?

No. It was nothing.

'When did this happen, exactly?' he asked, folding his notebook and slipping it back into his breast pocket.

Bob Julius gave PC Churcher the date. 'I remember it because it was my old lady's birthday. What a bloody birthday, eh? Two raids. We had to eat our dinner down the shelter. And then my dog goes missing.'

PC Churcher was staring at the old man.

'Will that be all now, officer? I'll get Bruiser home, my old lady's going to be made up.'

'Yes,' said PC Churcher, 'that's all for now, thank you, sir.'

PC Churcher was walking away to continue his beat when Alvin called after him: 'Hey! Wasn't that the night the Post Office mail van got done?'

35

Ruby had to run off the stage in the middle of the midday performance. There was 'flu going around – as if they didn't have enough on their plates with Hitler dropping bombs on their bloody heads – and she knew she'd caught it. Several of the girls already had, and were off sick.

She vomited in the tiny loo backstage. Mrs Henderson was there, rich as Croesus so everyone said, but as kind as a mother hen. Draped in fox furs and scented with sickly lavender that made Ruby's stomach turn over all the more. She tutted and cooed over Ruby.

'Oh dear – looks like you've caught it,' she said, laying a cool hand on Ruby's hot, sweating brow. 'Better go home, dear. Right now,' she added, as Ruby started to weakly protest.

She felt no better next day. She was sick again. Vi came by and eyed her beadily.

'Fuck it, not you too. They're all coming down with it, we're dropping like flies.'

Betsy came by a couple of days later. She had forgiven Ruby for forgetting their date, and was determined to prove herself magnanimous. She knew Ruby was on her own with no woman to care for her. She bustled around happily. Ruby needed her. Vi was no good where there was illness, so it was her, Betsy, who saved the day. Ruby's old dad with his dicky foot and Charlie and Joe were worse than useless when there was sickness in the family – men always were.

'Why don't *they* get it?' Ruby moaned, feeling useless lying in bed with her stomach turning over and over. 'I could look after *them*. But no. They're fine, aren't they? It's just me that's copped it.'

'Don't worry, dear,' said Betsy, bringing her a mug of hot Bovril. 'I'm here, aren't I?'

A week later, Ruby was no better.

Charlie came and stood in her doorway. 'Fuck's sake, Ruby. You look like death.'

'I don't know what's wrong with me,' she moaned. All she knew was that she was spending a lot of time stumbling back and forth to the chamber pot, being sick. Her head wasn't bad, she wasn't all snotty and bunged-up. Maybe it was something more serious. Maybe she had appendicitis. She'd heard you could die from that, if it burst.

'Better get the doctor out,' said Charlie, and turned and went off downstairs.

The doctor was there by mid-afternoon.

Ruby didn't ask how Charlie had achieved this miracle. Charlie always had money, she knew that much; he would have slipped the quack a few quid for this visit.

The doctor was old, fat, and he looked worn out. He blustered about the bedroom, stuck a freezing-cold stethoscope against Ruby's chest and back, palpated her stomach.

'Is it appendicitis?' she asked.

Joe came and leaned against the doorframe, concern on his face. 'Is it the 'flu, Doc?' he asked. 'She's been like it a couple of weeks now, does it go on that long?'

The doctor was busy prodding at Ruby's midriff. 'Last show?' he asked.

For a moment, stupidly, she thought he was talking about the shows at the Windy. But he was asking when her last period had occurred. Her periods had always been erratic. She thought back. 'I'm not sure. . .'

Now she was beginning to feel anxious. She thought it could be six, seven weeks since her last period, maybe even longer. She'd been so busy, working and seeing Cornelius – who hadn't been near her since she'd been off sick, the bastard – and thinking of fun and laughter and dinners at the Ritz, she hadn't even been noticing what was going on.

'Six weeks ago, I think,' she said.

'I think it must be longer.' The doctor's eyes held hers. 'You seem to be about two months pregnant.'

Ruby felt every muscle in her body freeze. 'You *what?*'

'It's morning sickness,' the doctor said, putting his stethoscope back into his bag and snapping it shut with finality. He stood up. 'Worse in the early stages – you should start to feel better soon.'

The doctor went to the door. Ruby's panic-stricken eyes met Joe's. Her brother was looking at her as if she was a stranger.

'You're saying she's up the duff?' Joe asked in disbelief.

Ruby cringed. She felt even worse now than she had before. Now she felt not only sick but ashamed. She could see the harsh disapproval in Joe's eyes; he thought she was a slag.

'She's pregnant,' the doctor repeated as he stood beside Joe at the door. He glanced back at Ruby. He knew the family, he knew she was unmarried, he knew *everything*. Ruby reddened and shrank back into the pillows.

With that, the doctor went off down the stairs and out the front door. Joe stood there, as if transfixed, staring at Ruby. Then suddenly he bellowed: 'Charlie! Get up here!'

She was just glad that Dad wasn't up here too. His health – always a problem – had been getting steadily worse. Now he was asthmatic, and what with his bad foot and that, he could no longer manage the stairs. Charlie and Joe had put a bed in the front parlour for him. *Thank God for small mercies,* she thought. Dad was a spent force now, and she was grateful for that, at least.

Ruby sat at the breakfast table with Joe and Charlie a few weeks later. She'd taken Dad in his breakfast on a tray. The sickness was still bad, but she could force down a slice of bread and jam, a cup of tea. What *really* choked her was the way her brothers looked at her. Mostly they didn't talk to her at all. But when they did, their eyes said it all. That she was disgusting, a tramp, a disappointment.

After the doctor's visit, Charlie was too furious to speak. But later, he had spelled out how it was going to be. She could carry on working at the salvage centre, do whatever the fuck she liked, until she started to show.

'Then we'll ship you off, maybe down to Aunt Martha's in Essex. You can have the kid, then I'll take care of what's to be done with it. Then you can come back here.' Charlie stared at her face, his lip curling in disapproval. 'I ain't even told Dad yet, Christ knows how he'd take it. He's ill enough as it is. And look, you daft mare – don't for fuck's sake ever get caught like this again.'

What's to be done with it. Those words rang around Ruby's head like a death knell. Like the baby growing inside her was a piece of rubbish, to be disposed of. Like she herself was an embarrassment, to be shunted aside where no one could see the shame she had brought upon the Darkes.

Charlie was terrifying when he was like this: cold and hostile, taking over, directing operations.

'Who did it then?' he demanded while they sat at the breakfast table.

Ruby sat there, silent. She knew what Charlie was capable of in the grip of one of his rages. She didn't want Cornelius hurt. She *loved* him. She hadn't broken the news to him yet, but she had every confidence that he would take care of her, and their child, even if he *was* married.

'Now come on. I said *who the fuck did it?*' Charlie shouted in her face, thumping the kitchen table with his fist. 'You tell me now, you bitch, or I swear . . .' He raised his hand.

'Easy,' said Joe, looking uncomfortable. Ruby was *expecting*, after all.

'Cornelius Bray,' blurted out Ruby in a paroxysm of fear. 'He works at the War Office.'

The rest of it poured out too. That she'd been working at the Windy, not the salvage yard; and it was at the Windmill Theatre that she'd met Cornelius.

36

Charlie ran over to the corner shop like a long dog. He barrelled inside, slapped the CLOSED sign up, and turned on Betsy, who was frozen in surprise behind the counter.

'Charlie?' she said, bewildered.

He rushed across to her and grabbed her by the arm.

'Ow! Charlie, that *hurts*,' cried Betsy.

'You been covering for her. Ain't you?'

'What . . . ?' asked Betsy faintly, eyes wild with fright.

'Now *don't* play the innocent, Bets. I'm talking about Ruby. She's up the duff. She's been lying to us, saying she was doing war work over at the salvage centre, when in fact she was playing the fucking *tart* at that Windmill place.'

'I didn't . . .' Betsy started.

Charlie shook her, hard. 'You *knew*. Don't tell me you didn't, because you ruddy well did. You two have always been thick as thieves.'

Not any more, thought Betsy. Now Ruby seemed to much prefer Vi's company to hers. In fact, she could now see that Ruby had only *made use* of her, while she was off having fun with Vi. And now look! It had all gone wrong for Ruby, which just about served her right.

'She asked me to cover for her,' lied Betsy. 'It was her idea. I wanted her to tell you, I told her so. You have to believe me, Charlie.'

Something about the earnest expression on Betsy's face calmed Charlie. He let go of her arm and passed a weary hand over his brow.

'What are you going to do then, Charlie?' she asked. It would reflect badly on him, on the entire family, Ruby having a child out of wedlock.

'Sort it out,' he said. 'What the hell else can I do?'

He went across the shop. Flipped over the sign. Opened the door. A copper was standing there.

37

PC Churcher dragged Charlie down to the local nick. Chewy, Ben and Stevie were hauled in too, and Joe, and they were questioned intensively over the mail van robbery. But making this shit stick was proving a lot harder than Churcher had first thought it would be. After long hours, Charlie and Joe and the boys were released.

But Churcher couldn't let it go.

This injured dog had opened up new possibilities. Patiently and diligently, he took statements from the dog's elderly owner and his wife, and then he kept an eye on the widow Tranter's house for a few days, and *then*, confident that he had something to go on, he reported back to his superior officer at the Yard. Churcher knew he would be in line for promotion if he could bring this case alive again.

'So, what you got?' asked his sergeant.

Churcher laid it out for him. Micky Tranter's widow and her connection to Charlie Darke, who was a known villain who had been questioned in the case though charged with nothing. Charlie had been seen twice this week going into her house; Mrs Tranter with the injured dog, and its owner's intervention in the street; and the fact that the dog had apparently been run over on the night of the mail van robbery.

'So you know what I think?' said Churcher in conclusion while the sergeant sat silent, taking it all in. 'I think Charlie

Darke and his boys *did* pull off that robbery. They ran over the dog with the van, it was injured. And Charlie took it to his fancy piece for her to sort out.'

'Maybe,' said the sergeant.

'We've got to take a look at that mail van, sir. It was found empty the day after the robbery and put in the pound over near Augustus Street, wasn't it?'

His superior nodded. Maybe Churcher *was* onto something. 'If the van hit the dog . . .' he said.

'It's a big dog. There'll be a bit of damage, maybe. And blood? Who knows?'

His superior officer looked sceptical.

'We'll see,' he said. 'Won't we?'

38

On Friday, Cornelius went to work in the War Office as usual, then went to Waterloo to take the train back down to Brayfield for the weekend. His taxi pulled up outside the station. He'd no sooner paid the driver than someone as big as himself came charging out of the shadows and yanked him off his feet and crashed him into a wall.

'What the *hell?*' he gasped.

All sorts of scum around these days, looking to rob innocent people of their valuables. Deserters and the like. The taxi driver took no notice, he just drove away. He wasn't about to get involved.

'Cornelius Bray?' snarled the man, staring straight into his eyes.

Cornelius stiffened. This wasn't anything as simple or straightforward as a robbery. The man knew him.

'Who wants to know?' asked Cornelius. His attacker wasn't familiar to him. He was tall, hard-muscled, dark-haired, and his grey-blue eyes were both icy and manic.

'Charlie Darke,' said the man, clutching harder at the front of Cornelius's camel-hair coat. 'You bastard, you got my sister up the gut.'

'*What?*'

'My sister. Ruby. She's pregnant. And it's yours.'

Cornelius's head spun with the force of this assault and

these words. He tried to assimilate the information he'd just been given, but all he could think was that this man looked crazy – mad enough to kill him.

'I didn't . . .' he started.

Charlie yanked him away, pulling him off balance, further back into the shadows where no one could see them. Cornelius staggered against the wall, feeling skin scrape off his hand, feeling the sting of it. His briefcase fell to the ground.

'*Don't* lie to me, arsehole. You got her pregnant.'

'Not me.' Now Cornelius was shaking his head. He'd been so careful. He hadn't wanted complications. He'd used French letters each and every time they'd had sex.

But remember that time when the condom split? asked a tiny voice in his brain. He stiffened, thinking fast. It *had* split, just once. And once was enough. But denial was his only option. He was married, his *wife* was pregnant. He couldn't complicate things any further, they were bad enough already.

'It wasn't me,' he said.

'Yeah, it was,' said Charlie, thumping Cornelius's head back against the wall to emphasize his point. 'You got her pregnant . . .'

'Well *someone* did,' said Cornelius, and his weak grin of denial enraged Charlie all the more.

He gave the posh bastard's head another whack against the wall. 'You sayin' my sister's a slut? She ain't. The poor silly cow thinks she's in love with you, says you've told her how much you love her too. So now you're going to do the right thing by her.'

'Did she tell you I'm married?'

Charlie froze. 'You're *what?*'

'Married. So you can pound me black and blue, but I can't "do the right thing", can I?'

'You *fucker,*' hissed Charlie. 'You been turkin' my sister and you're a married man?'

'Look,' said Cornelius, 'I can pay to get rid of it. Whatever she wants, I'll pay. It's not a problem.'

'What? My sister, go to one of those back-street abortionists with a length of wire and a packet of Omo to scour her out with? You're joking, mate. You'll pay all right. I'll be in touch to let you have the bill for your little pleasures, all right? You pay up for our girl, or I'll fucking kill you.'

39

The journey home was fraught and fearful after that. On the train, Cornelius was transfixed by the idea that Ruby's thuggish family might somehow contact Vanessa, and tell her about Ruby's condition. Vanessa's nerves were always taut as a bowstring; she was delicate at the best of times. Now, with the baby coming, she would be more than ever in need of peace and stability.

What if Charlie Darke got in touch with her and told her about Ruby and the baby she was carrying – *his* baby? Oh, it was his. For all his bold words when he'd been talking to Charlie, he didn't doubt that. Ruby had been a virgin when they met, and she was in love with him; he knew that. She wouldn't want any other man, she loved *him*.

He picked up his car at the station and sat in it for long moments, staring at the rain on the windscreen. Sighing, he started the engine and slipped the car into gear. He was in a mess, but it wasn't unsalvageable. Vanessa hardly ever came up to town. She loved the country and never wanted to leave it. Ruby was an East Ender, a London girl through and through; the two would never cross paths.

They *mustn't*.

Finally he turned into the drive and passed the brightly lit gatehouse. His mother – Lady Bray, widow of his late father

Sir Hilary – lived there. At other times he would have stopped, told his mother that she mustn't keep these lights on, and she would say, with all the hauteur of one born to privilege, 'Why shouldn't I? We're miles out in the country, is Hitler going to bomb us out here? I don't think so, dear.'

It was a conversation they'd had many times. She would be unapologetic, he would smile indulgently. But this time he didn't stop the car. He drove on up the long, winding driveway to the main house and pulled up outside. The last of the day's light was going, but he could still see its big outline, solidly comforting, black against the paler sky.

Brayfield had been in his family for four generations. Built of glowing rose-red brick with cream stone quoins at the corners, the Elizabethan manor house was a pink jewel set in acres of green. It had two outer gables and a smaller central one, and a stunning clock tower to one side.

Brayfield was, in every way, a grand house and he adored it. It was in his blood. It should be full of children, bursting at the seams with them. Now – at last – that dream would come true. Vanessa was expecting their first child, hopefully the first of many.

He parked beside the big circular fountain of Neptune that guarded the front entrance, and for the first time saw the other car there, a Riley. Frowning, he turned off the engine, got out, locked the car and went up the steps. The porch light was off because of the blackout. He slipped his key in the door, fumbling slightly, and was stepping inside, laying his briefcase aside, shrugging his coat off, when Mrs Hayter the housekeeper came hurrying along the hall, her stern face pale and anxious.

'What is it?' Instantly he was on the alert. 'Whose car is that?'

'I called the doctor. Mrs Bray . . .' Her voice trailed away. Her eyes lifted to the stairs.

His heart suddenly in his throat, Cornelius took the stairs two at a time and crossed the landing to the master bedroom. He threw open the door. The doctor was there, a thin little man wearing half-moon spectacles. His head turned as Cornelius came into the room.

Cornelius stared at his wife, lying there pale and sickly-looking in the bed. She was fully dressed in a white blouse and a beige rucked-up skirt. The front of the skirt had a bloodstain the size of a dinner plate on it. There was a prim-rose-yellow towel wedged up between his wife's slim legs, and the yellow was rapidly turning a dull brownish-red.

'Vanessa!' He ran forward, sat on the bed, clutched at her hand. 'My God, what's happened?'

'I'm sorry,' said the doctor. 'I'm afraid she's lost the baby.'

Cornelius felt like he must be going mad. 'No!' he shouted, springing to his feet.

Vanessa was crying silently. She looked appealingly at Cornelius. 'I'm so sorry,' she said. 'I've let you down again.'

'No! No you haven't, don't be silly. It's just one of those awful things that happen.'

'Yes. To me. Always to me.' Vanessa started to sob.

The doctor drew Cornelius to one side. 'Call the house-keeper up here, Mr Bray. She needs a woman with her, help her get cleaned up. And the baby . . .' He lowered his voice. 'It's in the toilet bowl. It's dead.'

Cornelius's stomach clenched hard with horror. He stood up and walked on numb legs to the door out onto the landing. This couldn't be happening. In one day, he had learned that his mistress was pregnant, which was a nuisance, a liability; and now this. Was it God's hand at work, punishing him for his sin of ungovernable lust? Because now his wife had lost their longed-for baby, which would have been cherished and adored.

He called the housekeeper up to attend to Vanessa. The

doctor beckoned him out onto the landing and, when Mrs Hayter had gone in to help Vanessa, the doctor closed the bedroom door gently.

'Mr Bray,' he said quietly, 'I'm terribly sorry.'

Cornelius looked at him. 'But these things happen, don't they? Every day of the week. And then people go on to have healthy babies.'

'Mr Bray . . .'

'Obviously she needs to rest more. I've told her about bending and stretching in the garden, we have a *gardener* for that sort of thing, I have warned her . . .'

'Mr Bray.' The doctor interrupted this feverish flow of words, his tone sharp. 'Mr Bray, I'm sorry, but I have to tell you that your wife shouldn't be put through this again.'

'What?' Cornelius's face was blank.

'She isn't physically or even mentally strong enough to bear children, Mr Bray. That's what nature's trying to tell us, and that's what I'm telling you now. She's fragile.'

'What? But surely . . .'

'Mr Bray.' Now the doctor's face was hard. 'Listen to what I'm telling you, for the love of God. One more miscarriage like this could kill her. I'm warning you.'

Cornelius turned away from the words that were hurting him too much. Of all the horrible, twisted jokes to be played on a man, this had to be the worst. His mistress was giving birth to a child he didn't want – and his wife had just lost the child he did want.

'I'm so sorry, Mr Bray,' said the doctor to his back.

Cornelius turned and looked at the little man. 'Get out of my house,' he said quietly.

'I'm sorry . . .'

'*Get out of my house you bastard!*' he roared.

The doctor gave him one last startled look and then hurried off down the stairs. He crossed the hall, and went quickly out of the door. It closed behind him. Into the silence came the sounds of Vanessa sobbing, and the muffled, soothing tones of Mrs Hayter as she tried to comfort her.

40

When he was sure that Vanessa was asleep and that Mrs Hayter was sitting with her, he walked out into the star-studded night and trudged down the long drive to the gate-house, lit up like a ship at sea in an ocean of darkness. He knocked on the door, then put his key in the lock and entered.

'Is that you, dear?' came Lady Bray's voice, from the sitting room.

'Yes, it's me,' he called back, and went in.

The fire was blazing away in the hearth and his mother was sitting in the same chair where she always sat, her elegant silver chignon glinting in the firelight, her chin sharply pointed, her blue eyes intense. She was working on a piece of bright floral tapestry on a frame, with her glasses slipping down her nose. She peered up at him over the top of them and said: 'What's the matter?' when she saw his face.

Cornelius slumped down on the sofa, dropped his head into his hands. He sat like that for long moments. Finally he let his hands fall between his knees and stared at her.

'She's lost the baby,' he said starkly.

'What? When? Why didn't that stupid Hayter woman come and get me . . . ?'

'This afternoon. I got back from the city to find the doctor there.'

'But Hayter should have told me.'

'I don't think there was time. When I got home, it was all over.'

'How ghastly for you,' said his mother, with sympathy. 'And poor Vanessa.'

Cornelius looked at his mother. She had never really liked Vanessa, had said before their marriage took place that Vanessa was not good stock: too skinny and nervy.

'Look at those hips,' she had said to him. 'Those are *not* good child-bearing hips.'

'She's heartbroken,' he said.

But he had once fallen in love with Vanessa's delicacy, her frailty. He felt big and strong with her. Only after the marriage did he discover that they were badly matched physically. He'd had to take his pleasures elsewhere – so what? Many other men did the same.

'Well, of course she is, the poor girl.' But he could see in his mother's steely eyes the thought that Vanessa's inability to give birth was reprehensible. She had warned him about just this outcome.

Cornelius was aware that there was a weight of responsibility upon him. For four generations, Brays had bred to continue the line, producing the requisite number of children to be sure the family name would live on.

But now, this. If what the doctor had said was true and Vanessa couldn't bear children at all, then what would become of the Bray line? Julianna, his sister, was married to Terence Wyatt, co-owner of a small merchant bank. But as yet there were no children. Perhaps there wouldn't be. It was a bad situation.

'And there's something else, something unfortunate . . .'

'Yes? Go on, dear.' His mother's head dipped as she applied herself to the tapestry. It was a ploy she often employed with her son: if he had to confess something, he found it easier if her eyes were focused elsewhere.

'There's a girl. She works at the Windmill Theatre, in town.'

'A girl?' She kept her head down. She knew her son had an excessively sexual nature: his father had been just the same.

'It's a bloody mess, I'm afraid. She's pregnant.'

Now the eyes came up and fixed sharply on his face. 'And it's yours?'

He nodded. Much as he might bluster about this, he knew that Ruby would sleep with no one else. The silly girl actually loved him. And he cared for her, of course he did, but she was from a different class. She was just for fun, like all the other beautiful young girls and exquisite young boys he sometimes enjoyed. He was *married*, for God's sake.

'It's mine. And her brother's demanding payment from me.'

'How much?'

'He didn't say. He said he'd be in touch, though. And he will be. I could see he meant it.'

'Is she intending to keep the baby, this girl?'

'Her brother says she'll have it. I suppose they'll get it adopted. She can't keep it, after all. She's a single woman.'

'Oh.' Then his mother said: 'So you'll have to pay him for . . . what? Their silence? Are they threatening to tell anyone about it?'

'No. They're not threatening that. They want Ruby compensated, that's all.' Cornelius let his head drop into his hands again. 'What a *mess.*'

'Look,' said his mother, putting aside her tapestry, 'you're tired. You're in no fit state to consider this right now. Eat something, get some sleep. Tomorrow, we'll talk again.'

Cornelius ran his hands down over his face and looked at his mother. 'You're right,' he said.

But tomorrow I still won't know what to do.

'Kiss me goodnight,' she said, and offered up her cheek.

Dutifully, Cornelius kissed her, and left the room, and walked back up the drive to the house that meant so much to him, and to the woman who couldn't even give him children to fill it.

His mother put aside her tapestry and stood up, stretching. Time for bed. Poor Cornelius, he never could see what was so plainly staring him in the face. The answer was obvious, and easy.

Tomorrow, she would explain it to him.

41

Charlie Darke's boys, Chewy, Stevie and Ben, were coming out of the Rag and Staff after a late-night lock-in when the men grabbed them. It was ten on three, they were drunk and taken unawares. They never stood a chance.

They were kicked, punched insensible and then hustled into a motor and driven to an empty warehouse in the docks. Bleeding and semi-conscious, they were tied to chairs. Then a big dark-haired pop-eyed Italian came in and stood looking down at them.

'Chewy Carson,' he said, starting at the one on the left. His voice echoed around the cavernous building.

Chewy was bald with a long dour face and brown eyes. He had a habit of chewing the inside of his lip when he was nervous. He was nervous now. 'That's you, right?'

Chewy said nothing. He spat out a tooth. Blood spattered Astorre's brightly polished shoes. Astorre smiled.

'And you're Stevie Boyd,' he went on, looking at the man in the middle, a dumpy, curly-haired and plug-ugly individual.

'So you must be Ben Morrison,' said Astorre to the blond one seated on the right. 'Been buying your wife presents, I hear.'

Ben said nothing. But he felt Stevie and Chewy's eyes turn on him, felt their derision like the sting of a whip.

'Been buying her fur coats,' said Astorre.

Fucking Moira, thought Ben. She'd been bending his ear night and day until he'd caved in and bought her the damned coat. Then – all right, admitted – he'd looked at a few cars, where was the harm in that? Joe had marked his card over it . . . but too bloody late, by the look of things. Moira had her mink. And *he* was in the shit.

'And I can't help wondering,' said Astorre, pacing around in front of the three bound men while his boys looked on, 'where you got that sort of cash.'

Ben tried to shrug. It hurt.

'There's always cash floating about,' he said.

'Particularly in mail vans,' said Astorre. 'You did that job, am I right? With Charlie and Joe Darke. Yes?'

'No,' said Chewy. 'Not us.'

'No?' Astorre stopped walking and stared hard at Chewy. Chewy could feel his heart beating so hard he thought he was about to faint. 'You sure?' asked Astorre.

'It wasn't us,' said Stevie, shooting a look at Ben that said: *You fucking fool, we'll get you for this.*

'Well, that's a pity,' sighed Astorre. His eyes were fastened on Chewy. 'You want to change your mind on that?' he asked.

Chewy shook his head: no. He was sweating; he *stank* of fear.

Astorre stepped closer. 'Sure?'

Chewy shook his head again. Whatever these bastards did to them, it would be nothing compared to what Charlie would do if *he* kicked off.

'Pity,' said Astorre, putting his big hands around Chewy's neck and starting to squeeze.

Chewy's whole head went purple. His eyes bulged out of their sockets, his mouth turned down in a grimace of pain. Ben and Stevie started shouting. Astorre squeezed, harder and harder. A wheezing groan escaped Chewy.

'No!' howled Stevie, struggling against his bonds.

'You can't . . .' Ben was about to spew in horror.

Astorre squeezed.

Chewy's eyes closed and his head went forward. Urine dripped from his chair onto the concrete floor. Stevie and Ben watched, mouths open, not believing it.

Astorre stepped back, avoiding the pooling liquid on the floor. Then he turned to the other two.

'Now,' he said. 'Suppose one of you tells me where the two hundred thousand pounds you and Charlie and Joe nicked from the mail van is hidden?'

Ben somehow got his mouth to work. The bastard had *killed* Chewy.

'They gave us three grand each,' he gabbled. 'Another three grand's to come. Six in total for me and Stevie and . . . and Chewy.'

Chewy was never going to collect his final payment. Stevie stared at Ben with wild hatred. He'd killed them. Killed all three of them. All the for the sake of that thick grasping bint Moira.

'And the rest?' asked Astorre. 'That's just nine thousand accounted for so far, which leaves one hundred and ninety-one thousand still to come.'

'It was divided between Charlie and Joe,' said Ben, tears of anguish running down his face.

'And where is it?'

Stevie and Ben exchanged desperate looks.

'We don't know,' said Stevie. 'That was the deal. Joe stashed his cut and Charlie hid his. Neither of them knows where the other's stash is hidden. They thought that was safest. And they never told us the details. Why would they?'

Astorre thought about this. Then he smiled.

'You're lying,' he said.

'No!' Ben sobbed. 'No. We *don't know*. We'd tell you if we did. But we don't.'

Astorre stepped in close to Stevie, sitting between the corpse of his mate and the fool who'd betrayed him. Astorre flexed his fingers, like a concert pianist about to sit down and play.

'Now. Are you sure you don't want to change your mind about that?' he asked.

Neither man spoke. They were dead already, they knew it. Ben shook his head, trying to choke back the tears. Astorre's shadow fell over Stevie and he felt his bowels give way as Astorre's big hands fastened around his neck.

'Sure?' said Astorre, his eyes locked on Stevie's.

Stevie didn't answer. He closed his eyes and prayed for death.

Astorre squeezed.

42

The van wasn't in the pound any more.

'Probably been scrapped,' said the desk sergeant when Churcher and his superior showed up at the station to ask about it. 'I'll look into it, and get in touch.'

The desk sergeant had the air of a man who had too much trouble on his hands to handle even a tiny scrap more.

'It's important,' said Churcher.

'I'll get in touch,' repeated the man, his eyes fierce. 'All right?'

'Fuck it,' said Churcher as they left the station. There went his dreams of promotion. There went all the things he'd planned. That bastard wouldn't even bother, he'd just leave it a few days and say the damned thing couldn't be found. He said as much to his sergeant.

'Nah, we'll take it further. Don't worry. We're going to get to the bottom of this.'

But Churcher was afraid that, in the overwhelming confusion of wartime, they never would. That Charlie Darke and his mob were going to walk about scot-free for the rest of their days. One of the two badly injured postal workers had recovered, but the other poor sod was a vegetable now, eating baby food and shitting into a nappy. Someone had to pay. And he just *knew* they'd done that heist.

Yeah, but prove it.

Without that van, they couldn't. If the van *had* been scrapped, that was the end of the line.

Nobody piled on weight under rationing, but Vi had wondered if the increase in Ruby's girth could be put down to all the fine dining she'd done with Cornelius. She didn't *think* so. And then Betsy, flapping the lip as always, let slip the real problem.

'You're pregnant, aren't you?' Vi asked Ruby straight out, backstage one day.

Ruby looked like she'd swallowed her tongue, her expression was so shocked.

'Oh, come *on*,' said Vi. 'How much longer did you think you were going to keep it hidden, for God's sake? Betsy's told me the whole sorry tale. Couldn't *wait* to spill the beans. Looked all sad about it, but I know her. She's pleased as punch. Thinks you've got your just desserts for being a bigger pal to me than to her.'

Ruby didn't know what to say. She didn't give a fuck about Betsy any more, Betsy with her wheedling treacherous ways. After this evening's performance, she was going to meet Cornelius for dinner. But this was to be no romantic candlelit assignation. Cornelius had suggested something to her, something truly shocking. And tonight, she was going to meet him, and they were going to discuss things.

It all sounded so logical, so reasonable, when Cornelius explained the plan to her. Yet in her head, Ruby was screaming, *This can't be happening.*

'I suppose it's his?' asked Vi.

Ruby nodded dumbly.

'Well, what are you going to do? Get rid of it?'

'I don't know.'

'You can't leave it too long, you know.'

'I know.'

'You have to do something. Make up your mind.' Vi took hold of Ruby's shoulders and stared into her frightened eyes. 'You have to take control in these situations, Ruby.'

Ruby stared at Vi. She'd tried to take control, to bust out of the prison of her family life. Look what had happened.

'He doesn't want to know, I suppose. He's had his fun,' sighed Vi.

Ruby stood up. 'I don't want to talk about it,' she snapped, and walked away.

43

Cornelius was outside the Windmill after the evening performance, with a taxi waiting. Without a word being spoken between them, he and Ruby got in and were driven to a hotel he had never yet taken Ruby to: five-star, flunkies everywhere, all waiting on your every whim.

They went up to the suite, and stepped inside.

Sick with nerves, Ruby stared at the woman sitting on one of the gold-brocade couches. She had a fine face, delicately boned, and a light thin frizz of blonde hair. Her eyes were pale. The woman looked up at the two of them as they came in. Her bony hands were clenched in her lap. She was elegantly dressed – obviously a lady. She got to her feet.

She looks even more terrified than I feel, thought Ruby.

Cornelius took off his coat and walked over to the woman and kissed her cheek.

Lady Bray had put Cornelius straight. He had railed against the idea at first, said she was mad, that this was crazy, but when he calmed down he had to admit that there was a grain of perfect sense in it. Of course, he didn't want to admit to his mother that Ruby was – well, not black but certainly just a little *dark* – no need to complicate matters. And in any case, he'd already resolved any problems on *that* issue in his own mind.

The woman didn't smile or even acknowledge the fact that he'd kissed her. She was staring at Ruby in shock.

'But . . . Cornelius, she's a *darkie*,' said Vanessa.

'She's not *that* dark,' he objected swiftly. 'Just a little, perhaps. Look, I've thought this through – it won't be a problem. The Bray family traits are very dominant, you know they are. We're all robust, blue-eyed, blond-haired. Like me and Julianna. As I'm sure my son will be.'

There was a short silence. The two women went on staring at each other.

'Vanessa, this is Ruby. Ruby Darke.'

'Good Lord, how apt,' sneered Vanessa.

Cornelius ignored that. 'And this is my wife, Vanessa,' he told Ruby.

Trembling, that horrible word *darkie* still ringing in her brain, Ruby crossed the room and held out her hand. Vanessa looked at it, ignored it, and sat down again. 'Shall I send for tea?' she asked Cornelius.

He shook his head. Ruby's hand dropped to her side. Her cheeks were burning. He gestured for Ruby to sit down opposite his wife.

'This is awkward,' he said, and Ruby felt a sharp pang of irritation with him. *Awkward?* This was *excruciating*. 'But we have to meet, all three of us, don't we? And we have to discuss the baby Ruby is carrying.'

'Because it's yours,' said his wife, eyeing him coldly.

Vanessa had been furious and hurt when he'd first confessed his sins to her. But his mother had spoken to her. His mother was always right, and she was right about this. It was the perfect solution. If Vanessa couldn't provide him with children, then someone else was going to have to do it.

Fate had seen fit to take two children from him, but now it was giving him another chance – with a baby that was half his, after all. It wasn't ideal; but it was a solution to a tricky problem. Yes, Mother was right.

'The baby is mine,' he said carefully, his eyes fixed on his wife's face. 'Darling, you can't have children. We both know that now, it's something we are going to have to accept. And Ruby is a single girl of . . . well, of mixed race, with no prospect of marriage, of a proper settled family life, because she's disgraced herself with this pregnancy.'

Ruby was staring at him. Now she felt more than irritated, more than embarrassed. She felt a surge of pure rage at this sanctimonious bastard well up and nearly choke her. But . . . she'd loved him. And now he was sitting here saying she was disgraced. When *he* had made her pregnant. It was the same with Charlie and Joe, they acted like she was a whore when her only crime had been to fall in love and to give herself absolutely to the man she had fallen in love with.

Of course, *he* got no blame. His wife might complain and cry about it, but she would accept it because what was the alternative? To be cast out, sent back to a grudging family to live out her life a sad spinster – because of course divorce was out of the question. Vanessa was tied to this man and to the decisions he made, for better or worse.

And now Ruby had been sucked into his orbit, and she was having the law laid down to *her*, too. Just like at home, where first Dad and now Charlie ruled the roost and was shouting at the top of his voice like a cockerel on a muck heap, dominating all around him. She was sick of it.

'The only logical outcome is that Ruby should have the child and that we should keep it as our own,' he said.

Both women eyed each other in outrage as the words were spoken.

Ruby's child would be taken from her.

And Vanessa, although she couldn't produce a healthy

baby herself, would have to accept this child as her own, nurture it, love it, see it grow safely into adulthood.

But it might look like her, thought Vanessa, eyeing the tall, beautiful, black-haired woman before her. She didn't know what she had expected tonight, but she *hadn't* anticipated a young woman as stunning as Ruby. The girl had a natural elegance about her, wearing a simple Empire-line red dress that almost – not quite – covered the growing bump of her pregnancy. If the child did look like Ruby, then how would she be able to face it, day after day?

She wouldn't. She knew it would be beyond her.

Seeing Ruby here, for the first time, Vanessa was struck by how healthy she looked, how robust; a perfect female specimen. While she . . . she was nothing. She was too weak to have babies. A thread of utter hatred uncurled in her stomach as she gazed at Ruby.

'What if it . . . looks like . . . ?' she asked hesitantly, still staring at Ruby.

'I've told you,' said Cornelius smoothly. 'I'm certain the child will be white, darling. *Positive.*'

'But what if it's not?'

'Then of course we'll have to think again,' he said. He wouldn't even consider that as an option.

The baby would be a Bray, he would *look* like a Bray. But if – God forbid – he should be dark like Ruby, then she was on her own and Charlie Darke could go and whistle for his money. Cornelius wouldn't want the child, and Vanessa would shun it completely. A black-haired dark-skinned baby, born to two fair-haired pure-white parents . . . ? It would be unbearable, impossible, out of the question. Vanessa felt enough of a failure already, without having to tolerate anything as ridiculous as *that*.

'No, it's . . . I can't . . .' said Vanessa, clutching nervously at her throat, her eyes frantic.

'But, darling, it is exactly what we want,' said Cornelius almost tenderly.

Ruby sat there like stone, listening to her lover talking to his wife in that intimate, caressing voice.

This is the woman he's committed to, she realized painfully. *With me, it was only ever just sex.*

Vanessa was shaking her head, torn in two by this. Her husband had taken a mistress; that was insult enough. Now he wanted her to accept his mistress's baby. But . . . oh God, she so *wanted* a baby. And here was her way to get one, with no questions asked, no painful sex, no chilling fear that her inadequate body might reject him, and worse, might reject yet another child.

'It can't work,' she said desperately. 'It *can't.*'

'Darling, it *can.* And I am going to tell you how.'

He explained it to the two listening women – his mistress and his wife – just as his mother had explained it to him. When Ruby started to really show, she would move into a house that Cornelius would rent well away from where she lived now. Vanessa would stay in a little place he owned on the Kent coast until the baby was born. Then they would bring the baby back to Brayfield, and Ruby would go home to the East End, and carry on with her life a great deal richer than she had been before.

'You're going to buy my baby off me,' said Ruby when he stopped speaking.

'Exactly,' he said, as if the prospect pleased him. 'No one will know that Vanessa has not given birth. We'll say she was delicate and needed the sea air to see her through the pregnancy. And no one need ever know that you had a child, Ruby.'

Ruby looked at him dully. The man she loved. The man she had been fool enough, *stupid* enough, to hope one day might love her. Who was now discussing her body and its contents like she was a commodity, to be bargained over, bought and sold. She felt it sting her, a knife blade straight between the ribs; her heart literally *ached* with the pain of it.

'Someone already does know,' she said at last.

'Who? Oh, you mean your brothers. But I told you, you'll be paid. Handsomely rewarded.'

'No, I mean Vi, the woman I work with at the Windy. She's noticed I'm filling out. And her sister, Betsy.'

'Then we must move soon, get things organized.'

The two women looked at each other with blank dislike. But . . . he was right. It made sense.

'But what if, when I see it, I can't . . .' Ruby hesitated, frowning. 'What if I can't bear to give it up?'

Cornelius shook his head. This was the stupidest question he had ever heard. 'Don't be silly. You're a woman alone, unmarried. The scandal would be dreadful, you'd be spat at in the street, ostracized. You can't keep the child. And wouldn't you want a good home, two comfortably secure parents, for your baby? Good schooling, the chance to grow up strong and educated and well-fed? Wouldn't you want the very best for him? I'm sure you would, and that is what we can provide.'

'I don't know . . .' she said uncertainly. *Him?* She looked at Cornelius, and now the very act of *looking* at him disgusted her. He was excited by this, seeing himself already as the father of a boy he could put down for Winchester, for Eton. A boy who would follow him to Cambridge and beyond.

'Talk to your brother,' he said. 'He'll advise you.'

'Charlie? All Charlie will do is milk you for every penny, don't you know that?' Ruby almost smiled; but it was a sour, bitter smile. Her great romance had come down to this: a cold transaction.

'I'm prepared to pay,' he said. He reached out a hand and took Vanessa's. 'Whatever it takes.'

Ruby sat there feeling like shit. She wanted to shriek, to stand up and slap his arrogant, smug face; but he was right. She couldn't keep the kid. And they could. They could give a child everything, she could only offer the poor little mite disgrace and a terrible start in life. People shouting *bastard* at it, and treating her like a pariah. She knew it. But it was bitter to admit it. Bitter and hard.

She sat there and stared at them. And she vowed then and there that when it came to striking the final deal, Charlie must bargain hard on her behalf. She wanted to take them for as much as she could.

44

Months went by and Churcher heard nothing about the van used in the Post Office robbery. In fact, after his initial excitement at the discovery of some connection between Charlie Darke's lot and the mail job, he'd all but forgotten about it.

So he was surprised to turn in for work one day and find himself called into his sergeant's office to talk about it. The super was in there, too.

'The van was definitely taken for scrap,' said the sergeant. 'To a yard over in Camden Town – Baker's.'

Then what the fuck are we doing standing about here? wondered Churcher.

'The yard was hit in a raid,' said the sergeant.

Shit.

'We went over there yesterday, it was flattened.'

Dead end then, thought Churcher.

'Crater the size of God's arse there, you wouldn't believe it.' The sergeant was eyeing Churcher. He was a good lad, ambitious. Diligent. The sort the force needed. He could see how gutted Churcher was at this news. And he enjoyed playing him, teasing him, just a bit. Just for a minute or two.

'But there were a few pieces at the back of the yard that escaped the worst of the blast,' said the super, getting to his feet and picking up his hat from the desk. 'Our boys over there have just phoned. The van's there. Come on, Churcher, look lively. Let's take a look.'

The yard looked like someone had taken a giant hammer to it and gone *splat*. It was raining, a thin, dismal, foggy downpour on a scene of devastation. Their spirits dipped. Of course it was bloody raining. It had rained a hundred times since the mail van robbery, and the van had been standing out in it. There wouldn't be a damned trace left of anything. What were they, crazy? They picked their way over smouldering bits of scrap with the yard's owner, who was inconsolable about the state of his formerly lucrative business.

'Look at this place, how am I supposed to make a ruddy living now?' he moaned.

'At least you weren't here when it hit,' said the super. 'This it over here?'

The owner nodded morosely.

The mail van was there, dust-covered but intact.

Churcher went eagerly forward, looking at the front bumper, the wheel arches. There was nothing on the driver's side, nothing that looked like a dent, a scratch, or even a smear of blood. Nothing.

'Bugger,' he said.

'Here,' said the super, bending over on the passenger side of the van. The sergeant and PC Churcher went forward, stooping down to look where he pointed. 'That's a dent, isn't it? And look – there's blood there, just under the wheel arch.' He stood up while they had a closer look.

Slowly, Churcher stood up. He was grinning.

'That's blood,' he said.

'It hit the dog,' said the sergeant in wonder. 'It hit the damned dog. Then Charlie Darke got out and shouted, "Back up a bit." And whichever of his boys was at the wheel backed the van up. Then he picked the dog up, chucked it in the back, and they drove the animal over to his fancy piece Rachel Tranter for her to see to it. It lived. She was out walking it to the shops . . .'

'And one of the Special Reservists came across her arguing with an old man who said it was his dog. It *is* his dog,' said the super.

'We've got him,' said Churcher triumphantly. 'We bloody have. We've *got* the thieving bastard.'

45

Cornelius was having such a worrying time with all the baby business and Vanessa's bad nerves that he had to take time out to relax. He had many friends, many contacts; in particular he was friends with a wealthy businessman called Astorre Danieri, who owned a gambling club in the West End and had other interests – some of them dubious – around the city.

'*Mi casa es su casa*, as they say in Spain,' Astorre would say to him with a grin. 'Come and meet the family.'

Cornelius did.

You knew where you were with suave urban crooks like Astorre. Cross them and they'd have your balls fried and served up as *hors d'oeuvres*, but do them a favour or two – and Cornelius was very well placed to do favours – and they were your friends for life.

Astorre was pleased to be associated with a man of standing like Cornelius Bray.

'Come and meet my friend, he went to Cambridge, did you know that? He was an MP, you know. He's the son of Sir Hilary Bray,' Astorre would say to his close circle of scary-looking friends, basking in the reflected glow of Cornelius's status.

'We call him the Palladium,' Astorre would say with a shout of laughter.

'Why is that?' the friends would ask.

'Because he's twice a night. Seriously, watch out: if it moves, my friend Cornelius will fuck it.'

There were benefits for Cornelius in this association, too; he found the border-edge criminal element extremely stimulating. He knew Astorre was always teetering just beyond the reach of the law, and he liked that. But Cornelius's high connections kept Astorre safe; and in Astorre's company, he was safe too – safe to explore the wilder sexual aspects of his own personality now that Ruby was off limits.

'My friend,' said Astorre proudly, introducing him to his family: the small insignificant woman who was his wife, and his three boys – Tito, Fabio and Vittore. All three had a cold, feral look about them. Tito was the eldest; already handsome and imposing with his ice-blue stare. One day he would take over Astorre's empire.

'Charmed,' said Cornelius, and chatted and put them all at their ease. He took dinner with the family, made them laugh. Then Astorre and Cornelius went to Astorre's club to flirt with the hostesses who moved between the tables, dispensing drinks.

'Which one do you like best?' asked Astorre, blowing out a massive blue plume of cigar smoke as he grinned at his friend.

Cornelius looked at him. 'The hostesses?'

'Of course, the hostesses. You like one? Pick one,' said Astorre while the music played and the hostesses skimmed in and out of the packed tables in their fake-French-maid outfits.

'The little blonde,' said Cornelius without hesitation. He had been flirting with her all evening, he liked her saucy over-familiar manner and her lush curves; he'd been picturing her naked, wondering what she'd be like in bed.

'That's a good choice,' Astorre congratulated him. 'Have her tonight. She's yours.'

Privately, Astorre thought Cornelius a fool. A highly bred Lothario, careless enough to be led by his cock into all sorts of trouble. *He* would never be so stupid, and neither would his boy Tito.

Astorre adored Tito. He had told him about the mail van loot, and about the three idiots who had gone to their graves rather than betray Charlie and Joe Darke's secrets.

'Then why not tackle the Darke brothers themselves, get it out of them?' asked Tito.

'You are young and impetuous,' said Astorre fondly. 'Those three were nothing, just foot soldiers. Start a fight with Charlie and Joe Darke themselves and the streets will be running with blood.'

'But we're not afraid of them,' said Tito.

'Of course not. But why not play a cleverer game? We have them watched. Sooner or later, they'll go to fetch the money, and when they do – we pounce.'

Tito wasn't over-pleased with this idea, but what the hell? They had plenty from their own businesses, without plundering the Darke haul. And Astorre's word was law.

46

Ruby's time was approaching fast. Her only contact with her old life now was Charlie, who kept calling round to keep an eye on her. Charlie had negotiated the deal for her. She had already been paid half the amount that Cornelius and Vanessa were willing to give for her child – ten thousand pounds. The final ten thousand – chicken feed to them, a fortune to her – would be paid when they had the child, *her* child, safe with them.

'After all, the sprog might be born dead or something,' said Charlie. 'They got a point, I s'pose.'

Ruby sat in the same window day after day, looking out on a street she didn't know, at people she didn't know either. She wore an old pawn-shop-purchase gold wedding band when she went out, to look respectable, but she rarely did. When she went to the shops, no one spoke to her because no one knew her. She liked it like that. She had her ration book, she went to the grocer's and bought food, but she talked to no one.

She had a story ready, just in case anyone enquired. She was a war widow, and she had been bombed out of the East End and that was why she was here. That was the story. But she never needed to use it, because no one asked, no one spoke.

She missed her friends at the Windy; in particular, she

missed Vi. But she didn't feel she could talk to her, not while all this was going on. Charlie said Betsy wanted to call on her, but Ruby had said a flat no to that. Betsy would be all sympathetic on the surface, gloating beneath.

Sometimes the sirens went and she had to go down the shelter, but mostly she just sat in the window, hugging her huge bump, feeling the child inside her kick like a centre forward and feeling a rise of joy at the movement – and then an overwhelming blanket of sadness would steal over her as she thought of what she must do.

It was going to be a girl, she thought. She was massively fat with the child, and boys only carried at the front, everyone knew that. So a girl it would be, a little black-haired girl like her, that she could dress up and play with and . . . but no. She had to stop that train of thought, right there.

The child – even if it *was* a girl, a useless girl and not the boy she knew Cornelius craved – was not hers. She had sold it, for its own good. She had to keep reminding herself of that. The child would benefit, and she had to hope it was blond, and male, for its sake.

She might be bereft and heartbroken, but the child would be happy, well-fed, cared for, given a far better start in life than she could ever hope to provide as a single disgraced woman of uncertain origin.

All too soon, it was time. Ruby awoke in the night and felt the cramping take hold of her. She staggered from the bed, her waters breaking as she stood up, liquid cascading down her legs. She staggered to the next room, and woke Charlie, who phoned Cornelius.

'One thing's for damned sure,' said the stocky Irish midwife Charlie had called in to attend her, without sympathy, 'you may not have felt it going in, but you're certainly going to feel it coming *out*. Now come on. Push harder.'

Ruby had never known such pain. She sweated and shuddered on the bed, spreadeagled and horribly uncomfortable on crackling sheets of old newspaper that the midwife had laid out underneath her.

Bitch, she thought, wishing for a kind word, for reassurance, for an end to this grinding awful pain that had started hours ago, after midnight. Now the bedside clock said ten past four.

But she didn't expect kindness from this woman – or from anyone else, come to that. She'd committed the cardinal sin of being unmarried and becoming pregnant. She was aware of the Irishwoman's sneering disapproval – but right now Ruby didn't even care. Her whole world had become boiled down, concentrated into this mammoth battle of endurance against a flooding sea of pain.

And then it started – the shriek of the air-raid siren.

The midwife stiffened and drew back. 'Damn, isn't that all we needed?' She lunged forward, starting to heft Ruby from the bed. 'Come on, better get you down the shelter.'

Ruby cringed away from her, teeth gritted as another unholy wave of pain hit her.

She shook her head.

'Come *on,*' said the midwife. 'D'you want one of those bloody doodlebugs to get this child before it's even born?'

'I'm not. Having this baby. In the fucking shelter,' Ruby managed to get out between gasps.

'Now don't be a silly girl,' said the midwife briskly, and bustled back in for another try.

Ruby's lips drew back from her teeth in a snarl. 'You deaf? I'm not going out to the shelter, I'm having this baby *right here.*'

'Then you're having it on your own,' said the midwife, jaw set and eyes unfriendly.

'Fine,' yelled Ruby to the woman's back as she left the

room and stomped off down the stairs. 'That's just bloody *fine,* for all the sodding use you've been so far!'

Downstairs she heard the raised voices – *his* voice, louder than the others.

The loud one. She remembered she'd thought that the moment she'd first seen him among his big group of mates. Voice like a foghorn; that was him, all right.

The back door slammed. The midwife was gone, heading down the garden to the Anderson shelter.

Another great boiling wave of pain was building in her midsection.

'Ah *shit,* here we go again,' she groaned, and clung to the old brass headboard as it hit her.

The siren stopped.

And then she heard something else: the hum of a motor. Shit. Doodlebug.

She pushed and heaved and writhed like an animal.

Just so long as the bloody motor kept going, she and the baby were safe. And him downstairs, him and *her,* the snooty cow, what were they doing? Had they gone out now to the shelter too, was she all alone, *completely* alone, in the house?

But no. She could hear their voices down there.

She actually felt glad the midwife had gone. The woman's overwhelming air of disapproval had been depressing Ruby for half the night. For the moment it was just her and the baby, battling against the odds, and she preferred that. Now, things were at a crucial phase. She could feel it.

And then the motor stopped.

Shit.

She kept pushing anyway, and then – oh miracle of miracles! – she felt something give deep inside her, and the baby, still attached to her by the thick red pulsing worm of the cord, corkscrewed out with a wet slither onto the papers. Then Cornelius appeared in the doorway, and

Vanessa, with her snooty face twisted in disgust at the mess and the blood.

Silence.

Then, suddenly, the baby started to cry.

Ruby saw their attention fasten upon it; a girl, her daughter, only not hers because she was giving her up right now, or maybe she wouldn't even get the chance to do that, maybe the child was going to die with its first breath . . .

The doodlebug struck. It felt like an earthquake must feel; the battered old building shook to its foundations. Vanessa let out a quavering cry of fear. The explosion rocked the bed. The lampshade swung crazily, but somehow the light stayed on, sending mad shadows dancing over the three adults and the bloody newborn. A shard of plaster cracked off from the ceiling and struck the edge of the bed before tumbling to the floor. Ruby leaned forward and put her hands over the little girl's head, a protective gesture, noting with wonder the wispy blonde hair still sticky with the birth fluids.

Missed us, thought Ruby, and the two of them approached the bed. *Killed some other poor sod stone-cold dead, but not us. Not this time.*

'Look,' said Cornelius to his wife. 'It's a girl – but look, she's blonde, you see?'

Ruby watched them both with hatred. Him big and golden, her small, mousy, thin, terribly refined. Ruby had never seen a more ill-matched pair than these two. Yet, here they were. Together. Cornelius Bray and his wife, Vanessa.

The siren started sounding the all-clear.

Outside was bedlam. Shouting, screaming, the horrible crackle of flames nearby. But in here it was quiet. They all stared, transfixed, at the baby girl.

Cornelius's eyes rose and met Ruby's. There was a hint of guilty unease in them, which surprised her. She'd never suspected he had even a grain of conscience in his entire body. 'The midwife will be back in a minute,' he said.

Another spasm gripped her and she gritted her teeth again, clutched a hand to the headboard.

Just the afterbirth, coming away.

Only it wasn't.

It was another baby, spiralling out to lie beside its sister. *Twins? No one had told her she was giving birth to twins!*

She touched the child's head and the eyes opened. A boy. The tiny scrap of hair was dark.

Ruby saw Vanessa take a half-step back, her lip curling in distaste. 'Good God, it's . . .' she started to say, then bit her lip, cutting the words dead.

Ruby heard the midwife returning and lay back, exhausted, amazed.

They would take the girl. That was the deal. But the boy . . . she stared at him writhing there, now starting to cry. Her heart leapt at the sound. They wouldn't want him; you only had to look at him to see that. The boy would be hers. A surge of pure gladness hit her then, where before there had only been sadness and pain. She had a consolation prize. She would give up her daughter; but she still had a son. She clung to that; it made it all a little easier to bear. Everyone would disapprove, look down their noses at her, but she would take it. She would have to. Because she was going to hold on to him, even if it killed her.

'Christ!' Now Charlie loomed in the doorway, gazing down at the two babies. One blonde, one dark. Twins, but not alike. Not at all.

The midwife had cut the cord and was now cleaning the girl up. The boy still lay there, abandoned, squirming, on the sodden newspapers.

'That's enough now,' said Charlie. He took a wad of notes

out of his pockets and started peeling them off. He handed some to the midwife. 'Here.'

'The boy . . .' said the midwife.

'Oh. Right. Well, cut the cord. I'll see to him,' said Charlie.

The midwife cut the boy's cord and tied it off. She placed the little girl in her mother's arms. Ruby looked down at her baby girl, feeling pure untrammelled love for the first time in her life. The Irishwoman went off downstairs. Charlie came forward without a word. Grim-faced, he took the baby from Ruby and handed her to Vanessa, who stood there, speechless, gazing down at the baby, while Ruby lay there in mess and blood like a butchered beast of the field, her purpose served.

Ruby saw Cornelius draw close to his wife, stare down at the daughter who was, after all, half his. While their attention was focused on the baby girl, Ruby reached out a gentle, shaky hand to touch the boy's head. Then Charlie came back to the bed, carrying a sheet. He lifted the baby boy into it, wrapped him securely.

'No . . .' said Ruby urgently.

'I'll see to this one,' he said.

'No . . .' said Ruby, feeling like her guts were being ripped from her as she heard the baby start to wail. '*No!*'

'Now don't be stupid, I've got to get shot of it,' he told her bluntly.

And he was gone, out of the room.

She closed her eyes. Tears spilled over as she watched Vanessa go too, leaving with her little girl.

She lay back amid the blood and sweat, and sobbed exhaustedly into the pillows. The afterbirth would come away soon and then, *then*, if she could summon the will to move or even care what happened any more, she would get out of the bed and start to clean herself up.

How did I come to this? she wondered.

It had all started so easily; she could still see it, that bright room with the chandeliers, could still hear their laughter, smell the cigar smoke and brandy and the overwhelming scent of wealth. Like entering a foreign country. That's what it had felt like to her, on the evening when she first met *him*. She'd had a glimpse into another world – a world of ease and privilege.

But that world had never been meant for her.

'Ruby?' He was back. Her blond god Cornelius was standing over the bed, looking down at her, sweat-stained and hollow-eyed; the sad remnant of the woman he had used.

Now she looked at him and felt the last vestige of her once consuming love dissolve into hatred. She lay there, open for everyone to see, exposed, *ruined*.

'Go away,' she told him coldly.

'Ruby . . .'

'Didn't you hear me, you fucking bastard?' Ruby shouted suddenly. '*Fuck off!*'

He left the room. She watched him go, listened to his footsteps going down the stairs, then the door opening, then closing behind him. In the silence, she could hear fire engines roaring to the scene of the blast. Finding death and destruction.

She had her own tragedy here.

Her little girl was gone. Her son was gone.

Ruby lay back and let the hot, gut-wrenching tears come. Soon, she might begin to feel she could move, do something. Right now, she could only cry, and despair. And she swore to herself as she lay there that she would never, ever, fall in love and let a man use her again.

47

Charlie took the boy over to one of his contacts in Finsbury Park. He rapped on the door and it was opened by a bug-eyed monster with the face of a fly.

'*Shit*,' said Charlie, startled. The baby wrapped in his arms gave a whimper and he bounced it irritably against his chest.

The fly monster pulled its head off to reveal the plump and pasty face of Hugh Burton. Hugh gave a sly grin. He was wearing a long grubby white apron. 'Made you jump, didn't I?' he said, and it seemed to please him, the fact that he had given a hard nut like Charlie Darke a turn.

Charlie moved inside, shutting the door behind him. Burton gave him the creeps, but he was useful. Crazy, of course, but useful. He'd been a fire-watcher all through the Blitz and now he was also a rubbish man – that is, he disposed of people that gangs wanted rid of. He had the stirrup-pump that he used in his fire-watching work, and with it he transferred sulphuric acid from a bucket into a big vat he kept in the cellar, and it was there that he disposed of his victims. They melted to nothing in that stuff, bones and all.

'Got a job for you,' said Charlie, indicating the child in his arms.

Burton looked at the kid, then at Charlie. 'Cost you,' he said. 'Fifty.'

'That's fucking robbery,' said Charlie.

'No, it's fucking *murder*,' smiled Burton. 'I take the risks, you cover the cost. That's the way it works. You know that. And it leaves no trace,' he added. 'None at all.'

Charlie gave a disgusted click of the tongue and thrust the child into Burton's pudgy arms. Didn't he have enough to think about, without all this kid business from Ruby? Neither he nor Joe had seen Chewy, Stevie or Ben for months. They hadn't even shown up to collect their final payment, and that was worrying. Ben's wife Moira had been round, shouting the odds, asking what the *fuck* was going on. But the truth was, Charlie didn't know. His boys had simply vanished.

Charlie pulled out a wedge and peeled off five tenners, and gave them to Burton. He pushed them into his trouser pocket, and nodded. Charlie took one last look at his nephew, then opened the door. He paused there, looked back again.

'Throttle the poor little bastard first, will you?' he asked.

Another nod.

The deal was done. Charlie went out of the door, satisfied that the whole thing had been sorted away, neat and tidy. Just the way he liked it.

Jenny Phelps née Burton was whistling under her breath as she walked up the path to her brother Hugh's place. She was clutching a tea towel in her hands to keep the casserole she carried from burning them. She often did this, popped over to Hugh's with a morsel left over from her own family's meagre dinner, because he was useless, unmarried, a bit of a misfit really, the poor sod.

She put her key in the door, calling out 'Yoo-hoo!' like she always did.

As she swung open the door, it hit an obstruction. Not expecting it, she was taken off-balance. The casserole dish slipped from her grasp and smashed on the stone step, spilling the precious neck end of beef and gravy all over her stockings, shoes, the door, everything.

'*Bugger!*' she cried out. Her legs stung where the hot liquid had splashed them. That messy sod Hugh, he never cleaned, he was always leaving junk all around the place. What had he left here now, right in the way of the door . . . ?

She edged inside and looked down. Hugh was lying on the floor, face-up, wearing a long grubby white apron. His gas mask was nearby. His eyes were half-open. Jenny was a nurse and she'd seen a fair few corpses during the war, and she only had to glance at her brother to see that he was dead.

'Oh no – oh, Hugh,' she said, starting to cry.

A whimpering sound made her pause. At her brother's feet was a bundle. It was moving slightly. She crouched down and pulled back the blanket.

It was a tiny dark-skinned baby.

Having delivered the kid to the rubbish man, Charlie went over to the house where his sister was living. She was still lying in the filthy bed, alone. She looked up dully as he came into the bedroom. Saw that his arms were empty; saw that her child was gone.

'What did you do with him?' she asked, sounding numb; without feeling.

'Took it over to a friend of a friend,' said Charlie. 'He'll be looked after, brought up proper. Don't worry.' He looked at her, still lying there, wallowing in her own mess, the lazy cow. 'Ain't it time you got yourself tidied up? You can come back home tomorrow morning, it'll be as if nothing happened. You can go back to the ruddy Windmill, if you want to. Do what you like.'

Ruby turned her head into the pillows. 'I'm not going back there,' she said. If she hadn't been tempted away by all the false glitter of showbiz, she'd never have met Cornelius Bray: and she would never have known the agony of giving up her babies.

'No? Well, something else then.'

He didn't even care, she could hear it in his voice. The problem of her and the bastard kids was solved; that was all Charlie cared about. One job finished, on to the next. That was Charlie.

But her heart was shattered into tiny pieces. *One job finished, on to the next*. She couldn't do that. She couldn't pretend she hadn't just given birth. That she had a son, and a daughter; one dark, one fair.

But as usual the men in her life had taken charge, sorted it all out. Her dad had beaten her. Charlie had dominated her. Cornelius had *fucked* her.

Now it was over. That was the end of all that. She would never let a man control her again. Never again let one raise a finger to her. Never, ever, let one inside her. She swore it, on her babies' lives. Silently, vehemently, she swore that, from now on, things would change.

48

When Charlie left Ruby that night, he went on over to Rachel's. She was expecting him. He had to stop on the way and take shelter down the Tube when the wailing sirens told of another raid. He sat down there and thought about her. Only Rachel gave him any solace these days. Ruby was a fucking nuisance; couldn't the daft mare have kept her legs together? And her mate Betsy was no better, pestering for a walk up the aisle now she had his engagement ring on her finger.

Still, there were compensations to be had in Betsy's house. Her dad had got several of Charlie's boys into the docks already, and lots of boxes of goodies were falling onto the quayside and breaking open as a result, ruining the fruit and textiles within so that the boys just had to take them home and sell them at a nice profit – what else could they do?

Betsy and her marriage talk! Fucking women, who needed them? But he knew he needed Rachel. He lived for the times when he could go there, just talk to her or bed her, feel her silky skin against his, drown in the sweet hay-meadow scent of her hair.

He knew he was in love with Rachel Tranter, and that he would never give her up. Even if he *did* marry Betsy, and he supposed he would, he would keep Rachel too. That went without saying. And if Betsy found out and kicked off, fuck her. Who was the boss? He was.

When the all-clear sounded he trotted up the steps and walked on to Rachel's. He turned the corner into her street, feeling happier now he was going to see her, whistling 'When the Red, Red Robin' under his breath, and that was when he saw it.

The fire engines.

The crumbling masonry still falling, disintegrating.

A vast crater where the bomb had struck.

Rachel's house wasn't there any more. Neither was the whole row of houses that had spanned out on either side of hers.

They were all gone.

Every one of them, flattened as if they had never been.

He ran forward, flung himself at the spot where her front door should have been. There was nothing there but smouldering splinters.

A fire officer was grabbing him, trying to haul him back. 'Steady on, sir, it's still burning . . .'

It was. The debris was alight, and there was nothing there, no sign of life, just this awful, blistering *ruination*. He could see a remnant of Rachel's kitchen curtains, the green with tiny sprigs of yellow, being enveloped by flames. Somewhere in all that mangled wreckage was her bedspread, the one they had made love on, its rose-coloured softness turning to mush under the jets of water. He thought he caught a glimpse, a faint dim sparkle of her hair slide, the one he liked to pull loose from her hair before he caressed it, buried his face in it. He bent and snatched it up.

Somewhere under there was Rachel.

He was surging forward again, shouting her name, and now three reservists joined in. They held him back, preventing him from frying himself on Rachel's funeral pyre.

'There's no one left alive in there, son,' said an older man among them. 'There can't be. It was a direct hit. I'm sorry.'

'No! She's there, she's got to be there!' He was babbling, hurling himself against their mightier force.

'*No*. I'm sorry, sir. Very sorry. There's no one left.'

Charlie stopped struggling and stood there, staring in sick fascination at the devastation.

My God, they're right. She's dead under there somewhere.

And then he saw it: the blackened fingers of a woman's hand, an arm, a shoulder clad in dust-covered cream cotton, the blouse she so often wore. And there were some silken strands of hair, *Rachel's* hair. There was no head, though; no body. He was looking at part of a corpse, not the whole of one.

They released him, patted his shoulders. Rigid with shock, he stood there, his last living image of her strong in his mind – his Rachel, laughing and indulgent. He looked again at all that remained of her. Then he turned away and walked back, across the street, barely knowing what he was doing, barely caring.

Rachel's dead.

He could feel tears wetting his cheeks; he hadn't cried since he was a boy standing over his mother's grave. But he cried now, silent tears of utter grief.

'Mr Charles Darke?' said a voice behind him.

He turned. There were three coppers there, watching him intently.

'Who wants him?' he asked, without much interest.

Two of them stepped forward, one on each side of him; they grabbed his arms. He didn't resist.

'Mr Charles Darke, I am arresting you on suspicion of armed robbery involving one of His Majesty's mail vans . . .'

The words went on and on, but Charlie wasn't even listening. Nothing mattered any more. She was *dead*.

49

Joe was in a state of terror for weeks afterwards. He was waiting for the knock on the door, waiting for the police to come and get him, too. Or something even worse, maybe. There was still no news of Chewy, Stevie or Ben. Ben's missus Moira was still kicking off, wondering where her meal ticket had got to, the cow.

It felt sinister, somehow, all three going like that with no word. It was like someone had got to them maybe. He thought of Ben, stupidly spending out on flashy coats for Moira, and felt uneasy. Worse, with Charlie gone, for the first time in his life he felt alone. And afraid.

It would make sense to do a runner, but Joe found he couldn't do it. The rozzers were watching his movements anyway, he wouldn't get far. And there was trouble right here at home. Ruby was shot away since she'd dropped the sprogs. He knew about Charlie's involvement, that the girl had gone to the father, that bastard Bray, and the boy had been got rid of. A lot of money had changed hands, a deal had been done.

Now Ruby moved around the place like an automaton, cooking, cleaning, tending Dad, whose health was getting progressively worse every day. The old man had always doted on Charlie. Now Charlie was gone, held under arrest, and Dad seemed to find little else worth living for.

*

When she wasn't busy around the house, Ruby just sat at the kitchen table and stared at nothing. Out in the streets, there was noise, laughter. People were stringing up loops of bunting, hanging out flags. The war was over. Now it was VE day, a day of huge happiness, street parties planned, everyone busy and boisterous. Hitler was defeated, dead in his Berlin bunker. The world was delirious with summer and celebration.

Betsy came over to see her. Betsy was in bits too, her dreams of happiness and marriage shattered. Charlie was banged up, awaiting trial.

'I can't believe it,' she kept wailing to anyone who would listen.

'There's nothing we can do but sit tight and hope they can't make the prosecution stick,' Joe told her.

'But they will,' said Betsy dully. 'Ain't that the truth? He did it.'

So did I, thought Joe, his spine crawling with apprehension. But Charlie wouldn't finger him, not in a million years. Would he?

'What do you think, Ruby?' asked Betsy as they sat around the table, their faces as long as a wet weekend.

Ruby looked up. 'What?'

Betsy sent a quick glance Joe's way. This was what Ruby was like now. She had disappeared inside herself, withdrawn from them all. It irritated the hell out of Betsy.

'Don't you even *care* about Charlie?' she demanded.

Ruby gave a tight half-smile. 'Why should I?'

'For God's sake! He's your *brother*,' said Betsy.

'He's a bastard. Charlie's always been a bastard.'

'How can you sit there and say that?' Betsy was aghast.

'Yeah. Come on, Ruby. Blood's thicker than water,' said Joe.

'Is it?' Ruby was shaking her head now. 'Well, I'll tell you what, Joe. All I know is that he's not here throwing his weight around the place any more, and I like that. All I know is that Dad's lying in bed in the parlour and he's no trouble any more either – because the truth is he's pining away because Charlie's not here. And you know what? I'm just glad to be rid of them both. They've always treated me like *dirt*.'

Joe looked taken aback.

Betsy, shocked by what Ruby had just said, looked from sister to brother indignantly.

'Ain't you going to say nothing about that, Joe?' she asked, her eyes bright with unshed tears. 'Poor Charlie's in prison, and . . .'

'Don't be a silly cow all your life,' said Ruby, standing up. She leaned her fists on the table and looked at them both. 'All right, Joe, if you won't tell her, I will.'

'Sis . . .' Joe shook his head.

'Your wonderful Charlie was on his way over to the widow Tranter's on the night the police picked him up. Joe's visited him and he knows. *That's* how much he thinks of you, Betsy. He was off to see her. But you know what's ironic? Her house was flattened in a raid and her with it.'

'Ruby . . .' Joe was standing up too, shooting her warning looks.

'The widow Tranter's dead,' Ruby went on relentlessly. 'And your Charlie? He's heartbroken. He don't care if they bang him up for a thousand years, because what's life to him, without her?'

Betsy had gone white. She jumped to her feet.

'This is all *lies*,' she yelled, and lashed out, striking Ruby hard across the cheek.

Ruby recoiled. Her cheek turned red where she'd been struck. But she straightened and stared coldly at her friend.

'It's not lies, you fool. It's the truth. He's not worth your tears, he's not worth *that*.' Ruby snapped her fingers. 'He's betrayed you a dozen times over; he's a worthless conniving piece of shit.'

'Shut the fuck up, Ruby,' said Joe. Betsy was sobbing, racing for the door.

'It's not *true*,' she shouted back at Ruby.

'Yeah. It is.'

'You're not my friend any more,' yelled Betsy as she grabbed the doorknob. 'Don't you ever talk to me again, you lying bitch!'

'Happy now?' asked Joe, as the door slammed shut behind Betsy.

'Do I *look* happy?'

The broom handle was banging on the wall. Dad needed attention.

'Better get in there,' said Joe, his face thunderous.

'Yeah,' said Ruby, and went into her father's room to see what he wanted.

Joe dashed out into the street after Betsy. He caught up with her on the corner.

'Bets!' He grabbed her arm, pulled her round. Her face was streaked with tears.

'Is it true?' she asked him.

'Bets, don't . . .'

'Come *on*. I want to know. Is any of what she's saying true? People were talking about it weeks, months back. Charlie and the widow Tranter. And I asked you about it. You remember that, Joe? I asked you, and you said it was ridiculous, and *I* thought it was ridiculous too. Just stupid. That ugly dried-up old mare, and Charlie? Stupid. But . . . was it true?'

Joe stared at her face. He'd always liked Betsy. She was lively, she was fun. He was a serious, somewhat shy man and he found her liveliness beguiling. But . . . she'd always been his brother's girl. Now that could change. Charlie hadn't been interested in her much, not really. But Joe was. He always *had* been.

'It's true, Bets. I'm sorry,' he told her softly.

'No!' she flung herself into his arms.

Joe held on to her while she sobbed out all the hurt Charlie had caused her.

'Oh God, Joe, they won't take you too, will they?' She looked up at his face, and he thought how pretty she was, even red-nosed and tearful with her lovely eyes wet and bloodshot.

'No, Bets. They won't take me too,' he promised her.

'I couldn't stand that,' said Betsy, and buried her face in his chest. She clung to Joe like a rock. She *liked* Joe. And, after all, he had *his* share of the Post Office money somewhere – didn't he?

'They won't take me, Bets,' he repeated, holding her close.

But his promise could be an empty one. He knew it. The police were watching him. And he strongly believed that other people were too, blokes mixed up in the same sort of stuff as him. Without Charlie, he knew he was a sitting duck. But he wouldn't run. Especially not now.

50

Charlie Darke got thirty years for the mail van robbery, but the cash was never recovered. No one came for Joe. Charlie had seen him right. But Joe had other worries. Dad's will to live was severely weakened by the absence of his favourite child, and one night Ruby was bringing in his cocoa and dully wondering what had become of her life when she found him unconscious. Much as she tried, she couldn't rouse him. And his breathing was odd, wheezing and rattling in his chest.

She called Joe in.

'Better fetch the doctor,' he said, and left her with the old man.

Ruby sat there and watched her father. She felt no love for him. She was certain he felt none for her. No more could he tower over her with his belt, no more could he inflict pain on her. She had never known a moment's kindness or tenderness from this sad wreck of a man, and now, when he was slipping away from the world, she couldn't even bring herself to feel sorry.

She'd lost her babies. Ever since that awful night, she'd been consumed by misery. She'd been abused by men all her young life. Only Joe hadn't crossed her – but, being Joe, anything for the quiet life, he had stood idly by while Charlie and her father dealt out random smacks and more extreme punishment. He had never tried to intervene, and that hurt her. All the men she had ever known had hurt her.

But no more.

She stared at the pathetic remnants of her father and swore it. Now she was going to carve out her own path. No longer was she the quiet, gentle girl. Now she was a woman. She had suffered. And her suffering had forged a core of cold steel in her soul.

The doctor arrived, shooing her out of the way. He bent over the old man, checked his heart, while Joe and Ruby looked on.

'I think it's the end,' said the doctor, drawing back, putting his stethoscope away. He looked at them both. 'You should prepare yourself for the worst. I'm sorry.'

51

Ted Darke died that same night and was buried a week later, with no pomp or ceremony, beside his late wife Alicia. It was a simple funeral, attended by Ruby and Joe, plus a few of their father's old church friends. Betsy came, much to Ruby's surprise, and although she didn't exchange one word with her former friend, she clung on to Joe's arm throughout the ceremony and afterwards, out in the windy graveyard, she was there again, hanging on to Joe.

So that's the way it's going, thought Ruby.

She wasn't surprised. Ruby wasn't blind to Betsy's faults. Bubbly and supposedly warm-hearted, Betsy was in fact the ultimate opportunist. With Charlie out of the picture, naturally she turned to Joe. The Darkes still had a certain air of notoriety – and Joe was in charge of what had once been Charlie's mob now. Joe would be easier for Betsy to manage. Joe wouldn't be unfaithful. He just wasn't the type. And also, there was the matter of all those many thousands of pounds taken in the mail van heist, still unaccounted for. . .

Ruby managed to get through the tea and sandwiches back at the house, and was heartily glad when the last of the guests departed.

Finally, her and Joe were sitting alone at the kitchen table and night was drawing in. It seemed to her that a line had been drawn under everything. The war was over. Her babies were gone. Dad was gone. No more would they hear the broom handle banging on the wall. Their dad was dead, and Charlie had been put away for a long, long time.

'You. Betsy,' said Ruby curiously. 'Is it serious, Joe?'

Joe shrugged. 'Think so. Yeah. I know she was with Charlie, but I'm falling for her. She's good for me.'

Ruby stared at her brother. She doubted that, but still, if it made him happy, why not?

'You're not a bad man, Joe.' She sipped the whisky he'd poured them both. It was true. He was the better of the Darke brothers. And miles better than their drunken, God-bothering father had ever been.

Joe held up his glass in one meaty fist. 'To Dad,' he said.

Ruby clinked her glass against his. 'Yeah.'

They both drank in the silence of the night. No more bombing raids now. No more Dad. No more Charlie. The future stretched ahead of them, a blank canvas onto which they could write whatever they wished.

'It's been rough on you,' said Joe. 'Getting caught out like that. The kids. You know.'

'Yeah,' sighed Ruby. Her little girl was with her father, anyway. She'd be raised as a right little princess, spoiled to bits. Her little boy . . . a friend of a friend, Charlie had told her. At least he would be safe. At least he would be with a family, not condemned as a bastard with a disgraced woman to bring him up alone and unaided.

'Did Charlie tell you who had him? The little boy?' she asked hesitantly.

My son. My precious, beautiful boy.

Joe shook his head. 'No. He didn't.'

Joe felt bad lying to her. Charlie *had* told him what happened to the kid. Even hard-hearted tough-as-nails Charlie had been troubled by it, and telling Joe had almost been like a confession for him. But Joe wasn't ever going to tell that to Ruby. It would kill her, break her heart into bits. He was going to carry that grisly secret to his grave.

Ruby finished her whisky. It burned, all the way down. Seemed almost to cauterize, just for a moment, the pain that was always there in her heart. But only for a moment. Then the pain, the dull forever *ache* of missing her babies, was back again. She would learn to live with it. She had to.

'What you going to do then, Rubes?' Joe asked. 'Go back to the Windy? I know you said you wouldn't, but . . .' he hesitated.

But that was just after the babies were born, and you weren't in your right mind, Ruby finished for him.

And he was right. She'd been demented, hysterical and grief-stricken.

'No. I won't go back there,' she said. What for? To stand there like some sort of *object*, and let men ogle her, make use of her again? No, she wouldn't do that. It seemed to her that women were either shagged, shot or shat on, in this world. And she'd had enough of it. She wanted to make her own rules, not live by those imposed by someone else, just because they had a dick and she didn't.

'How about you?' she asked Joe. But he just winked. She knew the answer anyway. He would go on with his dodgy dealings and he would probably marry Betsy. And probably, one day, he would end up in the nick – just like Charlie.

'I might get the shop up and running again,' said Ruby. She had been thinking of it for a couple of weeks now, and it made sense. She had the money from Cornelius; blood money for her baby girl. She shuddered to think of that. Felt like shit about it. But it was done. All she could do now was carry on, somehow.

Joe looked at her in surprise. 'What, you? Run the shop?'

Ruby shrugged. *Run the shop.* It had a nice sound to it.

She would be in charge for once. She could organize every-thing, just as she liked it. She was *good* at doing that.

'Why not?' she asked. 'I've been having some thoughts about it. Why do just groceries? I think we should sell pins and needles, and tablecloths and stockings . . . and I've been thinking about taking over a market stall in the Portobello Road too, calling it a Penny Bazaar.'

He raised his brows, tilted his head and stared at her. 'Yeah, why not? If it makes you happy.'

Nothing would do that. All she could do now was go on. Do her best. Fill the void, somehow. Hold herself together. What else could she do?

Now someone was banging on the front door.

Tiredly, Ruby hauled herself to her feet and went through to answer it. She found Vi standing there, all glammed up as always. Vi gave her a brilliant green-eyed smile. There was a car at the kerb, its engine running, a chauffeur behind the wheel. The car looked suspiciously like a Rolls-Royce.

'*Wondered* where the hell you'd got to,' said Vi. 'Ready to rejoin the world yet?'

'Well, I . . .'

'Oh, I think so,' said Vi. 'War's over, babes. It's way past time.'

She was right.

Time for Ruby to rejoin the world. This time, on *her* terms.

BOOK TWO

52

'God, Joe – she's beautiful!'

Since that awful day when her babies had been taken from her, not a minute had passed when Ruby didn't long to hold them both. Now here she was, holding Joe and Betsy's first-born – her niece – and the pain of it was killing her.

Joe and Betsy had married not long after the end of the war, and it had seemed like they'd *never* have their yearned-for kids. But now – at last – it had happened. So Ruby had to force herself to smile, to behave as if she was delighted for them. She *was,* really. But it still hurt her to see their joy.

'What are you going to call her?' she asked her sister-in-law, who lay back on the pillows, her usually immaculate blonde hair all over the place. Betsy looked exhausted, but radiant.

'Nadine,' said Betsy.

Ruby gazed down at the slumbering infant, inhaling the sweet powdery smell of her.

Oh God – my babies . . .

'Were you in labour for long?' she asked.

'No, it was very quick. Four hours.' Betsy managed a taut smile for her sister-in-law. They had never rekindled the friendship they'd lost during the war, but she was married to Ruby's brother, they were *kin* – they had to be civil to one another.

'She's a marvel,' said Joe, holding his wife's hand and staring at her with loving eyes.

Ruby thought of her own labour, the doodlebug going over, her fear that they would be hit, that her babies would be killed even before they'd drawn breath. But they had survived. Now her daughter was with Cornelius and his family, named and raised by them. Her son . . . she had no idea. Charlie had never told her what had become of the little boy, only that he would be cared for.

She gave Betsy flowers, hugged Joe and congratulated him. She stayed for an hour – the longest, most tortured hour she had endured for years. Then she left, and went home to her solitary, luxurious flat above what had once been Dad's corner shop: now it was a big store. The emerald green 'Darke & Sons' sign was long gone. Now the sign was huge and burgundy-red, with DARKES picked out in black-outlined gold. The same signage appeared over the entrance to all her shops, on the bags and food packaging, and soon – if the wholesalers kept pissing her about like they were – that same name would be on the labels of the clothing range too. She had some plans for that.

Yeah, but it's just business, right?

The business had kept her sane.

But now . . .

Ruby listened to the echoing silence of the flat all around her. Her babies were out there. Young adults now. She felt her eyes fill with all the tears she'd been holding back for so long, so many empty years when she'd buried herself, *immersed* herself in work. They flowed like a river as she stood there in her sumptuously appointed flat. She didn't try to stop her tears, she couldn't. She was rich, she was successful, she had everything. But without them, without her babies . . . she had nothing. Nothing at all.

Her daughter was with Cornelius and Vanessa. They'd christened her Daisy; she had seen the announcement in the *Tatler* back in the day. Daisy, her beautiful daughter, had been raised as a lady, in comfort and style. Whereas her poor nameless boy . . . she had no idea what had become of him. She hoped he was happy, prayed he was well.

Maybe now it was time – well past time – that she made them a part of her life again somehow.

Next time she saw Joe, she tackled him straight away.

'The boy. My little boy,' she said, dry-mouthed, wondering if she was doing the right thing here. Opening a can of worms that would be better left untouched.

'What?' Joe was looking at her.

'*My* little boy, Joe. Charlie said he was with a friend of a friend. I want to know who, and where.'

Joe sat down with a thump. 'You're joking.'

'Do I look like I'm joking?'

'For God's sake, Rubes. All that happened back in the war. Twenty years ago, is it now? let it go.'

'I can't let it go. It's been playing on my mind so much. Have you any idea what it's been like for me? You've got a family, Joe. You've got Betsy and now you've got a daughter. What have *I* got? Nothing. Nothing at all. I want to know who Charlie left my boy with. He must have told you. He told you everything, back then. Didn't he?'

Joe glanced away from her face; his eyes were troubled.

'Charlie never told me a thing about it. He didn't want to talk about it, kept going on about how you'd shamed him, showed yourself up, acted like a slag.' Joe saw the expression on his sister's face and nodded. 'I know, I know. Things are changing now. Just a bit. But then . . . well, it just wasn't done, was it? An unmarried woman, keeping bastard kids.'

'So he told you nothing.'

'Nothing at all.'

'You still go to see him sometimes, don't you?'

'Sometimes. Not often.'

'He sends you a visiting order.'

'Yeah. He does.'

Ruby looked him straight in the eye. 'Next time you visit, tell him I want to see him. And in the meantime, I'm going to make contact with my daughter.'

Joe stiffened. 'That wasn't part of the deal. You know it wasn't. Bray won't have it.'

Ruby shook her head, her eyes flaring. For a moment Joe could see the bloody-minded businesswoman his quiet, unassuming sister had become – the one the papers now called the Ice Queen of Retail.

'*Fuck* Cornelius Bray. I don't care about deals, Joe. I want to know my own kids. Since when was that a crime?'

53

1962

When Kit Miller was nineteen, he was a Friday-night gang-ster, going around the clubs and pubs, the restaurants and arcades. Kicking up trouble for no reason other than he liked to. He'd left proper schooling at sixteen, and even then he'd been trouble. Any youngster who joined the school had to fight Kit in the playground, but he was artful, he never got the cane like everyone else in his class. When one of the old masters, Gerald Ratterton, left, he said he'd caned them all and Kit cockily shouted out, *Not me, sir* – and so earned himself a last-minute walloping off the old goat.

With school out of the way, he got a job through a youth employment agency in a bedding company. He knocked holes in the edges of beds day after day, for two shillings an hour. Pretty soon he thought, fuck *this*, and he left and found a succession of other dead-end jobs that paid similarly badly. He was a bookie's runner for a while, then finally he pitched up on the lorries, selling soft drinks door to door. After a week heaving crates of Corona about for pennies, he liked to let his hair down on a Friday night, get drunk and start to rip up the town with his mates.

He and his mates tore up Gasworks, the restaurant where one of the attractions – apart from the chance of seeing

Princess Margaret being fawned over by the underworld enforcer John Bindon – was a chess set with pieces depicting couples having sex in various positions.

Then they moved on to the next place, Sheila's, to cause more mayhem. And that was when Kit felt a heavy hand on his shoulder.

'Someone wants a word with you,' said the man standing there. He was built like a brick shithouse, with white hair and a face you didn't want to argue with.

'Tell them to go and fuck themselves,' said Kit.

He looked around, expecting to see his mates grinning. But they weren't there any more. They'd all scarpered. The cunts.

Kit stood there alone, with King Kong's bigger uglier brother breathing down his neck. He twisted sideways, away from the man, and elbowed him hard in the ribs. Then he followed through with a belter to the jaw. He wasn't running. He was standing his ground, fighting back. Kit always did. His mates told him he was stupid, but he saw himself as a gladiator, a fighter to the bitter end. He'd been fighting all his life, ever since he was a kid.

But now . . .

Kit was doling out his best work, but the man didn't seem to even feel it. He gave Kit a fast uppercut to the jaw, and Kit went down hard. Head spinning, he found himself being dragged to his feet and hauled into a back room.

Uh-oh, he thought.

His jaw felt like it was coming off. He rubbed it with one hand and stared around at the blokes assembled there – six of them. They all looked heavy, nasty. They were looking at him like he was excrement – but then he was used to that. Nineteen years of ducking and diving, he'd grown a hide like a rhino.

His mates had left him here to face the music alone. So what? He would face it.

'He's not a bad-looking kid, is he?' said the man seated behind the desk. 'Could scrub up, I reckon.'

They eyed up Kit like he was a piece of meat. He had a cocky bearing about him, a way of swaggering through the world as if ready to spit in its eye. He had good height, an athlete's bouncy energy, broad shoulders, curly black hair, dark skin. His face was arresting – his eyes in particular were startling, given his skin colour. They were a sharp, clear blue, and there was a quick intelligence in them that was there for all to see. His nose was straight, the nostrils widely flaring, and his mouth was sensual. Women turned to look at him in the street. Men too, sometimes.

'He's presentable. And he's got a good punch on him,' said the white-haired one who'd dragged him in here. 'Got balls. All the rest of 'em ran for the hills.'

'What's your name, son?'

Kit stared around at them all. 'I ain't your son,' he said stiffly.

'See? Balls like a tiger,' said the white-haired one, smiling.

'How'd you like a job?' asked the one behind the desk.

'Doing what?' asked Kit. He was bored to tears with the lorries.

'A bit of this, a bit of that. Nothing too difficult. But you do what you're told. Can you do that?'

Kit stared at the man behind the desk. He looked like trouble. He was forty, maybe fifty and very handsome in a strong and brutish sort of way. He was neatly dressed, with a square jaw, a neatly trimmed head of thick dark iron-grey hair and grey eyes, hard as chips of granite. He looked the sort that could drop shit on your head like a ton of bricks, if you weren't very careful.

Kit had got used to standing up for himself, summing up a situation quickly and knowing which way to jump. He changed jobs like other people changed their hats. He was rootless. He drifted around finding work where he could, if he could. He had no loyalties, no responsibilities. So if they were offering him a job, that was OK. But if he got bored, he'd piss off.

'I s'pose,' he said.

'All right then. You're on the payroll, as a breaker.'

Kit knew that a breaker was a heavy, a paid thug. Well, he could do that. He had been coping on his own for so long, he could do anything. He'd been in the kid's home, but then he'd left at sixteen, found work on the streets of the East End wherever he could, kept himself fed. He was a coper. He'd had to be.

'What's your name?' asked the man behind the desk again. He shook out a cigarette from the packet, placed it between his lips, snapped open a gold Dunhill lighter and lit it. Took a long, deep drag.

'Kit Miller.'

'I'm Michael Ward,' said the man behind the desk, wreathed in smoke. 'This is one of my gaffs. I got other places too. Other restaurants, a couple of clubs, some shops and stalls, and I do loans.' He picked up a pen and scrawled a note on a piece of paper. He held it out to Kit. 'Go round to this place in Lewisham in the morning. Watch yourself. They eat their own young down there. Get fifty quid off this geezer – he's late paying. I gave him one week, now he's asked for another. He's taking the piss. Lean on him hard. Think you can do that?'

Kit pocketed the piece of paper. 'I can do it.'

'What happened?' asked Kit's mate when he came out onto the street. 'I thought they were going to do you over proper.'

'Nah, they gave us a job,' said Kit with a grin.

'You're joking. Doing what?'

'Dunno yet. But fuck the lorries. This looks more interesting.'

54

When Astorre Danieri died, his eldest son Tito took control of his father's clubs and business interests.

At Astorre's funeral, Cornelius was in attendance. Since the war, he'd done well for himself. Now he was Lord Bray – the Right Honourable Cornelius Baron Bray – having been raised to the peerage as a life peer in 1958. He'd been appointed an Officer of the Legion of Honour in 1950, made a Knight of the British Empire in 1953 and an Honorary LLD by St Andrews in 1959.

Cornelius shook Tito's hand and conveyed to the old frail widow of Astorre his sincere condolences.

'Astorre was a great man,' he said. 'A true friend.'

'Thank you,' said Bella, and she turned away, weeping.

'You're too kind, your lordship,' said Tito, holding on to Cornelius's hand. 'Let's hope we can continue the strong friendship you first forged with my father, uh?'

Cornelius looked at Tito. Tito wasn't a boy any more. Now he was a big man, tanned and bulky. Tito was immaculately and expensively dressed. He had close-cropped hair that was turning from black to silver. He sported a small, neatly trimmed grey-flecked beard, but his eyes were the same: a stunningly clear, cruel ice-blue.

'That would be most agreeable,' said Cornelius.

'My father very much valued his association with you,' said Tito, still holding Cornelius's hand.

'I valued our friendship too, immensely.'

Tito's eyes were drilling into Cornelius's. Like Astorre, he wanted to nurture his association with this upper-class twat. It could be useful. Now he was in charge, things would be a little different. Astorre had blocked his, Tito's, wishes on many things, including that old mail van business. Tito had raged in silence about it. He felt his father's decision on that had been the wrong one. And now, of course, it was far too late. The currency was different. Even if he could have traced the cash, it was worthless and could only bring trouble.

'My father liked you,' he told Cornelius. 'So much so that he took photos. Many photos. To remember the happy times you had at his club.'

Cornelius felt his heart freeze in his chest. What was the conniving shit saying? He thought back frantically to all the times he had taken his pleasure at Astorre's place, with highly paid prostitutes, with hostesses, with boys, indulging in perversions that he knew must never come to light. He had never seen a camera. *Never.*

Which didn't mean that there hadn't been one, secretly recording it all.

'I think we understand one another,' said Tito, with a slight, cool smile. 'If everything continues as it is, no one will ever see those photos.'

There *had* been a camera. That fat cunning old goat Astorre had stitched him up. He'd filmed those sex sessions Cornelius had so enjoyed, and now Cornelius knew he was in Tito's pocket. Of course, he was pretty certain that his journalistic and police contacts would instantly bury any unsavoury details that might emerge, but could he be absolutely certain *nothing* would leak out?

No. He couldn't.

He swallowed hard. He wanted to grab Tito by the throat and throw him into his cheating old fuck of a father's grave. But he was old school, well tutored in the art of self-control when it came to doing business.

'We understand one another perfectly,' Cornelius agreed.

'Good. So we'll see you in the club one night next week . . . ?'

'Of course,' said Cornelius, and he turned away with a smile. His heart was full of black hatred for the dead father – and for the son.

But he knew he was going to continue his liaison with Tito.

That he couldn't turn his back on all that Tito had to offer.

He couldn't help himself.

And besides . . . he didn't seem to have much choice.

55

1962

'You look beautiful, darling,' said Lady Bray to her daughter.

Daisy Bray was turning back and forth before the mirror, looking at her reflection with a critical eye. Not so much beautiful as *distinctive* to look at, she thought.

She had very nice blonde hair, tumbling loose in artful tendrils from a French plait. She'd fought forcibly with her mother to prevent her from whisking her off to the Knightsbridge salon where Monsieur Albert would have inflicted a perm on her. She would agree she had lovely blue eyes, just like her father's. Piercing, and yes – beautiful. She'd agree to that. Her skin was good too, and she was tall – maybe too tall? – but nicely proportioned.

And now her mother had said she looked lovely! This was rare praise indeed, coming from chilly, buttoned-up Vanessa.

Daisy loved her dress. Yes, she thought all this coming-out business Vanessa insisted upon was impossibly old-fashioned, a leftover from the fifties – a last-gasp remnant of another time. But now she was glad she had laboured through all those tortuous fittings at the House of Worth in Grosvenor Street.

The dress was a swirling floor-length primrose-yellow shimmer of lace and chiffon, suspended from a nipped-in waist and a strapless, boned bodice. She fiddled about with it. She was clumsy and quick-moving. She worried aloud that her ample bosom might escape over the top of it if she moved too suddenly.

'Well, you *don't* move suddenly in it, darling,' said Vanessa. 'You deport yourself like the lady you are. You don't dash around like an idiot.'

Vanessa bit her lip, aware that she had been sharp with Daisy – *too* sharp. She stifled a sigh. She tried so hard, she really did, but she couldn't seem to help the resentment that haunted her every day. This feeling of resentment over Daisy's parentage had grown and festered over the years until it was like a solid *lump* in her chest, stifling her.

Every time she saw Daisy, she seemed to be searching for traces of Ruby Darke in her – and, oh God, the worst of it was, she was finding them too. The older and more troublesome Daisy became, the more Vanessa pushed her away. She just couldn't help it.

Chastened, Daisy stared at the dress in the mirror. It was the colour of spring, of optimism; she loved it. Better still, it hid her big bottom. She turned away from the mirror, watching her mother anxiously.

Vanessa sighed, sitting down on the bed in the master bedroom and holding out her hands. Obediently Daisy went to her, took Vanessa's thin cold hands in hers, and sat down beside her. 'I remember my own coming-out ball,' she said.

'Where you met Pa,' said Daisy. She'd heard the story a thousand times.

'That's right.' Vanessa's pale eyes were glazed for a moment, lost in the memory. Cornelius Bray had been a force of nature, completely bowling her over. He had been her first lover – and her last.

Not that he troubled her any more with all *that*. Thank goodness all that heaving and sweating was done with now.

She suppressed a shudder of distaste. She had never told Daisy how painful, how horrible all that was. She didn't want to frighten her. Marriage – a good marriage to someone suitable – was on the cards for Daisy. She'd been to the best girls' schools and completed a year at Egglestone being 'finished'; now she was being introduced to proper society. This was *not* the time to start making a bold-hearted spirit like Daisy nervous of what would happen in the future. It was her job as a mother to fill Daisy with confidence, to set her upon the path of life with brightness and hope, not misgivings.

Vanessa knew and hated the fact that her feelings towards Daisy would always be ambiguous. But still, she took her responsibilities as a mother seriously. But . . . oh God, Daisy was so young. So *innocent*. She had to at least warn her, if only gently . . .

'Look, darling . . . you will be careful tonight, won't you?' she said anxiously.

'*Mother* . . .' Daisy was half-smiling.

'Now don't take that tone,' chided Vanessa gently.

She knew her daughter, through and through. She knew how impetuous Daisy could be, throwing herself into this activity or that with reckless abandon. When Daisy rode a horse, it terrified Vanessa to see her daughter hurling her mount over jumps that always seemed much too high. Skiing at Klosters, she chose the dangerous black runs and rushed down them with screams of exhilaration, not fear. She might easily, Vanessa thought, throw herself into the arms of some opportunistic and – worse – unsuitable boy, just as recklessly.

'Don't drink too much,' she told Daisy. 'And – you know – be careful with the boys.'

Daisy knew what her mother meant, even though Vanessa had never once mentioned the facts of life to Daisy, not even when she'd reached puberty. She'd learned about it in giggled dorm conversations with her friends.

'I'll be careful,' she promised, although she thought 'careful' was dull, and to be avoided at all costs. She'd led a life of pampering and luxury; it had given her a feeling of absolute safety and self-assurance, in any situation. So she liked to push against the boundaries now and again. 'I wish you could be there,' she said.

Vanessa shook her head. 'Now, darling, you *know* I hate parties. Your aunt Ju will look after you.'

And who'll look after her? wondered Daisy. Aunt Ju, her father's sister, went crazy when she had a couple of gins down her.

They heard the doorbell then; the car was ready.

Vanessa dropped a quick kiss onto Daisy's smooth cheek. 'Have a marvellous time,' she said.

'I will.' Daisy picked up her stole and her bag, blew her mother a kiss, and ran from the room.

Left alone, Vanessa stared at the door. The silence of the London house closed around her. She'd come up to town specifically to help Daisy get ready for her big occasion, but she didn't like it here. Cornelius was out, of course, dining at his club, anywhere but here, with her. She knew she bored him. And now that the sex part was over and done, what else was there to be with her for?

Vanessa rose from the bed and went down to the drawing room to spend yet another evening alone. Tomorrow, when she got back down to the country, she would start replanting the roses. She had that to look forward to. And at least she didn't have Cornelius's witch of a mother to bother her any more. She'd died six years ago, and Vanessa didn't miss her at all.

His mother had never liked her. She had always believed her son could have done better – and it had been awful, her knowing about Daisy's parentage. Well, it had been her who had instigated the proceedings. It was her who had talked Cornelius into doing a deal with that common, awful girl Ruby Darke and *purchasing* a child since Vanessa had been unable to provide one. So . . . Vanessa had her mother-in-law to thank for that. She had Daisy: her daughter.

Only she wasn't, was she?

Not quite.

56

1962

'You Ray Cardew?' asked Kit of the man who was peering out of the barely open doorway at him.

It was ten to seven on the morning after his meeting with Michael Ward and his boys. Kit had thought to himself: the earlier the better, catch Cardew all unawares, half-asleep or doing the old lady.

It looked like his idea was sound, too. Cardew was a scruffy-looking porker of middle years, wearing a sagging cream-coloured vest and pyjama bottoms. His thinning hair was sticking up like he'd had an electric shock. His eyes were pale, and bewildered.

'Who is it?' floated down the stairs behind Cardew. A woman's voice, harsh from fags.

'I dunno,' shouted Cardew over his shoulder. 'Go back to sleep.' He turned his attention to the tall young man standing on his doorstep. 'Who wants to know?' he asked.

'Mr Ward wants to know,' said Kit, and he saw recognition flare in the man's eyes.

Cardew went to shut the door. Kit jammed his foot in it, and heaved. Cardew staggered back and fell onto the stairs as the door swung in. Kit pushed inside, shut the door behind him, and turned and tugged Cardew back to his feet. He stared at him from inches away.

'You owe Mr Ward fifty sovs,' he said flatly. 'And he wants it. Now.'

'I ain't got it. I don't keep that sort of money around the place. Who does?' Cardew was wheezing and wriggling against Kit's iron grip.

'That's what you said before. You been putting him off, and he don't like it. Now, he wants his money.'

'But I ain't . . .'

'You ain't got it. Fair enough.' Kit pulled the hammer out of his jacket and dragged the man along the hallway and through the open door into the kitchen.

'What the f—' gabbled Cardew.

Kit flung him face-first against the table. Cardew went sprawling across it. Kit grabbed the man's right wrist and held it down on the table's knotty pine surface. Cardew's eyes grew round with terror. He bunched his fingers into a fist.

'No!' he shouted.

'Open your fucking fingers or I'll do your knee instead,' Kit said. 'You *sure* you ain't got that money?'

'I ain't got it, I ain't . . .'

The hammer came crashing down on Cardew's index finger, right on the joint. Cardew screamed. Kit took aim on the next, Cardew's middle finger.

'You've broke my bloody finger . . .' he wailed.

'And I'm gonna break this one too. Then the next, then the next. Until you cough up Mr Ward's money. You got it?'

'Don't . . .' Cardew protested, but the hammer came down again. There was an audible *crunch* as the finger was shattered and Cardew groaned and sagged against the table, retching weakly, his knees buckling from under him.

Kit heard a sound behind him and turned just as a woman,

puce-faced with rage and with pink curlers sticking up from tufts of dyed blonde hair, picked up the frying pan and struck him with it.

Because he'd been half-turning, it missed his head but crashed into his shoulder. It bloody *hurt,* and Kit was torn between annoyance and amusement that the old slag had the bottle to tackle him. He grabbed the pan and snatched it from her hands, throwing it onto the floor.

'Don't you do no more to him,' she screamed full volume, drawing her pink quilted dressing gown around her and glaring at him in outrage. 'Don't you *dare.* Look.' She went to a drawer and with trembling fingers she drew out a purse. She looked at her husband, slumped over the table. 'Silly *sod*, I said he ought to pay, but he always has to push his luck. Here.' She licked a finger and counted out ten fivers. She thrust it at Kit. '*Here's* his filthy money, I hope it chokes him. You black *bastard.*'

Kit pocketed the fives. He'd been called worse. He slipped the hammer back into his inside pocket.

'Nice doing business with you,' he said, and left the weeping man and the glaring woman in the kitchen. He went back along the hall, and out the front door. Job done.

When Kit pitched up at the restaurant that night, he was shown straight into the back office. All the heavies were there, as usual. There was an unknown man there too, a big blue-eyed bastard with an air of absolute self-confidence, greyish hair and a little beard. There was a woman there, too, hanging off his arm; a gorgeous golden blonde who could have been in her thirties or early forties, it was hard to tell. Kit took the bundle of notes out of his pocket, and laid them on the desk in front of Michael Ward.

Michael put his half-smoked cigarette to the side of his mouth and counted the cash. He squinted up at Kit. He indicated the bloke with the beard. 'You met Mr Tito Danieri, Kit?'

'No,' said Kit, and nodded to the man.

'You done good,' said Michael. 'He kick up much?'

Kit shrugged. 'Had to bust a couple of fingers to make him see sense.'

Michael nodded. He couldn't give a fuck what Kit had broken. He had his money. He stubbed out his fag in an overflowing ashtray, then pushed four of the fivers back across the desk. 'That's for you,' he said.

Kit nodded and tucked the money away. He hadn't made that in a *week* on the lorries. This business was going to be a doddle. And it obviously paid like a bastard, too.

'Thanks, Mr Ward.'

'Use it to get yourself smartened up a bit,' said Michael. 'You're working for me now. I don't have rough-looking articles hanging round me.'

Kit looked down at his clothes. All right, he was no fashion plate. He was wearing his old frayed jeans, a T-shirt and a plaid jacket lined with fake sheepskin. He was comfortable in it. He'd never had to dress up before. Never needed to. But now he looked around at the men in the room, took in the black suits, the crisp white shirts, the black ties, the shoes polished to a mirror shine.

'Right,' he said.

'Good boy.'

He went back out into the restaurant and was through there and out on the street when someone called out to him. He stopped, and turned. It was the blonde woman. Kit eyed her assessingly. She was dazzlingly good-looking and she knew it. Everything was out in the shop window. The short skirt, the tight blouse, the heels, the heavy panstick make-up and the elaborately outlined ocean-green eyes. Yeah, she was an eyeful all right.

'What's your name? Kit, isn't it?' she asked, sashaying towards him.

'Yeah. And you are . . . ?'

'Gilda.' She held out her hand. The multitude of charms on her gold bracelet jingled as she moved. 'I'm a close friend of Tito's. He's an associate of Michael Ward's.'

Close? How close?

Kit took her hand and shook it briefly. 'What, like his girl-friend?'

'Something like that.' She smiled and her eyes swept down over him, then up again. 'You're a very good-looking boy, Kit,' she said.

'Thanks,' he said cautiously. *And you're hot as hell, but I'm not going there, not now, not ever.*

He was used to getting the come-on from girls. And occasionally from women, too; he had no objection to bedding older ladies. In fact, he preferred it. They were knowledge-able and usually up for no-strings fun – unlike some of the younger ones, who came over all hot and heavy when you least expected it. But this one was Tito Danieri's territory, and he wasn't about to tread on *that* bastard's toes over a piece of skirt.

'If you ever need any company of an evening, you could always drop by,' she said, and handed him a slip of paper.

He took it, opened it out. There was an address written on it.

Oh sure, he thought. *If I ever get tired of owning a pair of kneecaps, that's what I'll do.*

He smiled and handed the piece of paper right back to her.

'Sorry,' he said. 'Shitting on your own doorstep's never a good idea.'

Her eyes went from warm to flinty in an instant.

'Suit yourself,' she said, and turned on her heel. Then she

half-turned back, caught him staring after her. The smile reappeared. 'But if you change your mind . . .'

'Yeah. Thanks,' said Kit.

He wouldn't.

57

The Orchid and Holford Rooms at the Dorchester were so brightly lit and so beautiful that Daisy had to blink against the dazzle. She was a bit disappointed that Ma hadn't gone for the ballroom for this, her daughter's first-ever deb dance, but it was a dinner dance, so everyone met and dined at the Dorchester at nine o'clock, instead of meeting up after attending dinner parties all over the city.

Her closest friend Tabby Arnott-Smythe was there, clutching her arm excitedly, looking a picture with her brunette hair swept up and pinned with a tiara, wearing a ball gown of an exquisitely pale powder blue.

Daisy looked at her a little enviously. Tabby was so petit; Daisy towered over her. And men didn't like big women, did they? They liked to be made to feel manly, powerful, dwarfing the woman at their side or in their arms. She knew that. But she was just so damned *tall*, and so awkward too. Her clothes always seemed to be half-falling off her – and she frequently toppled off her high heels. She had Pa to blame for her height. Mother was short, like Tabby. But Pa was over six feet, and so was her Aunt Ju, who was here, tearing excitedly about the place. She was just as loud as Pa, and bristling – like him – with the Bray self-confidence.

There was a photographer circulating among the crowds before they sat down to dinner, and Daisy posed patiently for the shot that would appear in *Tatler*, announcing Daisy, daughter of Lord and Lady Bray, at her debs' dance at the Dorchester.

'You look fabulous,' said Tabby, and then it was a mad round of greetings and then she was sitting between two handsome young men, both complete debs' delights, and was so excited and so tightly corseted that she could barely force down even a mouthful of the exquisite food on offer.

Then, the dancing – the best part for Daisy, who loved to dance. She was whisked around the floor to old stuff like 'Night and Day', 'Cheek to Cheek' and 'These Foolish Things'. It was all *so* tediously old-fashioned, but somehow enjoyable too. Russ Henderson and his West Indians would be striking up later in the evening.

'Coloured folk,' said Aunt Ju, who seemed to Daisy more than a little drunk as she swayed along to the compulsive beat. 'How amusing. They call this calypso, don't they?'

Daisy didn't know what they called it, only that it was good. She danced with her two dinner-partners, alternating them like two favourite pairs of shoes.

'My turn,' said Simon Collins, whose father owned a massive construction company. He was short, red-haired, with a rough sort of male attraction about him.

Daisy felt more comfortable with the taller, more effete-looking Will Stone, heir to the Stone banking fortune. She was embarrassed that she hadn't considered the impact of heels when she stood in Simon's presence. She loomed over him.

'Perhaps we should sit this one out,' she said, and Simon coloured up with temper.

'I shouldn't bother with that Stone fella,' he said, puce with rage at what he perceived as rejection. 'He's *arse*, in case you didn't know.'

Arse? Daisy stared at him in bemusement. She had no idea what he meant, but it didn't sound very nice.

'Oh, Gawd, is the dwarf acting up again?' asked Aunt Ju, coming over clutching her drink as Simon stormed off. 'He's got a *huge* chip on his shoulder because Daddy is trade. But what's wrong with that, I say. His father, Sir Bradley, is very clever you know. He started out as a mining engineer, then got into building and bought up his own aggregate sources, made an absolute *killing*.'

'Oh – how?' asked Daisy. She was only half-listening.

'He bought up gravel pits close to communities, for building work. Transport's a huge cost in aggregates, I understand, so if you can cut down on that – and he did – you're quids in.'

'Simon told me Will is . . . arse,' said Daisy.

'Oh, well he is. Absolutely. And perfectly charming.' Aunt Ju looked at Daisy. 'You *do* know what arse is, don't you, darling?' At Daisy's blank look, Ju shook her head. 'My *God*, Vanessa has kept you tucked away out of sight, hasn't she? Wills is attracted to boys. Not girls.'

Daisy took this information on board. The band played on; they were banging on steel drums and the sound was huge, almost deafening, but very jolly.

'I just wanted to sit down,' she shouted at her aunt. 'Because I was so much taller than Simon. I didn't want to embarrass him. I think I ought to go and apologize.'

'Oh, let him stew, sweetheart,' said Ju.

But she liked Simon. She actually thought he was terribly attractive, very *macho*, even if a little on the short side, and if she kicked her shoes off, he wouldn't be short at all. She hared off in search of him, feeling a bit woozy from all the drink, and found him out in the corridor, smoking a cigarette.

'Oh – it's you,' he said, not looking very pleased about it.

'Yes.' Daisy stood there for a moment, not sure what to say. Her head was spinning slightly, she felt very relaxed, very odd. She wasn't used to men's moods. Her father was often away, in the city or on business; she had no brothers. 'I didn't mean to upset you,' she said at last.

'I'm not upset.' He took a deep drag, then stubbed the remains of the cigarette out on the heel of his shoe and tossed it carelessly down onto the carpet. He looked at her sharply. 'I suppose you think you're too good for me, the son of a builder.'

Daisy was outraged. 'How can you say that? I just felt embarrassed because I'm so tall. That's all.'

'You mean I'm *short*,' he said angrily.

'No, I didn't . . .'

'Well, you know what they say.'

Daisy looked at him, flummoxed. 'No. What do they say?'

He grabbed her wrist and pulled her sharply towards him. 'That they're all the same size lying down,' he murmured against her mouth, and kissed her.

Daisy recoiled in surprise. Then she moved back again, finding the contact pleasant . . . really, really nice.

'In here . . .' he was saying now, tugging her after him through a door. Half-laughing, Daisy fell through the opening with him. He flicked a switch. It was a suite, one of three hundred in the hotel. And it was, clearly, empty.

'How did you know it would be empty?' she asked him in surprise.

'Stupid. It's my suite.'

He was kissing her again. Then he bent and picked her up in his arms. Daisy clung to him, amazed at how strong he was. *A builder's son*, she thought, and hot on the heels of *that* thought came another. That her mother would be appalled if she could see her now. That Pa would be livid. But then, they weren't here. And she *wanted* Simon's kisses, she'd never been kissed before, not properly, like he was kissing her now, this was fun, this was an *adventure*.

Having carried her through to the bedroom, he placed her upon the bed as if she was precious, like a porcelain doll. He clicked on the bedside lamp so that the room took on a warm, romantic glow. Then he lay down beside her, his eyes sparkling as he stared into hers.

'See? Now we're *exactly* the same height.'

It was true. Daisy laughed, drink and excitement combining to make her feel reckless, ready for anything.

'Gorgeous, gorgeous Daisy Bray,' he murmured, trailing kisses over her collarbone. Daisy lay back. This was lovely. It felt so nice, his strong hands upon her. 'You know, I've been wanting this for so long,' he whispered, his mouth coming back to hers, covering it, invading it.

'I adore you,' he said, and now his hands were moving inside the tight bodice of her gown and she felt a thrill of sheer eroticism as his fingers grazed against her nipples. 'Oh, Daisy.'

Now he was nudging her legs apart, and she felt a tingle of foreboding but also she was so excited, she so wanted to understand things, to not have everything be a mystery to her any more.

This was what the girls had been whispering about in the dorm late at night. *This* was the thing that was so unknown, so fascinating. He was fumbling with the front of his trousers, unbuttoning . . . Daisy stared, she wanted to see.

'You ride, don't you?' he said, almost panting.

Daisy was staring, watching his fingers, wanting to know, wanting to see.

What was he asking *that* for? Of course she did.

'Yes,' she said absently. Silly question, surely?

'Then your cherry's already broken, I expect, and this won't hurt.'

And he pulled out his penis. It was very red, and extremely big. She had never seen a naked male penis before. And she had actually expected that Simon's would be short, like the rest of him; but it was powerful, beautiful, the big vein throbbing up its considerable length. Daisy looked at it and felt not fear but elation. She felt herself almost *melt* with desire for it.

'It *is* your first time?' he was asking, pushing between her legs, moving the flimsy protection of her panties aside.

She was nodding. *Just do it*, she thought frantically. She could hear her own breathing coming in feverish little gasps.

'I'll be careful,' he said, and placed it so carefully, so very carefully, against her.

Daisy gave a heave and pushed down, taking it in, her mouth opening in surprise at the size of it. She pushed crazily down, enveloping him, her arms flung above her head in complete abandon.

'Oh, you hot little *whore*,' he moaned, half-laughing because he'd been worried about her virginity, about hurting her, when she was so eager, so moist, so completely delicious.

It was over too quickly, that was all Daisy could think as he thrust and thrust at her. In moments, he was done, slipping away from her. But then he turned her onto her side and touched her smoothly, relentlessly, until pleasure – such startling, *unbelievable* pleasure – grabbed her whole body and shook it from stem to stern.

They lay in each other's arms after that, quietly, and Daisy half-smiled to herself. Now she understood. Now, at last, she knew; she'd finally become a woman. And it was at that precise moment that Aunt Ju flung open the door and hurled herself into the room like a hurricane.

58

'What we are going to have to do,' said Vanessa, pacing around the drawing room in the London house, 'is keep this quiet.' She stopped and stared hard at her sister-in-law. 'Cornelius must *never* know.'

Daisy sat in the big armchair, feeling as small as a whipped five-year-old. She had never, ever seen her mother so enraged. Vanessa's anger was whip-like and cold, lashing Daisy's composure. When her mother turned and looked at her, Daisy felt the full weight of Vanessa's disapproval and disappointment like a physical blow.

She shuddered and folded her arms around herself, just praying for this to end. It was two hours since Aunt Ju had burst in on Simon and her. Daisy couldn't even *think* about that, what Aunt Ju must have seen before she managed to scramble from the bed, before Simon, blushing scarlet, had staggered to his feet, adjusting his trousers.

She was still wearing the beautiful yellow Worth dress. But now she felt sullied, embarrassed, not beautiful at all. Aunt Ju was sitting opposite her with a face like thunder, while her mother, in her dressing gown, was marching back and forth in front of her, shooting her daughter looks that curdled Daisy's soul.

'How *could* you?' she kept saying over and over.

'I'm sorry,' Daisy said, time after time.

'*Sorry!*' When Daisy said it, it seemed to only infuriate Vanessa all the more. 'You silly girl! And thank *goodness* your father isn't here.'

Pa was never there. Daisy always missed her father, craved his attention, longed for his big warm presence, but tonight she could see that his absence was a mercy.

Now Vanessa was shooting black looks at her sister-in-law. 'And for the love of God, Julianna, what were you thinking, letting her wander off? You were supposed to be looking after her.'

'It isn't Aunt Ju's fault,' said Daisy.

'*Shut up*, Daisy,' snapped Vanessa. 'You've done quite enough damage for one night, just keep quiet now.' She turned to Julianna with a disgusted expression. 'Had they . . . I mean, had things progressed too far . . . ?'

Julianna exchanged a look with Daisy. 'Yes,' she said. 'I think so.'

'Oh *hell*,' said Vanessa, and slumped down in a chair, burying her face in her hands.

Daisy sat there looking at the pair of them, judging her. She *hated* that they were judging her. She knew her mother's strict moral code; she knew her mother was inclined to be . . . well, not cold exactly, but a touch remote. What she had experienced with Simon had been wonderful, warm, exquisite; and now they were cheapening it, turning it into a sin, something evil, something shameful.

'I should have known something like this would happen,' said Vanessa, staring at Daisy as if she didn't even know her. 'I should have known.'

'*Vanessa*,' said Aunt Ju, and there was a warning note in her voice. Daisy heard it, looked at her curiously.

'Bad blood always comes out,' Vanessa went on, still staring at her daughter.

Bad blood?

Aunt Ju stood up suddenly. 'That's enough, Vanessa,' she said briskly. 'She got a bit drunk, that's all, and did something silly. The poor girl's suffered enough, and God knows it's something that happens.'

Vanessa was staring at her sister-in-law with disgust now.

'Not to *me*. *I* would never have shamed my family, disgraced my good name, in such a way.'

Daisy cringed. 'I'm sorry . . .' she murmured hopelessly.

'Look, all I'm saying is that it's not the end of the world. We'll deal with it, whatever the outcome.'

'Oh, my God. You think there could be . . . ?'

'Hopefully not. But we'll see, won't we?'

'Oh, Daisy, how *could* you?' howled Vanessa, shaking her head. 'How could you be so *stupid*?'

'Oh, come on, Vanessa. Enough, now,' said Julianna.

'If it comes to that, he'll have to marry her.'

'Now you're talking rubbish, Vanessa. He's practically engaged to Breamore's daughter.'

Vanessa got wearily to her feet. She stared down at Daisy. 'How could you cheapen yourself like this? I've brought you up properly. But it's true, isn't it? Bad blood will always out.'

'What do you *mean,* bad blood?' Daisy burst out, hurt. 'I'm your daughter, yours and Pa's, how can you say a thing like that to me? There's no "bad blood" in me.'

Daisy looked from her mother to her aunt in bewilderment. She knew she'd done wrong. Drunk too much and behaved like a fool. But to castigate her like this, talk about her as if she was a slut – she just couldn't take it.

'No,' said Aunt Julianna briskly. 'Of course there isn't. Now, I think we're all overtired, and very soon someone is going to say something they really don't mean.' She looked pointedly at Vanessa. 'Let's just go to bed, forget about it.'

'*Forget* about it? Are you mad?' Vanessa was pacing again,

her face twisting in agitation. She stopped in front of Daisy, huddled there like a criminal in her armchair. 'I think it's best if she stays here in London with you for a while, Julianna. I'll think of something to tell Cornelius. I'm just . . . I'm just so exasperated I can't think straight. And you're right. We've all said quite enough.'

With that, she turned and left the room, slamming the door closed behind her.

Daisy flinched and shot to her feet. She had never been spoken to like this before. Like she was nothing. A disgrace. A flare of temper rose up in her as she stared at the closed door. Perhaps she had been stupid. But was it the crime of the century? Really?

'Don't worry about it,' said Aunt Ju comfortingly, putting an arm round Daisy's shoulders. 'She'll calm down. And hopefully it will all come to nothing.'

'She hates me,' said Daisy, trembling with anger and hurt.

'It gave her a bit of a shock, that's all.' *Because she hates sex*, thought Julianna. *And it's pretty plain that you don't.* But she didn't say it out loud. 'Anyway, it gives us the perfect opportunity to have some fun in the Smoke, just you and me, all girls together. Yes?'

Daisy shrugged listlessly. All she knew was that her mother was sending her away in disgrace. But then, it wasn't the first time she had felt the chilly weight of rejection from Vanessa. All through her growing-up, she had tried so hard to please her remote and rather reclusive mother, and she had always come away with the feeling that she had failed her somehow by being lively and hungry for life – that she could never live up to Vanessa's exacting standards of delicacy and gentility.

Bad blood. Her mother had hurt her before, but never so much as when she had uttered those two words – like she was a foreigner, an alien. Nothing to do with Vanessa at all.

'All right,' she sighed. She was being sent into exile, however nicely Aunt Ju tried to dress it up. Boarding school, finishing school, Aunt Ju's place in London, it was all the same to her. She just had to make the best of it.

59

1963

Kit was enjoying working for Michael Ward; he'd spruced himself up, got two bespoke suits, five shirts, some new shoes from Hobbs and a selection of dark-toned ties. He looked the business now, and Mr Ward was putting work his way on a regular basis. He often went two-handed with Reg, the big white-haired bloke who'd hauled him in from the restaurant. Reg was all right; a sound man, trustworthy.

So Kit was happy enough and he was beginning to see his old drinking mates for the losers they were as he settled into his job as a breaker. Michael Ward was big news. Like the Richardsons and the Frasers from South London, the Delaneys from Battersea, the Nashes from the Angel, the Krays from Bethnal Green and the Carter mob from Bow, Michael Ward ruled his manor with a rod of iron.

Michael was ready for anybody and anything. He had an arsenal of weaponry hidden away that staggered Kit the first time he saw it – there were Thompson sub-machine guns, shotguns, hand guns, grenades, swords, knives. He also had close ties to a trading place for guns called Port Road, where dealers traded in war souvenir weaponry – which could easily be converted back into useful life.

People came to Mr Ward for favours, and he was generous

to a fault, helping them out when trouble came their way – on the strict understanding that, should the favour ever need to be returned, then it would be, without question. He paid Kit a hundred pounds one evening and told him to get himself over to an address in Hoxton to do a favour for a man who'd found out his wife was fucking around.

Kit looked perturbed. 'I don't do women, Mr Ward,' he said.

Michael Ward looked slightly surprised that someone had just questioned his orders. But he took it well; Kit was only a kid, and a good kid at that; he'd learn. 'Don't worry yourself, boy, it's the bloke who's down for a caning. Not that you should be worrying too much about her. She's a right old shagbag, by the sound of it.'

'You don't want to be so hasty,' said Reg once they were in the car. 'Think before you even *blink*, boy. Mr Ward don't like having people talk back at him.'

Reg drove them over there. Kit took the rebuke, because he respected Reg. One thing that Kit had found distinguished Mr Ward's boys, they all had nice motors and soon, he knew, he would have one too, through one of the car dealers who paid money to the firm.

For now, he was content. He knocked on the door. When it was opened by a startled-looking chap with crooked teeth, he went straight to work. State of those gnashers, he figured he was doing the geezer a favour anyway, knocking them out.

'You Ted Rowles?' asked Reg, stepping in behind Kit and closing the door after them.

The man was on the floor, pleading with Kit not to hit him again. His face was a mass of blood where Kit had right-handed him. It was dripping down the front of his shirt, staining his trousers. He was shaking his head, clutching at his face.

'No! It's not me.'

'Liar,' said Kit, reaching down to drag him back to his feet.

'I'm not! I'm not! He's upstairs,' he managed to blubber.

Kit looked up. There was movement at the top of the stairs, a door slammed. 'Shit,' said Kit, and shot straight up there.

'See? Hasty. I told you. You never get nowhere if you're hasty,' said Reg, following him up at a more leisurely pace.

60

Tito was a major face in the East End now. He'd easily shouldered the Maltese out of the way and taken over their manor. He was feared and revered in equal measures, and he had connections as impressive as the biggest and best of the firms that ran the city. He had contacts in the police, and in Parliament. He had Lord Bray in his pocket. He was sorted.

There was a private party going on in the palatial flat over Tito's club. Tito's regular girl Gilda was there, a striking golden-blonde with ocean-green eyes and a taste for gold jewellery, which Tito kept her well supplied in. Gilda jangled when she moved, she was so laden down with gold. She wasn't wearing much else, at this precise moment. Neither was her pretty brunette friend, who was stroking Cornelius's hair.

The spectre of those photos haunted Cornelius. Because of that old bastard Astorre, he had to be nice to Tito, and Tito had asked him here, tonight, because he needed a favour.

'I have an acquaintance who's in a little trouble with the police . . .' said Tito, and went on to tell him about the son of a business associate, who had disgraced himself by snorting cocaine and then going on a ridiculous rampage, which he had topped off by urinating in the doorway of a church and then – allegedly – raping a fourteen-year-old girl.

'It's a bad business,' said Tito. 'If only there was something that could be done to rescue the boy from his own folly . . .'

Cornelius sipped his whisky; it tasted sour all of a sudden. 'I'll see to it,' he said.

'You will?' Tito's ice-blue eyes widened in fake surprise.

'I will, of course. As a favour to a friend.' *You blackmailing wop bastard.*

Tito relaxed and smiled.

'You are so good to me,' he said, indicating the doorway. 'And in return, look, I will be good to you.'

Suddenly there was a young man of about eighteen standing there; a very beautiful young man, with long straight black hair falling to his waist, a tanned and chiselled face and soft girlish blue eyes. He saw Tito sitting there and smiled, lifting a hand in greeting. Then his eyes drifted over and rested with interest on big, blond Cornelius.

'Isn't he perfect?' asked Tito, beckoning the boy over. 'Wouldn't you like to . . . ?' and Tito laughed, not bothering to complete the sentence.

The young man approached Cornelius and Tito where they sat, surrounded by half-nude girls, and Gilda. He looked at the girls with disdain, then turned his attention to Tito.

'Sebastian, this is Lord Bray,' Tito told him.

The boy nodded coolly to Cornelius, checking him over.

'Cornelius, meet Sebastian. He's yours for the night, if you want him.'

Cornelius knew he really shouldn't. He should be strong, resist temptation. But . . . Sebastian was the most fabulously beautiful creature he had ever seen.

After that first night, Cornelius met up with Sebastian as often as he could. In between the pressures of work, the dissatisfaction with his home life and the increasing nerviness of Vanessa, who was forever moaning on and on about Daisy ('She's impossible, she never does what I tell her, she's out of control') Sebastian was a sweet release.

Vanessa had wanted a child. He had *got* her a child. His child, too. Not the boy he had desired, of course, but it was far too late now to regret that. In between all *that*, the soothing balm of Sebastian was something he sought out more and more.

Never in Tito's club, though. He'd been caught once and he was still paying the price for that. Now he took Sebastian to discreet out-of-the-way places and they made love there. Afterwards he would buy the boy gifts. An Asprey wallet. A gold money-clip. Tiffany cufflinks and matching tiepins. Anything he wanted, he could have. And Sebastian wanted a lot. He knew his value, down to the last penny, and he was as skilled in bed as any Japanese geisha.

61

1965

The Darkes department store chain was growing strongly and that at least gave Ruby some satisfaction. She had invested the money Cornelius had paid for her little girl wisely. She had expanded her father's shop to a massive extent. She had acquired bombed-out premises near Marble Arch, Edgware Road and Oxford Street at knockdown prices, rebuilt, then ploughed all the profits she made straight back into the company.

Ruby had forced herself to live for her business. Every small thing about it had been a matter of great importance to her. She often stood in her stores, watching the customers, noting whether they turned left or right, what drew them, what pushed them away. She was always out on the floor, questioning the managers about stock levels, sales performance and new lines – because she had nothing else in her life, nothing at all. There was still food on sale, in separate food halls, but the clothes and the furnishings were the big sellers now. Post-war, people had just been grateful to be alive. But now it was the 'Swinging' Sixties. Now, they wanted to forget austerity, to celebrate. To live the dream.

'What we're selling now is a lifestyle,' she told her accountant. 'Not just the right clothes, but the right teacup, the right suitcase and bed linen, the right *style*.'

'You're expanding too fast,' he told her gloomily, blinking through his thick black-rimmed glasses at the figures.

Ruby looked at him kindly. Her thin, myopic, grey-haired accountant Joseph Fuller would always be an overly cautious man. He had guided her well so far. However, she was not such a fool as to let an accountant run her business for her. Her years in retail had given her confidence in her own sound judgement.

'Joseph, I told you: one year's for growth, the next is for consolidation. That's not fast, that's sensible.'

'Manufacturing costs are sky-high. The wholesalers keep pushing the prices up, and what can we do? They've got a captive market.'

Ruby knew this all too well. The latest price hike had sent her raging around the office for days. Finally, she'd sat down, Jane her secretary had brought her a cup of tea, and she had worked out what to do. It was, admittedly, a desperate plan. But she had to do *something*, or the wholesale bastards would be fleecing her until her dying day.

'I've been thinking about that,' she told Joseph.

'Oh?'

'I think we should cut out the middle man,' said Ruby.

'Cut out the *wholesalers*?' He stared at her as if she'd gone mad. 'Ruby. Be careful. You'll be blacklisted.'

To be blacklisted by the Wholesale Textile Association was no small thing. Ruby knew it. But it seemed to her that the wholesalers had had it all their own way for far too long.

'I've been talking to the Cohen brothers in Leicester.' Ruby had been up to their factory three times, wining and dining the manufacturers and their wives. 'They've accepted an order – a *direct* order – for two thousand dozen men's Y-fronts and string vests.'

Joseph was pale with shock. 'They must be suicidal.'

'On the contrary, they'll do well out of the deal.'

'It's crazy.'

But the two thousand dozen men's underwear order sold out in no time. The Cohens – urged on by Ruby – had taken a big risk, but it had paid off. Encouraged by this success, the Cohen brothers continued to defy the WTA and threw in their lot with Ruby.

'Don't gloat,' said Joseph, months later.

'Can't help it,' said Ruby, showing him the new Darkes label on every garment out on the shop floor.

Now she had her own manufacturing base, and no whole-salers to divvy up with.

'We give the Cohens mass-production orders, they give us rock-bottom prices, we can pass some of those savings on to customers. Everyone's a winner.'

62

Ruby met with her old friend Vi for tea and cakes at a Lyons Corner House.

'You're working too hard,' said Vi, sweeping majestically in. Vi hadn't changed. Despite the fact that she could have afforded a bucketload of Chanel now, she still stuck to her favourite scent, which followed her everywhere like a fragrant ghost – Devon Violets. She still had her helmet of auburn-dyed hair, her cupid's-bow mouth slashed with scarlet, her artfully blackened eyes. She was forty now, but remained an exceedingly handsome woman.

'I like working too hard,' said Ruby. She was proud of all that she had achieved. From a single corner shop, she had expanded Darkes over the years until she now had fifteen department stores, countrywide.

'Yes, because you have absolutely nothing else in your life. You don't even have a lover.'

Not having a lover was something Vi saw as a disaster. She was now married to one of those eager stage-door johnnies who had applauded her at the Windmill, a nephew of Lord Albemarle who had no sons to inherit. As a happy consequence of her judicious marriage and Lord Albemarle's death, Vi was now *loaded*.

But while dear boring old Anthony languished in the Oxfordshire countryside tending his thousand-acre estate,

Vi loved to come to town and meet up with one or other of the young men who kept her 'company' on these visits.

'I don't *want* a lover,' said Ruby with absolute truthfulness. 'What would a man do for me? Try to dominate me? Tell me what to do?'

Vi rolled her beautiful eyes. 'Darling, you don't actually have to *listen* to him. Just enjoy his company.'

Ruby smiled. 'And then what? Kick him out of bed?'

'Absolutely.'

Every time they met up, Vi went on about this. For years it had been the same. Now Ruby just changed the subject. Vi was a good friend – the best – but *God* could she go on. Ruby thought of Cornelius, the only man she had ever loved, and how disastrously wrong it had all gone for her after that. She despised him now. No, she *certainly* didn't want another man in her life.

'Ask me how the business is going,' she said, brushing aside these troubling thoughts as their tea and cakes arrived.

'No,' said Vi. 'I won't. You've buried yourself in that bloody job of yours because it stops you thinking about your kids. Admit it.'

Ruby's jaw tightened. 'Shut up, Vi.'

She knew Vi was right. And now . . . now she was going to do something about that. But she didn't want to discuss it. Not yet. Soon, she promised herself, she was going to do it: make herself known to Daisy. She'd already hit an obstacle on her son, though, because Charlie was refusing to send her a visiting order, the bastard. Joe was pushing him over it, but so far – no result.

'The truth hurt?'

'I said shut *up*.'

It *did* hurt. And it *was* true.

'All right.' Vi sighed heavily. Business to Vi was a bore. It was for men to worry about making money; she just spent it. 'How is the business going?'

'Splendid. And without a *man*,' said Ruby, 'I'm sole owner. All my work is for my own benefit.'

'Sounds a bit lonely to me.'

'Well, it isn't,' lied Ruby, buttering a scone. It was. She *was* lonely. She wanted her life back, her lost life. Fuck it – she wanted her *kids*.

63

1967

Daisy was having a whale of a time. She was shopping, meeting up with friends, and giving her careless Aunt Ju the slip as often as she possibly could. She had never had so much fun in all her life; being away from her cold and repressive mother cheered her up in a way she could never have believed possible.

'I love London,' she moaned, swooping in and out of the shops in Carnaby Street, lingering over Quant and Biba as if they were mouth-watering treats to be devoured.

Not that Daisy allowed herself many *edible* treats. She was wishing she was thinner, daintier. Twiggy was the ideal these days – every girl she knew wanted to look big-eyed and waif-like – but Daisy had these damned *curves*. Then up ahead she saw a rather short, powerfully built young man with dark-red hair.

'Jesus!' she yelped, falling off her white patent heels in surprise.

'What?' Mandy, her friend, clutched at her in alarm. 'What's up?'

It was Simon Collins. She felt her heart give a treacherous lurch at the sight of him. She had half-believed herself to be in love with him after that night four years ago, and had longed for the sight of him. She had seen herself as some tragic figure, a thwarted Juliet parted from her Romeo. Her period had reassured her that there was going to be no pregnancy, but still she had nurtured this fabulous *crush* on him. Her first man, *ever.* That was something special, surely? And now here he was, walking towards her.

'Simon!' she burst out, beaming.

She hurried towards him. And saw him recoil at the sight of her. It was then that she noticed he was with a slender young woman with long straight mousy-brown hair. Both Simon and the young woman were staring at her as if she had landed in a spaceship.

'It's me,' she said, aware that her voice sounded gushy, but unable to stop it somehow. Her loose top plummeted from her shoulder, exposing her bra strap. She scooped it back up, embarrassed. 'Daisy Bray. The Dorchester. Remember? My deb's dance?'

'Oh! Yes.' Simon's face was brick-red, as if fearing she was about to say something shocking.

Like what? wondered Daisy. *Hi, I'm the virgin you fucked in that fancy hotel room?*

In irritation she stared at him, waiting for him to respond, to say *something*. I've missed you. I'm sorry. Piss off. *Anything.*

'This is my fiancée, Clarissa,' he said instead. 'Clarissa, darling, this is Daisy – Lord Bray's daughter.'

The girl nodded, watching Daisy as if she might bite. Daisy, however, was watching Simon. What *had* she been thinking? It was true. Aunt Ju had been right all along. He was extremely short. He wasn't *that* handsome. Now she could see that it had all been an illusion, brought about by that magical night, that first night of adult freedom. She had drunk far too much and fallen into bed with a completely unsuitable man. No wonder her mother was furious with her.

'Well . . . nice to see you again,' said Daisy lamely, and Simon and Clarissa moved on along the crowded pavement.

Daisy stood there, appalled at her own stupidity.

'Who the hell was *that?*' asked Mandy as they linked arms and strolled on. 'That funny little man, he blushed like a girl when he saw you.'

'Nobody,' said Daisy. And it was true. The day seemed blighted somehow. She'd made a fool of herself. Flung herself at life again, been careless. She could see it now, so clearly. She felt hotly embarrassed to think that she'd actually let that creep have her.

'Tom's throwing a party tonight at his place,' said Mandy, forgetting all about Simon in an instant. 'Are you coming?'

'Of course,' said Daisy, pushing Simon from her mind. She was going to Tom's party tonight, and she was going to forget all about Simon, and her deb's dance, and the drunken humiliation of her night at the Dorchester. She was going to forget it if it killed her.

64

Tom's place was heaving with bodies writhing along to 'Paint It Black' by the Stones. He had a projector lined up on a blank wall, throwing multicoloured psychedelic images in a twirling, whirling mass that Daisy tried not to stare at because it made her feel giddy.

She couldn't speak to anyone, the music was too loud. As soon as she and Mandy came in the door, Mandy peeled off and was lost to sight. Daisy stood there alone, until Tom came by and pushed a bottle of beer into her hand. She drank it cautiously. She didn't want to see some other callow youth as handsome as Hercules, through beer goggles.

'We won it, isn't that fab?' shouted Tom in her ear.

'Won what?' asked Daisy, puzzled.

'Won *what*?' He laughed out loud. 'The fucking World Cup, that's what. We beat Germany 4–2. Isn't it great?'

'Oh. Yes. Terrific.' Daisy had absolutely no interest in football.

'You're pretty,' he shouted.

Daisy looked at him. She didn't have much interest in *him*, either. This was no Hercules. Tom was lanky, badly dressed, and he had wisps of beard clinging to his soft girly chin. So he thought she was pretty. What was she supposed to reply to that? *Well, you're not!* sprang to mind, but she had been raised to have impeccable manners; she couldn't shake the habits of her upbringing. She shrugged, smiled, and sipped the beer, which was warm and ghastly.

'Dance?' he yelled.

Daisy shook her head.

'Come on!'

Damn it.

They writhed about among the other heaving bodies, and Daisy kept having to slither away from Tom's groping hands. Finally, she'd had enough. She muttered an excuse to him and fought her way to the hall. She couldn't see Mandy anywhere. The Beach Boys were pounding out 'Good Vibrations' now. There was a weird smell in the air; she knew it was drugs.

She pushed her way up the staircase past snogging couples and started looking in the bedrooms. Pretty soon, she wished she hadn't. It looked as though an orgy was in progress. Mandy could have been one of the writhing shapes in any of the beds, but she couldn't be sure. And the music was too deafening for her to be heard, even when she shouted Mandy's name.

'Hi,' yelled a looming male shape in stonewash jeans and a LOVE T-shirt. His breath stank of cigarette smoke. 'You want to . . .' He indicated a bedroom.

'No,' said Daisy. The scene at the Dorchester sprang into her mind, the sheer humiliation of being caught in the act. It made her tremble to even think about it.

'Come on,' he said, catching hold of her arm.

'I said *no.*' Daisy yanked free and hurtled down the stairs. She pulled open the front door and ran out onto the path, inhaling clean night air. She went out into the road, and there was a taxi, the blessed yellow light glowing in the darkness. She summoned it, got inside, and went home to Aunt Ju's.

*

'What the hell happened to you?' asked Mandy next day when they met up, her eyes bloodshot and bleary behind big sunglasses.

'I was tired. Wanted to go home,' said Daisy.

But home wasn't Aunt Ju's. Home was Brayfield, which now she missed with an ache that was almost physical. These days, she was too embarrassed by her own behaviour to risk a visit. She felt displaced, disgraced. Nevertheless, she tried to be happy with her lot, she really did; she'd settled into London life, which seemed to be one mad continuous whirl of parties, shopping and generally not giving a damn. She'd even passed her driving test and Dad had promised her a Mini.

'Ally Pally soon,' Mandy told her with a grin.

'What's that?'

'The Fourteen-hour Technicolour Dream,' said Mandy. 'Pink Floyd are playing.'

'Aunt Ju will never let me go.' Aunt Ju behaved more like a slipshod gaoler than a true auntie – no doubt under strict instructions from Vanessa.

'Idiot, don't tell her you're going. Tell her we're visiting my folks in Cambridgeshire.'

'Do they actually live there?'

'Of course not.'

'She might check.' Daisy didn't think Aunt Ju would. Aunt Ju was more concerned with her own busy life than with supervising her niece's.

'Don't tell her until the day before. Then once we're gone, it's too late.'

Daisy felt a thrill of fearful expectation at that. She loved kicking over the traces, almost as much as she dreaded reprisals when the fun was over. Behaving badly brought attention – and any attention was better than her usual quota, which was none.

65

'I'm pleased with your work,' said Michael Ward to Kit as they sat in the back room of the restaurant one night.

'Thanks, boss.'

That meant a lot to Kit. He respected Mr Ward. Looked up to him. Mr Ward was a mean, hard bastard, but he was also straight as a die. All his boys had a lot of time for him. He looked after them. He was looking after Kit very well indeed. Kit had a brand-new motor now to drive around in. A penthouse flat had been organized. He had pussy on tap, and he was making a real name for himself around the manor.

'Reggie says you're a good boy, a thinker.' Mr Ward's granite-grey eyes crinkled at the corners as he blew out a plume of smoke from his cigar. 'That's a rarity, son. And the boys like you.'

Kit was proud to hear that. The boys were hard nuts but they had quickly taken him into the fold. At first he knew he'd been too impulsive. There had been a ruck or two with other youngsters who saw him as a threat to their own positions, but he had quickly sorted those out. Now he'd outgrown the need to run full-pelt into silly situations. He found the Ward organization provided him with something he had never had before – that feeling of being part of a family, accepted and watched over. He liked it.

'You heard about Reggie?' asked Michael Ward, tapping ash from the Cohiba he was smoking. He watched Kit closely.

Kit nodded. There had been a rumour that Reggie, the big white-haired geezer who had been Mr Ward's number one man, was retiring from the game due to ill health. Kit knew Reggie had a hernia, an old sports injury from his younger days in the boxing ring, that played him up. More and more he had been leaving the strong-arm stuff to Kit and to others.

'He's dropping out,' said Mr Ward. 'You want to take over, head up the breakers?'

Kit couldn't believe it. His face split into a wide grin.

'That a yes?' asked Mr Ward.

'Yeah, boss.'

'This means you can pick and choose your own jobs,' said Mr Ward. 'Delegate any you don't fancy. And it means you keep an eye on things.' Mr Ward stared into Kit's eyes. 'You watch my back, son. Anybody thieves off me, you let me know. Anybody tries to cross me, you sort them out. You know the drill. Reggie taught you.'

And it was as simple as that. Kit was in charge of Mr Ward's boys.

To Kit, it was like winning the pools.

'How's it going then, Kit?' asked Gilda as he passed her in the bar.

Kit paused. He'd been at pains to avoid contact with Gilda since she'd first propositioned him. She was sitting at the bar, flaunting her long tanned legs in a white miniskirt, her golden-blonde hair spilling down her back, wearing a tight-fitting black top that hugged her opulent breasts. She wore a ton of elaborate make-up that made her sea-green eyes look even more beautiful than they already were. She also wore a gold charm-bracelet, gold necklaces, bangles, earrings. She *dripped* with gold. All presents from Tito, Kit guessed. She looked good enough to eat, and she knew it.

'Fine,' he said. 'Just got promotion.'

'I know.'

'Oh? How?'

'Pillow talk with Tito.' She tapped her nose. 'Michael likes you. Everyone's been telling him how good you are. Including me.'

Kit thought this was an exaggeration of her own influence. He'd been watching her and Tito together, and they didn't seem that close. Mr Ward didn't seem that close to Tito, either. Kit's feeling was that Michael Ward tolerated Tito as an occasional business partner: but there was no love lost there.

'You know what?' Gilda was smiling. One of her long-nailed fingers was running up and down the stem of her Babycham glass on the bar. The charms on her bracelet jingled. 'I bet you're more than good. I bet you're very impressive.'

Kit looked straight into her smiling green eyes. She wasn't talking about the work now.

'Get you something?' asked the barman.

'Beer,' said Kit.

'What, you having a drink with me? That's progress.'

'Just a word,' said Kit.

'Oh? Just one? I expected two.'

Kit half-smiled. The barman brought his beer and put it down on the mat. There was no charge; there never was for Mr Ward's boys.

'Thanks,' said Kit, and took a long, cool mouthful. Then he turned to Gilda and said very quietly: 'Not your place.

Not mine. Go to the Long Bar in Maidstone, and watch you're not followed. Next week, let me know a day.'

With that, Kit swallowed the rest of his pint, and turned and walked away.

66

1967

Charlie had finally relented and let Ruby visit him in prison. She had never been within spitting distance of a prison before. Wandsworth depressed her instantly, with its disinfectant stink and its air of sad hopelessness. She was ushered by a prison warder into the visiting room with a large group of others. Though Ruby had dressed down for the occasion, she still stood out. She was taller than most women in the room, and darker, and more elegant.

Looking around at the others, she was struck by how poor they looked, how haggard, how beaten down, and she understood. Bad enough to be dirt-poor, but to have a husband or a boyfriend or father inside was more than most women could stand.

The prisoners were filing in now. She kept her head down. Already she'd had enough of this place and she wondered if she was doing a stupid thing, coming here. It had been quite an experience, just getting it all arranged. The Home Office had wanted her photograph, and they had to approve her visit or she couldn't come.

Now she almost wished she hadn't bothered to go to all that effort. Her and Charlie had never got on. All too often she had been the target for his brutality. Bullish Joe had been able to stand up to him; she had not. But she had to do this. This was about her son.

Just get on with it, she told herself.

'Sis?'

Ruby looked up. There was a stranger standing there. At least, that was her first thought. But after a split second she recognized this aged man as Charlie, her brother. He didn't smile. He sat down on the other side of the small table that acted as a barrier between the visitor and the visited. Strange that the first thing Ruby's mind did was leap back to her childhood. Charlie had always triggered a flinch response in her, like Dad – even now, as an adult, she expected a cuff around the ear.

She remembered all those times he had sat there grinning and watched their dad pummel her with his fists or lash her with his belt, never trying to intervene. Slapping her himself, time and again. At least Joe had always had the decency to get out of the room when all that happened. But Charlie had relished it.

Ruby looked around. The warder was standing at the side of the room, watching everyone. Any trouble, he'd be there in an instant. That reassured her.

She looked back at Charlie. His eyes were the same. But they were sadder, like they'd seen too much. And his curly hair was thin now, his scalp showing palely through wisps of it, and its blackness had faded to white. His face, once so full of life, was still and almost devoid of expression; deep lines ran down beside his mouth, and his eyes were almost lost in folds of loose skin and a network of wrinkles.

Charlie sat down, folded his arms over his chest.

'Now don't tell me you've come to pay me a social visit at last, Sis,' he said, half-smiling.

Ruby eyed him coolly. 'Why the fuck would I? You always hated me, just like Dad did.'

Charlie threw back his head and laughed at that. He didn't deny it.

'Then what you doing here?' he asked her, tipping his head on one side in a movement she knew so well.

He was still a scary, intimidating man. It was all in the eyes, in the body movement. Joe had told her before this visit that Charlie was Category A, kept in a maximum-security block away from the 'regular' cons, and considered to be a danger to the public.

'Everywhere he goes inside, he's signed on,' Joe had said.

She had asked what that meant.

'Like when he goes from the workshop to the cells, he's signed in by a warder, and when he's out in the grounds there's an escort and a dog handler with him, and when he comes back indoors, he's signed for again. He's checked every hour of the day and night. His cell's impregnable.'

'What, they think he's going to make a break for it or something?' asked Ruby, horrified and fascinated.

'Maybe. Or do somebody who looks at him the wrong way. You know Charlie.'

Oh yes. She knew Charlie all right.

'So, what you doing here then? Asking after my health?' he asked.

'I don't care about your health,' said Ruby.

'What then?'

'The baby. The little boy. I want to know who had him,' said Ruby.

She hadn't ever contacted Daisy like she'd told Joe she would. To her shame, she had lost her nerve. Tried to work herself up to it, and failed. She felt a crushing weight of guilt over Daisy. She had been *paid* to give up her daughter. But now, at least she had summoned her courage to find out about her son. She *had* to get some answers.

Now Charlie really *did* laugh. He laughed so hard Ruby

thought he was about to have a stroke. She *hoped* so. But not before he told her what she needed to hear.

'What's funny?' she asked when his laughter wore itself out.

'You,' said Charlie, the smile dropping from his face, leaving it hard and mean. '*You're* funny. All these fucking years and not a visit, not so much as a kiss-my-arse or nothing. Now suddenly you pitch up and tell me you're a concerned mother. Don't give me that bullshit.'

'I want to know where he is.'

'Yeah. Well.' He shrugged again.

Ruby had never hit anyone in her entire life. Now she found herself wanting to fling herself across the table to smack his big meaty head so hard it would bleed.

'So where is he?' she asked.

Charlie stared at her. This pleased him, she could see it; that she wanted something from him, that he had her at a disadvantage. 'He's dead,' he said.

Ruby felt her stomach drop away. '*What?*'

Charlie leaned forward, rested his elbows on the table. Ruby leaned back.

'Chap who used to do fire-watching in the war,' said Charlie, smiling and speaking in a low hissing whisper. 'He got rid of things people didn't want. Had a vat of sulphuric down in the cellar. People who'd crossed them. People who wouldn't pay up. And,' he leaned closer, his voice dropping, hardening, '*bastard black babies.*'

Ruby tried to draw breath and found she couldn't. She had to gulp, hard. Clutch at her chest with both hands. She stared at his hated face.

'You're lying,' she gasped out.

Charlie sat upright again, looking at her like she was the lowest form of life.

'Like you give a shit,' he said. 'Talk about history repeating itself. Mum was a slag, and so are you. She had it off with a black who worked in a jazz club, she did. I remember it all like it was yesterday. Took boiling-hot baths and drank gin to try and lose it, you know. Maybe that's why she died when you were born. Maybe she did some damage inside. I ain't lying about the kid. And you never cared up to now. So what's changed?'

Dead? Ruby was still trying to take it in. The horrible, loathsome words pouring out of his mouth . . . *a fire-watcher in the war. . . sulphuric . . .*

She couldn't get her breath. All she could hear was a pulse, beating hard in her head. Her chest was a sea of pain.

Her baby.

Dissolved in acid.

She swallowed hard, tasting bile. 'Does Joe know about this?' she asked faintly.

'Yeah. Sure he does. When your sister behaves like a tart, what you supposed to do? You cover her tracks, you don't want your family disgraced. Joe understood that.'

Joe had known about this?

Ruby jumped to her feet.

'It was just a bit of filth, to be disposed of,' said Charlie, and he actually looked *pleased* to be saying these awful things. 'Bad blood only makes bad blood. Best to do away with it. Kid would only have been trouble. And be grateful – you made a good bit of wedge out of the girl.'

'You *bastard*,' said Ruby.

She turned and fled the room.

'*Nice of you to come and see me, Sis!*' roared after her, and the sound of his laughter was echoing around her head as she went through the prison gates.

She sagged against the wall outside, her stomach churning. She doubled over, and was suddenly sick.

'You all right, love?' called one of the men at the gate.

She wiped her mouth, panting, crying.
Her baby.
And Joe had known.
Not answering, she reeled away and headed for home.

67

The more Kit learned about Michael Ward, the more he admired him. Mr Ward was a big figure in the East End, deeply feared and respected, and a patron of many charities. He raised thousands for the Aberfan Disaster Fund, when a slag heap smothered a Welsh village school, and kept donations flooding in to the Hackney Road Queen Elizabeth Hospital for children. Michael Ward dined with peers of the realm at gentlemen's clubs in the West End, held court with film stars.

But Kit had no illusions. His boss had a hugely impressive public façade and some friends in very high places, but he was also a crook. He was paid protection all around the city, and his breakers and enforcers made sure that no one slacked when the time came to cough up.

The business kept Kit on his toes. He was always sending his lads off to this arcade or that shop to chase late payments. Some of the venues he visited in person, just to keep his hand in, keep his ear to the ground. Or, when a venue was new, Mr Ward himself sometimes showed up, to make sure that everything was done as it should be.

So it was Michael Ward himself who kept the appointment he'd made to see the owner of the new department store near Marble Arch. He was ushered into the office of a tall dark-skinned woman in her forties, elegantly dressed in an ivy-green business suit and white shirt. Her sleek black hair was tied back in a bun and there was a no-nonsense look in her beautiful brown eyes.

'Hello, I'm Ruby Darke,' she said, indicating that he should take a seat while she went round behind the desk and sat there.

Truth to tell, she was rushed off her feet and barely even noticing who the hell she was speaking to. Sometimes she didn't know how she coped at all, but running the company had at least kept her busy over the years, taking her mind off what could have been. If only it could also stop her reliving that visit to Charlie, and hearing again all those foul things he'd said.

Her business was sprawling out now. She had enthusiastically followed Marks & Spencer's brilliant idea of a nationwide distribution network to move chilled and dried foods around the country with speed and efficiency. Darkes now boasted a fleet of thermostatically controlled refrigeration vehicles to carry chilled meats and poultry, so that fresh produce as well as frozen could be provided to the consumer. A big consumer panel had been taking up much of her time, and she now felt that she knew everything she needed to know – in fact, *more* than she needed to know – about the merits of fresh chicken over frozen.

'I can't spare much time, I'm afraid,' she said. 'I don't usually see sales reps at all, I generally leave that to the buyers. And it's pretty late in the day . . .'

'Ah, well,' said Michael. 'That's all right. Because I'm not a sales rep.'

On the phone to her secretary Jane, he'd said he was.

Ruby looked at him. Took in the sharp suit, the iron-grey hair, the hard grey unblinking eyes that held hers. He was, she realized for the first time, an extremely attractive man. His appearance was wealthy, cared-for, beautifully groomed.

But . . . the only time in her life she'd seen a similar expression in a man's eyes was when she looked in her brother Charlie's. Joe's had that look, too, but to a lesser degree. It was a look that said: *I don't give a fuck who you are; I'm in charge here.*

'Then what are you? Exactly?' she asked, all thoughts of poultry gone from her mind.

She'd had the week from hell and now she had this dangerous-looking, frankly *gorgeous* man in here playing silly buggers. Ever since she'd visited Charlie, she hadn't been able to get what he'd said out of the forefront of her mind, and this Saturday was the christening of Joe and Betsy's second child, a brand-new baby boy. She was going to attend, and she was going to get some straight answers out of Joe if it was the last thing she did.

'Just a businessman,' said Michael with a light shrug. 'I like to offer my services to people to make sure they have no problems. Keep out the unruly elements, and so on.'

Ruby stared at him. Now she knew exactly what he was.

'Don't you usually send the breakers in first?' she asked.

'What?' He stared at her, wrong-footed.

'The breakers. Soften the mark up a bit.'

This intrigued him. She knew about his business. He half-smiled.

'Not when the mark's a lady. Besides, I don't want to break you.' His smiled widened slightly. His eyes teased hers. 'Yet.'

Ruby stared right back at him. 'I have a brother who can handle security for me,' she said. 'Perhaps you know him: Joe Darke.'

Joe was still doing his iffy deals, but that was nothing to do with her. She didn't want to know about Joe's 'business' – it just reminded her of the bad old days with Charlie. But Michael Ward wasn't to know that.

The grey eyes blinked, once.

'I know Joe. Top man.'

'So you see, the issue of protection for my business is already covered. But thank you for the offer.' Actually, she wouldn't dream of asking Joe for help. She knew he still did the loan-sharking and other stuff, but she didn't want to know about it: she never had, not even when Charlie was out on the loose and involved in it all.

Michael smiled slightly. 'I never knew he had a sister. Never connected the two in my mind. Joe Darke and Darkes the store.'

No, a sister's not worth talking about. Not worth mentioning, not among the men of the Darke family, she thought.

'Well, he has,' she said. 'And I'm it.' Ruby stood up in one smooth movement. 'And now, if that's all . . . ? I have a busy schedule.'

Michael thought that maybe this was a bluff. Maybe she *wasn't* Joe and Charlie Darke's sister. Michael knew Charlie had gone down for the mail van robbery during the war. He knew he was still doing time for it. He knew Joe had taken over the reins. But a sister called Ruby? He'd never heard a word about that.

He'd seen Ruby Darke occasionally in the business pages. She was clearly intelligent, which was good: he hated dumb women. And she was fabulous to look at. He'd already decided he wanted her in bed. The famous Ruby Darke – the Ice Queen, they called her – intrigued him. Unmarried, childless, relentless in her pursuit of profit. And yet . . . hadn't there been stories about a wild past as a Windmill girl? Stories she had always sidestepped with a brisk: 'No comment.' And she was as stunning in the flesh as she was in the papers. Cold as permafrost, yes – but a beauty.

'You don't look like Joe,' he said.

Ruby knew that. She was dark-skinned, exotic-looking;

Joe was pasty-white. She said nothing. All that was her business, no one else's.

'Well, I think that's all for now,' he said, when the silence stretched out between them, and stood up and held out a hand. 'Thanks for your time – Ruby.'

Ruby took his hand warily and shook it. His hand was hot and dry, his grip very firm. It felt electric, unnervingly thrilling, just that simple contact.

'How about dinner one night?' he said.

'No,' said Ruby, and let go of his hand as if it had burned her.

'No? Well, if there's ever anything I can do for you . . .'

'There isn't. There won't be. Goodbye, Mr Ward.'

68

'Come on, sweetie, let's play,' said Sebastian excitedly.

Cornelius lay naked in bed, watching the boy fondly. Sebastian was jumping around the room in the nude, his skin glowing golden over long, taut muscles, his coal-dark hair cascading like a dark waterfall around his powerful shoulders, his cock bouncing on its little cushion of black pubic hair. This was the first time he'd brought Sebastian here, to his own London house in its peaceful leafy square, and Sebastian was thrilled.

'Come on, lazy,' said Sebastian, coming to the bed and yanking the covers back. He was holding a scarf. 'Come *on*, I want to try this.'

Cornelius gave a groan. Sebby wanted to try *everything*. No outer limit of sexual deviance was too extreme for him. Now he looped the pastel-toned Liberty scarf around Cornelius's neck.

'What . . . ?' Cornelius was laughing.

Leaning in, laughing too, Sebastian tied the scarf in a tight knot. Cornelius felt his throat constrict.

'Good *God*,' he objected, his voice coming out a breathy whisper. Sebby's head dipped and his hair brushed teasingly down over Cornelius's stomach. He felt the boy's lips touch his penis.

'See? It works,' said Sebby. 'It's true, it enhances sexual performance, you see?'

Cornelius wrenched the damned thing from around his neck. His erection was sudden and mighty. Yes, it *did* work. But he didn't like it.

'Oh, don't take it off,' objected Sebby.

Cornelius threw the scarf aside. 'I've no taste for being throttled,' he said.

'Don't be such an old fusspot,' said Sebby, jumping off the bed and heading for the fruit bowl on the side table, his buttocks jiggling enticingly. He picked up a tangerine. 'See, you hold something like this in your mouth. Keeps the airways open. Try it.'

'No,' said Cornelius.

'Then *I* will,' said Sebby, popping the fruit in his mouth. He snatched up the long scarf and went over to the big mahogany wardrobe, throwing the doors open. Carelessly he pushed aside garments, throwing a couple out onto the floor.

'Hey!'

Sebby held up a hand and Cornelius fell silent, watching his young lover. Sebby was reaching up, looping the scarf around the clothes rail inside the wardrobe.

Cornelius watched, smiling.

'Mmph,' said Sebby past the fruit, beckoning him over.

'Oh, for God's sake.' Cornelius left the bed and strode over there. Sebby indicated that Cornelius should tie the end of the scarf around his neck and hoist him up, just a little.

'This is stupid,' said Cornelius, but he did as the boy wanted.

He was alarmed to see Sebby's face turning bright brick-red the moment his feet left the wardrobe floor. But Sebby was making *it's OK* movements with his hands.

'What . . . ?' Cornelius didn't like this at all.

Sebastian spat out the tangerine.

'It's all right,' he wheezed. 'Oh, it's good. Look . . .'

Sebby was right. He had a large erection. Cornelius was transfixed, staring at it.

'Yes, that's all very well, but . . .' Cornelius stopped speaking. Sebby's eyes were *shut*.

He felt a hot thrill of fear.

'Sebby?' he said quickly. 'Jesus – Sebby!' he shouted, and tried to lift the boy up. He could only lift him a little. He was heavy. Scrambling, straining, half-sobbing with effort, he put a hand to the boy's heart, and could feel nothing. 'My God, no. No! *Sebby!*'

Tito got there shortly after midnight. A white-faced Cornelius, wearing a silk paisley robe, let him into the house. He led the way upstairs to the master bedroom. Cornelius nodded towards the wardrobe then collapsed onto the bed, his head in his hands.

Tito stepped over the pile of clothing on the floor, and opened the doors. Sebastian was hanging there, blue in the face with his tongue protruding from his mouth. He was obviously dead.

'I didn't know what else to do, who to call . . .' said Cornelius hopelessly.

Tito glanced back at him, seeing the desperate eyes, the face wet with tears. Carefully, he closed the wardrobe doors. He crossed to the bed.

'Can I use this phone?' he asked, indicating the one on the bedside table.

Cornelius nodded. 'If this gets out, I'll be *ruined*,' he said.

Tito made a call, then hung up.

'I'll take care of it,' he said, patting Cornelius on the shoulder. 'Give me a front-door key, then get dressed and go downstairs to the drawing room. Ignore anything you hear. Just stay in there.'

Cornelius did as he was told. Later, *hours* later, Tito knocked on the drawing-room door and handed him back his key.

'All done,' he said.

'I'm very grateful,' said Cornelius shakily.

'These things happen,' said Tito, and left.

Sickly, Cornelius crawled back upstairs and fell onto a bed in one of the other rooms: he couldn't stand the thought of going back into the master bedroom, where he had romped so carelessly, so happily, with Sebby, and where Sebby had died.

'Christ,' he moaned, choking on his tears.

Sebby was gone.

And even worse – he knew that he was now more than ever in Tito's debt.

69

The christening of Joe and Betsy's second child Billy was held not too long after Ruby had visited Charlie inside. All Betsy's side had come, the women in feathered hats and slim-fitting suits; even her mother and her elderly father had made a big effort.

Vi had turned up in a chauffeur-driven Rolls, looking incredibly glamorous in a lilac silk gown and matching hat. She had her husband Anthony, the present Lord Albemarle, in tow.

Mr and Mrs Porter were suitably overwhelmed by this ugly but titled individual. They behaved as they always did around their eldest daughter – slightly stunned, like a pair of sparrows who'd somehow bred a swan.

On Joe's side there were a couple of his heavies and their wives, plus Ruby, who had come unescorted in a little clip-on fascinator hat and a figure-skimming apricot-coloured shift dress. She went everywhere unescorted. She was used to it. She was the Ice Queen, all the papers said so. Unmarried. Childless. Cold to the bone. Entering a room alone, walking into a party on her own, none of that held any fears for her. Her harsh upbringing had paid dividends, in the end. Made her tougher.

She was one of the godparents for little Billy, and had to stand up alongside three others at the font with the vicar and renounce the devil and all his works. Later, back at the house when there was a crowd around the cutting of the christening cake, Ruby took the opportunity to take Joe to one side.

'I want to talk to you,' she said straight away. 'About Charlie.'

Instantly Joe's expression of happy fatherhood changed; became secretive, closed-off.

'Charlie said you were asking him about the kid,' he said.

'I told you I was going to.'

The music came on – the Monkees singing 'I'm a Believer' – and tables were being pushed back. Betsy, the baby cradled in her arms with the beautifully embroidered silk and chiffon christening gown spilling down like a white waterfall, sent Joe a look that said: *What are you doing?*

Joe mouthed back: *Just a minute.*

'Thought you'd have a family of your own by now,' said Joe to Ruby. 'A proper one. You know. Husband. Kids. Nice house. Take your mind off all this.'

'I don't need a husband,' said Ruby. 'And I'm in the process of buying a nice house.'

This was true. She'd grown restless at the flat over the store. She'd hunted down a lovely Victorian villa in the countryside near Marlow and put in an offer.

'And I have two kids,' she said.

'You *had* two kids. You ain't been poking around with that Bray lot, pestering them for a look at the girl, have you? Because I warn you, Sis, they won't stand still for that.'

'They're my children,' said Ruby.

She wished she *had* contacted Daisy, but she'd lost her nerve. Several times she'd been *this close* to doing it, to making herself known to her daughter. But every time, her courage deserted her.

'No.' Joe shook his head. 'You *sold* that little girl.'

'You know damned well Charlie pushed me into it. And I was wrong to let him. I was young and stupid—'

'And now you're old and stupid,' cut in Joe. He turned his back on Betsy's desperate mouthings. 'Look, Ruby – all that's the past. It's too late to turn back the clock. You think either one of those kids would want you anyway, once they know the truth?'

Ruby was eyeing her brother coldly, but he'd hit home with that one. She had sold her daughter. Every day, the guilt over that tormented her. She had been too weak, too afraid, to fight Charlie over her son. She should have done better by her kids; she knew that. But she hadn't. And now, she wanted – *so much* – to make amends.

'Charlie said my boy was done away with,' she said.

Joe hesitated. 'That's right. I'm sorry. He told me at the time.' His eyes skipped away from hers. 'I couldn't tell you, Rubes. Don't look at me like that. I had to lie to you. How the hell could I tell you *that*?'

'What's going on?' asked Betsy, bustling over with the baby whimpering in her arms. Two-year-old Nadine was clinging to her leg, whining for attention. 'Joe, we have guests . . .'

Ruby looked at baby Billy, so pretty in his christening gown, and couldn't help but think of all the things that she had missed with her own children. Their christenings, yes – but also their first days at school, their first boyfriends and girlfriends, the everyday joys and pains of a family life. She'd been cheated of all that.

'Clear off, Betsy,' snapped Ruby, wanting to swat the woman who had once been her best mate away like an irritating gnat. It was painful, to see the baby close-up like this. When she'd held baby Nadine shortly after her birth, it had cut her like a knife. And now time had gone by again – and Joe and Betsy had Billy to complete their family. And what did she have? Nothing. She had to talk to Joe about this now. It was *important*.

Betsy's face scrunched up in outrage. She was already royally pissed off because Vi had pitched up with such a flourish, and upstaged her without even seeming to try. Now *Ruby* was acting up.

Ruby confronted her one-time friend. Betsy hated Joe spending time with anyone but her. She'd been sick with temper when Vi had befriended Ruby, consumed with envy when Ruby made a success of her life – and twisted up with bitterness over Vi's elevation to the aristocracy.

'Go on – clear off,' said Ruby again, her voice harder.

'You going to let her speak to me like that?' Betsy demanded of Joe.

Vi came up, looking concerned. 'What on earth are you all up to? People are looking.'

'Nothing, Vi.' Joe turned to his wife. 'Give us a minute, Bets, OK?' he said.

'I don't know *what* this is all about, but I don't think this is the time or the place, do you?' said Betsy hotly, her eyes skipping angrily from Ruby to Vi and back again.

'A minute!' snapped Joe, and Betsy subsided and sloped off to her folks. Vi went with her, casting questioning looks back at Ruby. Joe turned to his sister. 'I'm going to get stick for a week over that,' he informed her.

'Good. You deserve it. You *lied* to me.'

'Let it go now, Rubes. The boy's gone. The girl's happy.'

'The boy was dark-skinned, like me,' said Ruby softly. 'Did you know that?'

Joe stared at her face. 'No. What? What d'you mean?'

'The girl was pure white, but the boy was dark.'

'Jesus. I didn't see the kid. Charlie never said.'

'Is that why Charlie had him murdered? Charlie and Dad hated me because I looked a little coloured, a little *dusky*. So did the baby. I guess that was all the reason Charlie needed to see the poor little sod off.'

Joe was silent, taking it in. 'Jesus,' he said again, shaking his head. 'Can that happen? One twin white, the other . . .'

'I think it's rare,' said Ruby. 'But when there's black blood in the family, it can happen, yes. It can come out. Didn't you ever wonder why Cornelius Bray kept the girl, and not the boy, too?'

'No. I didn't. Look, it's all dead and gone now, Ruby. Black or white or fucking *purple*, what's it matter? The little nipper was a *bastard*, and you were Charlie's sister. That was what bothered him. That people were going to laugh about it behind his back, the high and mighty Charlie Darke who ran the streets, he couldn't even control his own sister, she was putting it about like a common whore and having kids out of wedlock. Sorry. But that was Charlie, you know it was.'

Ruby was silent for a long moment. 'I hate him,' she said.

Joe shrugged. 'You think he cares? Don't make me laugh.'

'Did you know the man who did it?' asked Ruby.

'Fuck it, no, I *didn't*. And you know what? Even if I *did*, I wouldn't tell you his name. All that's water under the bridge, girl. Do yourself a favour. Forget it.'

With that, Joe turned his back on her and rejoined his wife and his family, all of them laughing and smiling on this happy day.

Ruby stood alone, an outsider as always, and watched, and thought: *No. I can't forget it. I wish I could, but I can't.*

70

'Steady,' said Kit. 'Don't rush.'

Gilda smiled at him, and lay back on the double bed in the room they'd rented for the night. They'd met up for a drink in the Long Bar near Maidstone, then driven away in their separate cars, very careful that they were unobserved and not followed.

They weren't. Kit made absolutely sure about that, and finally they pulled into a cheap little hotel on the outskirts of a small town, and booked a room.

'Shit. I've stayed in better dosshouses than this,' said Gilda when they were shown up to the room.

It was shabby, to say the least. There was peeling nicotine-stained wallpaper, tired dusty light fittings, rugs so threadbare you had to be careful not to get your feet caught in the open loops and go arse over tit.

But there was a bed. Gilda went straight to it, and threw herself back on it, bouncing up and down a few times to test the springs. They bit back.

'Ow! You know what, my gran had these old metal springs,' she said, laughing. 'You used to get on the bed and there'd be this big dip in the middle, your bum would be touching the floor. Fuck me, I wouldn't have thought there was a bed this old left in the *world*.'

Kit locked the door and watched her, bouncing around and giggling like a teenager. He had to smile.

'It's a bed,' he said. 'Beyond that, who cares?'

Kit sat down, swung his legs up onto the bed. It was a damned uncomfortable bed, she was right about that. But he was in it, with Gilda, and she was an itch he had been trying to resist scratching for a long time. Gilda swooped on him immediately, her mouth fastening over his like a suction hoover.

'What's the hurry?' he said, easing her away.

Gilda smiled and lay back. 'I've fancied you ever since I first saw you,' she sighed, sitting up to peel off her coat. She flung it aside. 'And it's mutual, isn't it?'

'Yeah,' said Kit, pulling her back to him.

He'd had lots of women, but Gilda was something special. She was forbidden fruit, for a start. Everyone knew that Gilda was Tito Danieri's bit of fluff, and that Tito was a hard man, into all the rackets, and not to be crossed. Also, he was in tight with Mr Ward. Kit wasn't comfortable having Gilda because of his loyalty to Michael. So he had resisted her – even when she'd made it pretty obvious that she was hot for him.

Now, he'd given in to the impulse. But on his own terms, not hers. Out of the way where no one could see. A few brisk bonks and then it would be over, he promised himself. She'd be out of his system and no harm done.

'Let's get our clothes off . . .' said Gilda, pulling at his tie.

'Easy,' he said. 'We've got all night.'

'It'll take all night, to do all that I want to do to you,' she said, her ocean-green eyes smoky with lust.

There were clearly some advantages to the older woman. Kit lay back and let her remove his jacket, shirt and tie. She ran her hands admiringly over his taut muscles, then slid her hand down, right down inside his trousers to feel his erection. She moaned and pulled off her pants, the gold charm-bracelet rattling with every move she made; then she knelt up on the bed and straddled him.

Gilda unbuttoned her cream-coloured blouse, and slipped it off her shoulders in a slither of silk. Then she unhooked her white bra and let the straps fall down over her arms so that he could see her dark-nippled breasts.

She smiled into his eyes and unfastened his belt, unzipped him.

'Lift up,' she ordered.

Kit raised his hips off the bed and she pulled down his trousers and underpants.

'Oh, that's better,' she said, stroking him, then moving a little and guiding him easily inside her. She moved down onto him with a gasp, wriggling her hips to take him right inside.

Kit felt like he was about to come straight away, but he held back even though he was excited almost beyond bearing. This was *Tito's* girl. He was breaking his own rules here, he *knew* this was wrong. But, oh, it was good. She'd been taunting him for so long, enticing him, and now, at last, they were here.

'You're beautiful,' he said, grasping her breasts.

'You too,' she groaned, and set to work.

It was a long night, and Kit woke in the morning exhausted and satisfied, with Gilda's arm across his chest and the gold charm-bracelet right in his eyeline. A horseshoe, a fish and a shamrock for luck.

Luck. Would they need luck for this? He thought they would.

He wondered if Tito had bought the bracelet for her – he probably had – but the thought was an uncomfortable one and he swept it aside. All right, he felt bad about this. But not *that* bad. All through his life he had been like this – it was as if something had been cut off, cauterized, somewhere deep inside him. He didn't think he had the capacity to care deeply about anything. He didn't think he would ever lose his head over any woman, he was sure he would never fall in love.

But here he was. With Gilda.

He saw that she was awake too, her sea-green eyes smiling into his.

'I don't know anything about you,' she said.

He kissed her lightly. 'What do you want to know?'

'Oh, I don't know. What you like . . . ?'

'I like you.'

'I *know* that. What you hate. What frightens you . . . ?'

'Nothing frightens me.'

'*Something* must.'

Kit lay back and thought about it. 'Fire,' he said at last.

'What?'

He shrugged. 'I don't like to feel the heat of a fire. Weird, yeah? So come on. What frightens *you*?'

Gilda's smile slipped. 'Tito frightens me,' she said.

Kit said nothing.

Suddenly she smiled again and put her arms around his neck. 'Kiss me,' she ordered.

Michael was asking his contacts about Ruby Darke. He found her so fascinating. So cool, so remote. And yet so downright *sexy*.

'Her brother Charlie's in stir,' said Michael's mate over a cognac.

'He did the Post Office robbery, back in the day,' said Michael. He knew about that. Everyone did.

'After which his brother Joe took over the family firm.'

'Yeah, but where does Ruby fit in?'

His friend smiled. 'She don't. There was a big scandal, Ted Darke's missus was playing away with some coon in a jazz club. Got herself up the duff with Ruby. It's a wonder the old man didn't murder the girl, but word is he was a bit of a religious nutter: Thou shalt not kill, et cetera. Ruby's straight. Into legitimate business, that's all.'

'What about the mother?'

'I heard she died having Ruby, the poor cow.'

71

It cost them just a pound to get in to the Happening at Alexandra Palace. They were wearing their lacy minidresses, lots of beads. Mandy also wore a too-large white ten-gallon hat that kept falling over her eyes, and a yellow poncho.

Late into the evening, Daisy heard that someone had been stabbed at the back of the hall but the police didn't come because they had to get an entry warrant and at midnight it was clear that the gig would be over before *that* happened. Up on stage, the Crazy World of Arthur Brown was dressed in an insect costume.

Daisy could only see the stage at a far distance, and the searchlights winked on and off constantly, alternately dazzling her and then leaving her blind. She could hear the roar of the Gibson guitars and the shrieking gutsy wail of Eric Burden and his New Animals. There was a huge screen hung from the balcony, and projected onto it in multicolours was an amoeba or something, constantly dividing and reforming. Daisy thought that if she stared at it for long enough, she'd go mad.

'Isn't it *great*?' demanded Mandy, jigging about alongside her in the midst of a huge, heaving, sweating throng of other bodies.

It was pretty great. Pretty scary too, ten thousand people packed into the Ally Pally for a mad night of psychedelic fun. Mandy rummaged around in her string bag and then shoved a pill into Daisy's hand.

'It's just speed,' she said. 'Nothing nasty – it just gives you a lift.'

Daisy took it and suddenly she felt supercharged, all senses heightened. There was a guy squatting nearby tripping out by smoking banana scrapings, and someone ripped a fire extinguisher from the wall and started spraying the crowd with it.

Daisy and Mandy got soaked, and instead of being furious with the fool, for some reason Daisy found this enormously funny. She laughed until she thought she was going to be sick, and started thinking about her staid, boring mother, who would be so outraged to see her daughter in such a happening place.

'I'm liberated,' shouted Daisy, and started ripping her clothes off.

'You're high as a kite,' said Mandy, trying hard to get Daisy's clothes back on.

On top of the Ally Pally's organ, forty feet up in the air, a man in a purple shirt was beckoning others to follow him. People in floral shirts and hipster loon pants started climbing the scaffolding. One man had a lit candle gripped in his teeth. Another was swinging like a monkey from the scaffolding, about to fall.

'Please come down from the scaffolding!' blared a loudspeaker suddenly.

Nobody took any notice.

'If you don't get down from the scaffolding, the show will be stopped!'

Daisy found this hilarious. The people kept climbing upward. She ran forward to join them, but then all the lights went out. When they went back on again, everyone was coming down off the scaffolding. A long-haired young man with a white-painted beard came down near her and grinned at her and passed her the plastic daffodil he'd had clamped between his teeth.

'A token of love,' he said. His eyes looked like saucers.

'Let's have a love-in,' said Daisy, and suddenly this seemed like the most excellent idea. She and Mandy stripped naked but for their beads and coloured headbands, and the young man and his friend did the same. Mandy supported Daisy from behind, and the young man's friend held him from behind, and the two connected, Daisy's thighs locking around the young man's waist as he stood there with his friend's arms around him. It was a moment of complete communal love, with everyone around them observing and encouraging them to let it happen.

'Man, this is so real,' said someone beside Daisy's ear. The young man penetrated her briskly and everyone crowded around them. She felt a part of the whole, accepted, wanted, desired. Then it was Mandy and the friend's turn, and they joined together in a frantic scrabble, Daisy and her partner supporting them, fondling them, loving them.

Someone was saying Pink Floyd were on the stage, but the noise and the crush of people were so intense that Daisy found she didn't even care. Her head was starting to spin from the heat; she felt parched. She felt . . . very odd.

She reeled away to the side of the great hall and slid down the wall. She sat there, thinking she was about to be sick. People passed by her, huge giants looming over her. She felt the stickiness between her thighs and frowned in confusion. How had that happened? Had her period come early or something . . . ? And where were her clothes?

Her stomach contracted once, hard, and she leaned over and vomited on the floor.

'Jesus,' she groaned, and Mandy lurched up to her and slid down beside her. Daisy had no idea where their clothes had gone. Mandy's hat and poncho had vanished somewhere, into the crowd. But Mandy was ever resourceful. She was holding two jackets. She gave one to Daisy, who was now shivering, and put the other one on herself.

The music played on, the lights strobed. They sat there for an hour, too weak to move. Then at last Mandy said: 'Let's go, shall we?' and they staggered outside.

It was two o'clock, and still there were people going into the hall.

'What's it like in there?' asked one couple passing by the two girls in their jackets and – apparently – little else.

'Groovy. Really happening,' said Mandy.

Daisy felt too sick to speak.

There was an ambulance out here, someone was being shoved in the back, there was blood . . .

Daisy couldn't look. Her first happening, and she'd been sick and thought she was going to pass out. And . . . oh God, she thought she'd done something really stupid. Hadn't she *fucked* someone, someone she didn't even know? Hadn't she done that again, when she had *sworn* she wouldn't? Her mind felt wired, scrabbling around like a rat in a cage, but her body was exhausted. Mandy hailed a cab, and they fell in the back of it, and went home.

72

1968

'More flowers? God, that man just don't know the meaning of the word *quit*,' complained Ruby.

Jane, her PA, brought the huge bouquet of creamy-white roses into Ruby's office over the flagship store. It was the third bouquet she'd received from Michael Ward.

'Don't knock it,' said Jane with a wry smile. She was a plump, immaculate and silver-haired matron, extremely efficient, long-married and merry-eyed. 'Mine don't even know what flowers are *for*.'

Ruby stood up and took the bouquet from her. 'Is there a note . . . ?'

'Yeah, it's here, look.'

Ruby read it.

Roses for a Ruby. Call me.

His number was written underneath.

Ruby gazed at it, and wondered. Mr Ward was a very handsome man with his iron-grey hair and his steely grey eyes. He oozed a brutal confidence. He scared her. All right, he attracted her too. She had to admit that.

But . . .

She'd already done the whole love thing once, in her youth, with Cornelius. It had been painful beyond belief. To start over again, try again with another man . . . she didn't want to do it. It would hurt too much when it all went wrong. And it would; she knew it would.

'I'll put them in water then . . . ?' suggested Jane, while Ruby stood there, staring at the note.

Ruby shook herself. 'Yeah. Thanks, Jane.'

No, it was safer to cling to her business. They were launching a new wine department to run alongside the food halls, and it had taken up most of her time to debate with her team the merits of the various wines and choose which wines to select. They had settled on eighteen wines, plus vermouth, sherry, beers and cider.

'Liebfraumilch at ninety-five pence a bottle, that's a good deal,' had been Jane's input. 'Us ladies do love a sweet wine.'

So the Liebfraumilch had been included, along with a good selection of other whites and reds.

What remained of Ruby's time was taken up with wondering if she could get up the nerve to meet with Cornelius and ask if she could see her daughter. She quailed at asking him, though. She knew he'd be angry at the very idea. And she hadn't seen him face-to-face in years.

She saw him often in the press: Lord Bray was a very influential man now, chairman of many charities and active in politics in the upper house. It always shocked her when she saw his photo. He was still her Cornelius, more *white* than blond now, with crinkling lines around his eyes when the camera caught him smiling.

Yes, he was older, but he was still the devastatingly attractive charmer she had known. If she saw him in the flesh, would she turn back into the star-struck idiot youngster she had once been, falling out of the Windmill Theatre straight into his arms?

'You gonna put this man out of his misery soon?' asked Jane, pausing at the door with the bouquet in her arms.

'Mr Ward? I don't think so,' said Ruby, sitting down behind her desk and reaching for last month's figures.

'Shame,' said Jane. 'You could use some fun in your life.'

'I have the business,' said Ruby with a brisk smile. Jane was starting to sound like Vi. Going on about fun all the time, when Ruby really wasn't interested. She'd thrown herself into business to hide from her own feelings. What else could she have done? Shit happened. All you could do was tough it out, get on with it.

'That's work,' said Jane. 'That ain't fun.'

'So you say.'

'I *do* say. You gonna do that thing of lying on your deathbed saying you wished you'd spent more time at work? I don't think so. Love's what counts, girl. Family. That's the stuff that matters in the end.'

Family! Apart from Joe and Betsy and their kids, she had none. She was pleased that Joe seemed to have drawn back a little from all the shady deals and thuggery he'd once been so deeply involved in with Charlie. Oh, he was still operating on the fringes of it all, she knew that – but she thought that Charlie's fate had sobered Joe a lot, made him more careful. Joe was a family man these days. But what was she?

She had cashed in on her daughter.

Sacrificed her poor son.

Sold her soul to the devil, in fact.

As the door closed on Jane, Ruby turned her attention back to the figures. Maybe she didn't even *deserve* happiness. Maybe she was just wicked, through and through. She concentrated on the figures, forgot the rest. She had to, or it would drive her crazy. Tonight, when she got home, she would think about all this again. About her children. She promised herself she would.

73

1968

'Oh, for God's sake, Daisy, this is *ridiculous*,' said Aunt Ju.

They were sitting in the waiting room in Harley Street. It was a beautiful high-ceilinged Georgian building, staffed by discreet white-coated nurses and one of the best private doctors in the country.

'I can't believe you've been so stupid. Again.'

Daisy sat there, ashamed. She *had* been stupid. Her wild night out with Mandy had come at a cost. As the months had wound on after the happening, she had become aware of a monstrous itching in her genital region. She could remember dimly that she'd had sex with someone that night, but she didn't know who. And now she had this horrible *itch*.

She suffered it in silence and then in despair and desperation went to Aunt Ju, who instantly whisked her off to her doctor.

'Crabs,' he pronounced, when Daisy had been examined and Aunt Ju was ushered in with her to hear the diagnosis. He wrote a prescription and Aunt Ju snatched it from him, casting a withering look at her niece. 'This'll clear it up. And, young woman, you should be more careful who you mix with in future.'

'I have never been so embarrassed in my entire *life*,' said Aunt Ju as she left the building with a cringing Daisy. She shook her head in disbelief. 'For the love of God, Daisy, what on earth have you been up to?'

Daisy hung her head in shame. She'd even frightened herself this time. She'd awoken on the morning after the happening feeling dry-mouthed, foul-headed and sick. She remembered snatches of what she'd done, how she'd behaved, and was appalled. 'You won't tell Mother, will you?' she begged.

'No. I won't. But only because I want to spare her feelings, and your father's too. They're so good to you. Cornelius bought you that car just a week ago.'

Daisy thought about the little car, her Mini. Red and shiny as a Christmas bauble, and she loved it. But that was always Pa's answer to everything: throw money at it. She didn't see him much.

Aunt Ju raised an imperious hand as a cab approached. 'I think it's best if you go home, Daisy. I really do. I don't know what to do with you any more. You're twenty-four years old, and all you do is get into trouble. You need to just *grow up*. You are worrying me to *death*.'

Considering Aunt Ju never seemed to care much what she did or where she went, Daisy thought this was a bit rich. But she didn't say so. She was in enough trouble as it was, doomed to be sent back to the country, without Mandy, without any hope of entertainment or simple downright *fun*.

But maybe Aunt Ju had a point. Maybe she was just too damned *old* now for happenings, love-ins and all that shit.

Kit was busy with the clubs and bars and restaurants, sending Mr Ward's boys out here, there and everywhere, raking in fistfuls of money and heading off trouble. He was also busy with the voracious Gilda, meeting up with her as often as he could in far-off locations around the home counties. They would drive there separately, meet up, make love, then go home separately the following morning.

This was what he was in the act of doing in his beautiful, treasured Bentley Tourer, driving over a little hump-backed bridge over a river somewhere in the lush Hampshire countryside. There were froths of tall creamy flowers all along the edges of the lane, and in the field below they were cutting some green stuff or other, he noticed – and then a red Mini was lurching towards him, filling his windscreen, and he accelerated, pulling the wheel hard to the left to avoid crashing into it. He shot over the bridge, hearing a shriek of metal as the other car swerved and bumped the edge of it. He slammed on the brakes, switched off the engine, and jumped out.

The Mini was over the other side of the bridge, its wheels embedded in greenery, its side scraped to bare metal. Kit went to the driver's door and flung it open.

'You fucking fool, what d'you think you're doing?' he shouted.

A dishevelled blonde girl looked up at him, her face sheet-white.

'What am *I* doing?' she shot back in a crisp Home Counties accent. '*I'm* not the one who was in the middle of the road.'

'I wasn't in the middle of the road. I was coming over a single-lane bridge at a reasonable speed, and your driving is *crazy*.'

Daisy thought that this was too much. She'd been humiliated in London, cured of her embarrassing problem and was now at home, at Brayfield, bored and wondering about a job, fending off her mother's probing questions about why Aunt Ju had sent her home so suddenly. She'd taken the Mini out for a spin, just to kill an hour or two – and had nearly ended up getting killed herself by this maniac.

Although . . . he was quite a handsome maniac. He was

very well dressed in a sharp suit and tie, about her own age, she thought, with dark skin, black curling hair and startling blue eyes. He looked prosperous – he was driving a Bentley, after all. But even without the car, his bearing alone would have commanded attention.

'You might ask if I'm all right,' she said.

'*Are* you?'

'I'm quite shaken up, actually. I think the least you can do is buy me a drink.'

He stared at her. 'You've got some front.'

'We can call in the garage on the way to the village and arrange to get the Mini towed.'

'A *lot* of front.'

'My father has a Bentley too.'

'Does he?' Kit was looking at her. She was pretty and she did look pale and genuinely shaken after that narrow scrape. If she'd been travelling any faster, the Bentley would have mangled that Mini into mush. He wasn't in a hurry to get back today. So why not? 'OK, come on then,' he said, and walked back to his car.

Daisy scrambled out of the Mini's bucket seat, slammed the door and locked it. She ran to the Bentley and got in the passenger side, flashing him her brightest smile. 'You can turn around in the drive of Campbell's farm, it's just up ahead,' she said.

They sat in a corner of the pub in the village. He bought the drinks to the table and sat down. The Move was blasting out 'Fire Brigade' from a transistor radio perched on the end of the bar.

'Thanks,' said Daisy, taking a hasty gulp of white wine, tapping her foot to the beat.

'You live around here somewhere?' he asked.

She nodded. 'At Brayfield.'

'So you live in a place here, right here in the village?'

'I live at the house, which is about half a mile in *that* direction,' said Daisy, pointing. 'It's been in the family for generations – the house, the land, the church, the village.'

He shot her a look. 'Wait up. Your family *owns* this village?'

'Yep.'

Kit took a drink, shaking his head in wonder. This explained a lot. She was just a crazy little posh tart, overindulged by a rich mummy and daddy.

'What was that stuff they were cutting under the bridge?' he asked.

'Watercress. There have been cress beds here for centuries.'

'So do you work?'

She shook her head and necked the rest of the wine. 'You do, I suppose?' she asked him almost sympathetically.

He smiled. If your family owned a village, gainful employment obviously wasn't on the agenda. 'Yeah. I do.'

'Doing what? May I have another of those please?'

Kit looked at her. She was very direct, with that ingrained self-confidence the rich always had. He went to the bar, and returned with another glass of wine.

'Thank you. Now, what do you do?'

I break people's legs if they don't pay money to my boss, he thought. 'I work for Ward Security,' he said instead.

'Where? In London? You've got a Cockney accent.'

He nodded, sipped his pint. 'East End,' he said.

'Then what are you doing down here?'

Kit was thinking of the wild night he'd just shared with Gilda. What a woman. While this little hoity-toity tart . . . he looked at her . . . she was pretty, but unformed. There was something almost familiar about her, maybe he'd seen her somewhere before.

'You ask too many questions,' he said.

'I know.' She laughed and threw back the wine. 'My aunt Ju's always saying so. Another?'

'I don't think so,' he said, and finished his pint and stood up. 'I've got to be getting back. Can I drop you at the house?'

'OK.' Daisy stood up. 'Can we see each other again then?'

'What for?' asked Kit. God, she was irritating. Like a kitten, batting its claws at your ankles as you passed by.

She shrugged and smiled coquettishly. 'I don't know. A drink or something?'

Kit sighed.

'We could meet up in London,' said Daisy. She'd work on Aunt Ju, get herself back in her good books. Use the infallible Daisy Bray charm. She was using it now, but it didn't seem to be having much effect. Men usually swooned over her. But this one wasn't doing that. It offended her, and made her all the more determined.

She was scrabbling in her overstuffed bag, pulling out paper and pencil. 'If you give me your number . . .'

'I'm *not* giving you my number.'

'Then take mine.' She scribbled on the paper and thrust it into his hand. 'Here.'

'Oh, for fuck's . . .' he muttered, and pocketed the piece of paper just to shut her up.

He went out to the Bentley, Daisy trailing him.

'You will call, won't you?' she asked, smiling.

'Sure,' he said, and they got in and he started the engine and drove the half-mile to the house. He turned into a narrow opening and passed a gatehouse, then drove up a winding gravel track that eventually opened out onto a big turning-circle with a dormant fountain with dolphins and a half-man, half-fish set in the centre of it.

'That's Neptune,' said Daisy.

Behind that, the house stood like a monolith, multi-gabled,

its rose-red bricks and cream-coloured corners glowing in the midday sun.

'You're fucking joking,' said Kit, pulling up in front of it.

'Home sweet home,' said Daisy.

'Serious?'

'Yep.' She looked at him. He was gorgeous, she'd liked him on sight. Even if he *had* pranged her beloved car. 'You *will* call . . . ?' she asked hopefully.

'Sure,' he said again. He wouldn't. Young chicks – posh or otherwise – did nothing for him. They wanted too much, a level of feeling and commitment he knew he was unable to give. He preferred older ladies, who understood his no-strings outlook better. And right now he had Gilda, who was more woman than most men could cope with anyway.

'Right,' he said, when she showed no sign of getting out. 'Got to go.'

'Well, it was nice meeting you,' said Daisy. 'Thanks for the drinks.'

'That's OK.' *So get out of the bloody car.*

'Bye then.'

'Bye.'

She opened the door. 'Phone me.' She blew him a jokey kiss.

'Sure.'

She closed the door and he started the car and drove off. Daisy heaved a sigh, stumbled up the steps and went indoors. She didn't see Vanessa, watching her from her bedroom window, appalled that her daughter had just got out of a car with what looked like a foreigner driving it.

Who on earth could that be? wondered Vanessa. *And where's the Mini?*

Daisy had blown him a kiss. Vanessa wrapped her arms around herself and shuddered at the thought of her daughter being in any sort of relationship with a person of colour. That couldn't happen. She turned from the window just as the Bentley reached the bottom curve of the drive and vanished from sight. At that instant, she saw its driver lob a small scrap of paper out of the window and into the shrubbery.

'Who was that?' asked Vanessa when she came downstairs and found Daisy unloading the contents of her carpet bag onto the table in the hall.

'Hm?' Daisy looked up, wide-eyed and innocent.

Vanessa wasn't fooled. Her daughter had a talent for deviousness; she still hadn't got to the bottom of what had been happening in London to make Julianna send Daisy back home.

'That *dark* person in the Bentley. Someone's chauffeur? Whose?'

Daisy rolled her eyes. 'He's not a chauffeur, he's a businessman. He's in security. I'm afraid . . .' Daisy bit her lip . . . 'I'm afraid I pranged the car just a bit, on the bridge.'

'Oh, *Daisy.*' Vanessa had warned and warned again that she had to drive carefully, but would she listen? No, she would not.

'But it's OK, just a scratch, and I've arranged for the garage to collect it. Kit was passing and very kindly gave me a lift back here.' Daisy omitted the drinks in the pub. She didn't think Vanessa would like the idea of her daughter drinking with such an exotic-looking man. But the village gossips would probably filter it all back to her waiting ears, anyway.

'That's his name? Kit?'

'Kit Miller, yes.'

'Is he local?' She'd never heard about anyone called Kit Miller in this vicinity. She was certain she *would* have, surely . . . ?

289

'No, London . . . just down here on business, I suppose.' Daisy thought for a moment. 'He said he works for Wade . . . no, *Ward* Security.'

'And you're all right? You weren't hurt at all?' Vanessa took Daisy's shoulders in her hands and gazed anxiously into her face. She was responsible for Daisy's safety.

'Not in the slightest.'

'Good.'

Daisy had found her purse and was now piling all her belongings back into the bag. She turned to her mother with a bright smile. 'Going up for a bath,' she said.

'Right.'

Vanessa watched Daisy run off upstairs. Her reckless, *infuriating* daughter. Vanessa had the strong feeling that if she knew even a tenth of what Daisy got up to, she'd turn grey overnight.

74

1969

Michael Ward was surprised when she called him at last.

'It's Ruby Darke here,' she said, sounding very businesslike.

'Oh! Right.'

It was a long time since he'd sent that third bouquet of roses. *Third time lucky*, he'd thought. But he hadn't really believed it. Here was a woman who, despite her luscious looks, was cool, right through to the bone, a dedicated businesswoman. He respected that. After the third time, he'd thought, no more. But here she was, calling him.

'I just wanted to thank you for all the roses you sent.'

'Pleasure.' *What, a year later?*

'And to accept your invitation to dinner. If it still stands.'

'Fine.' He sat up straight, starting to smile, just a bit. 'Where would you like to go?'

'Surprise me.'

They went to the Connaught. Ruby thought that Michael Ward was even better-looking than she remembered, his striped grey-and-blue tie perfectly complementing his healthy tan and grey eyes.

'You look wonderful,' he said to her after the waiter had brought bread and water and taken their order for starters.

Ruby nodded, acknowledging the compliment. She'd tried her best to look good, but she hardly knew what to put on for an actual 'date'. She'd *never* dated – not since Cornelius had blundered into her life and wrecked it. After putting on and ripping off half the dresses in her wardrobe, she had settled on a claret-coloured jersey dress that discreetly skimmed her tall figure. She had selected nude sandals, a small clutch bag. She had added ruby stud earrings, and piled her thick black hair up on top of her head in a severe, elegant topknot.

Michael Ward looked at the woman on the other side of the table. He wasn't bullshitting her. He really thought she was the most stunning woman he'd met in years. And her air of quiet calm, of extreme and almost frosty reserve, intrigued him. It was in complete contradiction to the way she moved, with the sinuous grace of a jungle cat. Her cocoa-brown eyes, flecked with warm chestnut, looked sad sometimes when her guard came down. Which didn't happen very often, he guessed.

'What?' Now she was staring back at him.

'You're beautiful,' he shrugged.

'No. I'm not,' she scoffed.

What's he playing at? wondered Ruby.

Here was a man of wealth and power. He could have any nubile twenty-year-old he desired. She was *old*. Almost fifty. She had a shedload of miserable weighty baggage she was carrying around with her. But while he was here, and while he was busy trying the honey-tongued routine on a woman who was old enough to see through it, then fine: she was going to exploit him.

She'd been thinking it all over, and had finally decided that Michael Ward was *exactly* what she needed right now. Not for sex, though. For information.

Their starters arrived – prawn cocktail for her, avocado for him. While they ate, she said:

'You said once that if there was ever anything you could do for me . . .'

'Ah.' He gave a half-smile and put down his fork and stared at her. 'So that's it. You want something.'

'Well, you said it.'

'And I meant it.' *Only I'm a bit gutted you're here for that.*

'Well then.'

'OK, shoot. What is it I can do for you?'

Ruby put down her knife and fork. She could see she'd annoyed him. She'd been too direct, too unwilling to play these little parlour games. But she'd started, and she was damned well going to finish. She'd been turning it all over in her mind, wondering how to get the answers she needed, and she'd come up with only one solution.

'I want you to get to my brother, Charlie Darke. He's in Wandsworth. I want to know what really happened to my son.'

So she had a son, big surprise. Michael stared at her, waiting for more.

'He was taken away by Charlie when he was born,' added Ruby when he said nothing. 'It was during the Blitz in London. I was unmarried. I believed Charlie was taking the boy to a good home. A *married* home. You see?'

Michael was still staring.

'OK, what?' asked Ruby.

'When did you last go on a date?' he asked.

A long, long time ago. 'Not your business. When did *you* last . . . ?'

'Six years ago. And it wasn't a date, strictly speaking. I took my wife out to dinner on our anniversary. She was ill and we both knew time was short. Six months later, she died.'

'I'm sorry.'

'Long time ago.'

'No it isn't.'

'You're right.' He gave that half-smile again, picked up his fork and continued eating. 'It don't feel that long ago at all. I still wake up sometimes and imagine she's there. Then I open my eyes, and she isn't.'

'And your point is . . . ?'

'You've carried all this around with you for a long time. Since the war. Now, all these years later, you want answers? The kid's grown up now. Probably he's a married man, with kids of his own. Is it fair to barge into his life after all this time?'

The waiter came and cleared their plates. There was a long pause and then Ruby said: 'He's probably not grown up at all. He's probably dead. But I want to know for *certain*, do you understand?'

'But you said Charlie . . .'

'I've been to see Charlie. He says he took my boy to a mate of his who was a fire-watcher in the war. That he . . . disposed of him.' She couldn't go further than that. Her hand trembled as she reached for her glass and drank deeply. Picturing Charlie's sneering face, and those ugly, horrible words pouring out of his mouth. *Dissolved in acid. Her baby boy.*

Their main course arrived. Ruby looked at her lobster and felt suddenly sick.

'You OK?' he asked.

'Fine.' She drank again, felt a little better.

'You're saying this friend of Charlie's did away with the kid?' Michael wasn't touching his meal, either.

'That's what he's saying. I want to know whether it's true or not. I want to know who this friend is, where he lived, I want . . .' Her words were tumbling over one another and suddenly her voice cracked with strain.

'Whoa, slow down.' He reached out a hand and put it

over hers, on the table. 'What about Joe? Don't he know the details?'

She shook her head. 'No. I've asked. Charlie's the answer. Charlie's the key.'

Michael squeezed her icy-cold hand briefly and then released it. He picked up his knife and fork and started in on his steak. 'You know, as a date, this is a bit weird.'

'I'm sorry.'

'Don't be. Eat your dinner. I'll get someone to have a word with your brother.'

75

Sebastian Dorley's father, Richard, had been searching for his son for a long time. Sebastian had left the family home in Leicester at sixteen, after he'd confessed to his parents that he was gay.

'It's your fault,' Richard had told his wife angrily. 'Giving him a poofy name like that. Sebastian! What for the love of God is *that* all about?'

But his mum had taken it well, on the whole. Cried a bit, but said if he was happy, then so was she. Richard, however, couldn't accept it. This was now Richard's greatest grief. He had behaved like a complete fool, lashed out in anger at his beloved son, driven him away.

So, Sebastian had gone to London. They hadn't seen or heard of him since. Andrew, Sebastian's older brother, had gone down there, searched for him, but he couldn't be found. Their boy was lost.

But now – it was a miracle! – Sebastian had written, said he was fine, they weren't to worry. He'd given no forwarding address, but he had enclosed a picture. He'd grown his hair long, and – good grief! – was that *eyeliner* he was wearing? But it was him. It was their boy.

'My baby,' cried Sebby's mother, smiling tearfully at the photo, running her fingers lovingly over the face of her youngest child.

'Don't upset yourself,' said Richard. He hated to see her cry; it made him feel helpless.

'Who's that with him?' asked Andrew, peering over his mother's shoulder. 'That white-haired bloke.'

Richard looked at the man in the photo. He was standing right beside Sebastian, his arm around Sebby's shoulders. Richard frowned.

This 'white-haired bloke' was unmistakable. It was the Tory peer, Lord Bray.

76

'I got a new charm,' said Gilda excitedly, as they lay in bed in another random, impersonal hotel room. The outskirts of Cheltenham this time; Kit certainly got around these days. They'd arrived after dark and would depart in the dark, separately, this morning. Fingers of light were already penetrating the gloom and Kit was getting restless. You couldn't be too careful.

'Look,' she said, propping herself up so that her tits rested on his chest. She jingled her multi-charmed gold bracelet in front of his face. He wasn't very keen on the heavy jangling thing. She wore it all the time, and it made him think of her being in chains to that bastard Tito. Which, truthfully, he supposed she was.

Gilda was indicating the new addition. It was a black heart. 'It's ebony,' she told him. 'I bought it for myself. You can't give me gifts, I can't wear anything you buy for me, so I bought this for myself. A tiny dark heart that will remind me of you whenever I look at it.'

Her eyes were anxious as they rested on his face. 'You like?' she asked.

'I like,' he smiled, and turned over, nailing her to the bed. He kissed her once, very gently. 'I like very much,' he said.

She slipped her hands around his neck and pulled him

in for a closer clinch. Finally Kit drew back. 'Time we were leaving,' he said.

She groaned. 'Kiss me once more,' she asked.

He obliged.

'I hate Tito,' she sighed against his mouth.

Kit moved back a little. 'What?'

'He's a bastard.'

'In what way?' Kit thought he knew in what way. He tried not to think about it. He hated to even hear Tito's name mentioned when they were together. He couldn't stand the thought of that fucker sliming over Gilda.

'He'll screw any woman with a pulse. And he likes hanging around with the aristocracy, giving himself airs. Like that pervert Bray – you seen him? The things *he* gets up to would make your hair curl, believe me.'

Kit considered this. He knew of Lord Bray. Everyone did. Could he be Daisy Bray's father? Yes, he could. Poor bitch. No wonder she was so shot away.

'If you can't stand Tito, why don't you leave him?' he asked. It was a stupid question: he knew it. But he hated this, snatched moments with her while she belonged to that bastard. Once, he'd been cool with the situation. But now, every time he saw her with that fat fuck, he wanted to punch his lights out.

Gilda gazed at him, her expression sad.

'He took me off the streets when I was eighteen,' she explained. 'He's kept me ever since. He won't let me go. Tito *never* gets dumped. It's only over when *he* says it is.' She sighed and cuddled in closer against him. 'Kit . . . I'm so in love with you,' she whispered.

Kit jerked back in surprise. Her eyes were steady as they held his.

'Well, you can't say you're *that* shocked,' she laughed.

Kit felt uneasy. He didn't want her love. At the start, this had been all about fun, indulgence, happy escape. And the fact that she was tied to someone else – yes, someone *dangerous* – had only made it all the more appealing.

'You could say you love me too,' she prompted, half-embarrassed.

'I love you too,' he said obligingly. He had always firmly believed that he could never truly love anyone except possibly himself, and sometimes even *that* was a big ask. But he could see from her widening smile and her brimming eyes how much it pleased her.

'There. Was that so hard?' she teased.

Kit rose from the bed and looked down at her. She was quite an eyeful, and he was very fond of her. In fact, just lately, he'd been *living* for these secret meetings.

Is this love? he wondered.

Christ. It was. He was in love with Gilda.

'Time we were going,' he said, and this time she got out of bed and started to dress.

77

Cornelius was just going into the upper chamber when someone caught his arm. He turned in surprise, with a quick spasm of alarm. He'd been jumpy since that incident with Sebby, starting at shadows. He felt he'd moved into some dark and dangerous place, driven there by his own moral bankruptcy.

Tito had dug him out of *that* hole. But now Tito's demands had picked up. He called on Cornelius constantly to get his lowlife pals and employees out of trouble. Cornelius felt his own standing among his peers waning as they colluded – reluctantly – with him to cover criminal tracks. People had started to avoid him.

And a couple of journalists had been sniffing around, asking him about his association with Tito.

'Is it really wise, Lord Bray, mixing with someone like that? Allegedly, Mr Danieri has countless criminal connections and . . .' They'd scuttled up to him, notebooks poised, eyes hungry for a story.

'No comment,' said Cornelius, hurrying on.

But they persisted.

'I have no association with Mr Danieri, he's a distant acquaintance,' he blurted out, once.

They persisted.

'Consult your editor,' he snapped. 'This is harassment.'

Of course he knew that his network of contacts would shield him from any smear. But still . . . when Richard Dorley grabbed his arm outside the Lords, his instant reaction was, *Oh God, they've found me out. This is it. It's all over.*

'Lord Bray?' asked the man.

Cornelius stopped in his tracks and looked him over. This didn't look like any reporter he knew. The man was shabbily dressed, grey-haired, with a haggard and desolate air about him. Cornelius flinched when he looked into the man's dark eyes. They reminded him of Sebby's.

'Who are you?' asked Cornelius, heartbeat accelerating.

'I'm Richard Dorley, sir. My son . . .'

To Cornelius's horror, the man's eyes filled with tears. He blinked and fiddled in the pocket of his raincoat. Pulled out not the handkerchief Cornelius had expected, but a photograph.

'I'm very busy,' said Cornelius, starting to walk away. A couple of people he knew well were ambling past, looking curiously – and, he thought, disapprovingly – at Cornelius talking to this shambolic little man.

Richard caught his arm again.

'Just look at it, will you? Please?' he asked, brandishing the photo in Cornelius's face.

Cornelius looked. His innards froze as he saw a couple there. Sebby smiling at the camera, and himself standing there at Sebby's side with his arm draped around the boy's shoulders.

'I'm trying to find him. It's my son, Sebastian,' said the man. 'He sent the photo to his brother a while ago. His mother got very upset. And I promised her that I would come to London and track him down and bring him home. Andrew – my eldest son – recognized you in the photograph and said that's Lord Bray. He said *he'll* probably know where Sebastian is, he's right there with him . . .'

Cornelius stared dumbstruck at the incriminating photo. He had his arm around the boy's shoulders, cuddling in close to him. They looked like lovers.

Jesus.

'I haven't seen him about in a long time,' said Cornelius, taking hold of the photo. He'd say he would show it around, get it off this man, dispose of it.

But Richard snatched it back. 'So you do know him?' he asked.

'No,' said Cornelius, flustered. 'We met briefly, that's all. I don't know him.'

He walked on into the upper chamber. As he did so, he felt a bead of moisture trickle down between his shoulder blades. He hadn't even realized it, but he was sweating.

78

'I thought I'd take a spin down to the South of France in the spring,' said Michael to Ruby a couple of weeks after their dinner at the Connaught.

'Oh?'

This wasn't what she'd expected. This time they were doing lunch in the art deco Savoy Grill, and what she'd *expected*, what she *needed*, was that he would get straight down to cases and tell her what was happening with Charlie.

She was finding him increasingly attractive. He had an air of being able to handle anything, however dark, however dirty; his power was an aphrodisiac to her, and that surprised her because she had always believed that she had power enough of her own without having to find it in a man. Also, men with power over her had hurt her so much in the past.

Now she was feeling her stomach lurch a little every time she heard his voice on the phone; she was feeling that long-forgotten flush of excitement when he came into a room. But all that was a distraction, she *had* to concentrate on what really mattered here.

She had abandoned the idea of contacting Daisy. Daisy was happy, settled. Ruby knew it would be selfish of her to ruin Daisy's stability. She hated it, but she felt it was right that she stayed away. But her boy was another matter. Charlie *had* to be tackled.

'I thought about Cannes. It's nice, they've got these great big boulevards,' Michael was going on. 'Palm trees swaying in the breeze. The best hotels. You'll love it.'

'*Me?*' Ruby nearly choked on her cocktail.

'Yeah, you. This is an invitation to come with me on a little jaunt. Just for a couple of weeks.'

'But . . . I don't know. I have the business to think about.' She was shocked that he had offered. Shocked and a bit scared. She hadn't had a close relationship with a man in so long. *Jesus, it's probably healed over by now*, she thought with a stab of mirth.

'You have managers, let them manage.'

'I don't know . . .' She hadn't taken a holiday in . . . well, she had *never* taken a holiday. Not really. Sometimes she shopped or went to the park or to the beauty salon, but her mind was always occupied. Not so much with business, though: now she was becoming more and more obsessed with staying away from her lost daughter, and tracing her poor nameless son.

'Only,' he said, looking very serious all of a sudden, 'there'll be things going on, Ruby. And it's best we slip out of the country while all that happens, do you see?'

Ruby took a deep breath. 'You mean Charlie.'

He nodded, glancing around to be sure they were out of anyone's earshot. 'Exactly. Now, how far do you want me to go, in relation to that?'

'Get him to tell you *exactly* what happened to my boy. No matter what happened, no matter how bad it is, I want to know.'

'And if he won't play ball . . . ?'

Ruby's eyes grew cold. 'Get it any way you can.'

Michael looked at her consideringly. 'Not much love lost there, then.'

Ruby drained her drink and placed the empty glass firmly upon the table. She looked straight into Michael's eyes. 'I hate him.'

'Then a little break for the pair of us, don't you think? A nice trip down to the Côte D'Azur.'

'All right. OK. I get the message, I'll come.'

'At last!' said Vi when they met up for lunch and Ruby told her the news about the holiday. 'I was starting to really worry about you. Who is he? Is he nice-looking? Come on, I want the details.'

Ruby smiled, but bearing in mind the motivation behind their trip – that they should be out of the country when whatever befell Charlie took place – she felt she ought not to be too specific.

'I met him through the business. He's . . .' Ruby hesitated, trying to find the words to describe the sheer physical impact of Michael Ward . . . 'very attractive.'

'Good *girl*,' said Vi. 'And rich, I trust?'

'Yes. I suppose he is.' Ruby was torn about the trip. It might be lovely . . . but all the while she was getting her jollies, Charlie would be getting quite another sort of treatment. She shouldn't give a stuff about that, but she did.

'Not separate bedrooms . . . ?' queried Vi.

Ruby snapped back to attention. 'Of *course* separate bedrooms. Vi, I hardly know him yet.'

Vi sipped her tea and eyed her friend with cynicism.

'Not still pining after that arsehole Cornelius, I hope?' she asked.

'Of course not. That was *years* ago.'

'He's done very well for himself. You know he's a friend of Anthony's? Cornelius got him into White's.'

'Well, good for him.'

'I think I would have died of curiosity by now, in your place,' said Vi.

'Meaning?'

'Meaning *Daisy*. His daughter. *Your* daughter.'

Ruby said nothing. She had been dying of curiosity and stifled love for too many years to count, suppressing the almost animal, *visceral* need she felt to see her daughter, to know her. Daisy's welfare must come first, not her own feelings. She knew Daisy was well looked after, she knew Vanessa had longed for a child and that she would lavish care on one. So she had to rein in her impulses, and leave Daisy alone. It was hard, though. *Crucifyingly* hard.

'Surely you'd like to see her, at least?' said Vi.

Ruby looked at her friend. Vi thought she had never seen so sad an expression in anyone's eyes before.

'Of course I want to see her.'

'Why don't you then? You could see her, perhaps even speak to her. She wouldn't *know* you were her mother.'

'No,' said Ruby. 'I can't do that.'

'Rubes . . .'

'*Drop* it, will you, Vi?' Ruby managed a smile. 'Or should I say Lady Albemarle?'

'Do you know, I nearly purr every time I hear that,' said Vi with a shiver of bliss. '*Lady* Albemarle. Isn't it wonderful?'

Ruby smiled. 'Is *Anthony* wonderful?' she asked. Vi never really mentioned her relationship with the staid, rather elderly Anthony.

Vi gave her a wry look.

'Now that really would be asking too much, don't you think?' she said briskly. 'A thousand acres, a fabulous home in the country and another in town, pots of money and a ladyship . . . and then to expect your husband to be the life and soul of the party? No, darling. Anthony is . . . nice. So I think, overall, I've done pretty well. Don't you?'

79

They drove down to the South of France in Michael's Aston Martin, stopping off at Nice before proceeding to Cannes. Ruby couldn't quite believe that she was here, cruising along the Croisette in the vivid sunshine, while Michael played his favourite audio tape of Matt Monro singing 'On Days Like These'.

'That's from the new Michael Caine film, isn't it?' she asked. '*The Italian Job*?'

'That's the one.'

'But the man was driving . . .'

'A Lamborghini. Along the Grand Corniche, I think it was.'

'Or was it the Alps? He crashed in a tunnel. The Mafia got him and pushed the wreckage of the car over the cliffs. They threw wreaths down after it.'

'Well, we're not going to crash,' he said.

Ruby believed him. Michael was a great driver – smooth, considering, observant. He spoke French – not fluently, but enough. She didn't speak a word of it, although she loved its lyrical sound. She had never driven, either.

In fact, she had never really lived. That was coming home to her now. Something deep within her was changing. She had been frozen in time after the babies were born and then so cruelly lost. All her feelings had become locked away; she had withdrawn from the world, hidden herself away behind the cool, efficient façade of the businesswoman. Forgotten about the world of pleasure, and sensation.

She glanced at him as he drove.

He was *so* good looking. His hands were strong on the wheel. The sleeves of his open-necked white shirt were rolled up to his elbows and the muscles in his arms were impressive.

'What?' he said, glancing back at her.

'Nothing,' she said, and fixed her eyes on the road instead.

She swallowed nervously. All the way down here, when they had stopped in hotels he had, without even asking her, booked two rooms, one for each of them. She liked it at first, but gradually it began to grate on her nerves. Didn't he *want* to sleep with her? She felt at the same time pleased that he respected her wishes, and affronted that he did so.

Now he was booking them in to the Carlton. Separate rooms again.

Oh, for God's sake, thought Ruby, half amused, half angry.

He kissed her politely at her door as the porter took their bags, showed them their rooms.

'I'll see you for dinner at eight, down in the bar. OK?' he said.

She nodded, bit her lip. Suddenly she was so furious she wanted to hit him. These were *fabulous* rooms, with endless views stretching away over the crystalline-blue waters of the Med. Rooms made for romance. But Michael just kissed her goodbye and went along the hall to the room next door.

Ruby unpacked, bathed, changed into white linen trousers and a turquoise top. Then she opened the balcony doors and walked out, inhaling the hot salty breeze and a faint sweet tang of lavender. *This is so wonderful.* But she felt unloved and resentful. She wanted to *share* this with Michael.

But maybe he just saw her as a companion. Maybe – oh *shit* – he was still in love with the memory of his wife.

That thought sunk her even further into gloom. She went back into the room and flung herself on the bed. She glanced at her watch. It was only five o'clock.

Maybe he thought that she was just in this for the favours he could do her. Like getting the truth out of Charlie. And . . . wasn't she?

Well, she had been. That had been at the forefront of her mind when she'd first called him. Three bouquets, and she had thought: all right, here's a man with influence, a man who knows the underworld and how it works, someone who isn't scared to break down barriers. He could help me. So – at last – she had called him, and now . . . maybe *right now,* his people were beating the details out of Charlie.

But things had changed. Being with him over the past week or so, spending leisure time with him – a completely alien concept to her before now – had begun to skew her feelings in quite another direction.

The cold, controlled Ruby was retreating. Now she was remembering the Ruby she had been as a young girl . . . but it had all been beaten out of her, first by her father and Charlie, then by that uncaring bastard Cornelius. She had been looking desperately for love, and instead disaster had befallen her.

Hadn't she learned her lesson by now? It was dangerous to love, dangerous to trust. And she had *sworn* she would never love again. And yet . . . here she was. In danger of falling for Michael Ward.

'Oh *God,*' she moaned against the pillow. Three hours until she could see him again, hear his voice. She sat bolt upright. '*Shit,*' she said loudly.

She got off the bed, slipping on her sandals. She grabbed her key, then went to the door. She stepped out into the hall, and hurried along to his door before she had the chance to change her mind. She rapped on it.

He opened it after a few seconds. He was towelling his hair dry, and wearing another pristine white towel around his waist. Water droplets beaded his chest, rivulets running down from the dark hairs there. Ruby almost moaned. He looked startled to see her there.

'You all right?' he asked.

Ruby stepped into the room and closed the door behind her. 'I'm fine,' she said, and lunged at him and put her arms around his neck and kissed him. She felt his whole body stiffen in surprise, then relax. He dropped the hand towel and fastened his arms tight around her waist.

The kiss lasted so long Ruby felt light-headed from lack of air when it finally stopped. She almost blurted out that she loved him then, but she stopped herself in the nick of time.

'This is nice,' he breathed, working his hands up under her turquoise tunic. His hands fastened over her breasts and Ruby let out a shuddering groan of pleasure. 'No bra.'

All right, fair enough. He hadn't said 'I love you' either, he was still probably hung up on his wife. Right now, Ruby didn't even care. She was too caught up in the moment, feeling his strong hands roaming everywhere, sliding over her skin, dipping down inside the elasticated waistband of her flimsy white trousers to cup the cheeks of her behind and pull her in close.

Then he tripped her, and suddenly they were on the floor, on the carpet, and he was pushing the tunic up and over her head, throwing it aside, and pulling down the white trousers, throwing aside the towel he'd been wearing around his waist, and he was so beautiful, so strong, kneeling naked between her thighs, almost grinning down at her.

'Why'd you take so long?' he managed to say. 'I've been dying to do this . . .'

'I thought you didn't want me,' she panted, pulling him close, pulling him in. 'Ahhh,' she moaned as he slipped inside her.

'You're crazy,' he gasped. 'I adore you.'

It wasn't a declaration of love, but it would have to do. Now he was thrusting into her, and the pleasure was so intense that Ruby thought she was just going to die of happiness. She hugged him, murmuring endearments, until he could stand no more and he shuddered and grew still.

'Think I've got carpet burns,' said Ruby lazily, feeling so replete, so relaxed. She had forgotten how good this could be.

'Then let's get on the bed,' said Michael, and they went over to the bed and sank down onto it, kissing, caressing, making love all over again, until it was eight and time for dinner. Ruby didn't think about Cornelius or Charlie that night. Not even once.

80

Charlie Darke was hopeful of parole. He'd been careful to be on good behaviour for a while now, and here was his reward at last: he'd been downgraded to a Category C. No longer did he have to be escorted out to work, to bathe, to do any fucking thing at all. Now he had a small glimpse of greater freedom, even if he was still in stir.

But he quickly found there were drawbacks to this new arrangement. He was going out of the wing to his labour one day when a huge con coming in shouldered him hard. Charlie was a big bloke, but he was nearly knocked sideways by the impact.

'What the fuck you doing?' he said, and turned and whacked the cunt straight across the face.

The new man, bald, massive, with a drooping Sancho Panza ginger-brown moustache, only smiled and wiped a smear of blood from his mouth where Charlie had cuffed him. The screws went mental, hustling Charlie away, dragging the new one in the opposite direction.

Things settled down, and later in the day Charlie started making enquiries. The new man was from Maidstone, he'd arrived in Charlie's orbit yesterday.

'John Corah,' his contacts told him. 'Mean bastard. He's in A for rape and assault.'

'He wants to watch himself,' said Charlie.

He was offended that this new man had treated him with disrespect. He was one of the 'top' cons in this place, and he wasn't used to being treated as anything less than royalty. Everyone knew Charlie Darke, that he'd done the Post Office job during the war and the police had never recovered the haul. He was a legend. He wouldn't tolerate anyone taking the piss.

He was in the workshop next day and Corah was there again, sneering at him.

'What you looking at, you arsehole?' asked Charlie.

'Nothing,' said Corah.

'Watch your fucking step,' said Charlie, and got on with his work.

'*You* watch your step, you fucking fool,' said Corah.

Charlie hit the roof. '*What you say?*'

'Shut it, the pair of you,' said the screw nervously.

The whole thing blew up at teatime when they passed on the landing. Despite the screws being right there on the spot, Charlie found himself hustled into a cell by Corah. He'd been expecting trouble. The screws had clearly been paid to look the other way. He was on his own, and there were three men with Corah, waiting in the cell. Suddenly they were slapping him about, kicking him.

He was furious. He was *king* of this shit heap, and here they were, knocking him around like a Saturday-night barmaid. He let the six-inch nail he'd pocketed in the workshop slip down his shirt cuff and into his hand when the next one came at him. He whacked it into a big beer-bellied bastard's eye and felt it connect with gristle. Charlie twisted the thing and the geezer's eye popped straight out of his head in a shower of blood and rolled onto the floor.

'*Jesus!*' bellowed the injured man, scrabbling around on the floor in agony with his hands over his face.

Charlie stamped on the bloke's eye, pulverizing it.

The man writhed and screamed, blood streaming from the socket, splashing around the cell.

'Get him out of here,' said Corah, and one of the screws grabbed the injured man while the other two got the nail off Charlie and got him on the floor with more kicks and punches.

Finally, bruised and battered half to death, Charlie lay still, face down.

'All done?' asked John Corah, and pulled up a chair.

Twisting his head – the other two were on his back, he couldn't move an inch – he could see Corah, sitting there grinning.

There was blood and a squashed eyeball right in Charlie's eyeline. His head felt like shit where he'd been punched so hard.

'Tough nut, ain't you?' said Corah almost admiringly.

'You're dead,' grunted Charlie.

'No, you see, that's *you*, not me. If you don't answer a few questions.'

'Questions? What is this? *Take Your Pick?* Who are you, Michael fucking Miles?'

'Yeah, funny. Now tell me all about what you did with your sister's kid, back in the war.'

'You *what*?'

'The boy. Someone wants to know.'

'The boy's dead,' Charlie managed to get out.

'How. When. Who. Come on, details.'

'You serious?'

One of the men pinning Charlie down clouted him hard in the ear. Charlie's head started ringing like an alarm clock.

'All right,' he gasped. 'You want to know? It's nothing to me. I took him to a mate of mine in Finsbury Park. Rubbish man. Lots of the gangs used him. Bloke was a fire-watcher during the war, he had all the gear. Used to dissolve rubbish in a big vat of acid in the cellar. The kid's long gone. You won't find a trace. No one will. Who the fuck wants to know, after all this time . . . ?'

'None of your business. You see the deed done?' asked Corah, his eyes fixed on Charlie's bloodied face.

'I paid him to do it. He was sound.'

'So you didn't *see* it done?'

'He wouldn't have mucked me about. He wouldn't dare.'

'Big man, yeah?'

'Bigger than you, shit-face,' said Charlie, and that earned him another punch in the head.

'This bloke's name,' said Corah.

'He'll be dead and buried by now, you're wasting your time. Who wants to know this?'

'Shut the fuck up and answer the question. His name.'

'Hugh Burton. Sound. Dependable.'

'Good man, uh? He'd do a kid in acid.'

'It was a little black bastard. What else would any decent man have done?'

Even Corah felt sick at this. He liked kids, he had four little ankle-biters of his own. He stood up, put the chair neatly to one side.

'Give him a bit more,' he said, and left the cell to let his two friends attend to Charlie Darke.

Charlie was in the hospital wing by that evening, and by the following day he was making enquiries and planning a rematch in which John Corah would be carried out as a corpse. Fuck good behaviour, that bastard had it coming. But he was too late. Corah had already been moved to Leicester. And the governor had turned down Charlie's parole.

81

1970

'No,' said Aunt Ju. 'Absolutely not, Daisy. Out of the question.'

That was Aunt Ju's reaction to Daisy's request that she come up to London to stay for a little while. She was bored with the country. She wanted to be in London again, near her friends, and she *also* wanted to be there because that enigmatic guy called Kit Miller had never called her and so she had decided that she was going to take the initiative and track him down at Ward Security.

Daisy wasn't the type of girl to be deterred if a man didn't contact her. *She* would contact him instead. Why not? Everyone was liberated these days, you didn't have to wait for a man to do the running any more.

But why hadn't he? She was very good looking. She was young. She was fanciable. She had made it clear that she wanted him to get in touch. What was his problem?

'Oh please, Aunt Ju,' she whined. 'I'm really sorry I messed up. And I'd so love to see you.'

'Daisy – no.'

Daisy pulled a face and put the phone down. She found Vanessa in the drawing room, engrossed in gardening books as always, and got straight to the point.

'I'm thinking of going up to London for a while to stay with Aunt Ju,' she said.

Vanessa looked at her daughter and sighed. It was horrible to admit, but she found Daisy such hard work. *But then – she's not your daughter, is she?* floated into her brain.

Certainly, Daisy was nothing like her at all. In looks, she was very like her Aunt Ju, very like her father. Very blonde, very blue-eyed, robust and clear-skinned. And in character, she was just so *wild*.

If I'd ever had a child, my own child, would she have been like this?

Vanessa didn't think so. She was genteel, reserved. Daisy was just crazy, making up her own rules as she went along. Crashing cars. Attending those awful parties, getting herself deflowered – for the love of God! – at such an early age. So fortunate there had been nothing to show for that, but there could have been. She really didn't know what Daisy was going to get up to next.

But at the same time, she felt bad about her own antipathy towards Daisy. She had been so desperate for a child that she had thought she could handle it, taking on a child that her husband had fathered on another woman. Now she knew that she should never have done it.

Over the years the whole thing had become harder and harder to bear. Every misdemeanour Daisy committed only reinforced the truth: that she was not Vanessa's child, and that she would have to struggle forever to maintain an appearance of affection for the girl, even when – more often than not – she didn't feel it. All Daisy did was remind her that her husband had cheated on her, that she was a failure as a wife, and a failure as a mother too.

Daisy looked at her mother, who was watching her again with that *judgemental* look on her face. As usual, she felt the full weight of Vanessa's disapproval. Ever since she could remember, she'd felt that she was a great disappointment, that she could never live up to her mother's expectations.

'I can go and stay with Aunt Ju for a while, can't I?' said Daisy. 'What do you think? If you suggested it to her, I could go. Could you do that?'

Daisy knew that if Vanessa asked, Aunt Ju would cave in.

'All right,' said Vanessa. 'Why not? I'll phone her tonight.' And she couldn't suppress it even though she tried – that tiny, treacherous prickle of feeling that she later identified as relief. She was *glad* Daisy was going back to town. She could tend her garden, immerse herself in it. And forget about the rest.

82

Two of Michael Ward's men went over to Finsbury Park to see if there was any hope of tracking down Hugh Burton after all this time.

'Probably dead,' said Kit to his companion, Rob.

Certainly the house – the *row* of houses – wasn't there any more. Instead, there was a cable factory on the site. It was early morning and workers were flooding in through the gates to start their day's labour.

The two men stood there and watched all this activity.

'Parish records . . . ?' suggested Rob. 'Electoral register? Don't they keep that in the library?'

They went to the library first, but there was – unsurprisingly – no Hugh Burton on the register.

Next were the parish records. There were several churches in the area – Anglican, Roman Catholic, Methodist. If Hugh Burton had been in his forties during the war, then his birth date had to be around 1900 to 1910.

'Shit, this is going to take for ever,' complained Rob.

'What, you got a date or something?' asked Kit.

'Yeah, with a pie and a pint.'

'Later.'

The Methodist and Roman Catholic church records yielded nothing of interest, but the Anglican showed up not only Hugh Burton, born to a cabinet-maker and his wife, but a year later a sister called Anthea and a year after *that*, another sister, called Jennifer. The two men made a note of the address of Hugh, Anthea and Jennifer's parents, and gave the vicar a large donation to the church funds by way of thanks.

They went to the address. Finsbury Park again. And this time, the house, a Victorian villa in the middle of a row of others, was still standing. They knocked on the door.

A woman answered, looking flustered. She was a young, hard-faced blonde, heavily pregnant, a prodigious bump ballooning the front of her lime-green T-shirt. Above the bump her breasts drooped tiredly. There was a two-year-old perched on her hip and a four- or five-year-old clinging to her denim-clad leg.

Kit thought that someone *really* ought to tell the poor cow about Durex.

'Whoever it is, tell them we're not buying,' called a female voice from inside.

'Yes?' snapped the young woman, eyeing the two men.

'Hi,' said Kit, smiling. 'We're just down from Blackpool and we're trying to find a friend of our late father's called Hugh Burton. Or maybe his sisters? Anthea and Jennifer. Our dad always said we had to look them up.'

'No, sorry,' she said, and was shutting the door.

'Wait,' said Kit. 'Just a minute. I haven't told you the full story. Dad's just died and he's left Hugh and his sisters something in the will. So we'd really like to find them.'

The mention of a will stilled the girl's hand on the door. She hesitated. The two-year-old squirmed and she set him down on the rug. The four- or five-year-old promptly pulled the little one's hair with a grin, and the baby set up a howling fit to wake the dead.

'Hush, for God's sake,' said the young woman, and now another woman appeared behind her, an older, tireder-looking version of the ludicrously fecund woman in the doorway. Had to be her mother. She grabbed up the baby, shushing and rocking her. The four- or five-year-old ran off down the hall.

'It's a sad situation,' said Kit, looking sincerely into the mother's eyes. 'Dad often spoke about Hugh and his sisters, and now Dad's died but he's left them gifts of money in the will, and he always said he wanted Hugh and the girls to come to his funeral, and out of respect for his wishes, we've come down to find them.'

'Money?' The mother's ears had pricked up. 'How much money?'

'Why, do you know them?' he asked.

'Jennifer's my mother,' she said.

'Really? That's great.'

'Not really, it ain't,' said the older woman sourly. 'Her brother died during the war. And Aunt Anthea passed over a couple of years back.'

'Right. I'm sorry to hear that.' So that was the end of it. Hugh Burton was dead and gone, long since. Kit considered the situation. Michael would want details. 'Could I see Jennifer? Talk to her?'

'Well,' said the older woman as the four- or five-year-old decided now was the perfect moment to play trains up and down the hall, very loudly. Added to the wailing baby, it was hellish, the noise in there. 'You can try.'

83

'Hey!'

That evening, Kit was in the bar at Michael Ward's place. He turned at the girl's call. She was hurrying towards him. Blonde, pretty, young. Done up in a frilled smock, feathers hanging off beads around her neck, like a crazy milkmaid.

'Hi,' she grinned. 'Remember me?'

And now of course he did.

'You crashed my car,' she said.

'No,' said Kit. '*You* crashed your car, because you were driving like a maniac.'

'Pleased to see me?'

Kit gave her a reluctant half-smile. He seriously hadn't expected ever to see her again. He'd 'lost' her phone number. Eager young posh bints weren't on his agenda. He had beautiful Gilda with the sea-green eyes and the knowledgeable hands, jingling with gold and lush with promise. He was in love with her. Could never wait to see her.

Also, he had plenty of business to keep him occupied. He was off tomorrow to visit Jennifer Phelps at a place called High Firs, and he had told Michael just an hour ago how the whole Hugh Burton thing was going.

'That's good,' Michael had said.

'It's probably not,' said Kit. 'The daughter and granddaughter gave the impression we wouldn't get much out of the old girl.'

Michael was looking very fit and suntanned and relaxed, fresh back from the South of France. 'This is important to me.'

'Right.'

'So keep going with it, son,' he said.

Kit nodded.

'And well done. Didn't think you'd get this far with it, let alone any further.'

Then Kit had come out to the bar, and now . . . Daisy had turned up.

'How did you find me?' he asked her.

'So you're *not* pleased to see me,' she pouted.

'Have a drink and shut up,' said Kit, half-amused and half-irritated. 'White wine?'

'Please.'

Kit relayed their order to the bartender, who delivered their drinks.

'So,' he said, turning to Daisy. 'How . . . ?'

'Yellow Pages. Looked up Ward Security. *Went* to Ward Security, and was directed here.'

'That easy.'

'That easy, yes.'

Kit took a swallow of his beer and eyed her beadily. 'You know, some men would find that a massive turn-off. A woman chasing after them like that.'

'Do you find it a massive turn-off?' she asked coyly, and gulped down a mouthful of wine.

'That's good stuff, you should sip it.'

'Do you?' It was as if he hadn't spoken.

Kit shrugged and sighed. This was getting tedious. 'Daisy . . .'

'Are you involved with somebody? Is that it?'

'I'm involved with somebody, yes.' Involved right up to the hilt. *Now* would she take the hint?

'Is she as gorgeous as me?' asked Daisy with a smile, but he could see the hurt in her eyes.

Poor little rich girl, she just wants to be loved, he thought.

Gilda had filled him in about Daisy's father Lord Bray – a public school product with perverted sexual appetites. And Mummy? She did charity and the church flowers down in the country, probably. She was never really seen around town.

But somewhere in this batty little cow, Kit could see a faint echo of his own insecurities. He had pulled a crew of men together under Michael Ward's guidance, and *they* were his family. He liked his mates around him, because . . . he had never before had that strong feeling of belonging that he got from working for the firm. In the children's home it had been all shoes-off-slippers-on, all rules and regulations. He'd been glad to get out of there.

Now he made his own rules, up to a point. But the scars from his institutionalized upbringing were always there. He had a chip of ice in his heart. Only Gilda had ever come close to melting it.

'Let me buy you dinner,' he said, surprising himself. What the hell? He wasn't due to see Gilda until eleven; he had time to kill. The poor little mare didn't mean any harm.

'Great,' she said instantly, and drained her glass. 'I'm starving.'

84

1970

High Firs was a pretty nineteenth-century lodge set in a country park. Once it could have been the home of a prosperous wool-merchant. Now it was God's waiting room, stuffed full of the elderly.

Kit and Rob were led inside by a blue-coated young woman, through a day room where lots of old folks sat. Some slept, their heads drooping onto their chests, some watched TV on the small screen in the corner of the room. A couple of them looked up and smiled as Kit and Rob passed by. One of them, her face spotted with age, said to Rob: 'Do you speak Russian?'

Rob shook his head and they moved on.

There was a scent in the air that reminded Kit of the homes he'd grown up in – boiled cabbage, onions and Dettol, mingled with human body odours and strong soap. Holding his breath, he followed as the girl led them through the day room and out into a conservatory that had a look of long-faded grandeur.

Three more inmates were sitting out here, blankets made of multicoloured knitted squares draped over their laps. Two were dozing. One was letting her glasses fall down onto the chain around her neck. There was a little notepad on her lap, and in her shaking hands she held a ballpoint pen. She was watching them, her bony head with its thin white fuzz of hair wobbling on a neck that looked hardly strong enough to hold it up. Her cheeks were like softly collapsed balloons. Her bright blue eyes were hazed with age, but hopeful.

Christ, thought Kit. If he ever wound up like this, his fondest wish was that someone would have the decency to put a bullet through his brain and end it.

'Have you come to take me home?' she asked, her voice cracked and almost pleading.

'These people have come on a visit,' said the girl, ignoring the question just as Kit and Rob did.

Kit guessed that was what old age boiled down to, right there: speaking, and being ignored. Having the whole world forget that you and your needs existed. Until, finally, you – and they – didn't.

'Take a seat,' said the girl, while Jennifer Phelps watched them in bewilderment, her head waggling around as she followed their movements.

Kit and Rob sat down in a couple of creaking Lloyd Loom chairs, and the girl departed.

'This is nice,' said Jennifer, one hand clawing at her blanket to straighten it. She knocked the notebook from her lap, and Kit picked it up, put it back there. 'Thank you, dear. Don't I know you?'

Kit looked into the eyes. Bright, but vacant.

Lights are on but the dogs ain't barking, he thought.

'I don't think so,' he said. 'Mrs Phelps . . .'

'Call me Jennifer,' she said. 'The Duke of York was here last week, you know. Visiting the wards.'

'Jennifer,' Kit corrected himself. She thought she was in hospital. She thought royalty had visited the wards. There was no hope. He rolled off the spiel about his father dying and how he wanted to trace his father's old friend, Hugh.

'Hugh? Your father knew Hugh?' she asked. She was frowning hard.

'Yeah.'

'Well, that's amazing. Hugh never had time for anyone. Never had a kind word to say for a soul, either.'

Kit and Rob exchanged a look. Clearly, the old woman was nuts. But sometimes the very old and even the demented remembered what happened years ago with clarity, while yesterday was a mystery to them. Did her daughter ever come and see her here? Having met the hatchet-faced woman, Kit doubted it.

'Were you close? You and Hugh?' asked Kit.

Jennifer made a huffing noise. 'Hugh weren't close to *anyone*. And he was cruel. Used to pull the wings off flies when he was a boy, used to make me and my sister cry to see it.'

A psychopath in the making. A boy who would go on to become a man who disposed of 'rubbish' for gang leaders like Charlie Darke.

'Did you ever hear anything about a baby?' asked Kit. They were wasting their time here, but what the hell.

One of the other residents, bathed in sunlight in the conservatory, gave a bubbling snore.

'A baby?' Jennifer gave a croak of laughter, displaying a shocking mouthful of crockery, huge pristine white dentures that looked odd against her wrinkled, yellowing skin. 'Hugh weren't married. Never had it in him. Never even *looked* at a girl. Are you interested in poetry?'

Kit took a breath. 'Not really,' he said, and Rob got up and walked to the glass wall that separated them from the neat gardens beyond the conservatory's edge. Rob let out a loud sigh.

'I am. I write it. I'm quite good,' said Jennifer.

'Getting back to this baby . . .' said Kit.

'Just for my own amusement, you know.'

'That's nice. The baby . . . ?'

'I told you. Hugh weren't married. Now, young man, you just listen to this,' she said, and picked up the glasses that dangled on the chain around her neck and flipped over a page of her notebook.

Ah shit, thought Kit.

Her voice wobbling, Jennifer read aloud:

> *Bury me in wicker*
> *And garland me in flowers*
> *Then go off and have a drink*
> *Celebrate for hours*
> *For life it is a precious gift*
> *The greatest we are given*
> *So raise a glass and smile and laugh*
> *You're still among the living.*

Kit had never heard anything so gut-wrenchingly sad in his entire life. Jennifer removed her glasses and looked at him.

'What do you think of *that*, young man?' she asked.

'That's beautiful,' said Kit.

She smiled, her dentures twinkling like a toothpaste commercial.

'You're nice,' she said.

'Thank you,' said Kit, and stood up.

'You're not going, are you?' she asked anxiously, the smile dropping from her face.

'We have to go, yes,' said Kit.

'But I thought you wanted to know about a baby?'

Kit looked at Jennifer. 'Do you *know* anything about a baby?'

'Only the one I found on the night Hugh died,' she said.

85

Richard Dorley met up with Sammy Bell, who wrote for the *Globe*, in a fuggy corner of El Vino in Fleet Street. He set it all out for Sammy. That he believed respectable, married Lord Bray had been – maybe still was – having an affair with his son, Sebastian. He showed the journalist the photo.

Sammy Bell was a tired old hack, bald on top but with grey hair sprouting from his nose and ears and with huge bushy eyebrows. He was looking forward to retirement and a quiet life with the wife. But his newshound's nose twitched when he saw this. He hated the establishment – all those twats who broke the rules and never paid the price. Bray was right up there among the upper echelons. He would *love* to rattle the bastard's cage. And look at this. Clearly the old sod was turking the boy, you could see that from the cosy way they were standing there: a couple.

'You showed him this?' asked Sammy, downing his pint.

Richard nodded. 'He just said he'd met Sebby once, and hadn't seen him since.'

'Which could be true.'

'It could be. But now Sebby's gone off somewhere. He hasn't been in touch, and that's not like him. We're worried . . .'

'You could go to the police.'

'Sebby's not underage. He's not actually *missing,* is he?

He just ran off down here when we fell out. But that photo . . .'

Sammy knew what Richard meant. It was clear as day looking at this: these two were in a hot physical relationship.

'Can I take this?'

'I'll want it back,' said Richard.

'Of course.' Sammy whipped out a notebook and pen. 'I'll have a word with my editor, see if he's interested. OK? Give me your address and telephone number, I'll be in touch.'

Richard gave him the address of the B & B he was staying at, over in Rotherhithe, and his home phone number in Leicester. His son Andrew could relay any messages when he next phoned home from the B & B. The landlord didn't like anyone using the phone much; he'd made that very clear.

Sammy tucked the photo into his notebook, put the notebook and pen back in his pocket. He drained his pint and stood up, holding out his hand. Richard rose too, and shook it.

'I'll see my editor,' said Sammy. 'See what he says.'

'Thanks,' said Richard, his voice shaking now. 'It's made my wife ill, all this. When Sebby sent us this photo, it gave us some hope. I thought his lordship might know where Sebby's got to.'

'We'll see what we can do,' said Sammy. He wasn't interested in Richard's sob story – but he *was* interested in making Lord Muck squirm, if he could.

86

1970

Michael had invited Ruby to dinner at his restaurant, Sheila's, to tell her the news that Kit had relayed to him. Sheila was his late wife. He'd named the restaurant after her. Ruby wondered if he was still in love with Sheila. And if so – where did that leave her?

'The kid wasn't killed,' he said, after they'd eaten.

Ruby sat like a stone, her eyes fastened on his face as he said those words. Suddenly she screwed her eyes tight shut and released a huge breath.

'You OK?' asked Michael.

Her eyes opened. They were brimming with tears. She nodded, swallowing.

'Hey, don't cry. This is good news. Have a sip of wine.'

Ruby lifted her glass. A tear spilled over, and she wiped it away. She took a mouthful of the wine, and felt a little steadier. Her son was alive.

'Where is he?' she asked. 'I don't understand. Charlie took him to that awful man, he should be dead.'

'He was called Hugh Burton. We tracked down his sister.'

'You said he *was*?'

'Patience.' Michael made a calm-down gesture. He paused, lit a cigarette and took a drag. 'His sister's very old. She married and was widowed a long time ago. Her name's Jennifer Phelps. She's in a nursing home. She's lost a few marbles, but some of 'em are still hanging on for grim death.'

Ruby stared at Michael's face, digesting this. 'And she knew what happened to the baby?'

Michael nodded.

'She said she remembered that night as if it was yesterday,' said Michael, leaning closer, lowering his voice a little. 'She took her brother over a cooked meal every evening during the war; she only lived in the next street. He was single. Lived alone in the house where they all grew up. Hugh stayed on, didn't marry, looked after the parents until they both passed away – he was a misfit. A loner. Didn't care for company of any sort, male or female. That evening she got there and let herself in with her key, as usual.'

He paused, took a drink.

'*And?*' Ruby prompted. 'Come *on*, Michael.'

'And there was Hugh Burton, her brother, laid out dead on the hall floor. Heart attack.'

'The baby. What about the baby?'

'The baby was there too, but alive and well.' Michael sipped again. 'Seems there *is* a God. Jennifer said she was upset at finding her brother like that, she hardly knew *what* to think. There'd never been much affection between them, but this was her brother after all. She didn't know where the baby had come from. Hadn't a clue. So she grabbed a police reservist off the street, and he helped her with sorting out an ambulance to take Hugh's body to the local morgue, which was in the hospital. The baby was also taken to the hospital, and that was the last Jennifer saw of him. She said she'd wondered over the years, wondered what the baby was doing there – and Hugh being Hugh, she said she was probably better off not knowing. She said the police found weird stuff in his cellar. An acid bath. Traces of human and animal skin and hair.'

'Jesus.'

'You OK there?'

She nodded.

'Jennifer said she wondered how the baby got on. How his life went from there.'

Ruby's eyes widened in distress. 'So we *still* don't really know what happened to him.'

'We know he was safe. In hospital. Alive. After that, I'm guessing fostering, maybe a children's home. The authorities would have looked after him.'

Ruby was folding and refolding her napkin, her movements convulsive. 'We have to find him,' she said.

Michael looked at her. 'He may not want to be found. Chances are, he don't feel very friendly towards his mother. In his eyes, I suppose he was abandoned; unwanted.'

Ruby threw the napkin down. 'It was the stupidest thing I ever did,' she said hotly. 'Getting involved with Cornelius. *Trusting* him. I was such a fool.'

'You were young,' said Michael. 'We all act the fool when we're young. We don't see the consequences. It's only later when reality hits.'

Ruby's eyes were full of sadness as they held his. 'I don't think this is ever going to come out right,' she said.

'We'll make it,' he said.

But Ruby couldn't bring herself to believe that.

87

'No,' said Sammy Bell's editor. He squinted at Sammy through a pall of cigarette smoke, then looked back at the picture of Lord Bray and some gay-looking young bloke. 'No way.'

Sammy stared at his editor Brian Scott, fat as butter with his white nylon shirt stained yellow, sweat around the armpits, the buttons straining across his chest and stomach, wheezing and coughing as he puffed on his umpteenth fag of the day.

'What?' Sammy was surprised. He'd expected arguments, maybe. He hadn't expected a flat, unequivocal 'no'.

'I said no. Drop it.' And to Sammy's dismay, Brian tore the photo into shreds and dumped it in the waste bin.

'I said I'd give it back to the man,' he objected.

'Say you lost it,' said Brian. 'Better yet, say nothing at all. Don't get back in touch with him and don't pursue this.'

'Brian . . .'

'No arguments. We're a Tory paper, you silly fucker. You don't piss in your own tent.'

Sammy drummed his bitten fingernails on the arm of his chair.

'You got this bloke's address?' asked Brian.

'Yeah.'

'Let's have it then.'

'I thought you said . . . ?'

'Hand it over.'

Sammy handed over Richard Dorley's address.

'I just think . . .' he started, standing up, gutted by this put-down.

'I know what you think. You think you'd like to squeeze his lordship's poncey nuts in a vice. Well, so would I. But it don't work like that. You *know* it don't. Jesus! You're not retiring a minute too soon, you idiot. Off you go.'

Fuming, Sammy left the office. Before he'd even shut the door, Brian was on the phone.

88

Gilda was in bed with Tito one morning when she realized she was dead.

They'd spent the night together, and he'd been his usual self: brutally sexual, bruising her and then rolling over and snoring like a hog. She lay there long after he was asleep, dreaming of Kit, gorgeous Kit with his strong yet gentle hands and his beautiful body. Then she slept, and awoke to find Dan and Biffy, two of Tito's heavies, standing at the end of the bed.

'What's going on . . . ?' she asked, blinking, pushing her hair out of her eyes.

Tito was waking too, sitting up. He saw the two men there.

'You ready then, boss?' asked Biffy, his eyes glued coldly to Gilda.

She felt her skin start to crawl. She clutched the sheet to her, her fingers cold with sudden fear.

Tito turned his head. His ice-cold eyes bored into hers.

'What is it?' she asked, her voice rising in panic. 'What's happening?'

Tito let out a sigh. 'We need to talk,' he said.

'What? What about?' she asked, dry-mouthed.

'About you.'

'What?'

'You and Kit Miller,' said Tito. Then he looked away from her. 'OK, boys,' he said.

Gilda was dragged naked and screaming from the bed. Tito watched dispassionately as the two men hauled her out of the bedroom. The door slammed behind them and he could still hear her screaming. He sighed and went into the bathroom and turned on the shower to deaden the sound. It annoyed him.

89

'Shit – you again.'

Kit couldn't believe it. Daisy Bray really was the most audacious little mare he'd ever come across. She'd shown up once and he'd bought her dinner – out of pity. Straight after that, when she'd moved in for a smooch, he'd pushed her away and laid it all out for her – *again* – in plain English.

'I'm involved with someone, I told you,' he said.

'So?'

'So back off, Daise, for God's sake. What are you trying to do? Have a bit of fun, slumming it with dodgy geezers like me?'

'No! And are you telling me you're faithful to her? Because I don't believe it. There's no such thing as a faithful man. There's only a man who doesn't get the offers.'

That amused him. 'You're so cynical,' he smiled, wishing now that he *hadn't* bought her dinner, thinking that she'd seen it as encouragement, when he had only been trying to let her down gently.

It wasn't that she was unfanciable. She was. It was just she was such a *child*. She was like Tigger, bouncing around being lovable. And being bloody irritating at the same time.

Daisy shrugged as they stood outside in the rain, waiting for a taxi to pass by.

'My father has affairs all the time,' she said.

Kit looked at her. So she knew about all that. He couldn't tell whether this hurt her or not. She was looking pugnacious, like she didn't care. He thought her not caring was a thin veneer, nothing substantial.

'That's rough. I'm sorry,' he said.

Daisy let out a brittle laugh. 'Oh, it doesn't bother *me*,' she returned. 'I feel sorry for Ma, of course. He's always up here in London, hardly ever goes home. But then, it doesn't seem to really trouble her too much either. Sometimes I think she's glad of it, that it stops him bothering her. She'd rather hoe the long borders than get into bed with him, that's my feeling.'

Kit absorbed all this with interest. Hearing the intricacies of family life always fascinated him. Daisy's didn't sound like a happy family. Kit wondered if there *were* happy families. There must be. Somewhere out there.

The orange light of a taxi was emerging from the gloom. The rain was coming down harder, and Daisy, in her thin little Laura Ashley milkmaid's outfit, was starting to shiver.

'This isn't going to happen,' Kit told her more gently, hailing the taxi, which swerved into the kerb. 'Now go home.'

After that, he thought she'd got the message. But now, here she was again, waiting for him at the bar in Michael's place.

'Pleased to see me?' she asked with a grin.

'This has got to stop.'

'You bought me dinner, and I thought I'd reciprocate.'

Kit glanced at his watch. He was meeting up with Gilda out of town at eleven thirty.

'One dinner,' he relented. 'Then that's it. OK?'

They ate in the restaurant. She told him more about her family.

'Pa's in the Lords. Tell me about your folks.'

'Don't have any,' said Kit.

'What?' Daisy paused, a forkful of food halfway to her mouth.

'I don't have any family.'

'But you must.'

'Sorry. Nope.'

'But who brought you up . . . ?'

'I was brought up in a kids' home.'

'Oh God.' Daisy put down her fork. 'You poor thing.'

Kit shrugged. 'It wasn't so bad. Soon as I could, I got out, started earning.'

'No family at all . . .'

'None.' Kit gestured around him. 'My workmates are like a family, sort of. And Mr Ward, who owns this place. He's been real good to me.'

'I think I saw him earlier. There was this man, very handsome, middle-aged, everyone was being very polite around him.'

'Dark greyish hair? Grey eyes?'

'Yes. Very *penetrating* eyes. *Extremely* attractive. He was with a dark-haired woman, she was lovely.'

Kit nodded. Everyone knew that Michael Ward had a new squeeze, this career-lady Ruby Darke person he seemed to dote on. And why not? He'd been through a sad time, his wife Sheila dying of cancer. Having found his own slim slice of happiness with Gilda, Kit was glad that Michael had found a bit too.

Daisy chattered away as the meal progressed; and, true to her word, she picked up the tab at the end of it. They rose and left the restaurant, and he hoped she wouldn't move in for the goodbye kiss again, and spoil what had, despite his expectations, been a pleasant evening.

Daisy didn't. She was horribly disappointed, but Kit clearly didn't fancy her in the least; so she had to put up with it.

'Goodnight then,' she said, and put out a hand. 'It's been nice.'

'Yeah.' He took her hand, gave it the briefest, tiniest shake, then dropped it.

'She's very lucky, this whoever-she-is you're so devoted to.'

'I wouldn't go so far as to say *devoted*,' he smiled. But it was true. He was. It was an entirely new feeling for him. His stomach clenched with excitement just at the thought of seeing Gilda, tonight.

'She's lucky, anyway.'

Kit saw a cab approaching and raised his hand; but before the cab got there, a long black car swerved around it and screeched to a halt right beside them. The doors were flung open and three heavies got out and flung themselves at the couple. Kit, taken unawares, was forced into the car. And so, shrieking in shock, was Daisy.

90

'Just shut the fuck up,' said one of the huge bruisers when Daisy carried on screaming. He had black crew-cut hair and a big tanned face with small, mean features.

'I *said*, shut up,' he roared in her face.

Suddenly, Daisy was silent.

The man turned his attention to Kit. 'Tito ain't very happy with you. He wants a word.'

Kit's mouth went dry.

Tito.

Gilda.

Shit. Tito knew.

But they'd been so careful.

Daisy was crying now, terrified out of her wits.

'This is nothing to do with her,' said Kit. His heart was beating so hard it felt like it was going to come straight through his chest wall. 'She's nothing, just a stupid kid, let her go.'

'You don't want to be laying the law down here,' said the big black-haired one while his two companions sneered at Kit and eyed up Daisy with interest.

'She's a fucking nuisance, that's all,' said Kit. 'Gives me nothing but earache. Do me a favour, eh? Kick her out the bloody car.'

The black-haired one stared at Kit's face, smiling all the while. It wasn't a friendly smile. It was the smile of someone who holds all the aces. He reached around and tapped the driver on the shoulder.

The car stopped. The black-haired one nodded. One of the others flung open the door. Kit thought of going for it, trying to get out, to run, but he couldn't. They were half-sitting on him and there was a knife being shoved hard up against his ribs. One of the men grabbed Daisy by the arm. She set up a fresh shriek of fear as he tossed her out of the door. She landed in traffic, car horns blaring, brakes screeching as drivers swerved to avoid hitting her.

Daisy rolled over in the road, blinded by headlights. The impact of the fall from the car had jarred all the breath from her body. She lay there, winded, blinded, expecting at any moment that she was going to be hit, killed, finished.

She heard the car door slam shut; the engine revved hard and the car roared away. She opened her eyes and saw it shooting off into the distance. Sobbing in terror, she crawled to her knees. Another car roared towards her, then a red double-decker, headlights blazing. Not even knowing which direction she was going in, she scuttled aside, feeling her shoulder throb, feeling her knees stinging where the tarmac had scraped the skin away.

Somehow she reached the pavement and crouched there, shuddering, beside a lamp post.

'Stupid drunk, silly *bint*,' shouted a car driver from his open window, and roared onward.

The world spun. She grabbed the post and held on. Shit, she mustn't pass out. She took deep breaths, staggered to her feet, held on tight to the lamp post to stop herself from falling flat on her face again.

Everything hurt.

She looked around hazily, tried to get her bearings. She

saw the huge flashing multicoloured adverts all around her on the buildings. PLAYERS. GORDON'S GIN. LEMON HART. WRIGLEY'S. She saw the statue on the fountain in the centre. Eros. She was in Piccadilly Circus. She tottered back into the road as a taxi approached, its light like a beacon of hope in a world of sudden, shocking disaster.

She gave the driver her address. Her teeth were chattering now, she felt very strange indeed. 'And please . . . hurry.'

They took Kit to a room over Tito's club. They bundled him up the back stairs and into the big, grandly appointed room with its cosily roaring fire, sat him down in a Victorian nursing chair covered in gold-coloured velvet. They got out ropes. Kit surged to his feet, and they smacked him about until he sat down again. They tied him to the chair.

Kit groggily looked around the room, blood streaming from punch-cuts on his lips and nose, and it was only then that he saw Gilda, in the far corner.

'*Christ*,' he said aloud, unable to stop himself.

Gilda the beautiful, Gilda the chic and gold-laden, with her sea-green eyes and fabulous, fuckable body was beautiful no more. She was bundled up in the corner like a discarded rag doll, and even from some distance away, Kit could see that she was dead. Her throat was a ragged, open wound. But he could see – ah shit, he didn't *want* to see it, but he could see it anyway – that before the bastards had killed her, they had ruined her looks. Her nose had been slit, and her eyes, her beautiful eyes . . . they'd been dug out. All that was left were two bloody sockets. She was still wearing her gold lucky-charm bracelet. He could see the dark heart there, the one she had bought to remind her of him.

His stomach turned over and he had to look away or throw up with the horror of it. And now, the door was opening. And Tito Danieri was entering the room, looking at Kit tethered there; and he was smiling.

Daisy had paid off the cab, and staggered half-fainting, shaking like a leaf in a high wind, into Michael Ward's bar and restaurant. The bar was crowded, and she had to push her way in, force herself past bulky bodies. When the barman came near, she reached across and grabbed the front of his shirt. He looked at her, startled.

'Mr Ward! I have to see him right now!'

'I was here before her,' said a man next to her.

'It's about Kit!' she yelled, ignoring the man and directing her desperate pleas to the barman.

The barman looked at her white, deranged face. He moved to one side, Daisy still clinging on to the front of his shirt. He looked over her head. Daisy twisted round, and saw a young muscle-bound man with treacle-coloured hair and khaki-green eyes back there in front of a door. She let go of the barman's shirt and shot across the room, knocking over a trolley of desserts as she went.

'Sorry, sorry,' she muttered, stepping on trifle, nearly slipping, navigating her way on trembling legs around waiters and diners, heading for the man, the door, staggering, almost falling. She reached him.

'Miss?' Rob was looking at her curiously. She was very pretty, but she was obviously just another bloody drunk who couldn't take her booze and was out on a Saturday night playing havoc while people were trying to enjoy a quiet evening.

'I need to see Mr Ward, it's about Kit,' she said.

'Look, miss,' he started.

She could see it in his eyes. He thought she was spaced out on something. Maybe he had seen her here, with Kit. Maybe Kit had said to him what he had said to the men in the car. That she was a fucking nuisance, always sniffing around him. *Just a silly kid*, he'd said. That stung. She wasn't that at all. And she *had* to get help.

'Kit's in trouble,' she said urgently, hardly able to get her breath. 'Three men snatched us out on the street, they got us into a car . . . they threw me out . . . oh, Jesus, please believe me . . . please get Mr Ward, *please* . . . they've got Kit, they said. . .' She tried to remember what they'd said. About Kit upsetting someone. Couldn't remember the name. 'They said he'd crossed someone, they wanted a word.'

The name. Why couldn't she remember the name?

'Who?' asked the man.

I can't remember. 'Please let me see Mr Ward.'

'What's going on?'

The door had opened and it was him. It was Michael Ward, looking at the minder and then at her.

'She's saying Kit's in bother,' said Rob.

Michael was staring at Daisy, noting her bedraggled clothing and her bloodied knees.

'Bring her inside,' he said, and the minder ushered Daisy into the room behind the restaurant.

91

Kit knew he was going to die, and die bloody, here in these gracious surroundings. He thought with sick horror of Gilda, and what she must have suffered before death released her at last from the pain of it all. Now it was his turn.

Tito Danieri had come into the room, and his three heavies were standing around now, watching Kit, watching whatever was going to happen. Tito smiled down at him, and then looked across to where the dead body of his mistress lay.

'See, I don't like people poaching on my territory,' said Tito, as if that explained everything. 'What's mine is mine, I don't share with *anybody*, you got that?'

Kit said nothing.

Tito lunged at him, his eyes suddenly wild. He punched him hard across the face, once, twice, three times. Kit's head rung with the force of each blow. For a moment he thought he was about to black out. And that would be good. Maybe that would be the best thing that could happen to him. He could feel blood seeping from his lower lip where Tito's fist had broken the skin.

Now Tito hovered over him, breathing heavily, not smiling any more. His lips were pulled back in a snarl and his eyes snapped with malice.

'You think you're clever, touching that on the sly?' Tito

stabbed a finger towards the corpse in the corner. 'You got a lot to learn, boy. A *lot*. And I'm about to teach you.'

Tito walked away from Kit. He picked up a glass of amber-coloured liquid. Whisky, or brandy. Kit would have *killed*, right now, for a drink. Something to take the sting off what was to come. Tito threw the booze back in one hit, and replaced the empty glass on a small occasional table. Then he moved over to the fire. Kit's eyes followed him. It was only then that he noticed the poker, embedded deep in the hot coals in the hearth.

It was a plain, functional room, the room behind Michael's restaurant. Small, too. With Michael, Daisy and the minder in it, there was not much room left. But there was another occupant in the room, a tall slim exotic-looking woman with upswept black hair. She was staring at Daisy, then glancing at Michael.

'What's happening?' she asked anxiously.

'Kit's in trouble,' Daisy blurted out on a sob. 'Three men have snatched him.'

'Where are they taking him?' asked Michael, ushering Daisy quickly into a chair as she looked as if she was about to collapse to the floor.

'I don't *know*,' she wailed.

'Did they say anything? Give any clue?' he persisted.

'Michael, she's in a terrible state,' said the woman. 'Take it easy.'

'Ruby, keep out of this,' said Michael sharply. He crouched down in front of Daisy and looked up at her mascara- and sweat-smeared face. 'They must have said something. Think, sweetheart. Did they?'

Daisy opened her eyes wide. 'Tito,' she said.

'Tito? Tito Danieri?' asked Michael.

'That's it! He was upset with Kit. He wanted a word.'

'Shit,' said Michael, and stood up. He looked at the heavy. 'Rob. Get Eric, get Jack, let's get over there.'

'Who is this Tito person?' asked Ruby as the heavy hurried from the room. Her eyes were fastened upon Daisy. It was her all right. Daisy Bray. Her beautiful daughter. Scraped and bloodied and in deep distress. Everything in Ruby cried out to her to run to Daisy, to take the hurt away. But she had to stand here, act normally.

'He's not someone you'd want to cross,' said Michael, grabbing his jacket from the back of the chair behind the desk and shrugging into it. 'Look after her,' he said to Ruby, and left the room.

Ruby looked at Daisy, who had dissolved into tears.

'I thought they were going to kill us,' she managed to blurt out in between sobs.

'Michael will sort it out,' said Ruby, standing there ramrod-straight. She was staring at Daisy's knees, scraped red-raw. She swallowed hard and went to the filing cabinets behind the desk and took down the first-aid box. She stepped around the desk and went to where Daisy huddled on the chair, and opened the box and found cotton wool and a bottle of iodine. She wanted to hug Daisy hard, to reassure her, but instead she said: 'This might sting a little bit,' and started dabbing at the grazes.

Daisy sat there, biting her lip, watching the dark-haired woman with the gentle hands working on her abraded flesh, and gradually she began to feel a little calmer.

92

Tito was slipping the poker out of the fire. Kit could see the bottom four inches of it glowing, white-hot, as Tito turned with it in his hand. Now Tito was smiling at him, his expression almost gentle, as he crossed the room.

'You right-handed or left?' asked Tito.

Damage limitation. 'Left,' he lied, heart hammering. The one thing – the *only* thing – that scared him shitless, was the prospect of burning, of fire touching his skin.

'They call that sinister in Latin, did you know that? Dexter's right, sinister's left. Sinister as in dark, untrustworthy, not quite *right*. And that's you, isn't it, you little shit? Creeping around behind a man's back and taking what's his.'

Kit worked some spit into his mouth and managed to speak. 'Takes two,' he said.

'Yeah, well, we've *done* all that.' Tito tipped his head to the left, indicating the crumpled corpse that was Gilda. 'And *that's* not going to be happening again, is it? Which just leaves you. So hold out your left hand, you cunt. It's going to be a long night for you.'

Kit's fists were clenched. He looked at Tito with dumb insolence.

'Open his hand out,' said Tito, and they all piled in, Kit was powerless to stop them. They held his hand out, palm up. Tito moved in with the poker, and Kit could *feel* the heat of the damned thing where he sat.

Delicately, almost lovingly, Tito laid the white-hot tip onto the flesh of Kit's palm.

Kit thought he was going to pass out. The agony was almost unbearable. He was panting, unable to help himself. Tito held the poker there for what felt like hours, but it was seconds, just seconds.

Then the poker lifted, and it felt to Kit that half his skin had lifted with it. His hand throbbed hotly, sending dancing waves of pain shimmering up his arm. He gulped, swallowed, heaved in a mouthful of air. Sweat had broken out all over his body, and now the nausea followed. He looked at his hand. It was already starting to blister. His head drooped. He blinked. His crotch was wet. Involuntarily, humiliatingly, he'd pissed himself.

'Only I don't believe you're left-handed,' Tito was saying conversationally. 'What would I say, in this situation? The same as what *you've* just said. I'd save my good hand. So let's get started on the right one, shall we? Before we move on to other things.'

The heavies piled in, exposing his right palm just as they'd done his left. Tito moved in, grinning as Kit thrashed about in the chair, unable to stop any of this happening.

'No good fighting,' said Tito. 'You've asked for this, boy, and now you're going to get it.'

The poker came down against Kit's cringing skin and this time Tito was in no hurry to lift it up. This time he yelled out with the pain. Couldn't help it.

The smell was bad. The scent of his own cooked flesh filled his nostrils as Tito pressed the thing down hard onto his palm. It smoked, and it sizzled.

Jesus.

Kit was breathing hard, like he'd just run a mile. Both hands were a sea of agony now. Pain seized him, hugged him like a lover.

At last, Tito raised the poker. Smiled right into Kit's sweat-stinging, watering eyes.

'Now it gets even more interesting,' he said. He looked at a small bottle on the table. Kit's eyes followed Tito's.

Lighter fuel.

Tito walked over, picked it up. Sauntered back to Kit. Unsnapped the bottle and held it above Kit's head.

I don't want to burn, thought Kit. *Oh, shit no. Please don't let me burn.*

There was a knock on the door, and another heavy slipped inside.

Kit was nearly out of it. Almost fainting, his head rolling around like a punch-drunk boxer's.

'Tito,' said the heavy. Tito's hand stopped moving. He paused. 'Ward's shown up.'

Michael was waiting in the club below. Tito joined him at the bar.

'Give Mr Ward a drink,' he said to the barman, slapping Michael warmly on the back in greeting. 'What is it, Michael? Whisky?'

'Not for me,' said Michael with a calm smile. 'I've come for a boy of mine. Kit Miller.'

'Ah.' Tito signalled for the barman to set him up a tumbler of Southern Comfort. 'Now, Michael, I'll be straight with you. I've had trouble with that little cunt. He's been fiddling around with Gilda – you know Gilda.'

Michael nodded, thinking, *Kit you fucking fool.* 'Of course.'

'You won't any more. I don't do sloppy seconds.' Tito drank down his whisky in one hit.

'He's young and he's foolish,' said Michael. 'However, I

don't want any harm coming to him. We can come to some arrangement over this.'

'Only my thinking is, I'm going to *re*arrange his face, Michael. I'm sure you understand.'

'I do. Absolutely. But he's a valuable man to have around and I don't want to lose him.'

'I can appreciate that,' said Tito.

'So what can we do here? Come on, Tito. Be the bigger man, yes? What can I offer you in return for your leniency in this matter?'

Tito blew out his cheeks. 'I dunno . . .'

'Come on, Tito. We're businessmen. We work together. And we have other connections too, don't we? *Deeper* connections. I'd hate for us to fall out over this – it's nothing. So come on. Name your price.'

Michael was mad at him, Kit understood that much. He also understood that he was lucky to be breathing as Tito's thugs untied him and hustled him tripping and stumbling down the stairs and out into a car. Michael was already in the back, one of his boys at the wheel.

'What are you, a fucking idiot?' Michael was smoking furiously. 'I expected better of you.'

Kit felt bad that he had let Michael down. But right now he was living in a world of hurt. Both hands were blistering and the pain was beyond belief. He'd be no use to anyone for quite a while. He thought of Gilda, lying there disfigured and dead. He'd loved her, *really* loved her. And he had failed to protect her from this.

That *fuck* Tito.

'You got nothing to say for yourself?' asked Michael.

'I'm going to kill that bastard,' said Kit.

Michael slapped him once, very hard, across the face.

'You say anything else stupid like that and I'll kill *you*,' he said, his eyes like flint. 'You got off lightly. You deserved to be pulled up, you behaved like a *cunt*. You cost me dear. I've had to hand over a lot of wedge to pull your sorry arse out of this shit. Now don't start coming over all Magnificent Seven with me, because I'm telling you, do that and you'll have more than Tito and his boys to deal with. You clear on that?'

Kit swallowed and nodded. 'Daisy tip you off?' he asked at last.

'She saved your arse big time.'

Kit was shaking his head. 'He killed her. He killed Gilda.'

Michael was silent for a long moment. 'Just be thankful you didn't join her.'

But Kit kept thinking of her, his beautiful Gilda, crumpled like a disused toy in the corner of the room. His hands hurt like fuck and his pride was smashed. He'd wet himself in terror, like a little kid. His hatred for Tito Danieri knew no bounds.

He was going to get even, sooner or later, whatever Michael said.

He promised himself that much.

93

Vanessa had brought to Cornelius's attention that their daughter was keeping company with an unsuitable young man. He was coloured – that was bad enough. Cornelius put out a few feelers and soon discovered that the man was a thug by the name of Kit Miller, and he had heard from one of his underworld contacts that his old comrade Tito had caught his girl Gilda cheating with Kit. He questioned Tito about it, but found him surprisingly close-mouthed.

Tito only shrugged. 'These things happen. The incident passed off, and there are plenty more girls.'

The incident passed off.

Cornelius didn't think the incident would have passed off *quite* that easily. He knew Tito, and he'd seen Gilda with him on many occasions. The woman was beautiful, golden, a prize – a cut above the usual gangster groupies who swarmed around men like him.

But Cornelius didn't continue with the questions; he knew better. Tito could go off into spectacular bursts of temper at a moment's notice. He couldn't imagine that Tito would have taken the news of his mistress's infidelity lying down.

And Kit Miller had bandaged hands. Cornelius had him watched discreetly as he moved around town. His hands were bandaged for over a month; after that, the wraps came off.

'Looks like his palms have been burned,' said Cornelius's informant.

'I want to know more about him,' said Cornelius to his man, and back came the information that Kit Miller had come out of a children's home and started throwing his weight about on the streets of the East End, before working for Michael Ward – another powerful gang lord who might or might not have some business links to Tito – and quickly progressing up the ranks until he was head of breakers.

'They break legs,' said his informant, a weedy little man who ran an investigation agency working on the shadier borders of government. 'Hence, breakers. But he's gone on to greater things, apparently. Ward trusts him. Miller's his number one man.'

Nothing would get Vanessa up to town these days, and Cornelius rarely bothered to go home at weekends any more, preferring to stay in a cottage he rented on the wilds of the windy Kent coast. But this particular weekend he thought the situation with Daisy was serious enough to warrant a visit to Brayfield.

He still loved the place; adored it. Passing by the gate-house, he thought of his beloved mother, long gone now. Every day he missed her sound common sense and ever-indulgent love. The gatehouse had stood empty since her passing.

Perhaps now would be the time to gift it to Daisy, to give her the feeling of a stake in the place, her own home, of course, but conveniently out of London and – better still, because Daisy was a loose cannon and he knew it – within her mother's eyeline.

Vanessa was waiting for him in the gold-and-eggshell-blue morning room with the French windows that led out onto the garden. It was exquisite out there, the lawns manicured, the long borders overflowing with an artfully themed blend of pinks, mauves and whites. Vanessa poured all her love into that garden, and it showed. He went to where she sat on the love seat, seed catalogues spread out all around her.

'Oh – hello, darling,' she said, looking distracted as he bent to kiss her cheek.

'How are you?' he asked. It was like looking at a stranger. Once, he knew he had loved this woman. But there had never been a strong physical bond between them. For such an intensely sexual man as him, that had rung the relationship's death knell. The sad truth was, her sex drive had always been low; and his was very high indeed, even in middle age.

'I'm fine,' she said, and he could see that she was having to tear her eyes from the catalogues, having to wrench her mind from the garden and the following season. 'You're here about Daisy?'

Cornelius nodded and told her all that his contacts had told him.

Vanessa listened, thin-lipped, while he spoke.

'What are we going to do?' she asked when he finished speaking. 'I'm worried about her. I don't know what she's going to do next.'

'I think it's best we give her a project. Distract her. I thought Mama's gatehouse.'

'But will she leave London? What if she's in love with this . . . common awful person, this thug Kit Miller?'

'Daisy may be a bit wild, but she's not stupid. There's no future in it. He could never keep her in the manner she is accustomed to. And that would finish it before it started. She's used to a certain level and although she may be enjoying a touch of slumming now, it won't last.'

'You sound very sure,' said Vanessa doubtfully.

'I know Daisy. Please – just forget it.'

94

Richard Dorley was on the Rotherhithe ferry when it occurred to him that he was being watched. Twice before, he had felt that when he left his digs he was being followed.

Now, he could see two men standing by the rail, chatting. Every so often, one or other of them would lift his head and look straight at Richard. He knew he wasn't imagining it.

He had hoped to have heard from that newshound Sammy Bell by now, and he was just killing time. A thick mist rose off the river this morning, foghorns calling mournfully. The sun was a tiny butter-yellow dot high up in a pall of grey cloud. He could see his breath in front of his face. Autumn was coming and still he had nothing to tell his wife. He was killing time, riding the ferry, taking in the sights and smells of the river.

But now . . . these two.

They *were* watching him.

They were going to mug him, that was it. Take his money. This was a big city, he knew things like this could happen. They'd rough him up, snatch his wallet. He felt a stab of fear as one of the men glanced at him. The man's face was expressionless, like a statue's: there was no feeling there. No mercy.

The ferry docked and Richard hurried down the walkway, shaking, his legs unsteady, trying to get some distance between him and them. He walked as fast as he could, head down, not daring to look back, carefully keeping among the bustling crowds. Suddenly, the two men were walking on either side of him.

'*Hello*, Tony,' said the bulkier one loudly, smiling, grabbing his arm.

'We ain't seen you in ages,' said the other.

'Christ, we ain't seen you in *years*, you old dog,' said the bulky one.

Richard stiffened.

'Keep walking,' hissed the smaller one close by his ear, and he felt something – *Oh, Jesus, was that a knife?* – pressing into his side.

He kept walking. Didn't know what else to do. The crowd was thinning around them. He was too afraid to cry out for help. They hustled him along, chatting away as if he was an old acquaintance.

'Let's get a drink, shall we?' said the bigger one, and suddenly they were peeling off, away from the crowds, and then they were in an alley, restaurant businesses backing onto it, big industrial-sized bins lining it, huge silver chimneys already exhaling steam into the still morning air.

'Look,' started Richard.

Suddenly they were hitting him. He tried to run then, but they knocked him over and he fell to the ground, jarring all the breath out of his body. He curled into a ball on the cobbles and then they started kicking him. The pain was monstrous, never-ending.

Richard thought with startling clarity: *I'm going to die here*.

His whole body throbbed with pain. A steel-capped boot struck his jaw and he felt a distinct *snap*. A howling crescendo of agony enveloped his head.

'No . . . please . . .' he groaned, hardly able to get the words out.

But it went on. And on.

Finally he lay there, bloody, broken: finished. Too hurt even to plead for mercy. Consciousness was flickering in and out like a faulty light switch. He was retching weakly.

The big one grabbed his hair, jerked his head up. It felt like his head was exploding. He saw a face swimming in front of his eyes.

'Now listen,' said the man. 'You drop this, OK? You been bothering a friend of ours, you know what I mean?'

Richard nodded faintly. Couldn't speak. Couldn't *believe* this was happening to him.

'You know.' The man was nodding too. 'So let it go, right? Be a good boy. Walk away, while you still got legs to walk with. Understood?'

'Please . . .' Richard muttered. There was blood stinging his eyes, and he could taste it. His whole torso was afire. It was agony.

'It stops here,' said the man. 'You got it?'

'I got it,' panted Richard, and passed out.

95

It was a long hard haul but eventually they moved Charlie to Acklington, an old RAF Base where Hussein of Jordan had trained to be a pilot. It was a semi-open prison in Northumberland and he was still graded as Category C; no longer seen as an escape risk, no longer so readily inclined to violence.

For Charlie it was a revelation. He had freedom for the first time within Acklington's walls. Authority was relaxed. There were no dog patrols, no walls, only a single wire fence. Charlie was given work in the prison canteen, but he preferred to be outdoors so applied for work in the gardens and was soon given a try.

All the while, he was thinking about parole. Every time he was given his F75 – an assessment of suitability for release and behaviour in prison – he answered honestly. He'd done his time well, kept his head down. There had been a couple of minor rucks, and his run-in with John Corah, but overall he'd behaved himself, worked hard, passed a couple of GCE exams in maths and geography, shown that he could become a good citizen once more.

'Suppose someone shoved you in a bus queue,' came the question as one day he stood before the board. 'What would you do?'

Charlie, spivved up to the nines, his thin wiry hair combed, his face washed, his prison garb neat and clean and freshly pressed, looked around at the board. The governor was there, and a doctor, a psychiatrist, an education officer, welfare officer, works instructor and prison officer, plus the probation officer, Mrs Mason, who had been his staunch supporter over his last couple of years inside.

'I wouldn't shove them back,' he said, and smiled slightly. 'I'd value my freedom too much for that.'

He knew what they wanted to hear. He knew this was an elaborate game, like snakes and ladders. Answer correctly, toe the line, be nice, and you might ascend the ladder to freedom. Say something wrong, and you'd slide down the snake and be stuck in this pesthole until you died.

'Where will you live?' prompted Mrs Mason, her eyes saying, *Go on*.

They'd discussed this before; she'd guided him through the sort of things they'd be asking and told him they'd be very concerned about where he would live, what he was going to do with himself, once released.

'I have close family,' he said. 'They'll put me up until I can find my feet.'

Joe had continued to visit him inside. Good old Joe. The screws and even the governor knew that he had a brother. He never mentioned his sister. After that single visit, Ruby hadn't come near, the cow.

It took nearly a year. The board recommended Charlie to the Local Review Committee, which would be made up of the entire review panel who had sat before, plus a magistrate, a judge, a Home Office official and a high-ranking police officer.

That obstacle surmounted, Charlie's case was recommended to the Joint Committee. It ruled in his favour, and then the whole thing was assessed again by the Parole Board.

Finally, a recommendation was made to the Home Secretary.

In the end, Charlie was left feeling depressed by the length and intricacy of the process. He became withdrawn, certain that it wouldn't work, that he'd end his days inside. The medics gave him some pills. Six months dragged by, then another six. Then, just before Christmas, he was called into the governor's office. A welfare officer and his probation officer were there.

They were all smiling at Charlie.

The governor handed him a piece of paper.

On it was his release date: 1 June of the following year.

Charlie didn't know whether to laugh, or cry.

He was getting out. At last.

And when he *did,* God help that bitch sister of his.

BOOK THREE

96

1971

At ten past nine on 1 June Charlie was called down to the office after a sleepless night to sign for his bank book and for the few possessions he'd had when he'd been arrested all that long time ago – his clothes, a little cash, comb, a bunch of keys, some photos, an old watch and chain, and Rachel's hair slide.

He dumped the old clothes straight in the bin – he'd been out of the hostel with his probation officer already, and was wearing new. The assistant governor came down and told him that he had to report to his probation officer today, without fail. He had signed his lifer's licence. When the assistant governor had gone, he sat on his bed and looked at the hair slide, seeing her all over again – Rachel Tranter, the only woman he'd ever loved, and lost so brutally during the war.

Now he had only Joe and Betsy to rely on; they'd agreed to take him in. And he had a score to settle.

'That's not a return ticket, I hope?' the prison officer joked with him as he went to walk out the door of Maidstone with his train ticket in his hand.

'Not effing likely,' said Charlie, and the PO laughed.

Charlie walked down County Road to Maidstone East station, and waited for the train that would take him back to his old life.

97

It was all progressing fine at Ruby's latest London project. Soon there would be another Darkes department store open for business. The main shell of the building was up and now the builders had almost finished excavating the spoil to lay the foundations for the warehouse at the back of the store. Ruby was proudly showing Vi around the place.

'I'm not wearing a hard hat, it will *ruin* my hair,' said Vi when Ruby met her at the polythene-sheeted entrance clutching two of them.

Ruby had to smile. Vi was still as chic as a fashion plate, her attire faultless, her hair exquisitely cut and vividly coloured. Her nails were long and painted scarlet, to match her lipstick. Her eyes were rimmed with kohl. Vi moved, as always, in a cloud of Devon Violets.

Ruby felt a surge of real affection for her old friend, and compassion too. She knew that the young 'companions' Vi had enjoyed so much over the years were getting thin on the ground now. Yes, she was ridiculously wealthy; but for many of those hard-hearted young stallions who'd once feted her, she was now – quite simply – too *old*.

'Put it on. It's for safety,' insisted Ruby. Grumbling, Vi did so. Ruby led the way through the windy, echoing building's emerging skeleton, pointing out to Vi what would go where.

'Ground floor's for the food hall, plus women's, children's, and men's clothing.' Ruby pointed upward. There were staircases, but as yet no escalators. 'First floor, that's home furnishings, china, bedding, that sort of thing. Second floor, the offices.'

Vi was looking around, nodding.

'What do you think?' asked Ruby when she didn't speak.

'What I *think* is you've come a bloody long way from an East End corner shop.'

Ruby's smile widened. 'Do you think it's OK for Lady Albemarle to have a friend who's in trade?'

'More than OK,' said Vi, and gave Ruby a quick, impulsive hug.

Daisy met Kit for dinner. It was almost a year since the night when Tito had burnt him, and his hands were better. There were scars, but they would fade. The ones that showed, anyway. He still mourned Gilda. He still wanted to slit Tito's throat.

Since that horrible night, every time he saw Daisy she made him spread out his hands so she could look at the damage.

'Oh God,' she said. 'It still looks so bad.'

'It's nothing.' Kit retracted his hands. 'I'm sorry you got involved, that's all.'

'Well, if I hadn't, you'd have been in even bigger trouble than you were.'

'You're right.' Kit hadn't filled Daisy in on the finer details of what happened that night. He'd told her it had been a misunderstanding over a woman, and that Mr Ward had sorted it. That was all she needed to know.

But he couldn't get Gilda and her awful fate out of his head. It was *his* fault she'd died, he was weighed down with guilt. And one day, he would have his revenge on Tito. But for now, he was back at work, heading up Michael's workforce as usual, and tomorrow he would resume what he had been looking into for Mr Ward before the ruck – this kid that Charlie Darke had been trying to dispose of during the war. Actually, he had no real idea how to proceed with that. So he was going to retrace his steps, see if he'd missed anything.

As they sat down at the table and ordered their starters, Daisy was watching Kit closely. The waiter poured the wine: Kit tasted it, nodded his approval. He was so unreadable, but there was some indefinable *something* about him that made her keep coming back. All right, he wasn't interested in her. He had this strange hang-up about older women. But if she was here enough, close enough, surely one of these days he'd weaken and accept that they belonged together?

She raised her glass. 'To us, then. What a team, eh?'

'Hmph,' said Kit, but he raised his glass and obligingly clinked it against hers.

98

The first chance he got, Charlie peeked in Betsy's address book while she was out down the shops, and found Ruby's address in there, as he'd expected he would.

Marlow, for fuck's sake. Stockbroker country. Here he was, on his uppers, and sodding Ruby was out there living the high life. He told Joe he was going to catch up with some of the old boys on the manor, and set off to see his little sis.

When he arrived, he stood at the bottom of the drive for a long while, looking up at the beautiful Victorian villa she'd bought herself while *he* had been rotting away inside.

That *bitch*.

He walked up the drive and knocked on the door. Half-expecting a servant to answer, he was surprised when Ruby herself opened it. She was just the same. Dark. Pretty. She was wearing jeans and a light grey sweatshirt. Her half-smile died when she saw who had come knocking.

'Christ – Charlie!'

Instantly, Ruby tried to shut the door in his face, but he put all his weight against it and she staggered back. He shouldered his way inside, and shut the door behind him and leaned back against it; grinning.

'Now is that any way to greet your long-lost brother?' he laughed.

Ruby moved away from him. For one heart-stopping, sick-making moment, she had thought it was *Dad* standing there on the step. But no, it was Charlie. He'd aged even more since that time she'd visited him in prison.

'What the hell do you want?' she demanded shakily.

Joe had told her Charlie was getting out. But she had *expressly* told Joe not to ever give Charlie her address, and he had sworn he wouldn't.

Now here he was.

The bastard.

She couldn't forget all that he'd done to her. Tormented her with Dad in her youth. Laughed at her distress over his callous disposal of her son. She couldn't forget. And she *certainly* couldn't forgive.

'I'll tell you what I want,' said Charlie, approaching her. 'I want to know how you – my *sister* – could have got me done over in the nick.'

'What . . . ?' Dry-mouthed, Ruby backed away until she hit the richly carved wooden newel post of the stairs.

'You going to deny it? Don't bother. All those questions about the kid? It *had* to be you.'

'It wasn't her,' said a male voice from the top of the stairs.

Charlie looked up in surprise. He'd thought she was alone. But there was a man coming down the stairs; dark-grey hair, granite-hard eyes.

'Who the f—' started Charlie.

Then he saw the pistol in the man's hand.

'It was me who had you done over. I'm Michael Ward,' said Michael as he reached the bottom of the stairs. He pushed Ruby out of harm's way and kept the gun aimed steadily at Charlie's midriff. 'And you're Charlie Darke, right? And you think you can push your way in here and throw your weight about? Is that it?'

Michael drew closer to Charlie, who had gone pale, his eyes fastened to the gun.

'Come on, don't get the wrong idea, I don't want no trouble,' said Charlie, putting his hands up, a sickly smile playing on his lips.

'Don't you?' Michael's eyes were cold as flint. 'Then you're going the wrong fucking way about it. Get the fuck out that door, you cunt, or I swear I'll spatter what little guts you have all over this hall.'

'I'm going, all right?' Charlie backed up and opened the door and dashed outside.

'Good,' said Michael.

Michael moved forward and looked out at Charlie running away down the driveway. He stayed there for long, thoughtful moments.

'Do you think he'll stay away?' he asked as Ruby joined him at the door. She was shivering, like she was cold all of a sudden.

Ruby gulped. 'Charlie? No. I don't.'

Michael nodded slowly, then closed the door and took Ruby in his arms.

99

Kit stopped off in Bond Street and made a small purchase, then he drove the Bentley out to High Firs again. He didn't think he *had* missed anything, but he owed Mr Ward big time, and if Michael wanted this kid found, then found he would be. He didn't take Rob with him; Rob had no patience with the old folks, and his presence last time had only proved a distraction.

This time, Jennifer Phelps was not in the conservatory. She was sitting at the window in her pink-painted bedroom. Kit stood for several seconds in the doorway, unseen by Jennifer. She was staring at the window, but the seal had gone in the double-glazing and the glass had turned opaque. She was staring, in effect, at nothing.

Jesus, is this a good idea? he wondered.

He stepped around her chair. Her eyes raised and met his, her head bobbing on her thin neck like a marionette's. 'Oh!' she said. 'It's you.'

'You remember,' said Kit.

''Course I do.' The implication that she might not seemed to annoy her. Kit placed a rectangular sparkly-pink bag on top of the open magazine on her blanketed lap. She stared at it.

'Present for you,' he said, sitting down on the nearby bed.

'Oh.' Jennifer reached inside the bag and pulled out a

rigid A4-sized item covered in red leather. Looking bemused, she opened it out. Inside, it was lined with gold velvet and fitted out with pockets holding an assortment of pens, lined writing paper, notepads, envelopes and stamps.

'For writing your poems,' he said. 'Or letters. Or whatever you want.'

Her crabbed and trembling hands moved over the thing, stroking the plush gold nap of the fabric. She looked over at Kit. 'Thank you, young man. What a kind thought. I've been reading my books. Did you find the baby?'

'You remembered that too.' Kit took a breath. 'Do you remember anything else about that night? You found the baby at your brother's house . . .'

'Hugh was dead,' said Jennifer, her sparse brows folding into furrows.

'That's right. And the baby was lying at his feet . . .'

'Yes, that was it.'

'What then? Can you tell me again?'

'Oh! Well, I got the policeman . . .'

'The police reservist.'

'That's the one. And he was going to take the baby to the hospital in the ambulance, with Hugh – poor Hugh – but I didn't think that was right. We had an argument about it. I was very upset. I used the B-word.' Jennifer's mouth formed a dazzling grin, as if her own devilment amazed her. 'A baby, in with a corpse? That's not right.'

Kit's attention sharpened at that. The last time he called, she said that the baby had been taken to a hospital.

'So – wait up – you're telling me the baby *wasn't* taken to the hospital?'

'Yes, he was. The other place.'

'What other place?'

'The *hospital.*' Jennifer was looking at him with exasperation in her eyes. 'The hospital place, the home. *You* know.'

'A home? What, you mean, a children's home?'

'That's right. We took the baby there.'

'What, you and the reservist? The policeman?'

'The reservist took the child, he said that was where he was going to take him. To the children's home.'

Kit's heart was in his throat. She called magazines 'her books' and she called a children's home a hospital. This was crazy. And probably hopeless.

'Which children's home?' he asked.

'Oh, I don't know about that, dear. Only that it was in Fulham, that's all he said.'

'What did he say? Exactly?'

'Lord, I don't know. Something like "I'll take the poor little blighter over to the Fulham place, they'll look after him."'

100

'I don't like having him here,' said Betsy. She and Joe were in the kitchen. The dishwasher had broken down, the repairman was coming next bloody Christmas or sometime next *century*. Betsy was in a mood, slinging dirty plates into the sink with quick, irritated movements.

Joe let out a sigh. They'd *had* all this out several times before, when it became certain that Charlie was getting out soon. Well, now he *was* out, and he was staying with Joe and Betsy. They had enough room for one guest, and that guest was his *brother*, for Chrissakes, couldn't Betsy cut the poor sod a bit of slack?

'I don't like him being around Nadine and Billy,' continued Betsy when he didn't answer.

Joe didn't have much to say about *that*, either. Nadine was a pudgy, truculent six-year-old kid and little Billy was sunny-natured and quick moving. They were normal and they seemed happy. Neither of them appeared to have the slightest problem with their Uncle Charlie staying here.

'He's a jailbird, they don't ever change,' said Betsy, tugging on rubber gloves to preserve her manicure.

Joe leaned against the worktop and looked at her as she ponced around the kitchen. It was brand new, beautifully appointed. A huge fridge/freezer, enough cupboards to stock up for a siege, and yes, a bloody dishwasher – even if the damned thing *had* broken down. It was all new, the latest of many additions to the house. The place was redecorated top-to-toe once a year, and new furnishings were installed. Never second-hand, always new to replace the old stuff. He knew he over-indulged Betsy, he *knew* she was a high-maintenance pain in the arse, but she was his old lady and so he tried to give her everything she wanted.

Not that anything ever seemed quite good enough for her. Oh no. Her sister was Lady Albemarle, and that meant they were now invited to all sorts of black-tie do's. In Betsy's eyes, that meant she had to *compete* with the landed gentry. Which was, of course, impossible. So she was always dissatisfied, and it all somehow got to be Joe's fault. And now this. Charlie's arrival, his status as a bad boy, an undesirable (and shit, wasn't that what Joe was himself, only he'd had the good fortune not to go down for it?) and an embarrassment.

'Look,' said Joe, trying to find the right words so she didn't go off on one.

'Look *what*?' asked Betsy, plunging her gloved hands into the soap suds and crashing plates and cutlery about. 'Do you think it's right, a man like that around our kids?'

'Charlie loves the bones of our Billy and Nadine.'

'I don't care. He's a convicted criminal.'

Now Joe was starting to get mad. 'Hey, *I'm* a criminal if it comes down to it.'

'No you're not.' Betsy's expression was stubborn.

'Fuck me, girl, look around you,' snapped Joe. 'You're living in the lap of luxury, you wear dresses at fifty quid a pop, d'you think I got all this with a book of Green Shield stamps or something?'

'It's a nice house, I grant you,' she said, slapping a plate onto the draining board so hard that suds flew up and bubbles formed, floating in the air between them. 'And my clothes are fine, but they're not *couture*.'

'Oh thank *you* Lady Muck. I'll be sure to call in some fag designer next time you get kitted out for another one of these fucking do's we have to keep going to.'

Betsy's cheeks flared with angry colour. 'Don't take that tone with me, Joe Darke. And the house *could* be bigger. Joe, are you *sure* . . . ?'

'Now *don't* start again. You know it's no bloody good.'

She was going to harp on about the stash again. She was a bloody lunatic. His part of the Post Office robbery money! Years back, he'd taken some of it for a deposit on this house, and it had scared him witless doing that. He'd grabbed a bit of the loot and scarpered. Then he started thinking about Chewy, Stevie and Ben, what the fuck had happened to them? *Then* he'd nearly shat himself worrying about using such old money. Would someone suspect? Would the bank tell the police? Had the notes somehow been marked? For weeks he was creased up with anxiety.

But it had all been OK. And after that, he'd known it was pointless to touch the stash again. Years had gone by, decimalization had been introduced, and the old notes would now be impossible to use without alarm bells ringing loud and clear.

Joe was happy with what he had. With this house. With Betsy – even if she was a mouthy cow. And with his takings from the arcades, shops, restaurants and brothels on his manor. He wasn't greedy. Not like Bets, who wanted to live like her sister Vi – and never would.

'Oh, Joe . . .' said Betsy, turning to him with a pleading face and a wheedling tone of voice.

Joe thumped the worktop with his fist. Betsy jumped.

'Jesus, Bets, I've told you a thousand times, no. It ain't usable and there's no way to make it so. You're doing all right, for God's sake. This house has got six bedrooms and a double garage. It's *massive*. You ought to remember where you came from, girl. A rotten little two-up two-down with iffy wiring and a stinking privy in the backyard.'

Betsy's face hardened.

'Yes, thank you *very* much, Joe, you don't have to spell all that out to me yet again.' Betsy slapped knives onto the draining board and sloshed the water out of the bowl into the sink. She grabbed a tea towel and dried her rubber gloves, watching him with hostile eyes. 'I'm just saying, that's all. He slopes around the place all day unshaven. He *looks* like a con. And I don't like it.'

'Well, thanks for that, Betsy,' said Charlie, appearing in the kitchen doorway.

Betsy's cheeks flushed deep red but, despite her embarrassment, she held Charlie's gaze steadily. The state of him! Once he had been so gorgeous, a true leader of men. Now stir had made a wreck of him. She couldn't even recognize the Charlie she had once known, the Charlie she had very nearly married.

Her first, her only real love, had been Charlie. And the shaming part – the part Joe would never know – was that she had still harboured a passion for him through all the years he was inside. She knew she had settled for second best with Joe. Joe had never been exciting, the way Charlie was.

But now it was like it had all been a cruel illusion and she felt cheated and angry. Charlie was nothing to lust over. He was old, belligerent, bleary-eyed, unwashed and unshaven. Yeah, a wreck.

'What a cow you turned out to be,' said Charlie.

'Hey!' snapped Joe. Charlie was right, but this was his old woman. He couldn't have her bad-mouthed by anyone, not even his older brother.

'You want to be careful,' said Betsy, chucking the rubber gloves onto the draining board. 'One word from me about your behaviour, and your probation officer'll go mental. You could end up back inside.'

'My *behaviour*?' Charlie's face twisted with disbelief. He hated being beholden like this, but they were his family and he ought to be made welcome by them, oughtn't he?

Joe held up a placatory hand. 'She didn't mean that,' he told Charlie hurriedly. 'We'd never grass up anyone, *would* we, Betsy love?'

Betsy looked at the pair of them. She didn't want to upset Joe, but she hated having Charlie anywhere near her. Just seeing him reminded her that once they had been lovers, and she was so much better than that now. Having him here reminded her of how shabbily he had treated her all those years back, practically raping her one minute and then dithering over whether or not to do the decent thing by her. She'd *loved* the bastard, and in the end it had all come to nothing; she'd had to settle for dull, predictable Joe instead. Now she wanted to forget all about Charlie. But she couldn't. Day after day, he was in her face.

'No,' she said at last. 'I wouldn't grass. Of course not. It's just . . .'

'It's just that you don't want me here,' finished Charlie.

'No . . .' said Joe.

'It's OK,' said Charlie. 'Maybe I'll go and stay with little Ruby for a while, who knows?'

Despite the scare Michael Ward had given him, the idea tickled him. Maybe he would. So what if Ward had warned him off? He couldn't watch her *all* the time, could he? So Charlie could have some fun with Ruby, frighten the crap out of her like he had back in the day. *Fuck* Michael Ward.

Betsy's face twisted with black humour. 'Ruby? You're joking. After the way you treated her? I wouldn't go near, if I were you.'

'What's she on about?' asked Charlie, glancing at Joe.

'Oh, come on, Charlie,' said Joe, getting exasperated with all this. He didn't want to upset Charlie, but he didn't want Betsy to get stroppy and start giving him a shedload of earache, either. 'You know how it was with Ruby and you and Dad. You seriously think she's going to put out the welcome mat for you?'

Charlie hadn't told Joe or Betsy how Michael Ward had seen him off at Ruby's place. Nor would he. He had *some* pride. He thought of Ward, that *git,* giving him the hard word. Him, Charlie Darke. *No one* told him what to do, and he was going to have to teach Michael fucking Ward that lesson – and *then* he'd teach Ruby.

Charlie looked at Joe and Betsy in disgust. They didn't want him, and Ruby – his *sister,* for God's sake – didn't want him anywhere near. At least back at the hostel in Camberwell he had been made welcome.

'I'm going out,' he said, and turned away.

Joe followed him out of the kitchen. 'Charlie!' He caught his brother's arm.

Charlie stopped, looked at him. 'What?'

'I don't want us to fall out,' said Joe.

'We won't. I'll be on my way soon. I'll get my stash, and then . . .'

'*What?*' First Betsy, now Charlie. Were they both *mental*? Joe let out a laugh. 'Don't be so bloody silly. The stash ain't worth a bean, not any more.'

Charlie looked at his brother dully. 'What?'

Joe shook his head, exasperated. 'Shit, you've been inside too long, you poor bastard. Look, those notes are from the war. They were completely different to the notes in use even ten years ago. Now we've gone decimal. Decimal coinage, Charlie. *Everything's* changed. You can't use that money. You may as well just bloody forget it.'

Charlie was shaking his head, his expression confused. 'I didn't think . . .' he said.

'Sorry, Charlie.'

'All that time inside,' Charlie mumbled. It sounded like he was talking to himself.

Yeah, for something that's now worthless, thought Joe. *You poor sod.*

'I'm going out,' said Charlie, and this time Joe didn't try to stop him.

101

Charlie ended up in the pub that used to be his local, the Rag and Staff. Here, it used to be that everyone stepped very carefully around Mr Charlie Darke; he was treated with respect. Now, no one seemed to even notice him. He ordered a pint and stood there at the bar to drink it, ignored by and ignoring the other punters.

He glanced up as he drank, and he saw in the mirrored wall behind the bar a sad, tired old man draining a glass of Guinness. The poor old cunt had bags as big as suitcases under his eyes. His thin grey hair was plastered greasily to his scalp, his skin was mottled and pale, and there was a couple of days' worth of grey stubble on his chin. He looked like a down-and-out.

And then he realized it was him.

It was *him* he was staring at in the bar mirror.

His stomach knotted and his hand tightened around the glass as he emptied it and slapped it back down on the bar. Jesus! When had all this happened, when had he got so frigging *old*? He'd wasted his life away inside. His stash was worth nothing. The world had moved on.

The jukebox was playing songs he didn't even know, rubbish songs, not the stuff he remembered from his glory days. Even watching the news on the telly was like an out-of-body experience; they were talking about things that could have been happening on another planet for all he cared.

Inside, he'd felt safe.

Now, he felt alone in a hostile world.

Rachel, he thought, and his hand tightened over the hair slide in his pocket. He took it out, turned it over in his hand. The cheap jewels glinted in the subdued light of the bar.

'You want to sell that?' asked a voice.

Charlie turned his head. There was a geezer there in a denim jacket and jeans, with messy wheat-blond hair. 'You what?' asked Charlie.

The stranger shrugged. He addressed his next remark to the change he was sorting out in his hands. 'I can see times are hard and friends are few. That's a nice piece. You want to do a deal?'

He thinks I'm a tramp, thought Charlie.

Maybe Betsy was right. He *was* an undesirable. In prison, he'd been a big noise and he had managed to hold it together. But now he was outside he could feel himself crumbling apart, dissolving like a sandcastle when the tide washes in.

Places to go, things to do.

Like what?

'Fuck off,' he said to the man, and put the hair slide away.

'I was only asking . . .'

'Well, you've asked. And I've said no. Now clear off.'

'Hey, there's no need to be like *that*,' said the geezer, and that was enough.

Charlie turned and punched him right on the nose, feeling the crunch of bone and gristle as his fist connected. The blond bloke sprawled backwards, knocking into several other punters, who *also* went down in a heap. They shouted and swore as pints and tables and beer mats went flying in all directions. The man lay on the floor amid a tangle of table legs, handbags and shrieking women, touching a hand to his bloody nose and staring up at Charlie through tear-filled eyes.

'You *cunt*,' he said, and came up at Charlie very fast.

Charlie was even faster. He broke his empty Guinness glass on the bar. The man stopped dead in his tracks as Charlie waved the jagged edges of the glass in his face.

'You want to persist in this?' Charlie asked him. ''Cos really, mate, I would advise you to just piss off while you still can.'

'Look, I don't want no trouble,' said the landlady anxiously from behind the bar.

She was a big brassy brunette who had served Charlie his pint, commented on the weather, smiled and chatted. Charlie didn't know her. Years ago, he had known the land-lord well, an old RAF type with a handlebar moustache. Sid. He'd asked her, did she remember Sid? But she'd never heard of him. Now she was watching him like he'd grown two heads.

He dropped the glass on the floor and went outside.

He looked around. The traffic was so much heavier than it had been back in the day. So many more *people*, all rushing around, going where? He looked at the cars, the buses, so much noise, and there were billboards everywhere, plugging cars, drinks, clothes. *Darkes*, he saw across the road. *New store opening soon.*

Little Ruby. His dear sis, who'd been getting the pork sword off Michael Ward, who'd got him worked over inside. Yeah, there was a score to settle there. Things needed setting straight. He'd get Ward, he promised himself that. But first, *first*, he was going to kill that bitch sister of his.

He stumbled out into the road, a man on a mission, intent on crossing to the other side. He didn't even see the car that hit him at full speed, flinging him up into the air, arms and legs flailing.

Charlie crashed back down onto the tarmac amid blaring horns and the shriek of tyres and the shouts and screams of motorists. He lay there, eyes open but seeing nothing. Charlie Darke was dead.

102

'You'll never guess,' said Daisy, her eyes sparkling with excitement.

They were at dinner, the four of them: Daisy and Kit, Michael Ward and Ruby. Since the night of Kit and Daisy's abduction, this had become a fairly regular occurrence. The four of them got on, seemed to speak the same language.

'Go on,' prompted Ruby.

'Pa's letting me have the gatehouse,' she said, nearly hugging herself with glee.

'What gatehouse?' asked Kit.

'The gatehouse at Brayfield, silly. *You* know. You drove right past it when you took me home.'

'That will be nice,' said Ruby, although her heart sank to hear it. She'd thought that Daisy loved London best of all, not the country. She didn't want her disappearing off the scene. They'd become friends. Not close, but friends nevertheless. It was the most she could hope for, she knew that. 'You'll be near your mother,' she said, although it nearly choked her.

Daisy nodded.

'Mother hates town. I always stay with Aunt Ju while I'm up here. Of course, I won't be down there all the time – I'd hate that.'

'She must be very pleased,' said Ruby, and took a sip of wine.

'She'll barely notice I'm there; she'll be in the potting-shed as usual.'

Now Ruby was curious, despite herself. 'Doesn't your father spend time with her down there?'

'Oh no. Well, not much. Pa has the London house where he stays during the week, and he goes home at weekends. Not *every* weekend, though. Sometimes he's just too busy.'

Ruby nodded. *Busy with what?* But she thought she knew. Busy with women, busy with boys. Once the very mention of Vanessa and Cornelius would have made her green with jealousy. Now, she just pitied Daisy, to have them for parents.

But you're her parent, she thought. *What about you, Ruby? When did you ever give her the love she deserves, the love she so obviously craves?*

She hadn't. And now, she couldn't. The deal had been struck, she had to acknowledge that: and it was far too late to break it. All she could do now was enjoy Daisy's company. She was so lucky to be able to do even that. No point in craving for more. No more was on offer.

'I've got the keys,' said Daisy, looking across at Ruby with an angelic smile. 'Would you come down with me on Saturday, give me some advice on furnishings and things?'

'I don't . . .'

'Oh, please, Ruby. You've got such fantastic taste and I don't know anything about décor.'

'But your mother . . .'

'Oh, she's away. Visiting the folks.'

Ruby took a deep breath, like a high-diver going off the top board. She knew she shouldn't. But the temptation was too much. And if Vanessa was away, it hardly mattered: she would never know. 'Then . . . well, all right. I suppose so.'

'Great!' Daisy picked up her glass for a toast. 'To my gatehouse!' she said, and one by one, smiling, they all picked up their glasses, clinked them against hers, and drank.

'You two seem to have hit it off,' said Michael, pulling off his tie and unbuttoning his shirt.

It was later that same evening and Ruby was sitting up in bed, wearing her peachy Janet Reger silk nightgown, watching him pull off his clothes and leave them in a chaotic heap on the floor. Hers she had neatly folded and placed on a chair. The habits of order, of keeping things tidy, had never deserted her; but he was so untidy. Scrupulously clean, but a crazy man about the house. She wondered why his innate messiness didn't drive her mad, but it didn't.

Must be love, she thought.

'Me and Daisy? Yes. She's lovely.'

More and more Ruby was spending time here with him, in his flat over the restaurant. But . . . it was a woman's flat, not a man's. The colours were neutral, very feminine; Ruby guessed that Sheila had been a blonde. She could clearly see his dead wife's hand all around her. There was even a pale space on the wall in the bedroom, where a picture of her must have hung, and which Michael had obviously taken down to spare Ruby's feelings. But the dead wife still hovered all around them, like a wraith. Ruby actually disliked making love in this flat, in his bed, because of it. But she couldn't tell him that. How the hell could she?

'You're lovely too,' he said, throwing off the last of his clothes and climbing into bed, pulling her close for a kiss.

'Michael,' said Ruby.

'Hm?'

'If I tell you something, will you keep it to yourself? Tell no one else?'

He drew back a little, his expression curious, smiling. 'What's this then, secrets?'

'Promise?'

Something in Ruby's eyes made him stop smiling. 'Of course. What is it?'

'It's Daisy.'

'What about her?'

Ruby stared at him.

'Come on, Ruby, what?' he prompted.

'She's my daughter.'

Michael stared. 'You *what*?'

Ruby looked away from him. She shouldn't have said it. But the need to share this, the need to shout aloud to the world that Daisy was her child, her precious baby, had been overwhelming.

'She's my child. The twin of the boy we're looking for.'

'But you . . . but . . .' He sat up sharply, dragging his hands through his hair. Then he shot a look at her. 'Twins? Ruby, help me out here. Are you serious?'

Ruby flicked a look at his face. He seemed shocked. She nodded dumbly.

'But this don't make any sense,' he said. 'For one thing, Daisy's Cornelius Bray's daughter, his and his wife Vanessa's.'

'No. She isn't.' Ruby drew in a shuddering breath and told him about the night she'd had the babies, the deal Charlie had struck with Cornelius.

'But wait. Wait.' He paused, taking it in. 'Jesus, girl, you've really thrown me. Daisy? But Daisy's white. She's *white*. And the baby we're looking for is dark, you said.'

Ruby nodded. 'Cornelius is white, she's his child. But look at me, Michael. I have black blood in me.'

'You're beautiful,' he said. And she was, the most exquisite woman he'd ever seen.

'I'm half black, half white. I think . . . I think my father, my *real* father, was pure black. My mother was white. She died having me and my family hated me for it. That and the fact that I was living proof that she'd been unfaithful.'

Michael flopped back against the pillows and stared at the ceiling. His head turned and he looked at Ruby.

'You're shocked,' she said miserably.

'I'm . . . yeah, I'm shocked all right. I'm shocked at *you*. That night when Kit was done over by Tito, Daisy was in bits. But you were calm as calm could be, helping her get cleaned up . . . and since then, we've met up with her again, and you've always been polite to her, nice to her, but . . . for Christ's sake, Ruby: *she's your child*.'

Now Ruby felt a pang of irritation. 'So what would you have had me do?' she demanded. 'Fling my arms around her? Blurt out the truth? I couldn't do that to her. It wouldn't be *right*.'

Michael was staring at her face.

'You know what? Sometimes I don't understand you at all. Me and Sheil were never lucky enough to have kids, but I know for a fact that we couldn't ever have given them up. No way. Sometimes you're so bloody cold I can feel it coming off you, like ice.'

'Why? Because I didn't do the thing you think is right, the impulsive thing? It's *Daisy* I was thinking of. She's grown up with two loving parents . . .'

'Do you really believe that?'

'What?'

'You heard what she said this evening. Her mother's more interested in a shitting flower bed than she is in her. And Cornelius Bray's a perverted bastard – everyone in town knows that. He'd screw anything that moves, male or female. He'd stick it in a hole in a *fence* to get his kicks. He's not that interested in his daughter. And can't you see it in her?'

'What?' Ruby asked faintly. Why was he attacking her?

Michael twisted around and thumped the pillow, hard.

'Fuck's sake, Ruby. The poor kid's a screw-up of the first water. She'd latch onto anything or anybody for a hint of affection. She's wild, the poor little cow, into drink and drugs and all sorts. She follows Kit around like a lost pup. And there you are, standing back, keeping to the rules, being all reserved and proper about it. A deal's a deal, that's what you're thinking. And you're doing the best you can for Daisy by letting her get on with it? Ruby.' He grabbed her shoulder and gave her a slight shake. 'What that girl needs is *you*. Not that pair of upper-crust twats she's stuck with.'

Ruby swallowed hard, feeling her eyes fill with tears. 'You think I should tell her,' she said.

'I'm *certain* you should,' said Michael.

The tears spilled over and ran down her face. 'No. I daren't do that. I wanted to once, but now I know I can't do it. She likes me. She seeks out my company. But if I tell her the truth, she'll *hate* me. She'll think I abandoned her.'

'And she'd be right, wouldn't she?'

Ruby stared at him. 'I *had* to. I had no choice. Back then . . . it was hard. A half-caste girl with a dark baby and a white one? Can you imagine the shame that would have brought on my family? They were ashamed of me *anyway*. My God, it would have been unbearable. I would have been stoned in the street, I would have been an outcast . . .' Ruby started to sob in anguish.

'Ruby . . .' Michael was reaching for her.

'*Don't touch me!*' she yelled in his face, and she was off the bed in an instant, rounding on him. 'You don't understand. You have no idea what it was like. *How dare you judge me?*'

'I'm not. I swear . . .'

'Yes, you bloody well *are*,' she said, and stormed from the room, slamming the door shut behind her.

103

Daisy drove them down in the Mini to the gatehouse at Brayfield. Ruby followed Daisy from room to room, slowly becoming infected with the younger woman's enthusiasm.

'In here I thought I'd do something bright. Orange with accents of mauve.'

'That would look terrific,' said Ruby. It sounded hellish to her, but it was Daisy's place and Daisy was so excited that the last thing Ruby wanted to do was piss on her parade.

'You think so? Not too over-the-top?'

Ruby almost smiled. Daisy herself was over-the-top, might as well do the whole place out in neon. It would suit her personality.

'You all right?' asked Daisy. 'You were quiet on the way down here. Sorry. Did I railroad you into this? Was there something else you had to be doing . . . ?'

'No!' Ruby said quickly, forcing her smile to widen. She was still terribly upset about her fight with Michael last night, but she couldn't discuss that with Daisy. 'Just tired after a long week, that's all.'

'I've dragged you around here quite long enough,' said Daisy apologetically. 'Come on, let's get on up to the house and have some tea with mother.'

Ruby's jaw dropped. 'What?' she asked faintly. 'But I thought you said she was away.'

'No, she's here. Change of plan. Cousin Jeremy cancelled at the last minute. Come on,' said Daisy, already whipping along the hallway to the front door, jangling the keys as she went. 'I can't *wait* to get started on this,' she threw back over her shoulder.

'Um – Daisy . . .' Ruby was trailing after her, thinking that this couldn't happen, that she was on some sort of crazy collision course and she had to divert Daisy from it somehow. 'Daisy, I think I ought to be getting back . . .'

'Well, I can't just go and not call in on her,' said Daisy. 'She'd nag me to death if I did.' Daisy was ushering Ruby outside and relocking the door. Then she hurried over to the Mini. 'We won't stay long, don't worry.'

Ruby found herself getting into the car, and Daisy jumped in and revved the engine before shooting off up the drive towards the house.

Oh help, thought Ruby as Brayfield appeared through the curving line of trees. Daisy drove like a Formula One racing driver, and they were screeching to a halt in front of the big fountain of Neptune before Ruby could even think. Daisy turned off the engine.

'I'll wait in the car,' said Ruby.

'No no! Come and meet Mother, she's a stickler for manners and she'll only come out and get you if you don't come in, so you might as well give in right now.'

Shit, thought Ruby. Feeling like she was about to be shot, she climbed out of the car and followed Daisy up the steps. Daisy put her key in the door, and opened it, guiding Ruby in front of her into a large, cool, airy hall.

'Mother!' she yelled.

There was no answer.

'Perhaps she's gone out after all,' said Ruby, hoping against hope.

'No, she'll be in the garden I expect, come on . . .'

Daisy led the way through the hall and into a large room painted in soft eggshell blue and gold. Through the open French doors, Ruby could see two people at the far end of the garden, a man and a woman, the woman gesticulating, the man listening.

'There she is,' said Daisy. 'Come on,' she trilled, and she was out of the doors and hurrying across the grass.

Ruby was forced to follow, but her mouth was dry and her heart was beating sickly in her chest. She'd been stupid to come anywhere near here; she knew it. But the lure of Daisy was just so strong.

Daisy ran up to the woman while Ruby hung nervously back. It was Vanessa, all right. She was wearing faded jeans and Wellington boots with a white top. There was a spade in her hand and she was talking about rudbeckias to the bearded man, clearly the gardener, who listened with polite attention.

'Mother?' called Daisy, hurrying towards her.

Vanessa turned and her thin face lit in a smile. 'Darling!'

Daisy hugged her mother so hard Ruby thought she might break the fragile-looking Vanessa in two halves. So many years had gone by, and with them she could see that Vanessa had not aged well. She was slightly stooping, and her once-delicate complexion was scored with many fine lines from hours spent toiling in the sun.

'And who is . . . ?' Vanessa started to say, looking past her daughter to see who she'd brought with her.

As instantly as Ruby had recognized her, Vanessa saw that it was Ruby. Her face fell, and drained of colour. She stared for a long moment, then turned to the gardener. 'Um . . . if you can carry on with that, Ivan . . . ?'

He nodded, and Vanessa handed him the spade, her eyes averted from Ruby now. She stepped out of the border and onto the lawn.

'This is Ruby, a friend of mine, I asked her to come down and look over the gatehouse with me,' said Daisy, glancing between the two older women. 'Ruby, meet my mother.'

Ruby swallowed hard. 'Hello,' she said, and held out her hand.

Vanessa hesitated and then touched Ruby's hand, very briefly, with her own. 'Hello,' she said.

Ruby wished the ground would open up and swallow her whole. She shouldn't be here. This wasn't the deal. Cornelius would be furious about this, she knew it. But . . . oh, so what? Let the bastard squirm. He deserved it, didn't he?

'Um, look . . . I'm sorry, darling, but I'm very busy at the moment. If you could take Ruby back to the house and make her some tea?' said Vanessa.

'I know, I know,' sighed Daisy. 'You're dividing the perennials, right?'

'You see? You could be a gardener,' said Vanessa, smiling slightly.

'No, I couldn't. I've just picked it all up from you. I hate gardening.'

'It's a beautiful garden,' said Ruby, feeling she really ought to say something.

'Thank you,' said Vanessa, and her eyes were full of freezing-cold wrath as they bored briefly into Ruby's.

What the hell are you doing here?

Ruby could almost read Vanessa's thoughts. She wanted to say it was a mistake, that it wouldn't happen again. But she couldn't. Daisy was standing right there, and now she was telling Vanessa about her plans for the gatehouse's interior.

'Sounds perfectly ghastly, darling,' said Vanessa.

'Well, Ruby *loved* the idea,' said Daisy with a mulish smile, linking her arm through Ruby's.

Oh God, let me just die now, thought Ruby in anguish.

'Does she?' Vanessa's smile was fixed. 'Well, you know I do have rather traditional tastes, Daisy.'

'Old-fashioned,' joked Daisy.

'Traditional,' said Vanessa firmly. 'Now, if you will excuse me . . . ?'

'All right, we're going, we're going,' tutted Daisy in fond irritation. 'I'd hate to tear you away from the long border.'

As they walked arm in arm back to the house, Ruby glanced back; Vanessa was staring after them, and there was such hatred in her eyes that Ruby shuddered and looked quickly away.

Vanessa rejoined Ivan. She could feel herself trembling with rage.

How dare that woman come here!

'What a stunning woman,' said Ivan.

Vanessa looked at him, startled.

'That woman,' repeated Ivan, nodding towards Daisy and Ruby as they went back into the house. 'So exotic.'

Vanessa couldn't help glancing down at herself – at her cracked nails, her grubby gardening clothes. Ruby looked ten years younger than her actual age. And Vanessa knew she looked ten years *older* than hers. She snatched up the fork, her face set in fury.

'Ivan, if you ever see her on this property again, then get her off it. Straight away. You understand?'

Ivan stared at his employer. He'd been with Vanessa for ever, and this was the first time he'd so much as heard her raise her voice. He was shocked.

'Of course,' he assured her.

'Let's get on with it then,' she snapped, and plunged the fork savagely into the earth.

Cornelius felt the bile rise in his throat when he got the call from Vanessa. Angrily she told him what had happened, that

Daisy had shown up with Ruby Darke. That *that woman* had the nerve to actually come to Vanessa's home and stand there smirking at her.

'You're not serious,' said Cornelius, incredulous.

'Does it sound as if I'm joking?' Vanessa's voice was bitter. 'You told me this wasn't going to happen. You said we had Daisy, and that was it. You paid Ruby Darke off and it would all be forgotten. But I'm telling you she was *here*, Cornelius. With *Daisy*. In my home.'

Cornelius was at the London house. He sat down on the couch, feeling genuinely sick with rage and anxiety at this news. He thought about Daisy mixing with that black bastard Kit Miller, and now – far worse – Ruby had clearly started to cultivate a relationship with the girl she'd given birth to. That wasn't part of the deal at all, and the sooner Ruby was taught the error of her ways, the better it would be.

'Daisy hasn't . . . said anything to you about Ruby?' he asked.

'No. Nothing. It was a complete shock when she turned up here with her.'

So it didn't look as if Ruby had told Daisy the truth about her parentage. There was that to be grateful for, at least. But if he allowed the two of them to get closer, to form any sort of bond, then how long could it be before the truth came out?

It just wasn't on. Ruby was going to have to be made to see that, and keep away.

'I'll sort this out,' he told Vanessa. 'Don't worry.'

As soon as Vanessa rang off, he phoned the private detective he'd had look into Kit's background, and told him to find out what had been going on with Ruby and Daisy, how they had come to be connected. When all that was done, he phoned Tito.

104

'I hate these places,' said Kit.

'It ain't too bad,' said Rob.

'No? I grew up in a shit-hole just like this.'

They were in reception at yet another children's home. A couple of the ones they'd tried close to where that nutter with the acid bath lived had long since been closed down and converted to housing. But this one was still functioning, and just being inside it, smelling those old familiar odours of overcooked dinners and sweaty plimsolls, made Kit start to gag.

'You serious? You really stayed in a place like this?' asked Rob. Kit never spoke about his background.

Kit was nodding, looking around him. 'The place I was in only took you 'til you were eight. Then you were shipped out to another one that took you until you were twelve.'

'What, and then another one?'

'That's right. Then at sixteen, you're on your own. Out in the big wide world.'

'That's rough,' said Rob, thinking of his own close-knit family.

'Life's rough,' said Kit. 'So what?'

Kit remembered all those Christmases, Mother's Days, Father's Days . . . The feeling of abandonment, of something always missing. A family. A home. A *life*.

But he had a job to do here, so he shut down his own discomfort and concentrated on the job in hand.

As it turned out, he needn't have bothered.

It was another dead end.

105

Ruby refused to speak to Michael when he called her on the phone at her home. He sent flowers to her office, and she binned them. Finally, he showed up in person.

'It's Mr Ward,' said Jane. 'You ready to see him yet, or you gonna let him sweat just a little more?'

This was stupid. Ruby nodded. 'All right. Show him in then.'

'Must have been *some* fight,' said Jane, going back outside and keeping her hand on the door while saying: 'You can go in now.'

'Thanks.'

Michael Ward walked past her into Ruby's office. Immaculate as ever, iron-grey hair smooth and tidy, grey eyes serious in his tanned face.

Jane pulled the door closed while making a *Whew! Hot!* shaking motion of her hand. Ruby ignored her. She looked straight-faced at Michael as he sat down.

There was silence in the room.

'All right,' he said at last. 'I'm sorry. I don't know what *for,* exactly, but here I am, apologizing. OK?'

'Oh, and you think that makes it all right, do you?' fumed Ruby. He'd hurt her. She'd been reeling from rediscovering Daisy, and had been looking for his support. Instead, he'd blundered in and upset her with stupid accusations.

Michael exhaled sharply. 'Look, Ruby. You shocked me, OK? But then, that's you all over, isn't it?'

'What?' Was he going to lay into her again, was that what he'd come here for?

'You. You say nothing, *tell* me nothing, then you come out with these shocking things and expect me to react like you're telling me nothing of any importance. You don't ever tell me a thing, Ruby. Not a fucking *thing.*'

Ruby stared at him. Yes, he was attacking her again, and right now that was almost more than she could stand.

'Even when we're in bed, you say nothing,' he was ranting on. 'I'd like to know what you like, what you *don't* like. What pleases you.'

'*You* please me.'

'Well you never tell me. What am I, a fucking mind reader?'

'Michael . . .'

'No, let me finish. You hold everything inside yourself and then, whoosh! Suddenly it bursts out of you like water from a dam. And it's shocking. It takes a bit of getting used to. So I'm sorry if I reacted in a way that you didn't like, but you knocked me sideways. I just wish you'd *talk* to me more, Ruby. Tell me things. Tell me what you like. Tell me what you don't like . . . Why don't you do that?'

'I don't like your flat,' said Ruby suddenly.

'What?'

'I *hate* your flat. It's got all your wife's stuff still in it, and I understand you're still in love with her, why shouldn't you be?'

'What . . . ?'

'And that space on the wall opposite the bed, there was a painting or a picture hanging there – a picture of *her*, I suppose – and you took it down to spare my feelings, but the mark's still there, I look at it every time we're in bed together and it kills me.'

Michael shook his head and ran a hand through his hair.

'It wasn't a picture of my wife,' he said. 'It was a copy of a painting, Renoir or something. I always hated it, but she liked it. When she was gone, I thought: Why not sell the thing? So I did.'

'Oh.'

'Yeah, "oh".' He was smiling slightly. 'And I don't keep the flat as some sort of shrine to Sheila, of course I don't. Yeah, that's her name: Sheila. I named the restaurant after her. I loved her very much and I'll never forget her, but now I'm in love with you. I just don't give a shit about furnishings, wallpaper, any of that stuff. The flat's as it is because I never did that and she did. If *you* want to do it, redecorate, do whatever you damned well want with it, then go ahead. I don't mind. You see what I mean, you crazy mare? This illustrates exactly what I've just been saying. You say nothing, then bang! Out it comes in a rush. Has this been bothering you for long?'

'Ever since I first came to the flat,' she admitted.

'You're so clever and such a fool.'

'I know.'

'So, am I forgiven?'

He loved her. There! He'd said it. 'There's something else. My brother died. You must have heard.'

'Charlie?' He was watching her face. 'Yeah, I did. You and Joe must be pretty cut up.' His mouth twisted. 'But then, the same thing again. I've been waiting for you to tell me, and this is the first I've heard of it from you.'

I'm not cut up, thought Ruby. But it was too long and too painful a story to discuss. She really didn't want to talk about it. Joe had called her, told her about the accident. Charlie had wandered drunk out into a road and been knocked down. The driver hadn't stopped.

She knew she ought to feel sorry. This was her *brother*. But really all she felt was relief. Relief that, at last, Charlie was really, properly gone.

106

'We'll have the wake at our place,' said Joe. 'Give the poor bastard a proper send off.'

Betsy agreed willingly, much to his surprise. He knew how she'd hated having Charlie around. But then – a chance to show off her house, her possessions, to all their mates? She couldn't pass that up. If she'd objected, it could have turned nasty. Big as he was, and tough as he was when it came to managing his manor, he had been pussy-whipped by Betsy for his whole married life and he knew it. What Betsy wanted, Betsy usually got. But – for once – here she was, being all agreeable.

Charlie's death had upset him, the sheer stupid futility of it. He found the funeral hard to get through. All the breakers and the part-time boys and their wives were there at the church to pay their respects, then everyone went back to his place in Chigwell. Before very long Betsy, forgetting the solemnity of the occasion, was preening herself in a three-hundred-pound black skirt suit and showing off her latest fixtures and fittings to all the other girls.

Ruby was there too, wearing a sober black jersey shift dress, a simple string of pearls and black court shoes. She hadn't wanted to come, but she knew that her absence would look strange so she had been forced to attend.

'You've got to go,' Vi told her when she confessed to her closest friend how much she was dreading it.

'Why? They're bound to be talking about Charlie, saying what a great bloke he was. He was horrible. A bloody monster. I can't face it.'

'Yes, you can. You're his sister. If you didn't show up, how would that look? Just tough it out. That's all you can do.'

She knew Vi was right. But still, it was torture and she couldn't wait for it to be over.

'I'm glad you came,' said Joe in a quiet moment. 'I've got Charlie's belongings, I'm wondering what the hell to do with them.'

'What belongings?' asked Ruby. She didn't want to even *think* about Charlie's things, far less see them. 'There can't be much, can there? He wasn't long out of prison. Just stuff his things up in the loft and forget about them.'

'Bets don't like old rubbish about the place. You know her, this house is a bloody show home.'

Ruby looked at him. So fearsome, Joe Darke was. And yet henpecked by a five-foot-nothing woman. Joe's big pudgy face was troubled. For the first time, Ruby noticed the black stubble on his jaw was flecked with grey, and his hair had turned white at the temples. There were hollows like tramlines on either side of his mouth, a perpetual frown etched on his brow.

He's getting older, Ruby thought. *Hell, we all are.*

'I could do with a hand sorting through it, Rubes. We're all the family he had, you and me. I don't want to do it on my own.'

Bugger it. She didn't want to do it, but look at him: Joe was really upset by all this.

'All right,' she said. 'I'll give you a hand.'

★

Joe was right: there wasn't much left of Charlie's. His meagre belongings were in a bag in one of the guest bedrooms; they spread everything out on the bed and stood there, staring down at the bits and pieces – all that was left of a life lived on the wrong side of the tracks.

There was a little double photo folder; a hunter pocket-watch with a low-grade chain and sovereign attached; a black comb, ingrained with greasy dirt; some socks, underpants, trousers and shirts that had seen better days; a bank book with bugger-all in it; and a woman's cheap hair slide.

'What a load of tat,' said Ruby, picking up the slide and turning it over in her hands. 'Except for the watch and chain, I suppose.'

'That was Dad's. I'll keep that. And what about that thing. It's a woman's hair slide, isn't it? Don't know whose it is. There's not much else.'

Ruby put it down with an inner shudder. She didn't know why Charlie had kept such an odd thing.

'I know it's all useless, but I can't just sling it, can I? Think you're right. I'll just put it all up in the loft, out of Betsy's way.'

'Put *what* out of Betsy's way? What you two doing in here?' said Betsy, appearing in the doorway.

'Just sorting through Charlie's stuff,' Joe said quickly.

'What for? Hurry it up, we've guests downstairs – I can't manage this lot on my own.'

'Sorry, babe. We'll be right down.'

'What's that . . . ?' asked Betsy, coming into the room and peering down at the slide. Her lips tightened as she looked at it.

'Bugger me.' Betsy picked it up and turned it over in her hands, her face sneering. 'I bet that's *hers*.'

'Who?' asked Ruby, curious.

'That ugly cow he kept sneaking off to during the war. She got blown to kingdom come one night, German bomb. And good bloody riddance, I say.' Betsy flung the slide back onto the bed. Her cheeks were pink with irritation. 'Rachel Tranter, that was her name. Married to that spiv. You remember, Joe?'

'Yeah,' said Joe. 'I remember Tranter and his mob.'

'He was always sneaking off to see her,' said Betsy, her mouth twisted. 'Sodding *cow.*'

Joe's face was expressionless, but Ruby thought this must have hurt: Betsy's obvious annoyance that Charlie had pursued someone else, not her.

'All water under the bridge now,' said Ruby.

'Yeah.' Joe heaved a sharp sigh.

'Hurry it up, will you, Joe?' Betsy snapped, and left the room.

They listened to the tap-tap of her heels as she hurried back downstairs to her guests.

'What's that?' asked Ruby, picking up the brown cardboard folder. 'Photos?'

She flipped the thing open; Joe was busy stuffing everything else back into the bag.

Ruby caught her breath. In one side of the folder was an image of a man who looked very like Charlie – obviously their father, Ted. And in the other side, there was a photo of another face she knew. She was looking at *Daisy.*

Joe glanced at her. 'What is it . . . ?' he asked, peering over her shoulder. 'Oh. That's mum. Never took Charlie for a sentimental sort, did you? He must have had that for years.'

Ruby stared at the photo. Of course, Joe was right. The clothing, the colour of the print, the carefully staged nature of it, the dated background – this wasn't, *couldn't* be Daisy. She'd never before seen a photo of her mother. There had never been any on display in her father's house.

'Dad must have kept that, passed it on to Charlie,' said Joe while Ruby just stared at it.

'But they never had any time for her,' she said at last.

'Didn't mean they didn't love her though, did it?'

'Dad said she was a disgrace.'

'Come on, Ruby. His old lady had been giving the ride to a black jazz-club trumpet player.'

'Only because *he* mistreated her.'

'You don't know that.'

'I knew *him*. He mistreated me too, remember?'

'Yeah.' Joe looked almost shame-faced for a second. 'He loved her, Rubes. But he hated her too. She'd made a public fool out of him by presenting him with a half-black baby. How d'you suppose he must have felt about that? And then it just got worse, didn't it? All that anger between them, it was never resolved. She died having you. Complications. So all that rage in him just went on . . .'

'And was directed at me,' finished Ruby, her eyes angry. 'I know.'

Joe sat down on the bed with a sigh. 'It's all past and done now, Rubes. All that bad blood, all that bad feeling. It's done. It's gone.'

Ruby closed the folder gently and clutched it to her breast. 'Can I keep this?' she asked, feeling choked. Her mother had looked so young, so hopeful in the picture. Just like Daisy did today.

''Course you can.' Joe stood up. 'Come on then, let's get back down there. I suppose we'd better show willing.'

107

When Ruby got back to Marlow that night she felt wrung out. It had been a hard day, making nice and smiling pleasantly when people told her time and again what a 'diamond geezer' Charlie had been. She was so pleased to get home – but that pleasure was roughly cut short when she went to unlock the front door.

Suddenly she was shoved violently from behind. Reeling with shock and from the savagery of the impact, Ruby fell forward into the hall, striking her elbow and the side of her head on the polished marble floor.

Pain rocketed up her arm. Her head literally spinning, she looked up in abject terror and saw a man standing over her, dressed in dark clothes, gloved up, his face hidden by a knitted mask. She could only see his eyes, which were pig-like and mean.

She was being burgled.

'I don't have any money here,' she blurted out, her heart rocketing in her chest, trying to crawl away.

He knelt down, grabbed her hair and whacked her head down against the floor.

Ruby shrieked.

'I don't want your money, cunt,' he growled. 'I'm delivering a message.'

A what? Ruby, eyes watering, her face twisted with fear,

could hardly understand what he was saying. His accent was thick Glaswegian, and further muffled by the mask.

'I don't understand . . .' she managed to get out.

'Oh, you will.' He whacked her head once more against the floor. 'I *said*, I'm delivering a message. You keep away from Daisy Bray, or trust me, *bitch,* you'll get more than a bang on the head next time. You got that?'

'What the . . .'

'*Got it?*'

Her head where he was gripping her hair so hard was agony. But despite the pain, despite her terror, fury started to stir in her. Daisy was *her daughter*. Vanessa and that bastard Cornelius, what right did they have to do this, to try to stop her having contact?

'Say it.'

'I'll . . .' Her voice was wobbling, trembling. Tears of anguish were flooding down her cheeks. She didn't want to say it. Didn't want to stay away from Daisy. She *couldn't*.

'*Say it, bitch.*' He shook her head. She felt strands of hair coming loose from her scalp, wondered if she was bleeding.

'I'll leave Daisy alone,' she gulped out.

'Good. Make sure you do.'

He thumped her head back down against the floor. Pain exploded once again, she screwed up her eyes and thought *Stop, please just stop*.

When she opened her eyes, there was no one there. The front door was standing open, admitting the cool, still night air. She was laid out on her hall tiles, shuddering with rage and crying in pain.

Her attacker was gone.

108

'And that's all he said? Just that – "Keep away from Daisy"?' asked Michael, chain-smoking with ferocious concentration.

She'd phoned him moments after her attacker had gone. He'd come straight over, two of his boys arriving with him – she recognized Kit, and Rob – and she had never seen him looking so angry.

Ruby sat there with him in her own home and thought she would never feel safe again. Her head ached, but more from tension than from the impact with her hall floor. The man had pulled out a chunk of hair from her scalp, and yes, it had bled a little. Her elbow was throbbing, but she thought it would be OK. She would live. But would she ever again feel safe here?

'That's all he said,' she murmured.

'What was he like? Can you describe him?'

'Mean piggy eyes. A thick Scottish accent. He had a mask . . .' Ruby shuddered and ground to a halt.

'You think this is Cornelius?' asked Michael.

Ruby looked him dead in the eye. 'Of *course* it's Cornelius. This is my fault. I was getting close to Daisy. I went to Brayfield with her, I was just going to the gatehouse, that was all, and I thought Vanessa was away, but she wasn't. Daisy insisted we go up to the house to call in on . . . on Vanessa.' She had nearly said *her mother*. But Vanessa wasn't

414

Daisy's mother. *She* was. 'I could see that Vanessa was furious. And she would have told Cornelius.'

'And so he got someone to pay you a visit,' said Michael, pacing around the room.

He felt sick to his stomach at the thought of anyone having the gall to do this to Ruby. If this was Cornelius, then damned sure it was one of *Tito's* boys who'd done the job on Ruby. *Fuck it.*

This situation was getting out of hand. He did business with Tito, they were tied together in all sorts of ways and also on a new deal on the London Docklands Strategic Plan. He wished to Christ they weren't, but there was no way of getting out of it now.

The old docks, once a prime target for Hitler's weapons during the war, were now largely defunct because the new giant container ships couldn't get up the river. They had to stop at Felixstowe. This meant that everyone who was willing to buy in – and there were huge government incentives to do so – was now sitting on eight square miles of prime building land. There were fortunes to be made. Tito and Michael were on their way to becoming millionaires.

But . . . now this. Michael felt soiled by his links with Tito. He'd always disliked the man, who swaggered around town puffed up like a toad on his own self-importance. But there was no way, at this late stage, to extricate himself from the deal. And there was no way he could break his word, his solemn promise to his dead wife. He *couldn't*. He turned, stared at Ruby. She looked subdued and vulnerable.

'You shouldn't be here on your own. It isn't safe.'

'I'm fine,' said Ruby. She wasn't, not at all; but she liked her independence. Hell for her would be moving into that flat of his. She'd bought this big Victorian villa and furnished it with care. This was her *home*. She'd worked hard for it, she loved it. She wasn't about to be scared out of it by Cornelius Bray.

'Ruby . . .' Michael was looking at her as if she was crazy.

'Stay the night with me,' she said.

'Of course I will. But after tonight . . .'

'Let's think about that tomorrow.'

And it was nice, sleeping in his arms, waking with him; she knew she could get used to it.

She awoke early – she always did – and he was still there, sleeping soundly beside her, brown-skinned, muscled, but somehow almost vulnerable in sleep. She slipped quietly from the bed, feeling the twinge of resistance in her arm from yesterday. She touched her head, was aware of soreness there, but nothing too bad. It could have been so much worse, she knew that.

Ruby pulled on her dressing gown and crept out of the master bedroom and downstairs to the kitchen. Dawn was breaking, spilling multicoloured light onto the hall floor through the stained-glass panels on either side of the front door.

She found herself looking at everything differently now. She loved this house so much, but perhaps she should have stayed in her apartment over the store. Maybe she needed better locks; maybe those exquisite stained-glass panels beside the front door would have to go.

But then – how could she have stopped what happened? Her attacker had been hiding outside, somewhere in the shrubbery; she'd been taken completely unawares.

'Oh!' Someone was in the kitchen. She clutched a hand to her chest as she saw the tall, muscular dark-skinned man standing there, his white shirt hanging open, wearing black trousers and a tousled look as he paused in pouring hot water onto a mug of instant coffee.

'Sorry,' said Kit. 'Did I startle you?'

'No, you're fine,' said Ruby, although he had. Her heart

had burst into a gallop when she'd seen him there; but it was just Kit, after all. 'Can you do me one of those?'

'Sure.' He took down another mug from a hook on the dresser. Then he looked at her. 'Sorry. I wake early, just needed a drink.'

Actually, he hadn't slept properly ever since the Tito thing with Gilda. He still missed her, and mourned her bitterly, and was wracked with guilt over her death.

'It's OK, make yourself at home,' she said, and went over to the big marble-topped island in the middle of the room and perched up on a stool, pulling yesterday's paper towards her and scanning it briefly. Evonne Goolagong had beaten Margaret Court in the women's singles at Wimbledon, and some Russian cosmonauts had died in their Soyuz space-craft. Tens of thousands of people had turned out in Red Square to pay their respects. And the submarine HMS *Artemis* had sunk in Portsmouth harbour, trapping three sailors on board. The same old mixture of misery and glory.

'Did Rob stay the night too?' she asked Kit, pushing the paper aside.

He nodded, busy with the coffee.

'You both sleep OK?'

'Fine. You take it black?'

'Yes please.'

'Sugar?'

'No.'

He brought the two mugs over to the island and put them down, pulled up a stool.

'Feel a bit better now?' he asked, his eyes scanning her face.

'Yes. Thank you.'

'The boss was very upset. Someone trying that on you.' Kit took a sip of the coffee. 'So what was it about? You got any idea?'

Ruby thought of saying it was nothing. She didn't particularly want to relive it right now. But she liked Kit, and she knew Michael trusted him implicitly.

'I was being warned off contact with Daisy,' she said.

'What?' Kit stared at her. 'You mean *crazy* Daisy – Daisy Bray?'

Now Ruby had to smile. 'Why'd you call her that?'

'Because she's a fruit loop.' He grinned. 'A nice girl, but mad. Why would anyone warn you to keep away from her?'

'It doesn't matter.' She definitely wasn't going into all that. She sipped her coffee and started to feel stronger.

'Well, it must matter.'

'No. It doesn't. Michael said you're still looking for the baby,' she said, trying to sound casual but failing. 'Are you having any luck?'

'Maybe. I don't want to get your hopes up too much, but it looks like we might have a lead on that.'

Ruby nearly choked on her coffee.

'Steady,' said Kit.

Ruby's eyes were dead serious as they stared into his. 'You mean that? You might really find him?'

Kit shrugged. 'We might. We're certainly trying.' He looked at her steadily.

'What?' asked Ruby.

'Nothing.' Kit glanced away.

'Come on, what?'

He looked back at her, his expression sheepish. 'It's just that I can't understand it. A mother, giving up her child. No, wait. I'm sorry. I shouldn't have said that. You must have had your reasons . . .'

Ruby felt the pain of it all over again, like a knife in her chest.

'I did,' she said. 'I did have my reasons.'

'Only . . .' His eyes were troubled. '. . . I don't see how

that boy could ever forgive you for it, for giving him away, for not caring what happened to him.'

'I did care what happened to him,' said Ruby. 'It tortured me every day. It still does.'

Kit looked straight at her.

'Go on,' said Ruby. 'Whatever you're thinking, just spit it out.'

'Maybe he won't want to know you. After all this time. Maybe . . . I'm sorry, but I got to say this . . . maybe you won't ever get your boy back, not really. Not even if we do track him down.'

Ruby felt her eyes filling with tears.

'Hey,' said Kit hastily, reaching out a hand. 'Me and my big mouth.'

'No, it's OK. You're right. He might never forgive me for giving him up. And I'd understand that.'

There was silence while they both drank coffee.

'What about Daisy? Why were you being warned off her?'

'Michael hasn't told you?'

Kit shook his head.

'They were twins. The boy and the girl. Daisy's father took her because his wife couldn't have children.'

'Cornelius Bray,' said Kit. 'You and he . . . ?'

'We had an affair during the war.'

'So Cornelius kept Daisy, but your brother took the boy.'

'Michael told you about that?'

'Yeah, he did.'

'I hope you find him,' said Ruby. 'I really do.'

Kit nodded. It was weird, Ruby being Daisy's mother. She was the wrong *colour*, for a start. But he hadn't questioned Michael over it, and he wasn't about to step on Ruby's toes, either.

'And what about Daisy?' he asked. 'You see a lot of her these days, don't you? She doesn't *know* . . . ?'

'No. She doesn't.'

'Are you going to tell her?'

'No, I'm not.'

'And are you going to stay away from her, like he wants you to?'

Ruby took a deep breath. 'I don't see how I'm going to be able to do that,' she said.

'But you said you would.'

'Yeah.'

'Cornelius Bray ain't going to be very happy with you.'

'No.' Ruby picked up her mug and took a sip. 'He's not.'

Kit had left Ruby in the kitchen and was crossing the hall when he saw Michael coming downstairs, buttoning his shirt cuff. They exchanged a long look. Kit went and met his boss at the bottom of the staircase.

'This was Tito, wasn't it?' said Kit with barely controlled anger. 'Him and this Bray character are in tight together. Shag little boys together, I heard.'

Michael let out a sharp breath. 'Kit,' he said. 'Drop the Tito thing.'

'You know he did this,' said Kit.

'Leave it,' said Michael, and walked past him, across the hall.

'You know this was Tito,' Kit called after him. 'So what now, boss? You just going to lay down and let him walk right over Ruby?'

Michael stopped walking. He turned slightly, looking back at Kit. His face was expressionless. Then he smiled, very slightly. 'I'm going to forget you said that, Kit, because you're my number one man and I like you. Just don't ever say anything like that to me, ever again. OK?'

Not waiting for a reply, Michael went into the kitchen, and closed the door firmly behind him.

But Kit didn't think he could ever bring himself to toe the party line over Tito. At night he dreamed sometimes of Gilda, tossed aside like a broken doll, Gilda with her lucky-charm bracelet and its dark heart, the one that she'd bought to remind her of him. Awful, painful dreams. No, he didn't think he could bring himself to drop the Tito thing – any more than Ruby could oblige Cornelius Bray by keeping out of her daughter's life.

109

New Year's Eve 1971

Daisy sighed and wandered from room to room in the gate-house. She was pleased with what she'd done here. Now it looked nothing like it had when she was a child, after Nana Bray had lived here. Daisy had played sometimes in the empty rooms, marvelling at the old floral wallpapers throughout.

Now it was completely different. There was vivid orange on the walls, and huge comfy purple sofas with orange cushions, deep shag-pile purple carpets and the odd splash of lime green in the ornaments and glassware. And tonight she planned to *party*. It was the end of the old year, the start of the new. Why not?

Everyone she knew was invited, all her old pals, even the interior designer who had helped her kit out the gatehouse was coming, with his boyfriend. Of course, her parents wouldn't come – and just as well. It would be too wild for their taste, Daisy knew. Ruby couldn't come because she was travelling on business or something, and that had disappointed her because she liked Ruby so much.

Now Kit had pulled out. Phoned her this morning – the morning of the party – to say he was busy and couldn't come. Just that.

'Busy?' She'd tried to keep it light, but she was very hurt. She *adored* Kit, and she couldn't understand why Kit didn't like her. He was a real man, not like those shallow trumpeting hoorays her parents kept trying to push her into going out with. She'd tried so hard with him. Short of stripping naked and lying in his bed in wait for him, she couldn't think of a single other thing she could do to convince him that she was available for him, day or night.

'Yeah, I'm sorting out some stuff.'

'Stuff? What "stuff"?' Daisy knew she shouldn't be questioning him like this, that men hated it when females came over all heavy on them, but somehow she couldn't help herself. Her whole mind had been focused on him coming to this party – she didn't give a *shit* if no one else turned up, she wanted *him* to come.

'Business stuff, Daisy.' Now he sounded exasperated.

'But for God's sake! It's New Year's Eve.'

'Daisy – I can't come. I'm sorry, but there it is.'

'Right.' Daisy felt her mouth grow stiff. She swallowed hard, holding back tears. 'Well, thank you. Thanks for letting me know.'

'Daisy . . .'

'No, that's fine. Absolutely *fine*. Goodbye.' She slammed down the phone. When it rang again, seconds later, she didn't pick it up. She had the caterers coming in a couple of hours, she was going to take a long hot bath, relax, maybe smoke a joint or two. Get in the party mood. Even if there didn't seem to be any point to that any more.

'What do you think?' asked Vanessa.

Cornelius stood at the drawing-room windows at Brayfield. Even with the windows closed, he could hear and almost *feel* the visceral thump-thump-thump of the sound system roaring away down at the gatehouse. He glanced at the clock on the mantle. Midnight had come and gone. The New Year had been welcomed in. Now it was two in the morning, and the party was still in full swing.

He turned away from the window and saw his wife's anxious face peering into his. This was an annoyance – he didn't often bother to come home any more, but this time Vanessa had insisted. It was New Year's Eve, she didn't want to spend it alone. And she wanted him on hand in case there was any 'disorderly behaviour', as she put it.

Christ – other people had daughters they could be proud of, fine girls who got married and behaved themselves. From what he was hearing now from Vanessa, Daisy was a complete liability and had been so for quite a while. He suspected that the worst of Daisy's behaviour had been concealed from him for some years, by Vanessa, and by his sister too.

'Think I'll go up to bed,' he said.

'*What?*' Vanessa's mouth dropped open. 'But, Cornelius, what if—'

'What?' he snapped, annoyed because this *wasn't* how he'd planned to spend his evening. He had wanted to go to the club with Tito, see a little action. Not be stuck here with Vanessa bending his ear over Daisy.

'What if something happens?' she asked.

'Nothing's going to happen. They're just young people enjoying themselves.' He opened the door and was halfway across the hall when the phone started ringing on the console table. 'Get that, will you, darling?' he said, and started climbing the stairs.

Agitatedly, Vanessa snatched up the phone. 'Hello?'

She heard a garbled female voice, pounding music. Vanessa glanced towards the drawing-room windows, in the direction of the gatehouse. The music – if you could call it that – was in perfect rhythm with the noise coming from out there.

She couldn't hear what was being said. Cornelius paused on the stairs.

'Who is it, at this hour?' he asked.

'I can't hear what they're saying,' said Vanessa. She gripped the phone tighter. 'Hello! Hello?'

She looked up at Cornelius and her eyes were frightened. 'I think it's someone calling from the gatehouse. A girl, but I can't hear what she's saying. It could be Daisy.'

110

By the time they had walked to the bottom of the driveway, Vanessa was in a state of high anxiety and Cornelius was seriously annoyed. There were more than twenty cars parked outside the gatehouse – and there was Mandy, Daisy's friend, running towards them as they rounded the corner of the drive.

'What is it?' asked Cornelius, grabbing her.

'Daisy! It's Daisy, I can't get her to wake up . . .'

'What? Is she drunk?' They were all hurrying towards the gatehouse, which seemed to be throbbing, there was so much light and noise spilling out of it.

The front door was open, and they hurried into the hall. There was no point in speaking any more, you couldn't hear a word above the din. Cornelius dived straight into the sitting room. There were people lying about on sofas, smoking joints. There were empty bottles of booze, there was a table strewn with remnants of food.

Vanessa followed him and stood there and stared in horror. There were drink stains all over the newly laid carpets; someone had been throwing food at the wall. The place was a mess and it stank to high heaven of strange substances, spilled booze and sweaty bodies. She grabbed hold of Mandy, shook her and shouted: '*Where is Daisy?*'

Mandy took hold of Vanessa's hand and hurried up the

stairs with her. There, in the master bedroom, was Daisy, sprawled out on the floor beside the hideous purple-covered bed, two young men watching her uneasily.

Vanessa drew in a horrified breath. Daisy was white as uncooked dough, her face sheened with perspiration. There was a ligature of some sort around her upper arm, and there was a puncture mark on the inner bend of her elbow.

'Oh my *God*,' said Vanessa, throwing herself to her knees beside Daisy and grabbing her wrist, feeling frantically for a pulse. She looked up furiously at Mandy and the two young men, who were edging towards the door. 'Who did this? What has she been injected with? *Who did this?*'

Cornelius was snatching up the phone, dialling 999.

'Ambulance, please. Yes.' He gave the address. 'It looks like an overdose. I've no idea of what.'

He put down the phone and turned towards Mandy. 'You. Get out.'

'But I . . .'

'Didn't you hear me? Crawl off into whatever hole you came from,' barked Cornelius.

That said, he followed Mandy down the stairs.

Vanessa knelt beside Daisy and smoothed her feverish brow, hoping she wasn't going to die. But – oh God – she looked so ill. And Mandy was right. She was unconscious.

Seconds later she heard car engines start. Abruptly, the music died. There were many footsteps in the hall, mutterings, the odd sheepish laugh. More cars started. Then after a while there was silence downstairs.

Vanessa got to her feet and went over to the door. She looked down into the hall. There was no movement now. The door was standing open.

'Cornelius?' she called shakily.

There was no answer.

Of course. He couldn't be found here, not with his daughter

drugged-up and unconscious. He had gone, back up to the house. She returned to Daisy and fell to her knees beside her. Alone – as so often she was – she waited for the ambulance to arrive.

111

'It was heroin,' said Berenson, the consultant at the hospital. 'A large dose. She's very lucky to be alive.'

Vanessa was almost too shocked by this to speak. But she had spent so many years as the wife of a prominent politician that she rallied – always – with phenomenal speed.

Heroin.

'This mustn't go any further,' she told the man, an old friend who played golf with Cornelius. 'No police. No press. You understand?'

The consultant nodded. 'Of course.'

He left her then, sitting alone at Daisy's bedside. Vanessa hardly knew what day it was. She had travelled in the ambulance with Daisy and then waited hour upon endless hour, and now it was daylight, dawn was creeping over the horizon and she was thinking, *Where did we go so wrong?*

She sat there and gazed at Daisy's pale, unconscious face. All right, Daisy was not her natural child. But she had tried her best with the girl; she believed that she had loved her as much as she possibly could, given her everything she could want. Maybe too much?

But they had tried never to spoil Daisy. It wasn't their fault. Daisy was just . . . wild. And she seemed to have this notion that she was unloved, when that wasn't true. They weren't demonstrative parents, they didn't hug or kiss very much, but surely the fact that she was loved by them went without saying? She was *their child*.

Only . . . she wasn't. She was Cornelius's child, yes, but got on that whore Ruby, not on his wife. Vanessa had hoped never to have to see or hear from that slut ever again, but it seemed she was everywhere, in the business section of the papers, in magazine articles, even showing up in Vanessa's home, with Daisy.

But then . . . Vanessa had been unable to have children. Daisy had been her one chance to achieve the impossible. And Daisy was her father's child; Vanessa had loved her, if only for that. While always – she could admit this to herself, but to no one else – there was always that feeling that Daisy was never truly hers, that she was very much *Ruby's* child.

Vanessa had never felt so alone, so completely frightened and bewildered by the world around her. She understood her garden, the soil, the plants, all that; but this . . . She couldn't even begin to comprehend why Daisy could have allowed some fool to inject her with that ghastly stuff. Or – horrible thought – had she done it to herself? Was she so unhappy? Had they – her parents – *made* her unhappy?

'She needs to rest now, that's all,' said the consultant, returning to Daisy's bedside in the morning. 'By this afternoon she'll be awake and she'll be able to talk to you. Until then, you should go home. Get some rest too.'

Vanessa went home, to find Cornelius waiting for her in the drawing room.

'How is she?' he asked, standing up.

Vanessa stared at him.

'Vanessa? Is she all right?'

Vanessa's mouth twisted. 'Oh – you mean your daughter?'

'Come on . . .'

'What, Cornelius? Are you going to tell me I'm overtired?' Vanessa slapped her bag down in a chair and let out a harsh laugh. 'Funnily enough, I am. I've been sitting and waiting to hear whether or not our daughter – no, let's get this right: *your* daughter – was going to die. I was there at the hospital for *six hours*.'

Cornelius let out a sigh and reached for her. 'Now, darling, you know I couldn't stay, I couldn't be implicated in anything like that. You saw Berenson? I called him. Did he sort things out . . . ?'

'Of course I did. And he covered for you, don't worry. There'll be no questions asked. That was the first thing you thought of, wasn't it? Your precious reputation. Well, maybe you ought to think about that a bit more when you're up in town having . . .' Vanessa paused, groping for the words, her face twisting in disgust '. . . *relations* with young women. And young men.'

Cornelius grew very still. 'What have you been hearing?'

'What, aren't you going to deny it?'

He let out a breath. 'Of *course* I deny it.'

But Vanessa had heard him in his role as a politician deny things that five minutes later he had coolly implemented. Cornelius was the suavest, the smoothest of liars. She knew that.

'Who told you such a ghastly thing?' he wanted to know.

'Oh, no one who would let it go any further,' snapped Vanessa. She wasn't going to tell him that his own sister had dropped this bombshell, when Vanessa had been chatting to her about Cornelius being so busy up in town.

'Darling, he's busy all right, and not just with the women, I hear . . .' Ju had said in her artless, blundering way.

'What do you mean?' asked Vanessa.

And Ju had told her everything. About Cornelius's close connection to Tito Danieri – a *gangster*, for God's sake – and about the beautiful dark-haired boy he had been seen hanging around with in a club.

'He was all over him, apparently,' gushed Ju excitedly.

Someone had taken a photograph, and it was rumoured that Tito's heavies had smashed the camera. Smashed the photographer up, too.

'Come on, Vanessa, I want to know,' said Cornelius roughly, his smooth veneer slipping, just a bit.

'I told you. No one who would pass it on to anyone, except to me. And you know I won't, either. But you should be more careful, Cornelius.'

'Look, that's enough of all that nonsense,' he said, turning away from her. 'The main thing is, is Daisy going to be all right?'

'She is. No thanks to you. I don't know whether she injected herself or someone else did it for her, but that was an overdose of *heroin* in her system. It could have been fatal.'

Cornelius looked aghast. 'Do you seriously think she'd do that to herself?'

'I don't know. I don't feel I know her. I don't know *what* she's capable of. All I know . . .' Vanessa choked on tears now. 'All I know is that she's beyond me. I've tried so hard with her. But she's *wild*.'

'I don't know what you mean.'

'Ask Julianna. Ask your sister. Daisy's out of control, she has been for a long time.' Now Vanessa broke down and started to sob, long, tearing exhausted gasps that shook her skinny frame.

'Darling – don't . . .' Cornelius pulled her in close to him, held her.

'I don't know what to do with her any more,' cried Vanessa.

Cornelius made soothing noises, but he wondered bitterly how Vanessa could have allowed this mess with Daisy to escalate to this level. It could *ruin* him. Didn't she realize that? Much more of this, and there would be Talk. He couldn't have that. He could see that he was going to have to take this situation in hand.

112

Daisy couldn't remember very much about that disastrous New Year's Eve party. She only knew that she'd been miserable. She'd tried to jolly herself up with a lot of drink and a pill or two. Then she had found herself up in the bedroom and someone . . . she couldn't remember who . . . had said, try this, and had tied up her arm with a plastic thing that hurt a lot. Then the sting of the needle. After that, nothing.

Expecting to be given a very hard time by the folks – she knew she deserved it – Daisy was surprised when she was allowed to recuperate at Brayfield without so much as a mention of her appalling behaviour. Pa was, as always, mostly absent. Vanessa was, also as always, mostly in the garden. Daisy was left alone.

At first she just stayed in bed. Then, when she was able to get up, she wandered around the big house, pale and shivery, feeling the horrible skin-crawling after-effects of the drugs. For a long while she couldn't sleep properly for vivid, terrifying nightmares, and she didn't eat very well either.

But slowly, surely, her body mended itself, although her mood remained black. Her life was a mess. Now her home, the one she had poured so much love and attention into, was a mess, too; one sunny day, when she felt strong enough, she walked down to the gatehouse and opened the door and went in.

She just stood there in the hall, looking at the chaos that no one had yet thought to do anything about. Tears were pouring down her face. She didn't feel she had the strength or even the will to sort this out. A car passed by on the drive, but she took no notice.

What's going to happen to me? she wondered bleakly.

She could feel her entire being spinning out of control. The folks had even talked about a psychiatrist, professional help. Maybe they were right, maybe she was just crazy. Her mind groped around for logic but couldn't find any. She thought of Kit, how upset she'd been when he rejected her yet again. She wondered if he'd tried to see her. She could have *died* that night. And would he even have cared? She was just 'that fruit loop Daisy' to him, mad and sweet, but not his type.

She had never been denied anything in her life; but she couldn't have Kit. She could see that so clearly now. So she was going to leave him alone. Why keep punishing herself by trying to summon up feelings that weren't there?

Her mind made up, she took a deep breath and dried her tears. She left the gatehouse, locked the door, and walked back up the drive to the house.

There was a large dark-blue car that she didn't recognize parked in front of the house when she got there. She went indoors and heard voices and laughter in the drawing room. The door to the drawing room was ajar. She didn't want to see anyone so she closed the front door as softly as she could and crept across the hall to the stairs.

'Daisy!'

Damn.

She turned, pasting a wan smile on her face. Vanessa was

standing there, flushed, in the open doorway, not wearing her usual uniform of jeans, blouse, jumper and Barbour but a floral-sprigged cotton sundress with a pale primrose cardigan. She had a smear of lipstick on her mouth, even a touch of mascara on her lashes.

So what's the occasion? wondered Daisy, her spirits sinking even further. She didn't want to make empty conversation. She wanted to go up to her room and never come back out again.

'We have visitors, Daisy, come on,' said Vanessa.

Daisy crossed the hall with all the enthusiasm of a prisoner going to execution. They stepped into the room and she saw to her surprise that Pa was there, holding court with his broad back to the fire, his thick mop of white hair aglow, an arm propped casually on the mantelpiece. Filling the room, as he always did, with his huge presence. There were three other people in the room: a ruddy-faced older man and a thin woman she didn't recognize, and . . .

'Simon?' she blurted out.

He turned towards her, drink in hand. He'd gained a little weight, she saw, but he was still essentially the same: red-haired, short, densely muscular, brutishly attractive with twinkling hazel eyes; the same Simon Collins who had taken her virginity at the Dorchester.

'You do remember Simon, don't you?' said Cornelius, leaving the fire to walk over to the younger man – dwarfing him, and placing an arm about Simon's chunky shoulders.

Oh gawd – didn't Aunt Ju call him the Dwarf . . . ?

'Yes, of course,' mumbled Daisy as Simon Collins was brought towards her by her father.

Simon kissed her politely on both cheeks.

'And these are Simon's parents,' said Vanessa. 'Sir Bradley and Lady Collins.'

Daisy was trawling her memory for details. Hadn't Aunt

435

Ju said that Simon's father owned a building company? Hadn't she said the family were 'trade', but very respectable? Yes, she had. They owned gravel pits: aggregates. That was it.

And hadn't the last time she'd seen Simon been a disaster, with him looking embarrassed and announcing that the girl walking with him down Regent Street was his fiancée Clarissa, one of Lord Breamore's daughters?

She glanced at his left hand as he turned and accepted a drink from her father.

No ring.

But then, Simon was so macho that he probably wouldn't agree to wear one.

'You're looking beautiful,' said Simon, staring at her in a way she found discomforting.

'Thank you,' she said. She knew she didn't look beautiful. She was scruffily dressed in an old jacket, jeans and sandals, and she was still looking – and feeling – washed-out from her brush with her own mortality.

What on earth's all this about?

She sent a querying look to her mother, but Vanessa was deep in conversation now with Lady Collins. She glanced at Pa, but he was making Sir Bradley laugh. She was marooned on an island of awkwardness, with Simon her only companion.

'It's been years,' said Simon.

'Yes,' said Daisy.

'Too long,' he said.

Daisy stared at him curiously. 'The last time I saw you, you introduced me to your fiancé.'

'Ah. Well, yes. Clarissa.'

'How is she?'

'Haven't a clue,' said Simon with a shrug. 'That fell through.'

'And before that,' said Daisy, 'the Dorchester. My deb's dance.'

Simon's eyes locked with hers. 'Quite a night.'

'You took my virginity.'

'I know. I enjoyed it, too.' He lowered his voice even further. His eyes caressed her face. 'You were fantastically hot, for a virgin.'

'I was drunk out of my skull.'

He was still very attractive, she had to admit that. And in flats, like she was wearing now, he didn't seem so short.

'Thought you might be married by now,' he said, sipping champagne. 'All sprogged up.'

Daisy shook her head. A brief vision of Kit floated through her brain, but she booted it straight out. Kit was gone, the past. Now, she had to somehow find a future.

'I was lucky not to be "sprogged up" that night. Actually, I *could* have been, for all you cared.'

'I think your aunt put paid to that, interrupting us like she did.' His hazel-flecked eyes were smiling into hers. 'But you were so delicious. And so surprisingly big-breasted under that demure yellow dress. I love large nipples. Yours are huge. I've never forgotten them, they've haunted my dreams.'

'Simon . . .' Daisy could feel herself blushing. For God's sake, her parents were in the room.

'I wanted to bite them, to eat them,' he went on, lowering his voice to a husky whisper. 'As a matter of fact, I'd like to do that now. I intend to do that, the first chance I get.'

Daisy felt a hard twinge of desire then.

'I'm very glad you're not married yet,' he said more softly.

'Why's that?' Daisy was trying to keep her voice steady, but failing.

'Because I want to marry you. I've already spoken to your father.'

Daisy glanced across at Pa. No wonder Sir Bradley looked flushed with pleasure, his face almost as red as his hair; no wonder his wife was looking like she'd won the lottery. Pa had organized this. Daisy felt herself shrivel with embarrassment as she realized that her father had spoken to her mother and Aunt Ju, and that he must know what she and Simon had done that night in the Dorchester.

'What did he say?' she asked faintly. She couldn't believe this.

'He said if you were agreeable, then he'd be very pleased to call me son-in-law.' Simon was standing very close now. '*Are* you agreeable, Daisy?'

Daisy stared at him. He was handsome, successful, vigorous. She felt as if she were standing on a precipice. Behind her, her wild past, Kit, loneliness, confusion and despair. Ahead – Simon. And marriage. A fresh start.

'My God. . .' she breathed, shocked by the suddenness of events.

'*Are* you?' he murmured. 'Because I want this, Daisy. I want to get you bedded and full of babies as soon as I can.'

It seemed an odd thing to say. Again Daisy found herself looking at Pa. Had Cornelius promised Simon and his gleeful parents' *money* to take his too-troublesome daughter off his hands? And – yes – more money if she produced children quickly, and got 'settled down' to maternity?

She stared at her father. Oh yes. He probably had. Money was, after all, Pa's answer to everything.

It wasn't exactly a romantic proposal. She barely knew Simon; all she knew, right now, was that her father was paying and that Simon was keen. And being desired was a balm to her hurt and bewilderment. Simon wanted her. She liked that.

'All right,' she said. 'Why not?'

'What?'

'I'll marry you, Simon.'

He stared at her a moment longer. 'You won't regret this,' he said, and then he turned and announced the happy news to his parents, and hers.

113

There had been only one children's home in Fulham in the nineteen forties and fifties, and Kit had been trying to find it but failing. He had the road right, but there were blocks of council flats there now. He went to the local post office and spoke to a harassed-looking man behind the counter there.

'In the forties and *fifties*, you say?' He stared at Kit like he was crazy. 'Who knows what happened? Come on, mate, there's people waiting to be served here.'

Kit withdrew. He thought about going back and talking to Jennifer again, but she was so frail that he didn't really want to bother her if he could avoid it. Instead, he went to the local paper and was shown into their archive section by a spectacled middle-aged lady who set him down and showed him how to work the microfiche.

'Do you have the year?' she asked.

Kit gave it to her.

She was shuffling papers, flicking page after page. 'That was near the end of the war. It could have been bombed,' she said.

'Yeah, it could,' said Kit. In which case, Ruby's quest was over and her child was dead. He didn't want to take her back news like that.

'Here we are,' said the woman, peering over the top of

her glasses. 'I'll leave you to have a look through then, shall I?'

'Thanks,' said Kit.

He didn't know what he was looking for. Some sort of news, some sort of *explanation*. The home had been there; now it wasn't. He trawled through page after page of fetes and disputes, strikes and hit-and-runs, carnivals and minor riots.

And suddenly, there it was:

Tragedy Strikes at Children's Home

Three fire brigades were in action on Thursday night when an electrical fault resulted in the deaths of all twenty-eight children residing at the Manor Park home. Two staff also perished in the blaze, which was brought under control in the early hours of Friday morning.

'*Fuck*,' Kit breathed, feeling sick to his stomach.

'Have you found anything?' asked the woman, bustling over.

'Yeah.' *More than I wanted.*

He switched off the microfiche and stood up. 'Thanks for your help,' he said, and left the room, left the building.

All those kids! Poor little bastards, they hadn't stood a chance. He walked back to his car, and got in. Drove over to Michael's place, and told him what he'd found.

'There were no survivors?' asked Michael, lighting a cigarette.

'Not among the kids. Maybe some of the staff got out, but it didn't say.'

'That was the only home, the only one the kid could have been taken to?'

'Yeah, boss. I'm sorry.'

'He's dead then.'

'For sure.'

'This is going to break her heart.'

'I know.' Kit shrugged his shoulders. 'But look, at least now she'll *know*. We'll be able to find a grave site, I should think, if she wants that.'

'Yeah. Maybe.'

'At least she'll be able to close the book on this. Let it go at last.'

'Yeah.' Michael's eyes were sad. He wished he didn't have to break this news to Ruby, but he had to. 'There's that, at least.'

He told her after dinner that night. Ruby took it on the chin, the way she took everything. But later that night, in bed, he heard her crying into her pillow, trying to muffle the sound, trying not to disturb him.

'Hey,' he said, pulling her close. 'Hey, come on.' He thought of Kit's words to him earlier in the day. 'At least you know now. We could find a grave, maybe.'

'No! I couldn't stand that.'

'I had to tell you. I knew it would hurt, but isn't it better to know?'

'No. It isn't,' sobbed Ruby. 'Before, I could hope, couldn't I? Now, I can't. Now I know it's a dead end. That I'm never going to see him again.'

He couldn't argue with that, she was speaking the absolute truth. He just held her, until she cried herself to sleep.

Ruby was inconsolable.

Her dream of finding her nameless child was over.

This was the end.

114

1974

'I suppose twins run in your family?' asked Simon.

Daisy lay back in the private hospital bed, exhausted but happy, fascinated as she stared at these two tiny babies her husband was now cradling in his arms.

'No, they don't,' she said. 'I thought the twin thing must have come from yours.'

'It doesn't matter,' he said, beaming with pride as he cradled his two boys. 'They're perfect.'

Daisy lay back and watched him. Simon had been as good as his word; within a year of him and his parents calling at Brayfield, he had married her; and she'd been impregnated on their honeymoon in the Seychelles. Pregnancy had mellowed her a little. She'd been too frightened to drink in case it harmed the babies, and for the first time in her life she took care of her body, nurturing it with good food and gentle exercise.

Now, here was the result. Two healthy children, with their father's red hair and dark-blue eyes that she suspected would soon turn to hazel. Simon's genes seemed to have overpowered hers. Just like Simon's will so often did.

'What shall we call them?' he asked, glowing with paternal pride.

'We've already chosen the names,' said Daisy, yawning. *Or you have.*

'Matthew and Luke,' said Simon. 'Like the Bible.'

'More visitors,' said the nurse, popping her head round the door.

It was her mother and father, coming in with flowers and chocolates.

'You are *such* a clever girl,' said Cornelius to Daisy, taking one of the babies from his son-in-law with extreme care. He grinned at Simon.

And you're going to give Simon a handsome pay-off for this, thought Daisy.

But she couldn't feel too annoyed. She was too sleepy, for one thing. The birth had been difficult, and in the end she had been rushed down for a caesarean as the babies were beginning to get distressed. Her stitches hurt. Her breasts were sore. She felt like she'd been picked up by a whirlwind, spun around, then slammed back onto the earth.

What had happened to her? She felt strange, somehow outside herself. The old Daisy would have been out partying now, boogying along to 'Tiger Feet' and wearing leathers like Suzi Quatro when she sang 'Devil Gate Drive'.

Motherhood had happened to her.

She gazed at her two boys as they were passed around and generally adored, and felt such an overwhelming wave of love for them that tears pricked her eyes. Was this how Vanessa had felt, when she'd given birth to Daisy? Daisy didn't think so. She wanted to think that, but she didn't. She couldn't.

'Daisy says twins don't run in your family,' Simon was saying, and she caught a look – *what was that?* – that passed with lightning speed between her mother and father.

'They don't,' said Cornelius. 'This is just a happy bonus,

isn't it? Two babies, instead of one. Two grandchildren to spoil, how marvellous.'

Simon gave Daisy a smile, but she knew what he was thinking and she was glad the babies had his red locks and not her blonde ones or he would think she had slept with someone else. Simon was hellishly jealous, which was flattering in one way but in another, a complete nightmare.

'Have you chosen names?' asked Vanessa.

'Matthew and Luke,' said Simon.

'Lovely.'

Two months after the birth, she was at home, with Ma and Aunt Ju visiting.

'He's not so bad after all, is he?' asked Aunt Ju, cuddling Matthew.

'Who, dear?' asked Vanessa, cuddling Luke.

'The Red Dwarf,' laughed Ju.

'Don't call him that,' said Daisy, looking around as if Simon was about to emerge from the woodwork.

'Don't look so worried, dear, he's away on business, isn't he?' Aunt Ju smiled across at her niece. 'Isn't a red dwarf a star that explodes spectacularly? In which case it's quite fitting really, as a nickname for your husband.'

Daisy half-smiled, but she felt embarrassed. It was true, Simon had a typical redhead's temper, blowing up in an instant. She always had to be careful not to annoy him. But, apart from that, he was a good husband, providing her with everything she could possibly want or need.

She had this big if rather charmless house out in the country, a white-painted monolith that Simon had picked out, not her. Daisy knew she was very, very lucky to have him – even if Pa had 'bought' him for her, showering his family with gifts and establishing connections for them that would otherwise have been beyond their reach.

She was so relieved that all the madness of her youth was over. When she looked back at her life now, her own behaviour frightened her. Marriage might be dull at times, but it was a safe harbour and she was glad of it. Look at Patty Hearst, for God's sake – heiress to a colossal fortune, but she'd been caught on camera, toting a gun and raiding a San Francisco bank. Patty had gone right over the edge – and now Daisy could see that, so easily, the same thing could have happened to her.

'When will he be back?' asked Vanessa, placing the baby tenderly in his crib.

'Simon? Oh, about a fortnight,' said Daisy. Actually, she rather enjoyed these times when business took him away from home. It was peaceful, just her and the twins. No explosions of temper, no walking on eggshells.

She did love him, a bit.

But it didn't worry her too much, when he was away.

She was on the bed in the master bedroom feeding the babies when she heard his key in the door.

'Hello!' he called.

'Up here!' Daisy called back.

Simon came up the stairs, loosening his tie, pulling open his shirt collar. He looked hot from travelling, but smiled when he saw her there.

'Hi, darling.' He came over and kissed her, smoothed a hand over each baby's head.

'Good trip?' she asked.

'Hellish. Nice to get back.'

'I won't be long,' said Daisy.

'No, carry on.' He sat down on the bed and watched his sons suckle at her blue-veined breasts.

'They're fuller than ever,' he said, fascinated, watching Matthew tugging at the teat.

'That's all the milk,' said Daisy.

'Do they get sore?' he asked.

'Sometimes.' Daisy looked at him. She knew he didn't want to hear about cracked nipples and nappy-changing. All that stuff bored him rigid. 'So did the deal go through?'

'Fine.' He shrugged, his eyes fastened to her chest. 'Christ, that's quite sexy.'

Daisy said nothing.

'Missed me?' he asked.

'Of course.' Had she? She wasn't sure.

'God.' He patted his crotch. 'Look at this. I'm hard.'

'I can't, yet . . .'

'Three months, the man said.'

'I don't know . . .' She didn't *want* sex yet. Right now, she was so wrapped up in the babies, so permanently exhausted, that she wondered if she would ever want sex again.

'Just carry on with what you're doing,' he said, and pulled back the covers, easing Daisy over onto her side while she still fed the twins.

He knelt up on the bed, unbuckled his belt, unzipped himself, pushed his trousers and pants down onto his thighs.

'Simon . . .' protested Daisy.

'Hush, my beautiful girl,' he said, and pushed up her nightdress so that he could get inside her.

It hurt, quite badly.

'Simon,' Daisy complained.

'Hush,' he said, and carried on.

115

'I think this is it. I'm finally going to tell her,' said Ruby to Vi, as they sat in Harvey Nicks' restaurant.

Vi's red-rouged mouth opened in surprise, her coffee cup poised halfway to her lips.

'But you said you wouldn't. And you were warned to stay away.'

Ruby let out a shuddering sigh. 'She's had twins.'

'Yes, you told me.'

Ruby thought about it. Michael had told her the news, he'd heard it on the City grapevine. Cornelius had been bragging around town about the arrival of his grandchildren.

Daisy – *her daughter* – was a mother now.

She knew that Daisy had married into the Collins family. They were in construction, apparently, and very rich. Ruby hadn't pursued the point about Daisy becoming a mother with Michael – she knew he'd come over all angry and protective if she did – but she did mention it to Rob, who was now her permanent minder.

'Do you know where they live, Daisy and her husband?' she asked him.

'Not a clue,' said Rob.

'Can you find out?'

'Piece of piss,' he said. And he did.

So now Ruby knew that Daisy and Simon Collins had a house in the Berkshire countryside. Rob gave her the address, and Ruby wrote a letter – and now, to her great joy, Daisy had phoned her, and agreed to meet up.

'Vi,' Ruby said deliberately. '*I* had twins.'

'I know.'

'She gets that from me, doesn't she?'

'She must do.'

Ruby frowned. 'Do you think her husband might suspect . . . ?'

'What, that Daisy's mother isn't who he thinks she is? I doubt it. And why should he even care?'

Ruby looked down at her coffee cup. She picked up a mint, turned it over, then put it back on the plate.

'Those are my grandchildren,' she said fiercely. 'I've never had Daisy. My boy . . . my boy died before I ever knew him. And now there are grandchildren, and I can't go near them, can't be their grandmother. All Cornelius cares about is appearances; he doesn't give *that* for Daisy's happiness. And as for Vanessa, my God!' Ruby let out a sour little laugh. 'All she wants to do is pick dead heads off roses!' Her eyes were vivid with emotion as they stared into Vi's. 'I could love those children *so much*. I could give them so much love, so much attention.'

Vi took a gulp of scalding-hot coffee. She put down her cup.

'And so you're going to let the cat out of the bag. After all these years.'

Ruby swept her hands up over her face and then threw her arms wide.

'I *have* to, Vi. It's been eating at me for so long, and now I really can't bring myself to stand back any more.'

'Ruby . . .'

'What?'

'Daisy might hate you for it. All those years, and you don't think she's been very happy . . .'

'I haven't seen her in quite a while. But no, she never seemed really happy. She seemed lost, somehow.'

'Maybe you were imagining that.'

'No. I wasn't.'

Vi reached out and grasped her hand. 'Look, Ruby, at the moment you're friends, aren't you? Even if you don't keep in touch very much. But if you tell her, she might turn against you. Have you thought about that?'

'Yes. I have. And I *have* to risk it.'

'And what about Cornelius? Or have you forgotten that the last time you got close to Daisy, he sent the heavies in?'

'I haven't forgotten.' Ruby's eyes strayed across the room. There was a bulky young man in a suit sitting there, sipping coffee – Rob. Her minder, who drove her everywhere and watched her every movement on Michael's instructions, ever since that terrifying brush with Tito's rampaging Glaswegian. Vi's eyes followed hers.

'I'm glad to see that Michael Ward's looking after you, but still . . . is it really wise to stir all this up?'

'I have to,' said Ruby simply.

She met Michael at his flat that evening. It was transformed; as invited, Ruby had redecorated. It was a chic, contemporary home now – no lingering memories of his late wife, Sheila, remained.

'I'm going to tell Daisy I'm her mother,' she said as they sat on the sofa after dinner, sipping wine.

'I'm glad you warned me,' said Michael.

'Well, aren't you going to try and talk me out of it? Vi did.'

'How do you think she'll react?' he asked.

Ruby's face was suddenly a picture of anxiety. 'I think

she'll hate me. Vi's right. And Kit said the same when I talked to him about finding my boy.'

'When was this?'

'Oh, a long time ago. After that night when Tito's boy paid me a visit, we talked in the kitchen the morning after. Kit thought my boy would hate me, for letting him go.'

'He could be right.'

'He could be. But I'll never know, because I've lost him, and there's nothing I can do about that.' Ruby gulped and blinked back sudden tears. 'But Daisy and her children, there's still a chance we could be close. They're *my blood*. And I have to let them know that.'

Michael eyed her steadily.

'What?' she asked. She had thought he'd kick up over this, had even braced herself for it.

But all he said was: 'Keep Rob close.'

Ruby was very still, staring at him. A shiver of fear crawled up her spine.

'Cornelius has kept this quiet for years,' said Michael. 'He wants to go on keeping it quiet. This could hit the fan, big style. Smear his reputation – he *loves* his reputation – and he's got contacts that wouldn't think twice about ensuring your silence. So be careful.'

116

'Well, this is unexpected,' said Daisy, coming into the restaurant and finding Ruby at the far table, the best in the room – Michael Ward's.

Ruby was sitting there alone. Rob was over at the bar. She stood up when she saw Daisy, and the two women exchanged brief hugs and kisses before sitting down.

'What can I get you, Miss Darke?' asked the waiter, coming straight over.

'Some wine? White?' Ruby looked at Daisy.

'I can't drink yet. Breastfeeding. Just some water, please.'

The waiter departed. Ruby felt her guts churn with inner turmoil. Finally, she was going to *do* this. She'd lost her courage so many times, but now she *had* to do it. She'd dressed carefully for this meeting, in a soft blue dress and matching accessories. She looked outwardly serene, but she had been sick twice overnight, and now her head was pounding with stress – but she was going to do this.

'I haven't seen you in a while,' said Ruby. 'I'm glad you came. I thought we ought to catch up.'

'It's been two years,' said Daisy a bit frostily. She remembered inviting Ruby to her New Year's Eve party at the gatehouse – and Ruby had declined, pleading business pressures. Kit too. It should have been a happy occasion. Instead, it had been awful, a cataclysmic turning point in her life. 'I was surprised to get your call.' She stared at Ruby and then she smiled, thawing a little. 'But it was a nice surprise.'

'How are the children?' asked Ruby.

'Fabulous. A nightmare. I'm run ragged, but they're adorable. Thank God I've got a nanny now to help out. Jody's terrific.'

The installation of Jody as nanny to the twins had been a major triumph for Daisy. Simon hated the idea, it went against all his working-class beliefs, but for once she had stood her ground and refused to be overcome by him. There had been real distressing knock-down, drag-out fights over the issue, but finally Simon had conceded. So Jody was a permanent fixture, and Daisy felt a little less frazzled all the time.

Ruby thought that Daisy *did* look tired. And when she relaxed and her face fell into repose, there was a vertical frown-line between her brows and deep furrows beside her mouth that hadn't been there before.

'Twins,' said Ruby, and then the sommelier brought the wine. A waiter arrived with a basket of freshly baked bread. He took their order – pasta for Ruby, salad for Daisy. Then they both departed. 'That must be wonderful.'

'Double the trouble, double the work,' said Daisy, but she smiled as she said it. 'You know, I can't believe how much my life has changed, Ruby. I really can't.'

'Your husband must be pleased.'

'Simon? Oh, he's delighted.'

'Twins run in families, usually.'

'That's what Simon said. But there are no twins in my family, or his.'

Ruby caught her breath. Now was the moment when she should speak. But she couldn't. She just couldn't push the words out of her mouth. Once they were out . . . oh my God, then Daisy would hate her, and her father would find out, and she had been warned . . .

The waiter arrived with their food, and the moment was gone.

'This looks great,' said Daisy, falling upon the food like a starving woman. 'I'm still eating like a horse, so I figure that, if I just eat salad, I can have big meals and still lose some of this baby weight.'

'You look absolutely fine,' said Ruby.

Daisy pulled a face. 'Simon doesn't like me porking up.'

'Better than fine. You look beautiful.'

'Well, *he* doesn't think so.'

Then he's a fool, thought Ruby. She looked across at Daisy, her beloved daughter, and thought, *No, it's no good, I can't do this. I don't want her to hate me, I couldn't bear it . . .*

'I suppose business is booming, as usual?' asked Daisy with a smile. 'You're such a powerhouse, Ruby. I really admire that.'

'Business is OK.' Nowadays, the business pretty much ran itself. She was just the figurehead really – little Ruby Darke, that quiet girl who had been frightened of her own shadow, who had sacrificed so much – a life, a husband, a family – and buried herself in work instead.

She knew that people perceived her as fortunate beyond words. That she had everything, with her luxury lifestyle, her business plaudits, her palatial home.

But inside, she still felt like that scared little girl. And she knew all too well what she had lost. She could *see* it, right in front of her. She had lost her daughter. She had lost – for ever – her son. Other people had their families around them, were cocooned in a soft comforting blanket of familial love; she was not. Apart from Michael, who was busy today, doing deals as usual, and Joe and Betsy and their children – whom she rarely saw – she was utterly alone in the world.

She sweated all though their meal, trying – and failing – to get the words out.

Just say it, she thought, time and again.

She couldn't.

Finally, after coffee, Daisy looked at her watch and sighed.

'This has been so lovely, Ruby. But I have to get back, the boys . . .'

She was going to lose the chance to do it.

She *had* to do it.

'*Daisy*,' she blurted out as Daisy was getting to her feet, groping around for her bag.

Something in Ruby's tone arrested Daisy's movement. She stopped, and sank back down into her chair, her eyes on Ruby's face. 'What is it?' Daisy gave a brief, nervous laugh. 'What's up, Ruby? You look like you're about to tell me the roof's fallen in.'

'It's . . .' Ruby swallowed. Her throat was parched. She reached for water, took a hasty swig.

'Well, go on. It's . . . what? Ruby, you're making me feel worried now.'

I have to say it.

'Daisy.' Ruby's hands were gripped tight together on the tablecloth. 'The twin thing.'

'Yes? What about it?' She stared at Ruby's fear-filled face and her smile fell away. 'Ruby, what on earth's wrong? You're frightening me.'

Ruby gulped. 'Oh, Daisy, please don't hate me . . .' she gasped.

'What? Why would I hate you? You're my friend.'

Ruby closed her eyes, shook her head and said: 'I had twins once. Long ago.'

Daisy's mouth dropped open. She was silent for a long moment, then she said: 'But . . . I didn't think you'd ever been married.'

'I wasn't. I had illegitimate twins. During the war.'

Daisy was staring at Ruby's face. 'My . . . God. And what happened?'

This was the hardest part of all. Ruby took another gulp of water.

'My daughter was taken away by her father. Raised by him and his wife. She couldn't have children.'

'And the other one . . . ?'

'My son.' Ruby choked on the words. Daisy reached out and put a warm hand over hers. 'He was taken away from me too. By my brother.'

'Good God.' Daisy's face was pale with horror.

'He wound up at a children's home, but it burned down and he died there.'

'Oh, Ruby, I'm so sorry.' Daisy's eyes filled with tears. 'How awful.'

'So . . .' Ruby said, blinking and swallowing. Daisy squeezed her hand encouragingly. This was *so hard*, '. . . so I've lost him completely, I can never get him back. But my daughter . . . she's alive, and I realize that you're only given so many chances in this world, and so I have to *take* this chance.'

'You're going to get in touch with her then? Tell her all this?' asked Daisy, holding tight to Ruby's trembling hand.

Ruby was breathing hard. She felt like she'd run a mile. Her whole body was shaking now, and she felt sick again.

'Daisy,' she said unsteadily, 'I *am* telling her all this. Right now.'

117

'What?' Daisy was staring at Ruby. Her fingers, which had been stroking Ruby's hand on the table, suddenly froze.

'Daisy . . . it's true. I'm telling her now. I had twins. You had twins. They run in families. They run in *our* family. Daisy . . . darling Daisy. You're my daughter.'

Daisy could only stare. What the hell was Ruby *talking* about?

'Is this . . .' Daisy was shaking her head, her mouth twisting up in a grim semblance of a smile . . . 'What is this, some sort of sick joke?'

Ruby bit her lip. 'No. It's not a joke. It's the truth.'

Daisy looked down at her hand. Quickly, she withdrew it.

'*Wait* a minute,' she said, clutching at her head now, her eyes fixed on Ruby as if she'd suddenly gone crazy. 'Now wait,' she almost shouted. 'This is crap, right?'

'No. This is the truth.'

'It can't be the truth. God's sake, *look* at you. Look at *me*.'

'Is everything all right here, ladies?' asked the waiter, coming over, alerted by raised voices and the curious glances of other diners.

'Everything's fine,' said Ruby firmly.

He went away again, but he didn't look convinced.

'Look, Daisy . . .' started Ruby, leaning closer, lowering her voice.

'No! No, *you* look.' Daisy didn't bother lowering hers. 'This isn't possible. Ma never liked you and now I can see why, it's because you're a *liar*!'

'Daisy!'

'No, come on. You can't be serious. You're dark-skinned, you're what my sainted mother would call "a bit of a mixture".'

'Or "having a touch of the tar brush"?' offered Ruby. She could see that nothing she said was going to lessen Daisy's fury. Better to let her get it all out, what the hell. 'Daisy, listen to me. My white mother had an affair with a black jazz player, and she had me. So yes, I'm "a bit of a mixture". And I . . . I'm sorry, Daisy, but I had an affair with your father.'

'My God,' wailed Daisy.

'At first I didn't know he was married,' said Ruby quickly, afraid Daisy might just bolt and not hear this. 'He didn't tell me. Then, when I became pregnant – God, Daisy, you have no idea what it was like for me. People didn't have illegitimate children then. It just *wasn't done*.'

Daisy was shaking her head steadily, like a metronome. 'This is all lies. Why are you doing this?'

'Why *would* I do it, Daisy?' asked Ruby intently. 'Why would I hurt you? I have no reason to. I've bottled this up for so long, but now I *have* to tell you the truth, and I just have to hope that, sooner or later, you'll accept it. You're my daughter. I'm your mother. Your true mother, your birth mother. Not Vanessa.'

Now Ruby was reaching for her bag, groping inside. She pulled out a polythene bag containing a brown-coloured card oblong. With shaking fingers she pulled the thing out and handed it to Daisy.

'*Look*, Daisy,' she said urgently. 'Look at the photo. That's your grandmother – my mother. See how much she looks like you?'

457

Daisy gulped and opened the folder. Inside was a picture of *her*. Only it wasn't. It was old. Sepia-tinted. It wasn't her at all, but somehow Ruby had mocked this thing up. Got a picture of her and made it look like something taken during the war.

Daisy threw the folder onto the table and surged to her feet.

'This is mad,' she said loudly. 'You're *crazy*. I'm not listening to this any more.'

'Daisy . . .' Ruby stood up too, hating the pain and confusion on Daisy's face, hating the fact that she had caused it.

'No, don't say another word,' Daisy said, and spun on her heel and almost ran from the restaurant.

118

He was waiting for her out on the House of Commons terrace, as arranged. Daisy hurried over to where he sat, watching tourists crowding avidly onto the riverboat down on the riverside for a trip along the Thames. There was an open bottle of chilled Chablis, one of mineral water and two glasses in front of him.

'Daisy!' Cornelius stood up, hugged her.

Daisy stiffened, didn't hug her father back. He felt her pull away, and stepped back a little, looking down at her curiously. 'What is it, darling? You sounded odd on the phone. Has something upset you? Is it Simon? Are the babies ill?'

Daisy shook her head and sat down. All she had told her father on the phone was that she had to see him, and he'd invited her here, for drinks. She'd phoned home, too, alerting the nanny to the fact that she expected to be late back.

'No, everyone's fine.' She sat down and looked across the table at him. He poured the water out for her and she took a hasty gulp. Shivered slightly. There was a cool breeze coming off the river, and the drink was cold too. She felt chilled, right through.

She couldn't stop staring at him. Her father. He was still a big, imposing man, suntanned and with that striking thick thatch of silver hair and those wide, seemingly guileless blue eyes. If what Ruby had said was true – which of course it wasn't – then he'd seduced Ruby, lied to her, deceived Vanessa. Daisy had always felt that deep down her father was an upright man, a man of principle. But . . . was he?

'So what's the matter?'

Daisy just sat there, wondering where the hell to start.

Had he lied to Ruby, lied to Vanessa, lived with those lies for years by not telling her the truth about her birth? He was a politician. Ruthlessness ran through his veins. But not with his family, surely? But then . . . look at how briskly he had arranged for Simon to come back into her life. She knew he had paid Simon to take her on. She *knew* that. Knew everyone thought she was a screwball and so a sweetener would be in order.

'What is it?' asked Cornelius again, feeling slightly unnerved by Daisy's unblinking stare.

'I had lunch with Ruby Darke today,' said Daisy at last.

'Who?'

'Ruby Darke, the owner of the department stores?'

'Oh? Yes, I've heard of her.'

'She's . . .' Daisy took another swallow of water to moisten her parched mouth . . . 'Pa, she said you had an affair with her.'

'She said *what*?' Cornelius let out a bark of laughter.

'An affair. That's what she said.'

'And when was this supposed to have happened?'

'During the war.'

'The woman's a fantasist,' said Cornelius.

'She said she had two children by you. Twins. There was a boy that her brother got rid of. He was dark-skinned, she said. You didn't want him. And there was me.' Daisy's eyes were frantic. 'She said that mother couldn't have children of her own, that you all agreed that you would take me and raise me. And that's what you did.'

'Daisy . . .'

'*Is it true?*' Daisy asked, tears springing into her eyes.

'Of course it isn't true,' said Cornelius earnestly. 'This Darke woman, from what I've seen of her, she's half-caste . . .'

'Don't call her that, it sounds horrible.'

'But how could you possibly be her daughter? Look at you. You're pale, you're blonde; you're the image of me.' Cornelius reached out a hand to touch her, but Daisy flinched back.

'She told me that could happen with mixed-race parents. One twin nearly black, the other white. And I know that's true. I've heard of it.'

'Daisy. Darling. What are you saying? This is all *nonsense.*'

'Why would she tell me, if it's not true?'

'God, I don't know. I know Vanessa doesn't much care for her and has left her off a guest list or two. Perhaps the feeling was mutual, perhaps this woman's cooked all this up to spite her.'

Daisy absorbed this. It sounded absurd. This was a monumental bombshell to drop on anyone, over a mere social snub. She thought back to all the times she'd been with Ruby. Ruby cleaning her up after that scare she'd had with Kit; Ruby going to the gatehouse with her, but being noticeably reluctant to go up to the house. Vanessa's stone-cold reaction to her. Daisy stared at her father. A politician, a practised liar. Her face grew very still.

'It's true, isn't it?' she said at last.

'Daisy, no.'

'Only it sort of makes sense. A lot of other things, little things, they all seem to add up now. And – oh God, yes – Aunt Ju telling mother to shut up after I got drunk and misbehaved at my deb's dance; she said something about "bad blood" and I never knew what she meant, it's puzzled me for years. *This* is what she was talking about. The fact that I'm not her child. That I'm Ruby's.'

'Daisy, darling, I promise you . . .'

But Daisy was standing up, staring down at him as if she'd never seen him before.

'Don't bother,' she said, and left him sitting there.

The moment Daisy left, Cornelius surged to his feet. He felt almost dizzy with rage that this was all blowing up in his face when he had tried so hard to suppress it. It seemed to him grossly unfair – *unbelievably* unfair – that a simple mistake made when he had been young and foolish should still have the power to disrupt his life.

He had a good life. A beautiful home, a wife who was always there. He could please himself, see to his own desires exactly as he wanted. But this . . . this *woman* continued to be a thorn in his side. If people knew about this, then his reputation would be damaged and his standing, his career, could be compromised. And he couldn't allow that to happen.

He left the House and went out into the road to flag down a taxi. He got in, gave the name of the place, and sat there, seeing nothing, as the cab wove through the traffic. That *bitch* had ignored the warning, and now things would have to get really dirty.

He got out when he reached his destination, paid the driver and went into the club. Tito was there, sitting on one of the stools at the bar. His ice-blue eyes widened when he saw Cornelius coming in, looking distraught.

'Trouble?' he asked.

Cornelius nodded, still so furious he could barely utter a word.

'Take a seat,' smiled Tito, patting a stool. 'Tell me about it.'

119

Daisy got down to Brayfield late in the evening, and charged into the drawing room where she found Vanessa watching television.

'Daisy! Why didn't you let me know you were coming?' she said, smiling, starting to get to her feet.

'No, don't get up.' Pale and drawn-looking, Daisy hurled herself down onto the other sofa and stared across at her mother.

Her mother.

Daisy felt like her whole world had shifted, plunging her into hideous uncertainty. Everything she had once believed, all that she had lived by, was now called into question.

'I had lunch with Ruby Darkc today,' she said.

'Oh.' Vanessa's face seemed to freeze.

'You don't like her. I could see it when I brought her here.'

Vanessa gave a slight shrug. 'She just doesn't seem our sort of person, that's all.'

'Is that the only reason you don't like her?'

'I don't know what you mean. I barely know her.'

'You know her well enough to take her child off her, apparently,' said Daisy.

'I . . . *what* did you say?'

'Ruby told me all about it. About her wartime affair with

Pa, and that you couldn't have a child of your own and so you took hers. Me. I'm *her* daughter, not yours.'

'Daisy, this is ridiculous. I hope you haven't been troubling your father with this rubbish?'

'Oh, God forbid I should trouble anyone. I've only just learned I'm a bastard, born out of wedlock. And that I had a brother, a *twin*, but you didn't want him, did you? Because he was dark-skinned, like Ruby. The pair of you wanted a white baby. Someone you could easily pass off as your own.' Daisy's eyes bored fiercely into Vanessa's. 'Well, aren't you going to say anything?'

Vanessa swallowed and looked away from Daisy. 'Your father denied all this, of course,' she said stiffly. 'Didn't he? Just as I do.'

'He denied everything.' Daisy's eyes were sparkling with tears and malice. 'But d'you know the funny thing, the one person who seems to *radiate* truth is Ruby. Not Pa. Not you.'

Vanessa looked back at her. 'Daisy. This is all nonsense.'

'That's what he said, too. I didn't believe him. And I don't believe you.'

'I have no idea why she's trying to stir up trouble like this . . .' started Vanessa.

'Did you have a script? Have you been looking at it together, the pair of you?' Daisy gave a sour laugh. 'That's what he said too. That it was just Ruby being bitchy because you'd forgotten to invite her into the inner circle along with all those dried-up harpies you fundraise with. Well I don't believe Ruby's that shallow, and furthermore I don't believe she'd give a *fuck* about your meetings and your charitable functions and all that crap anyway.'

'Daisy . . .' Vanessa was squirming in her seat.

Daisy pulled her hands through her hair. 'Did he phone you, is that it? Has he pre-warned you about this?'

'I haven't spoken to your father since last weekend.'

Daisy dropped her hands, her face naked with hurt and bewilderment. 'For God's sake,' she said, starting to cry. 'Won't one of you at least have the decency, after all this time, to admit to the truth?'

Vanessa stood up, her face cold.

'Daisy,' she said firmly, 'I have no idea what you're talking about.'

'Fine,' snapped Daisy, jumping up. 'You won't admit it. OK. But I don't want to see either of you any more. And I *don't* want you near the children.'

'Daisy!'

'And I don't want you near *me*.'

Daisy drove around after she left Brayfield, aimlessly, not knowing where to go or what to do. She ended up in London, at Michael Ward's restaurant, where she found Kit at the bar.

'Oh, it's you,' he said. 'Thought you'd left the country or something.'

He hadn't seen her for ages. He'd heard she'd got married, had a couple of kids. She'd dropped out of the London scene, and he hadn't expected to see her again. Now, here she was. And the last thing he needed right now was Daisy.

It had been a hard day, he'd received some bad news. He'd been visiting Jennifer on and off for a long time now, taking her little presents, chatting to her; but today, when he'd gone out to High Firs to see her and take her some new pens, she was nowhere to be found. Her room was empty, the bed stripped. He'd found the manageress, and asked her what was going on.

'Jennifer Phelps?' The manageress was shaking her head. 'I'm terribly sorry, she died last night. Went peacefully in her sleep, bless her.'

He left the home, still clutching the pens he'd bought for

her, feeling bereft. They hadn't been *close*, of course – he rarely got close to anyone – but he'd enjoyed her company, dotty as she was, and he knew she enjoyed his. Now the poor old duck was gone, and he felt sad about it, sadder than he would have expected.

Added to *that*, he'd been doing the rounds for Michael this afternoon, getting on with business, and that fat fuck Tito had cruised by with some of his boys, and Tito had grinned at him, mocking the fact that Kit couldn't do what he wanted to do, and smash the bastard's greasy face to a pulp.

He wanted – so badly – to do something about Tito. But Michael had said no; that they did business together, that it was impossible.

So tonight he didn't want to hear about anyone else's troubles; he had enough of his own. But Daisy looked like she'd been knocked sideways by something. He sighed. 'All right, come on, what's up?' he asked.

'Nothing,' she said. 'Get me a glass of wine, will you?'

Kit summoned the barman.

'Shit! No. I can't drink, give me an orange juice.'

The barman popped open a bottle of Britvic and decanted it into a glass. Daisy snatched it up and drank it, straight down. Then she turned and looked at Kit. She had to talk to someone about this, she *had* to.

'Ruby told me something today,' she said.

'Oh yeah? What?'

'She says I'm her daughter.' It poured out of Daisy then, the whole sorry tale. That Ruby had given birth to illegitimate twins, and Daisy had been taken by Cornelius and Vanessa, but the boy had been – apparently – passed on elsewhere.

'Right,' said Kit, draining the last of his pint as he listened to all this.

'What?' she asked, looking at his face. 'You don't seem very surprised.'

'That's because I'm not. I tried to trace that boy. Ruby's son. She told me you were her daughter. The twin of this boy I was looking for.'

Daisy stared at him. 'You knew, and you didn't *tell* me?'

'It wasn't my place to tell you.'

Daisy nodded her head, bit her lip. 'It's so awful. She said he died in a fire.'

'I'm sorry, Daisy,' said Kit. 'It's true. He was taken to a children's home, but it burned down. He's dead and gone.'

120

'Where the hell have you been?' asked Simon when Daisy dragged her exhausted body through the front door of their home at gone twelve that same night.

Daisy shook her head. She was so tired, wrung out by all that had happened, all these shocking new things she had discovered. That her mother and father were liars. That Ruby was her mother. That she'd had a twin, and . . . oh God, that she'd lost him, that she would never know him. Maybe that was why she'd been such a screw-up all her life. She was missing a part of herself, and maybe somehow she had always known it.

She dropped her bag onto the floor and took off her coat.

'Did you hear what I said?' Simon asked, coming and placing himself in front of her, red in the face with temper, hands on hips in indignation.

Even wearing flat shoes like she was now – and oh, she *detested* flats – Daisy noted that she was a couple of inches taller than her husband. *May as well give it up and wear four-inch heels*, she thought with a bubble of hysterical mirth.

'Yes,' she said, moving past him to get to the stairs. 'I heard you. Are the twins asleep?'

'Of *course* they're asleep. It's nearly one o'clock in the morning, what else would they be doing?' He caught her arm in a painful grip. 'Where have you been, Daisy? What have you been up to?'

'Up to?' Daisy could almost have laughed at that. 'I haven't been up to anything, Simon. I've . . . just had some really strange news. So I drove around a bit. Tried to take it all in.'

'What news?' snapped Simon.

'Can you let go of my arm? I just want to sleep.'

'Not until you tell me what's going on.'

'Nothing is going on. And I can't talk about this any more, not now.'

'Daisy!' He shook her. Daisy lost her footing and fell against him, feeling his fingers digging into the flesh of her arm. 'For fuck's sake. I've been worried half out of my mind, wondering where you were.'

'I'm not a dog, Simon. You don't have to keep me on a leash. I won't wander off, you know.'

'Won't you?' His eyes were hard as they stared into hers.

'You're hurting my arm,' she said, gritting her teeth. This was crazy and also rather funny. Simon and his family had bought into the posh Bray clan, but really, they'd been sold a pig in a poke. This explained so much! It even explained why she had always thought that Vanessa loved the *idea* of having a daughter – that she wanted a dress-up doll, a perfect little well-behaved replica of herself – rather than the boisterous reality that was Daisy.

She thought of that photo Ruby had shown her. The photo of her grandmother, but she hadn't believed it. She could still scarcely take it in, but Ruby's words resounded in her head over and over again. *Why would I lie? Why would I want to hurt you?*

'What?' Simon was glaring at her. 'What is it? What's going on?'

'Why don't you ask my father?' said Daisy. 'He'll tell you.

Or – no – maybe he won't. He's deep in denial at the moment. So's my mother. Only . . . oh dear . . . she's not actually my mother at all, as it turns out.'

Now Daisy started to laugh; it all seemed quite hilarious. She was stunned into silence when Simon slapped her, hard, across the face. Daisy fell to her knees and he dragged her upright again. Suddenly, she started to feel scared.

'You been drinking?' he asked. 'You *have*, haven't you, you silly cow? You know you're not supposed to drink, you're still feeding the twins.'

'I haven't . . .'

'Oh, shut up, Daisy. Why are you such a loose fucking cannon all the time? Why can't you just be a wife, be a mother? Isn't it enough I'm working my *arse* off day in, day out, without coming home to all *this*? What's all this rubbish you've got into your head now?'

'It's not rubbish,' said Daisy, feeling her cheek throb hotly where he'd hit her. My God – he'd *hit* her. 'Ruby Darke is my mother,' she told him forcefully. 'That isn't rubbish. That is the *truth*.'

'Ruby *Darke*? Are you crazy? That's the woman who runs the department stores, isn't it? The black woman?'

'She's not *black*,' said Daisy. 'She had a white mother, and a . . .'

'Daisy!' Simon was shaking her again. '*Shut up!*' he shouted straight into her face. Daisy flinched. 'You're drunk and you are talking *crap*. So just shut up and get the fuck up to bed, OK?'

He released her and Daisy staggered, clutching at the banister to stop herself from falling to the floor.

'I can understand you being upset,' said Daisy. 'I'm not exactly the purebred pedigree you expected, am I?'

Now Simon looked murderous.

'Shut your stupid mouth, Daisy. Go to bed.'

Daisy did. And Simon didn't come near her that night.

121

Ruby was working late, with Rob sitting patiently outside her office door. Jane had gone home. Ruby was mapping out her plans for the expansion of the childrenswear department, thinking of a new babywear designer, a schoolwear line, and a more appealing array of party frocks for little girls.

Finally the words and figures started to swim before her eyes, so she stretched, stood up, locked her desk drawers and the filing cabinet, and gathered up her black cashmere coat. She stepped out of her office. Rob looked up expectantly from his chair. She liked Rob: he was around the same age as Kit, with treacle-blond crew-cut hair, watchful khaki-green eyes and no tiresome chatter. She found his big, solid presence very reassuring – even though she hated the necessity of having him here.

'Ready, then?' she said.

He nodded and stood up. Together they went down in the lift and through the corridor to the staff exit at the back of the store. They passed the night security guard, just coming on duty. Rob opened the door and Ruby stepped outside. The night was frosty, the air bitingly cold.

There was a motor running somewhere out in the back alley, her car was waiting and ready. It wasn't glamorous back here. Front of store was immaculate, chic, polished to the nth degree; but here was the belly, the bowels of the store. Packing crates. Bins. Big sliding warehouse doors for goods inwards and out.

'Hey, Rob,' said the security guard, and Rob stepped back inside.

The motor had been idling, now it roared. Ruby looked around, surprised at the ferocity of the sound. Her car was a sleek, purring Mercedes and her driver Ben was old and not given to boy-racer stunts like this.

'What the . . . ?' she started, and the headlights blazed on, dazzling her.

The car was coming straight at her.

The noise of the engine was deafening, a high, shrieking whine. For a moment, Ruby stood there, frozen to the spot, disbelieving, and then when it was nearly on her she moved. She threw herself to one side, feeling herself being jolted and scraped as she hit the cobbles and rolled. She connected painfully, full-speed, with the wall of the store, knocking all the breath out of herself. She crawled to her knees, dazed, and stared after the car. Its red tailgate lights were on as it screeched to a stop twenty yards away. Then the white lights came on. The reversing lights. She saw a faint shadowy figure behind the wheel move, look back.

The car shot backwards.

Whoever it was, *he was coming to finish her off.*

There was a commotion and Ruby saw Rob almost fall out of the door, the security guard at his heels. She saw Rob reach inside his jacket and pull out a handgun. He took aim. The shots he fired off were deafening. Ruby flinched. The car halted abruptly, its back window cracking open in a shower of glass as bullets tore through it. The left-hand-side tyre collapsed, blown out. The car stopped moving and Rob took aim again.

Pow!

A bullet-hole appeared in the boot lid. Rob fired again and again, each shot hitting further to one side.

He's aiming for the petrol tank, thought Ruby with startling clarity.

But the assassin had had enough. The gears slammed and the car took off full pelt and veered crazily with a shriek of tyres and a squeal of metal rim, out and into the main road. Sparks flew from the back wheel as it spun, shredded tyre sprayed out. The car roared away into the distance, and was gone.

Rob was breathing hard. He slipped the gun back into his jacket and ran to Ruby.

'You OK?' he asked her, starting to haul her to her feet. The security guard was standing there open-mouthed. Someone had just tried to *kill* Ruby Darke.

Ruby collapsed with a scream. 'My arm,' she said, her teeth starting to chatter.

'Let's get you to the hospital.' Rob glanced around. 'Where the *fuck's* Ben got to?' He glanced at the guard. 'Miss Darke fell over on the icy cobbles, OK? You got that?'

The guard was nodding. The last thing he wanted was to get involved with this. He couldn't believe what he'd just witnessed. This bastard had a *gun*.

'I think it's broken,' said Ruby, feeling sick and dizzy with the pain.

'We'll take my car, it's just over there. Think you can walk it?'

Ruby nodded. As she walked, supported by Rob, she glanced fearfully again at the road, at the place where the car had vanished from sight. There was the smell of cordite in the air, of hot rubber from the tyres and scorched metal from the wheel rim. She'd told Daisy – and now here was the result. Cornelius had warned her, and he didn't make empty threats. The man in the car had been trying to kill her. And if Rob had been a second or two slower, he would have succeeded.

122

Michael was incandescent with rage when he heard what had happened. He'd visited Ruby at the hospital earlier in the evening, and she was sitting there in the hospital bed looking drawn and tired, her arm in a sling, Rob outside her door on guard. The arm hadn't been broken, as they'd feared. Just some ripped tendons. It would be painful for a week or two, but really she'd been lucky.

Really, she could have been *dead*.

Now Michael sat in the office behind the restaurant and looked at Kit as Kit filled in the blanks.

'This has got to be Tito,' said Kit. 'You know how tight he is with this Bray character.'

Michael nodded. His initial thought when he'd first heard about Ruby's near-miss was that this was payback over her brother Charlie, maybe Joe wasn't *quite* the limp dick he'd always thought he was. That somehow, somebody had tipped Joe off that Michael had been behind Charlie's death, and this was tit-for-tat.

But he'd dismissed that theory. Ruby herself didn't know that it was one of Michael's lot who'd run that bastard Charlie down. So she couldn't have let anything slip to anyone in a guilty moment, because *she didn't know*.

She was never *going* to know, either. The secret was his – and Reg's, because Reg had done the hit.

Reg would never spill his guts to anyone, Michael knew that. So this wasn't anything to do with *that*.

No, Kit was right. This was Tito.

Michael simmered with fury at that *punk* Tito daring to do something like this. Knowing his, Michael's, connection to Ruby, knowing he shouldn't dare. But doing it anyway.

Some people you had to do business with, that was a fact of life. Michael had tolerated Tito for years. As far as business went, that was fine; but he didn't want the creep any closer than that. He had kept Ruby well clear of Tito for a long time. But now, Tito had homed in on her once again, decided to do his perverted pal Bray a big favour by taking her out.

'You gonna let me do something about that fucker now?' asked Kit after a long silence.

Michael blew out a plume of smoke. 'I'll sort it,' he said.

Kit bit back the angry, impulsive words that sprang to his lips.

When are you going to do that, Michael? When are you going to let me give that bastard what he deserves?

He knew he couldn't say that. Michael's word was law.

But still . . . it hurt to know that yet again Tito had got away with it.

He thought of the horrible way Tito had ended Gilda's life. Mostly he tried not to, but it was a constant itch, a never-ending sore nagging *ache*, this need for revenge he felt.

It ate at him, all the time.

'Michael . . .' he started, knowing he mustn't say it, but wanting to.

'Kit,' said Michael, 'no. Now shut the fuck up about it, OK?'

123

Kit got home late that night, feeling wrung out after a day of nagging little worries and one or two damned great big ones too. This thing happening to Ruby. It could have been so much worse, and Kit could only be thankful for small mercies and for Rob's prompt actions. He liked Ruby. She was tough and she could appear cold, but deep down she was a sweet woman. He'd got used to her as a fixture in Michael's life, often around the restaurant or in one of the clubs with him.

He thought of the dinners they'd had in the past, Michael and Ruby, him and Daisy . . . oh yes, and now this Daisy business had blown up.

'Ah, fuck,' he breathed, and unlocked the door to his flat, snatching up the paper and the mail and flicking on the lights.

He tossed the letters onto a side table, shut the door, kicked off his shoes, took off his jacket, loosened his tie. Went over to the drinks tray and poured himself a whisky and necked it in one long swallow. It burned all the way down and then spread a cosy glow.

Better.

He glanced at the front page of the paper. Yesterday there'd been a general election. Today, Wilson was in power and the Tories had been kicked out. Kit hadn't even bothered to vote: he never did. He'd always felt detached from the rest of humanity – rootless, belonging to no one. Only Gilda had ever claimed his affection. Only Michael had ever won his allegiance.

He poured himself another before snatching up the mail and taking it over to the couch to read.

Bills and circulars. Damned things. There was also a large A4-sized envelope addressed to him in a loopy, stumbling handwriting he didn't recognize. He ripped it open, and there was a slip of paper inside, attached by a paperclip to a smaller white envelope. He looked at the slip of paper. The same loopy handwriting was there.

> *Mum said in her will that this letter should be forwarded to you.*
>
> *I got your name and address from your business card. Sorry, it was overlooked.*
>
> *Rose Bailey*

He looked at the envelope. It seemed to him as if the thing had been opened, then re-stuck. His mouth twisted grimly. It was months since Jennifer's passing, and her daughter and granddaughter had no doubt been busy dividing the spoils of her estate, and had then turned their greedy eyes on this envelope and wondered what could be inside it. If there had been cash in there, they would have nicked it, he was sure of that.

Remembering the load of horseshit he'd fed them when he'd met them, that his dad had died up in Blackpool and wanted to leave Hugh Burton some cash in his will, Kit had to smile. They'd been so gutted when their 'legacy' had turned out to be fuck-all.

He opened the thing up and spread out the sheet of paper it contained. It was a good-quality envelope, and the paper was thick – Kit was sure this was all part of the stationery set he had given Jennifer, and he looked at it with interest.

Kit, he read. *Dear Kit.*

The writing was Jennifer's, unsteady, nearly unreadable in parts, but the spelling was perfect. He read on.

I know you think I'm a very silly old lady and here's more proof of it! I forget things, you see. Things I should remember, things I try to remember. You know I said that reservist took the baby to a children's home in Fulham? Well, I got that right. But I never was able to tell you that I remembered something else. That place burned down. It was terrible, a tragedy. I forgot all about it but it came back to me. All those poor innocent children, lost to the flames! But the Principal survived, and she was sacked. It wasn't her fault, of course, but heads had to roll. Nancy Gifford was her name, and she lived for that job, she loved children so much and she couldn't have any of her own.

Anyway, where was I?

Yes.

She was so upset by it all that she went mad, poor thing, and they had to take her off to the asylum, but when they went to fetch her from her home, do you know what they found? A dark baby boy was there with her, she'd obviously snatched him from the fire and – thinking everyone believed all the children were dead – she told no one and kept him for her own.

Kit sat back, staring into space for a moment. For God's sake!

Then, his eyes skipping quickly over the page, he read on.

The child was taken to another home, not too far from the first.

Kit read the name of the home the surviving baby had been taken to. He threw the letter down onto the couch, exhaling sharply with the shock of it.

'Holy *shit*,' he said with feeling.

124

It was a grey misty morning and Daisy was walking the lanes near her home. She'd left Matthew and Luke with the nanny and had come out of the house, breathing in the fresh damp country air like a prisoner escaping Alcatraz.

Her home felt like a prison. There. She'd said it, if only in her head.

Her husband was her gaoler. She'd said *that* too, for the first time allowing herself to think it.

To make him happy, she had to be different from her normal self. And she had struggled to do that, ever since they'd married. But more and more she was aware that she was always, in his eyes, lacking somehow. That she was not the perfectly behaved hostess, the restrained companion at dinner dates and fundraisers. She had *opinions,* she was clumsy and careless, she had a free, breezy nature – and the very fact of all that seemed to make Simon furious.

And now she had this strange business to cope with. Months had gone by since she'd stumbled home in shock after seeing Ruby, her father and Vanessa. Months since Simon had reacted with such fury to the fact that she'd had a nasty shock. What she'd needed was a cuddle, understanding, sympathy; what she'd got was rage. He'd been away ever since, on business; and she was glad of that.

I hate my husband, she thought.

It was a startling realization. Daisy stopped walking. The hedgerows were dripping with moisture and thick with berries. Soon it would be Christmas . . . and she would still be miserable.

'Daisy?' The voice made her jump. She turned, and there was Ruby, standing with her arm in a sling and a beige trench coat over her shoulders. Behind her was parked a large car, pulled in tight to the verge. There was a grey-haired someone sitting behind the wheel, and there was also that same beefy, sexy-looking young man standing beside the car, watching Ruby, as he always seemed to do.

Daisy hadn't even heard the car approach, she'd been so lost in thought.

She paused, staring at Ruby. Then she said: 'I don't want to talk to you.'

'I know I shocked you. I know you're angry.'

Daisy shook her head.

'You didn't just *shock* me. You pulled my whole life out from under me. Made a mockery of everything I've ever been told, everything I've ever believed to be the truth.'

'You do believe me then?'

Yes. Daisy did believe her. But with *that* came other questions, unbearably painful ones.

'How could you do that?' she asked.

'What?' Ruby queried.

'Give me up. And the other baby, your son, *my* brother. How could you do that, just abandon us that way?' Daisy could feel herself shaking with the force of her anger. 'I have children. I could *never* do what you did.'

'Daisy, you don't understand.'

'No I don't. I can't. It's a mystery to me, how you could have done it.'

Ruby took a gulp of breath. 'I know you find it hard to understand. Of course you do. But those were different times.

So different, you can't imagine. I would have been an outcast. On the streets. Fending for myself. If I'd tried to keep you.'

Daisy shook her head even harder. '*No*,' she said firmly. 'I still couldn't do that. I could be thrown into the *gutter* and I would still never give my children up.'

'Those are fine words, from a girl who has never known a moment's poverty,' said Ruby sadly. 'I'm glad you haven't, Daisy, and you know *why* you haven't? Because I let your father take you from me. I had no choice. I had to think of *you*, not what I wanted.'

Daisy glared at Ruby. 'I don't want to discuss this. Go away. Leave me alone.'

And she turned and walked back to the house, the twins, her unhappy life.

'So how is it now?' asked Vi that lunchtime when she met up with Ruby.

'What?' asked Ruby blankly.

'The arm. You didn't tell me how it happened.'

'Oh. It's fine. I just slipped, it was stupid of me. It's still a little sore, but the sling's coming off the day after tomorrow, it's getting back to normal.'

Unlike her life. It felt to Ruby that everything was caving in around her. Daisy hated the sight of her. Cornelius had tried to kill her. If she didn't have Michael and the business, she felt like she would go stark, staring mad.

'We're having a weekend house party in ten days' time,' said Vi. 'A shoot.'

'Hm?'

'You know. Pheasant shooting. *Game* shooting, silly. Anthony gets terribly excited, and that's a very rare occurrence. You and Michael could come, we'd both love you to be there.'

'I don't know . . .'

'Oh, don't worry. We girls don't have to get involved, we can just hang about the house, drink tea and gossip, how's that?'

'Sounds fine,' said Ruby. Over the years she had occasionally been to Vi's country pile, but mostly they met up in town. A weekend away might do both her and Michael good. It would be a welcome distraction from all her many woes. She was very tense and – yes – very *frightened* these days. Just last night she'd been sitting alone, listening to records – the Hollies singing 'The Air That I Breathe' – and she'd found herself crying hysterically. Then Daisy had rejected her this morning. Yes, she needed a break.

'That's a date then. I guess Daisy reacted badly when you told her the truth?' asked Vi.

Ruby sighed shakily. 'I saw her this morning. She doesn't want to talk to me.'

'Give her time, she'll come round.'

But Ruby didn't think so.

125

Kit had always sworn that he would never go back to the place where he spent the first few miserable years of his life. But this was a job, he was doing it for Michael, and so he didn't see how he had any choice in the matter.

He drove over there, got out of his car in the parking area and looked up at the place he had once called home. His guts were churning with tension as he walked up the same steps. He was remembering running down another set of steps on the day of his sixteenth birthday, the day when yet another home could say that their duty towards him had at last been discharged.

He was remembering how he had swung out of the gates, laughing out loud with the joy of being free. But that evening, he had started to realize what freedom meant. Sixteen years old, and sleeping rough on a park bench with newspapers stuffed down his jacket to try and keep out the cold. Next day he'd tried to find a place in a hostel, but they were all full.

He came down with a bad chill, and after a week of freezing cold weather, of fending off assaults and threats, he turned up wheezing and sneezing at the Salvation Army place, where at last he was taken in. Then he started to take on low-paid menial jobs. From then it had been a step up to the bed factory and the Corona lorries. If Michael Ward hadn't got hold of him after that, he didn't like to think how he would have ended up. Dead in a ditch, probably. Or worse.

'I'm here to see Miss Page,' he said to the thin middle-aged woman who greeted him in the reception area of the hall. He'd phoned ahead, spoken to the Principal; she was not, thankfully, the same one who'd been here when he stayed. *That* one had been a tyrant – Mrs Anderson, he would never forget the name – with hairy warts on her chin and a beige twinset.

Jesus, he'd hated it here. He looked around – there was the same big mahogany staircase he'd got the cane for sliding down. The big stained-glass window above it, with its soaring angels and *In God We Trust*. Hadn't he put his foot through that once, kicking out in frustration at all the rules, all the regulations? The cane again, for that.

Three boys of about ten years old came hurtling down the stairs and ran off across the hall, ignoring him. Kit glanced at his watch. Lunchtime. He nearly gagged at the thought of the slops they'd served up back in the day. Spam fritters and watery shepherd's pie. Tapioca and thin custard. And the awful fucking greens, boiled to death and placed in front of him. On one memorable occasion, he'd refused to eat it, and the old bitch of a dinner lady had forced the stuff into his mouth.

There had been no privacy anywhere. Dormitories to sleep in, never a room of your own. He breathed in the smell, it was exactly the same. Cabbage and feet.

'Come with me,' said the woman with a smile, and he was led through the back hall and to the Principal's office at the far side of the building. He'd been back here for punishment, lots of times. Everything looked smaller, but otherwise the same.

She knocked at a richly embellished wooden door with a brass PRINCIPAL sign upon it.

She entered, ushering Kit in with her.

It was spooky being in here again. He had this weird sense of *déjà vu*. The same fireplace and the same fireguard, the flowers in the wheelbarrow tapestry, faded with age now. Framed certificates on the walls, books and sofas. Different sofas. Not the old red ones, these were cream-coloured. Flowers on the Principal's desk, that was different too. Mrs Anderson hadn't cared for flowers. Or for any damned thing, as far as he recalled.

'Mr Miller?'

The woman who rose from behind the desk, gave a warm smile and extended a hand, couldn't have been more different from the Anderson woman. She was thirtyish, verging on plump, in a royal-blue dress and crocheted white cardigan. Her hair was dark and styled in a messy pageboy, her nose was shiny from lack of make-up, and her eyes were alive with curiosity.

'Miss Page,' said Kit, and shook her hand.

'Please, take a seat.'

They both sat down and Miss Page smiled across at him as she patted a wad of files on the desk.

'Records,' she said in explanation. 'Raeburn Lodge prides itself on keeping records on all children who are admitted, ever since the place was built at the turn of the century.'

'This one was admitted some time after Manor Park burned down,' said Kit. He told her about the Principal at Manor Park, that she'd taken the blame for the fire and been sacked, and secreted a child – the only surviving child – at home with her. When she'd been taken off to the loony bin, the child had come here.

'At least, that's the information I've been given,' he said. 'As I explained, I'm looking into this on behalf of a friend, Ruby Darke.' He fished a piece of paper out of his breast pocket. 'These are her contact details, she'll verify what I'm saying. She lost touch with this child at birth, it was taken from her without her consent. She's been trying to find him ever since.'

Miss Page took the slip of paper, looked at it briefly, then tucked it away in her desk drawer. She glanced down, then back up at Kit.

'I hope you understand that I can only verify that the child was here,' she said. 'I can't supply forwarding addresses or anything like that.'

'I understand that.'

'Then let's have a look.' She opened the folder at the top of the file. 'What date was the fire?'

Kit told her.

She closed that file and sorted through another three before selecting one. 'But he didn't come straight here,' she said, busy turning pages.

'It could have been months later.'

'Ah.' She paused, smiling up at him. 'Well, this could take some time.'

'I'm in no rush,' said Kit, settling back.

'Perhaps you'd like to leave it with me . . . ?'

'No, that's fine.' This had all the hallmarks of another dead end. Kit sighed. He'd hoped he could have pulled this out of the bag for Ruby, but it didn't look too hopeful. If this last try went tits-up, that was it, there would be no more going forward. He'd have to abandon the attempt.

Miss Page was silent, shuffling papers, bent over them with complete concentration.

She paused. 'Um . . . didn't you say on the phone that this child was of mixed race?'

'That's right.'

'Only we would list that as MR, with Afro-Caribbeans as AC and Asians as A, or C for Chinese. And CA for Caucasian.'

'Right.'

'Oh, here we are. The only MR admitted in the six months after the fire's date was a little boy who'd been christened as Miller.'

Kit stared at her. *Miller?*

'Didn't you say your name was Miller? Are you a relative, then?' Miss Page was frowning at him.

Kit leaned forward, feeling suddenly dizzy with bewilderment. Obligingly, Miss Page turned the pages so that he could see the words. *Admitted, male approx two years old, MR. Christened & named as Kit Miller.*

The words seemed to dance in front of his eyes.

'Mr Miller? Are you all right?' she asked, her eyes anxious and kind. 'Do you know someone by that name? Do you know this Kit Miller . . . ?'

Kit gathered himself. He felt like he'd been gut-punched.

'No,' he said. 'No, I don't. Can you get me a copy of that?'

'Of course.' She went out into the corridor to the Photostat machine while Kit sat there, numb with shock, staring at nothing.

All this time.

All this *time*, he'd been looking for Ruby's lost son.

And not once, *not once*, had he realized that he might be looking for *himself.*

126

It was another charity fundraiser organized by Vanessa. She seemed to split her time almost equally these days between charitable events and the garden at Brayfield.

'What do you mean, you don't want to go? Of course we're going,' said Simon when Daisy objected.

So Daisy went, and sat there blank-eyed with boredom as the haw-haws around the table, who had paid monstrous amounts of money for the privilege of being here among the aristos and the celebs, drank too much and bid crazy money for this item or that.

Vanessa, up on the podium in sky-blue chiffon, was flushed with excitement and success.

Daisy watched her with a curious detachment. Her mother. Only not her mother at all. Her in-laws were on the same table as her and Simon, his father Sir Bradley puce-faced and jovial with pleasure, Lady Collins tight-lipped and sending Daisy dirty looks.

Daisy wondered if Simon had confided in his mother about her revelations. Certainly, her ladyship's attitude had changed towards her. Where once her whole manner had been fawning, now it was distinctly chilly. Maybe Simon had told her they were having problems. Which they were, that was true enough.

The thing was, Daisy couldn't imagine now why she had

married Simon in the first place. All she knew was that she had been in a bad place at that time, deeply unhappy and weary to the bone after the gatehouse party. So she had allowed her father to steamroller her into the marriage, and then while she was thinking *What have I done?* Simon impregnated her, and then there had been the twins, she was a married matron, she had the big house, the ambitious husband, the children, the nanny – and she was *still* thinking *How did this happen?*

She had floated around, teetering out of control, her whole life. Drink, drugs, anything to fill the void, to alleviate that feeling of being unloved, of being not quite what was looked for in a daughter. She was off all that now. She'd been clean ever since some fool had injected her with heroin; that had frightened her badly. But with a head free of drugs and drink came an awful, sick-making, anxious clarity. She was sitting here looking like a prosperous happy woman, but she was living a total lie. She was so, so glad when the evening drew to a close.

She wanted to go home *alone,* to look in on the twins, to be peaceful for once. But there was Simon, stomping around the master bedroom while she sat at her dressing table removing her earrings, staring at her reflection as if at a stranger.

'You see? It wasn't so bad, was it?' he asked, taking off his shirt and throwing it aside.

Daisy pursed her lips. 'Simon,' she said, 'it was fucking awful. And what have you said to your mother?'

He jerked to a standstill and stared at her. 'What? What do you mean?'

'She was looking at me all night like she wanted to kill me,' said Daisy.

'Oh, take no notice. Just in a mood about something, I expect.'

'You haven't told her anything? I mean, about what I told you, about Ruby . . . ?'

'God no. She'd go mental.'

'She doesn't like me.' Daisy had felt this for a long time. Sir Bradley, on the other hand, liked her very much. He was always trying to feel her up when he thought no one was looking. Maybe that accounted for his wife looking daggers at her.

'The less she knows about that, the better.' Simon's face was closed off, uncommunicative. 'And as I told you, I don't want to hear any more about it either. It's just rubbish, I'm sure.'

Daisy said nothing. Ruby didn't talk rubbish, she was sure of *that*.

'Simon,' she said.

'Mm?'

'I think I want a divorce.'

127

Kit drove down to Southend after he left Raeburn Lodge, trying to make sense of all these new things that were zinging around his brain.

He itemized them, laid them out one by one while he walked by the windblown shore and listened to the shriek of the gulls flying overhead. One: Ruby Darke was his mother. Therefore, two: that fruitcake Daisy was his sister. How could that be? Daisy was white as snow; he was dark.

Jesus, hadn't she come on to him? Hadn't she given him the green light?

He picked up a handful of stones and spun them so that they skipped out over the grey, white-flecked water. Three bounces, four . . . and oh *shit*, that was right, she had tried her level best to seduce him.

He'd heard that could happen. That somehow, deep down, people 'recognized' long-separated siblings or parents or cousins or aunts, and found them attractive. He didn't understand the colour difference between them, he couldn't make sense of that at all. But yes, Daisy had flung herself at him. And thank *Christ* he'd been tied up with Gilda, or he might easily have weakened. Daisy was gorgeous, but crazy. Usually he liked his women older . . .

Older.

It didn't take a shrink to work that one out, now, did it?

He dropped the rest of the stones, rubbed the sand and salty moisture from his hands. Stared out at the pounding waves, let the breeze cool his overheated face.

Well, now he'd found his real mother, and he felt . . . he didn't know *what* he felt. Like he wanted to see her. Also that he wanted to beat her brains out. Also . . . that he wanted to ask her why, *why*, did you do that to me? Abandon me that way? How could you, how could *anyone*, do that?

He thought of all those long, miserable years in the homes. Ruby Darke had condemned him to that. He thought of the bastard with the gas mask, who had fully intended to kill him but had died himself. And the fire! He turned his hands over, looked at the seared skin of his palms – Tito's handi-work. He'd always been so terrified of fire, of burning. Somewhere back there in his brain was a memory of the fire at the kids' home, he was sure of it.

And Ruby had condemned Daisy, his sister, to another sort of hell. He knew that Daisy had never felt that she meas-ured up to her parents' – or more specifically her mother's – expectations. Maybe that was why she had behaved like such a lunatic, maybe all that had been a cry for help, a *Hey, look at me. Please pay attention to me.*

Maybe.

He walked back to the Bentley and got in, slammed the door on the wind, the crash of the sea, the lonely call of the birds. In its hushed leather-clad interior, he thought of Michael Ward, his boss – but so much more than that: Michael had been a father to him, and the boys had become his family. Now he acknowledged that he had always wanted, desired, *craved* a family.

Now, it turned out he had one.

But . . . all he felt was *fury*.

128

Ruby was watching TV at home when the doorbell rang.

She glanced at the big sundial clock over the stone mantel-piece. It was seven thirty in the evening, Rob was in the flat over the garage, she was alone here in the locked, secured house. She had a panic alarm that she could press, summon Rob. But . . . she thought she could hear children, crying. She stood up, feeling her injured arm twingeing in protest, and went out into the hall. She approached the front door warily.

'Who is it?' she called. The crying children were louder now.

'It's me,' came the reply.

Ruby recognized that voice. She opened the door. There were two women standing there, each of them holding a screaming baby. One of them was Jody, the twins' nanny. The other one was Daisy, her blonde hair sticking out all over the place, wearing trainers and a body warmer over a white T-shirt. Her left eye was so swollen it was almost shut, and the shiny flesh all around it was turning blue.

'What the fuck . . . ?' asked Ruby, shocked. 'Daisy! What happened?'

'Oh, nothing very much,' said Daisy with a shout of near-hysterical laughter. Her one good eye was bright with unshed tears. 'I'm leaving Simon, that's all. And when I told him, he got rather upset. I hope you don't mind me coming here, but I just couldn't face Brayfield. And I really didn't know where else to go.'

Ruby stared, aghast. She had been warned to stay away from Daisy. Verbally and physically. But here was her daughter, needing help, needing shelter.

'Well, don't just stand there,' said Ruby, 'come in.'

While the nanny got the twins upstairs for a feed, a bath and then bed in one of the spare rooms, Ruby ushered Daisy into the drawing room and sat her down by the fire. She went to the drinks tray, poured a brandy, and took it back to her.

'Here. Drink up.'

Daisy took it, sipped at it. Ruby sat down opposite her daughter and stared at her. That eye was going to be all colours of the rainbow shortly. What sort of *animal* was that arsehole she was married to?

She wasn't surprised when Rob appeared, having used his key to come through the back door into the house. He must have heard Daisy's car.

'What's going on?' he asked, looking at Daisy's blackening eye, looking at Ruby.

'Daisy's going to stay here tonight,' said Ruby.

Rob stared at her in consternation. He had been told by the boss that Ruby had been warned off contact with this girl. She'd been first assaulted and then almost run over and killed because she hadn't toed the line. These people were serious in their intentions. That was all he knew. And now Daisy was here, right here, in the house.

'That's not a good idea,' said Rob.

Ruby stared at him coolly.

'Good idea or not, that's what's happening.'

'I'd better let the boss know what's going on.'

496

'Fine. If you have to.'

'I do have to.' Rob stood there, watching the women uneasily.

Ruby let out a sharp sigh. 'If you have something to say, Rob, please just say it.'

'Look, this is stupid,' said Daisy, starting to get to her feet, putting the brandy glass aside. 'I really appreciate you taking me in like this, Ruby, but . . .'

'Sit down, Daisy,' said Ruby, her voice suddenly commanding.

Daisy sank back down.

Ruby looked at Rob. 'Tell Michael that Daisy's here,' she said. 'That she is *staying* here, for as long as she needs to.'

'Jesus, Ruby . . .'

'Go and do it, please.'

Rob turned on his heel, his face grim. The doorbell rang again.

'What the fuck *now*?' he asked, and walked out into the hallway.

Daisy and Ruby exchanged glances.

'I don't want to cause trouble,' said Daisy.

Ruby exhaled. 'The trouble started a long time ago, Daisy,' she said more gently. 'None of it's your fault. Just relax.'

129

Rob was startled to find a dishevelled-looking Kit standing on the doorstep.

'She in?' asked Kit, moving past him into the hall.

'Yeah, she is.' Rob nodded to the drawing-room door. 'Through there. She expecting you? She never said.'

'No, she's not expecting me. But I've got to speak to her, it's urgent.'

'Fine.' Rob started to move ahead of him.

Kit stopped him with a hand on his chest. 'Leave me with it, yeah?'

Rob looked at Kit. He thought he looked like shit, which was unusual. Kit was a snappy dresser, usually he looked the business. But tonight, his shirt collar was grubby and his tie was pulled loose. His bespoke jacket was creased and rumpled. His flashy Italian shoes were muddy.

'You OK?' he asked. Kit was a mate, after all.

'I'm fine, just piss off for a bit, will you, Rob? Ruby and me need to have a chat.'

'Daisy Bray's in there with her.' There was a distant baby-like wail from upstairs. Both men glanced up, then Kit looked a question at Rob. 'She turned up with the kids and the nanny. Looks like her old man gave her a going-over.'

Kit went over to the drawing-room door and passed inside, closing it firmly behind him. Ruby was sitting there on one sofa, Daisy huddled over a nearly empty glass of brandy on the other. The fire roared and crackled between them. Ruby glanced up, saw Kit, and smiled.

His mother.

Could it be true?

It was. He *knew* it was.

Her arm was out of the sling, he saw, but as she stood up to greet him she still moved a little stiffly, like it was tender.

'Kit! This is a surprise.'

He approached her, like he always did, kissed her cheek. But this time he felt like he was moving in a surreal dream. Now he was aware that he was kissing his *mother's* cheek, and it felt so strange. Again he could feel that deep-seated fury, bubbling up in him.

'Well, it's been a day of surprises,' he said, and she sat back down and gestured for him to sit too. 'Hiya, Daise,' he said, looking at her.

She looked shattered. For the first time he noticed that her eye was bruised and blackening. It looked like someone had given her a nasty smack. What the hell was *that* all about?

He turned his attention to Ruby, who was smiling at him with a little puzzled frown. 'What does that mean?' she asked. 'A day of surprises? What surprises?'

Kit sat down. He leaned forward, hands clasped on his knees, and looked at her. Really *looked.* He couldn't see himself in her in anything but their colour; that was identical. But wait: she was tall. So was he. Anything else? No. If it was there, he couldn't see it.

'What is it?' asked Ruby, the smile dropping from her face. 'Is something wrong? Is it Michael?'

'Wrong?' Kit swallowed and shifted slightly in his seat. 'No. And the boss is fine.'

'What, then? There's something, for sure.'

'I went to Raeburn Lodge today, the children's home.'

'Why?' Ruby was staring at him in confusion.

'I had some news. An old lady I visited once or twice, she died.'

'I'm sorry.'

Kit was silent for a long moment. Daisy was staring at him.

'What are you talking about, Kit?' she asked him.

Kit glanced at her. 'She left me a letter. I didn't want to tell Ruby about it, I didn't want to get her hopes up just to let her down again.' He fished in his pocket, found it, handed it over to Ruby. 'This is it.'

Ruby slipped on her reading glasses and read it. She took a while, and when she'd finished she refolded the letter and handed it back to Kit. 'So that woman had concealed a little boy at her home . . . ? For God's sake. Do you think . . . is there any chance it could be him? It can't be, can it?'

'I spoke to the Principal yesterday, she dug out the records and she showed me them today,' Kit said, amazed at how calm his voice sounded.

He replaced Jennifer's letter in his pocket and pulled out the Photostat of the page of records pertaining to the mixed-race boy who'd been admitted quite a long while after the fire at Manor Park. He handed the copy to Ruby and she took it quickly, scanning the page.

'They categorized the races, you see?' said Kit. 'AC is Afro-Caribbean, C for Chinese, A for Asian, CA for Caucasian, MR for mixed race. There was only one mixed-race boy admitted in the six months after the fire, and that was the one listed there.'

Ruby was scanning the page. 'MR, MR, oh, here it is . . .' Suddenly she fell silent. She stared at the page, glanced up at him. Looked back at the page. Her face grew very still.

Slowly, with trembling fingers, she reached up and removed her reading glasses.

'It says . . .' she gasped out, her voice barely above a whisper. 'It says the boy was christened Kit Miller.'

Daisy was watching both of them in bewilderment. 'What's this all about?' she asked, confused.

Kit's eyes were glued to Ruby. 'Why don't you ask her?' he told Daisy.

Daisy's eyes went to Ruby's. 'What is it?' she asked. 'Will somebody tell me what's going on?'

Ruby looked as if she was about to be sick. She swallowed hard and looked first at Daisy, then at Kit.

'Oh God . . .' she moaned.

'Go on,' said Kit. 'Tell her.'

'Daisy . . .' Ruby hesitated.

'Yes? What is it?'

'Daisy,' said Ruby at last. 'Kit's your brother.'

130

'What is this?' asked Daisy with an unsteady laugh, looking first at Ruby, then at Kit.

Kit's eyes were burning into Ruby's.

'Kit . . .' Ruby started, then she faltered to a halt, shaking her head, not knowing what to say.

'Yeah, go on,' he said sourly. 'I'd like to hear this. I'd like to hear you explain how I got dumped in a kid's home and nearly *cremated*. I really would.'

Ruby seemed to have shrunk in her chair. 'I can understand that you're angry . . .' she said.

'That don't cover it.'

'I had no say in any of it,' said Ruby. 'None at all.'

'Wait!' Daisy intervened, holding up a hand. 'Just wait a minute. What is all this? You're both talking rubbish. Kit, you *can't* be my twin. Look at you. Look at *me*.'

'It can happen,' said Ruby, her voice trembling. 'I'm mixed race. It's rare, but it *does* happen, that when there are twins born, one can be white and the other darker.'

'Why don't you just say *black*?' demanded Kit.

'You're not black, though, are you? You're like me. Coffee-coloured, I suppose you'd call it.'

'That ain't what some people call it. Some people have called me *that black bastard*. Others weren't so delicate. They called me *nigger*.'

'I don't understand any of this,' said Daisy. She was staring at Kit. Her head hurt, she felt like hell, and she could barely see out of one eye. She found herself staring into Kit's bright blue gaze.

'Oh God,' she said suddenly.

Kit turned his head sharply and stared at her. 'What?' he snapped.

'Your eyes! They're exactly the same colour and *exactly* the same shape as mine.'

'So what? *You* had white skin and you could pass for a Bray. Your father wasn't ashamed to take you in. You were *acceptable*. But blue eyes or not, I wasn't. I was chucked on the scrapheap.' Kit stared into space in sudden realization. 'Oh shit, I've only just thought about this. That fucker Cornelius Bray's my father.'

'Look, don't go attacking *me*,' said Daisy hotly. 'None of it's my fault.'

'No, it wouldn't be. Little Miss Perfect, that's you. Or that's what they wanted you to be anyway. What a let-down for them.'

'Shut up!' snapped Daisy.

'Oh, the truth hurts? You're a screw-up, and no wonder.'

'Just shut up!' Daisy slammed the empty glass onto the side table and stood up. She looked at Ruby, not at Kit. 'I can't take this, not right now. I'm going up to see to the twins,' she said, and hurried out of the room.

'Well, you handled *that* well,' said Ruby, eyeing Kit with disapproval.

'Oh, did I? Sorry. It's just come as a slight shock, that's all. Finding out that my mother kept my *sister* but dumped me.'

'I didn't keep Daisy,' said Ruby tiredly, absently rubbing her arm. 'Cornelius did. He and Vanessa were childless. She couldn't have children of her own. When I became pregnant, it was agreed that I couldn't keep an illegitimate child.'

'You *bitch*.'

'Kit,' she said desperately, 'try to understand. I didn't even know I was expecting twins. When I gave birth – Daisy was first, then you came, completely unexpectedly. Cornelius didn't want a dark-skinned child. He wanted a golden baby he could pass off as his and Vanessa's own. So he just took Daisy. And you . . . my brother Charlie took you, said he'd pass you on to someone, a married couple. I couldn't stop him. I wanted to, but I couldn't.'

'You didn't *try*, did you?' asked Kit.

'Kit! You know I've been searching for my boy – oh Jesus, for *you* – for years. It's been hell, trying to find you. And then when I heard about the fire, and I believed you were dead, that was even worse. That was the end of all hope. It was horrible. But . . .' Now Ruby was staring at him in wonder, a slight tentative smile touching her lips. 'It's so wonderful to have found you at last. And that's it's *you*, of all people. I've always liked you so much, and maybe that was why. Because I knew you, deep down.'

But Kit was shaking his head, his eyes glaring into hers.

'You don't know me,' he snarled. 'You don't *care* about me. You gave me up when you should have fought to keep me. That's all I know.'

'Kit, no, that's not t—'

Kit jumped to his feet. He pointed a finger at her. Ruby shrank back into her seat. He looked capable of anything.

'You know what else I know?' he burst out. 'I'll tell you. I never want to see you or hear you or know anything about you, ever again. You keep away from me. You're *dead* to me. I am never, not while I'm breathing, going to forgive you for what you did. *Never.*'

131

As the days passed, Ruby remained in a state of confusion. Daisy stayed. Her daughter was with her, and now – double delight – she had her grandchildren in the house too, to fuss over. She felt deeply sad over Kit's reaction, but he would come round, wouldn't he?

'You don't know Kit very well, do you?' said Daisy when they sat in the kitchen a few days later, sipping coffee. Ruby had told her that Kit would mellow in the end, that he was just shocked by the news, which was understandable.

'He's more than shocked. He's devastated.' The swelling on Daisy's eye had gone down, and the skin was starting to turn yellow all around the socket. She looked accusingly at Ruby. 'He thinks you couldn't have loved him at all, to let him go like you did. Have you any idea what that feels like?'

Ruby stared at Daisy with pain in her eyes. 'No. I haven't.'

'Well, I have. You let me go too. Let me live a complete lie. I always felt that I didn't "fit" with my mother, I was always trying to win her approval. And of course I never succeeded. Now finally I know why.'

'I'm sure Vanessa did the very best she could for you. She was *desperate* for a child.'

'Yeah, so she took yours. And you let her. I can see why Kit's so wound up. He didn't even get the nice-upbringing option. All he got was *shafted*.'

Ruby took a swallow of coffee. 'I don't see what I could have done differently. I was in a desperate situation. I only wanted the best for you.'

'The best for me would have been staying with you.'

'No it wouldn't. I came from a household where bullying was endemic. I wouldn't have wanted that for you.'

Daisy gave a wry smile and pointed out the shiner her eye had become.

'Looks like I didn't *totally* dodge that bullet,' she said.

'Is it very sore?'

'It looks worse than it is.'

'What are you going to do? About Simon?'

'I'll phone him today,' said Daisy, her face falling. 'He's the twins' father. He has rights. We have to work out something so he gets to see them, I suppose. Although, truthfully, I wouldn't care if I never saw him again.'

'Are you definitely divorcing?'

'After this?' Again she indicated her swollen eye. 'I'm not a punch bag. And really, it was never a love match in the first place. I married Simon in a weak moment, when I didn't know where else to turn. And he . . . well, I think Pa paid him to do it.'

'Daisy, no.' Ruby was shocked.

'Ruby – yes. I think Simon got a hefty pay-off and his building company got a lot of lucrative contracts shoved its way, providing Simon took me as part of the deal and settled me down a bit.'

'That's horrible.'

Now Daisy smiled. Increasingly she was finding that – at last – she had something to smile about. A strange sense of peace had begun to steal over her since she had let Ruby into her life. All that unfocused longing and loneliness she had felt before was fading. Everything had been leading her to this place, to this woman: her mother.

'You know Pa. He *is* horrible. Look at what he did to you. Knocked you up and then whipped your baby off you. And he didn't even care about what happened to the other one – to his own son, for God's sake – because it didn't fit in with his rose-coloured plans.'

'Poor Kit,' sighed Ruby. 'But he *will* come round.'

Daisy was shaking her head. 'Ruby . . . no. You don't get it, do you? He won't. That's Kit's nature.' She thought in embarrassment of how she had come on to her own brother. Thank God he'd turned her down. He hadn't relented over *that,* and he wasn't going to relent over *this*, either. 'Once he's made up his mind, I'm afraid that's it. There's no changing it.'

132

'You are coming, aren't you?' asked Vi on the phone.

'What? To what?'

It was Thursday morning, and Simon had just shown up on the doorstep. Rob had ushered him and Daisy into the drawing room, and told Ruby they were in there. Jody was upstairs with the babies. Ruby lurked nervously in the kitchen, wondering if she should be in with Daisy, supervising.

'Leave them alone for a while, yeah?' said Rob, reading her mind. 'Let them work it out.'

'But what if he . . . ?'

'I'll stay in the hall. If I hear any sort of commotion, I'll go in.'

And now Vi was on the phone, saying, *You are coming aren't you?*

Ruby stared distractedly at the phone. Had she agreed to something? Her mind was in such a spin, she couldn't remember what.

Vi clicked her tongue. 'The house party, Rubes. The weekend. Do keep up.'

'Oh.' Ruby thought about it. She'd mentioned it to Michael, and he had seemed agreeable. But now she had Daisy here. She explained this to Vi.

'Well, that's good news, isn't it? Are you two OK now?'

'Sort of. I think.' Briefly Ruby thought of the hatred in

Kit's eyes when they'd last spoken. She had to blink back tears. She'd found her son, at last, after all those empty years of searching and hoping; and then that awful news of the fire, and then – such an unbelievable relief! – Kit had come and told her that he'd found the child. And even better, it was like a miracle, the child was *him*.

But he despised her.

Of course he did.

He had every *right* to. But it cut her to the heart.

'Well, look – bring Daisy too. And the babies, the more the merrier. Are you all right? You sound odd.'

'I'm fine.' Ruby forced a smile into her voice. She had Daisy back. She had her grandkids. She was unbelievably blessed. But Kit . . . the way he'd looked at her . . .

Now she realized in alarm that she could hear shouting coming from the drawing room.

'Look, Vi, I have to go.'

'You're coming though?'

'Yes. Absolutely. Why not.'

'Good show, girl. Catch you later.'

Ruby hung up the phone and quickly went out into the hall. Rob was leaning, arms folded, against the wall beside the closed drawing-room door. Their eyes met. Daisy was shouting. Simon was shouting.

'. . . if it hadn't been for my father pushing all those bloody *contracts* your way,' yelled Daisy.

'You *cow*!' returned Simon.

'Want me to go in now . . . ?' suggested Rob.

Ruby bit her lip and shook her head.

The volume of the shouting rose dramatically. Suddenly the door was flung open and Daisy stormed out.

'You're just a *bastard*,' Daisy tossed over her shoulder. She stopped and glared at him, hands on hips. 'And you know what? You're rather *short*.'

'You bitch. You're nothing but a flaming liability. You always have been,' snapped Simon, rushing at her, fists clenched in fury.

Rob stepped forward and planted a firm hand on Simon's chest. 'Whoa, pal,' he said. 'That's enough.'

'Get out of my fucking way, you shit. That's my wife.' Simon's face was as red as his hair as he tried to get past Rob. He lunged forward and made a grab for Daisy's arm.

Rob grasped Simon's wrist and twisted it. Simon gave a yelp and sank to his knees while Rob held his arm straight out behind him.

'Let go of me!' bellowed Simon.

Rob glanced at Daisy. 'You said all you want to say to him?' he asked.

Daisy folded her arms defensively over her middle and nodded. She was shaking.

'Come on then, pal, let's go,' said Rob, easing Simon to his feet and marching him effortlessly to the front door. Ruby opened it and Rob tossed Simon out onto the gravel. He scrabbled back up, glaring at them both.

'This isn't over,' he said hotly, dusting himself down.

'Yeah, it is,' said Rob, and shut the door.

133

Michael came by a few days later. 'So, Rob been looking after you OK?' he asked.

'Rob's a diamond,' she assured him.

It was a sunny day, hazed with gold as only an autumn day can be, a day when anyone would feel glad to be alive. They took their coffee out onto the terrace, lapping up the warmth and the countryside views. They stood in front of the balustrade and gazed out, looking down towards the russet, bronze and bright yellow woodland and the glinting river down in the dip of the valley.

'And Daisy's OK?'

'Daisy's wonderful,' said Ruby with an unstoppable grin.

'But you're pushing your luck having her here with you,' Michael reminded her. 'You know Bray hates the idea. He's made *that* clear enough.'

'I don't care what he thinks,' said Ruby. 'And, Michael, the babies are so beautiful, I'll take you up to see them in a while.'

'Not yet, hm?' Michael pulled her into his arms. She closed her eyes and inhaled the scent of him. Tobacco, Old Spice and clean skin.

'I love you, Michael,' she murmured against his neck.

'I love you too, honey. You know that.'

Ruby turned away, picking up her coffee cup from the

table beside the old, comfy wicker chairs. She smiled at him. 'I think Daisy's rather impressed by Rob,' she said. 'He tossed Simon Collins out of here like an empty tin of beans last week.'

'What, was he cutting up rough?' asked Michael in concern.

Ruby sneered. 'He's the type who only ever throws his weight about with women. He wouldn't risk it with a man.'

'Then I'm glad Rob marked his card for him.'

'It's Vi's party this weekend, you still on for that?' asked Ruby.

'Of course.'

Michael picked up his cup and it was then, at that precise moment, that Ruby felt something zing past her ear – maybe an insect or something? She flapped a hand, and then she heard another sharp report and a loud *crash* as a pane of glass in the French windows shattered. She looked at Michael and he was turning back to her – it seemed like he was moving in slow motion – and grabbing hold of her, pushing her to the floor.

Ruby's coffee cup exploded, then something went *whumph* into the cushion on the chair right beside where she lay. Michael pressed her face harder into the cold York stone of the terrace.

'Shit! Keep down, keep still,' he muttered beside her ear.

'What's happening?' asked Ruby, petrified.

They could hear that Rob was dashing through the drawing room and Michael shouted: 'Gun, Rob. Watch it! Ruby – just crawl back towards the door, keep as flat to the floor as you can, OK?'

Ruby did as she was told. More zings were whipping off the stonework; dust cascaded onto her head and hands as she crawled back indoors. Once inside, Rob grabbed her and pulled her out of sight of the windows, and Michael got back to his feet. He hugged her, hard.

'You OK?' he asked urgently.

'Fine, fine,' she muttered, shaking.

Rob was peering out around the edge of the French doors. The firing seemed to have stopped, for now.

'Probably down in the woods there – plenty of cover,' said Rob, and he ran back through the drawing room and out of the front door, slamming it closed behind him. They heard his car start up in the driveway and roar away, tyres squealing.

'Sure you're OK? Don't worry about this mess, we'll get it all fixed up,' said Michael, guiding her to a chair.

Ruby looked at his face. He thought she was worried about the *mess*? That was almost funny. But he didn't look amused. In fact, she had never seen him look so stony, so grim.

Someone had just tried to kill her.

This was the second attempt.

Pretty soon, she was sure there would be a third.

'It's him again, isn't it?' she asked unsteadily. 'It's Cornelius.'

Michael looked at her. It was without a doubt Tito's boys doing this, but yes, Bray was at the back of it. He stared out of the shattered window. Bray meant to see Ruby dead, and he would go on with this until he succeeded. It destroyed him to see Ruby so shaken up. He knew he had debts to pay, promises to keep, traditions to uphold. But some things, you just couldn't tolerate.

134

'Take out Tito and the whole thing stops dead,' said Kit.

He and Michael were in the office behind the restaurant that evening, Michael sitting stony-faced at his desk, Kit lounging in a chair opposite.

Kit wasn't sure *how* he felt about all this. Someone had tried to hit Ruby again. And Ruby . . . Ruby was *his mother*. Again he felt the confusion, the bitterness, the anger towards her. But if she were to die . . . he didn't want that. He didn't want a damned thing to do with her, but for sure he didn't want her laid out on a slab.

'Boss? You hear me?' said Kit, because Michael seemed lost in thought.

Michael gave a slight smile.

'I heard you. You're like a fucking parrot with this thing. "Hit Tito! Hit Tito!" Kit, I know you've got your own axe to grind here. The Gilda thing. But the time isn't right yet.'

'What, you're putting business ahead of Ruby's safety?' demanded Kit.

'Tito and I got a deal or two cooking,' said Michael. 'That much is true. But I have other concerns regarding Tito. Things you don't know about. And come on – what do you care about Ruby? You've already told me you wished she was dead and gone. What's changed?'

Kit shook his head. 'I didn't say that. I don't want her

dead, for Chrissakes. She's nothing to me, nothing at all. But I don't want *that*.'

Michael looked at his boy curiously. No longer a boy, though. Now, Kit was a force to be reckoned with and he was proud of him. Kit had been a bolshie nineteen-year-old tearaway when they first met: now he was in his thirties, and he was a man everyone treated with respect. He was Michael's right hand, and was greeted with deference everywhere he went. Only Tito dared do otherwise, giving him that mocking, shit-eating grin whenever their paths crossed. And Michael knew that it was because Tito believed Michael's hands were tied, that he would always restrain Kit from retaliation.

Tito thought he was safe.

'Yet you've been friends with Ruby,' said Michael. 'Her *and* Daisy. Now you're just going to cut that off, are you?'

'Yeah. I am.'

Michael let out a sigh.

'Tito's taking the piss,' said Kit. He looked down at his hands, at the angry scar tissue there. A constant reminder of what had been done to him, and to Gilda. A touching little memento of that *fuck* Tito. 'You know he is.'

Michael nodded in agreement. It killed him to admit it, but he knew Kit was right.

135

'I cannot believe that you would actually *do* this to me. Me, your friend. Of all people,' snapped Ruby.

It was the weekend. Vi and Ruby were standing in the long gallery of Albemarle House, looking out onto the estate. In the distance, far beyond the knot garden and the ha-ha, were the woods; they could just see the beaters moving along the edge of the trees, driving the birds towards the guns far beyond. Vi's husband Anthony was out there, ready and waiting with a few other weekend guests, including Michael.

'Anthony invited Cornelius and Vanessa at the last minute,' said Vi.

'Oh God.' Ruby paced around.

Daisy was settled in one of the many rooms here, with the twins and Jody the nanny. She – and Ruby – had come face to face with Cornelius and Vanessa in the hall when they'd all arrived at the same time. To say that it had been *awkward* was putting it mildly.

Ruby's first instinct was to flee, go home. But Michael was already out with the guns; she couldn't go out there and order him to take her home, right now. It would look odd. And she didn't want to order a taxi and go without him.

'You don't understand what you've done,' said Ruby,

trying to keep her voice even, though she was starting to panic.

'What do you mean? So what if Vanessa's here? It's about time you came face to face and buried the hatchet.'

'Vi, she wants to bury it in my *back*.'

'You've got to kiss and make up some time.'

Ruby stared at her friend in exasperation. She hadn't told Vi about the attempts on her life and now she could see that she really should have. Maybe *then* she would begin to understand.

'Look, it isn't that simple. There are things going on, things you don't know about.'

Vi was staring at her in wide-eyed incomprehension. 'Things like what?'

Ruby gulped down air, feeling panic take hold.

'I was warned off contact with Daisy. I mean *seriously* warned off.'

'How seriously?'

'Cornelius has friends . . . *gangland* friends.'

'You're joking.'

'Do I look like I'm joking? There have been a couple of incidents.'

'Go on.'

'Well, three. At first I think he only meant to scare me, but they've become more serious. Someone shot at me, Vi.' Ruby could see it all again, the terrace, the glass of the French doors shattering, Michael hurling her to the ground to protect her while bullets whizzed past her head. Rob had driven top-speed down to the woods, but had found no trace of the gunman. 'And someone tried to run me over. *That's* how I hurt my arm.'

Vi's mouth dropped open in shock.

Ruby nodded. 'It's true. And now look at this situation. I'm here, Daisy's here with the children, and Vanessa's here too. This is just going to antagonize Cornelius even more.'

'God's sake, Rubes.' Vi looked appalled. 'You should have told me this before.'

'What good would that have done?'

'Well, for a start I wouldn't have invited the Brays here at the same time as you.'

'So you *did* do it.'

Vi held her hands up. 'All right. Anthony knows Cornelius and he just suggested it vaguely, then I insisted because I thought that what was going on was just a remnant of all that's happened between you, and this would be a chance to put it to bed and forget it, once and for all. I had no idea it was this *serious*.'

Vi looked at her dear friend, her best friend in all the world, her lips thin with fury.

'Jesus,' she burst out, 'that *bastard*. I didn't have a clue. How could he *dare* do that to you?'

Ruby was staring dismally out of the long-gallery windows with their old, distorted diamond-shaped glass panes. 'Look, when the shoot's over and Michael's back – after dinner, OK? – I'm going to get him to take us home. I'm sorry, Vi, but I can't stay.'

'No. Of course you can't. I do see that, now.' Vi squeezed Ruby's hand. 'I'm so sorry, Rubes. For getting you into this situation.'

'You didn't know.'

'God if I *had* . . .' Vi flushed angrily.

'What could you have done? What could *anyone* do?' Ruby sighed.

They both gazed out of the window into the misty distance.

Suddenly, the white flag went up. The shooting began; the carnage had started. The beaters had driven the birds into the path of the guns. Ruby felt that Vi had just done something very similar to her.

'Sounds like they've started,' said Vi.

'So long as they hurry up and finish,' said Ruby grimly.

136

Ruby had never endured such a long, awkward day in her entire life.

'Good job it's a big house,' said Vi at one point, when Vanessa had passed Ruby straight by, snubbing both her – and Daisy – totally. 'At least you can more or less keep out of each other's way.'

The early break for elevenses was a nightmare. While Jody took the twins down to the kitchens to get their food, Daisy and Ruby had to endure light chat at the table with Vi's husband Anthony, Michael and the many others attending the shoot – but also with Cornelius and Vanessa. Afterwards, the men went out for the second drive of the day.

Michael paused with Ruby in the hall.

'Did you know they were going to be here?' he asked her.

'Not until we got here, no.'

'You want to go home?'

'No. Not yet.' She did, but she didn't want to spoil his enjoyment. 'After dinner.'

'Rob will stay with you.'

'Yes,' said Ruby. 'Please.'

'Go and have a lie down in your room or something. Read a book. We'll have dinner, keep his lordship sweet, then we'll be away.'

Daisy had Jody put the twins down for their nap, and

gratefully she settled down for a quiet rest in her room. Ruby did the same, pleased to see that Rob was taking up station outside her door. She lay on the bed and listened to the distant crack of the guns and thought about being here, so close to Vanessa and Cornelius.

It had been a shock, seeing him in the flesh after all these years. He was still handsome, but bulkier, the lines of dissipation embedded on his face, his cheeks mottled with red spider veins. Too much wine, too much low living, she guessed. His hair was pure white now. He was still a huge presence, louder than anyone else in the room, charming on the surface – but deadly underneath. Ruby imagined that women still found him attractive. But where once she had felt an overwhelming tug of sexual desire for him, now all she felt was hatred and fear. When Ruby glanced at him during lunch, she saw her own hate mirrored in his eyes when he looked back at her.

He'd tried to have her killed, after all.

And next time, he might even succeed.

137

Ruby must have slept. When she next looked at the clock it said nearly one in the afternoon. She couldn't hear the guns any more. She got up, splashed water on her face, and stepped outside into the hall. Rob looked up at her.

'They've finished shooting then?' she said.

He nodded. 'The mist is getting heavier. The birds won't fly in this weather.'

Ruby crossed the hall and looked out of the window. The morning had dawned bright and clear, but now she could see Rob was right, a solid bank of grey cloud was settling overhead. There was no wind stirring the trees. Autumn was creeping in, moving by stealth.

'Take a break, Rob. You must be stiff as a board, sitting there,' said Ruby, starting down the stairs.

He stood up. 'Where are you going?'

'Just down to the kitchen to get a drink, I'll be back in a second.'

'OK. Don't stray further than that though.'

'I won't.'

Ruby was almost at the bottom of the stairs when Vi came in the front door in a raincoat. She tossed it aside and smiled when she saw Ruby there.

'Been having a walk in the grounds,' she said. 'Starting

to rain now, that misty horrible stuff that sinks right into you. Where are you off to?'

'The kitchen, for a cup of tea.'

'Come into the drawing room, I'll get some brought up.'

Moments later, Daisy came down and joined them. She looked flushed. 'Rob was looking for you,' she told Ruby. 'I told him I saw you coming in here. He's outside the door now.'

'Have you seen Vanessa?' asked Ruby as the three of them huddled around the fire, drinking their tea and eating biscuits.

Daisy shook her head. 'Think she's in her room. I haven't spoken to her. Don't even know what to say to her really. I suppose I could say, I think I understand why I was always such a disappointment to you now.'

'I'm sure you weren't,' said Vi.

'Oh, I was.' Daisy seemed about to speak, then she paused.

'It's all right,' said Ruby. 'Vi knows.'

Daisy relaxed. 'She hasn't even tried to talk to me, you know. Not once, all day. Neither has Pa, but he's just pissed off because things haven't gone exactly as he planned, for once. He's probably *shitting* himself for fear any of this about you being my mother will get near the papers. And I bet Simon's told him it's all over between us. Actually, you know what? I think Mother's *relieved* it's all come to light at last. Oh God, I'm still calling her Mother . . .'

Now they could hear cars coming up the drive.

'That's it, shooting's over for the day,' sighed Vi.

'Good,' said Daisy. 'I hate the noise of the guns. And the poor birds falling to earth, dead,' she added with a shudder.

They went out to the front of the house. About fifty brace of pheasant were being laid out on the lawn, ready for a photo. All the men with guns were lining up behind the birds, ready for the snap to be taken. Anthony did the honours with his Leica. The flash illuminated the gloom of the afternoon.

'Come on, you lot,' said Vi, 'let's go inside and get warmed up.'

138

Brandy, coffee, sandwiches and pies had been laid out on the table in the main hall, and the fire there had been lit. Having done her duty, Vi left her husband Lord Albemarle to entertain his male guests. Vanessa still hadn't put in an appearance, so Vi escorted all the other women into the drawing room with Daisy and Ruby.

The afternoon wound on.

It wasn't until everyone was in their rooms dressing for dinner much later that Rob tapped on Ruby's door. She was in her dressing gown. She'd done her hair and make-up and was just laying out her black velvet dress on the bed. Michael was in the shower.

Ruby opened the door. Rob was standing there, beside a white and distraught-looking Vanessa. Her pale eyes fastened on Ruby.

'Vanessa?' she said, surprised.

'Is he with you?' demanded Vanessa, thin-lipped and quivering.

'What?'

'Cornelius. I haven't seen him since the men came back.'

'He's not with me. Of course he's not.'

Michael was stepping out of the bathroom, a towel around his waist. Ruby glanced back at him.

'What's going on?' he asked.

'Vanessa. She can't find Cornelius. You haven't seen him?'

'Didn't he come back with Anthony in the Jeep?'

'I didn't see him down in the hall with the others,' said Rob.

'Neither did I,' said Michael. 'Rob, go and tap on Anthony's door, see if he knows where he's got to.'

Rob went off along the hall. An uneasy silence fell as Vanessa stood there, staring at Ruby.

They heard Rob talking to Anthony, then Vi came to Ruby's door, looked at Vanessa, looked at Ruby and Michael.

'Cornelius came back with Anthony, didn't he?' asked Michael.

'No. He didn't. Wasn't he in with you?' asked Vi.

Michael shook his head. Rob came back along the hall and said: 'Did *anyone* see him come back from the shoot? Was he out on the lawn when Anthony was taking the picture?' he asked Vi.

Vi stared around at them all. 'No. I don't think he was.'

'Then where *is* he?' said Vanessa.

They all looked across the hall to the windows. Outside, it was nearly dark and the rain was starting to come down harder.

139

Within half an hour they had checked with the shooting party and their companions and the household staff: no one had seen Cornelius since they'd all returned to the house. He hadn't come back in anyone's car. Maybe he'd walked back? It seemed unlikely. But it was possible. So they checked all over the house. Cornelius wasn't there, or outside in the grounds immediately around it.

By the time that was done, it was full dark. Anthony summoned his gamekeeper, who had come up to the house and was now contacting all the beaters. No one had seen Cornelius return from the shoot. Some of them had seen him shooting, yes: but since then, nothing.

'He's still out there then,' said Michael.

The elderly Anthony was looking very upset. 'This is dreadful,' he said. 'I feel responsible. I hope no harm has come to him.'

'Of course it hasn't,' said Vi briskly. 'The silly sod's just wandered off and missed his ride, that's all. He's probably stumbling around in the undergrowth trying to find his way back to the house right now. Don't worry, Vanessa, I'm sure he's perfectly all right.'

All the men put on their coats, took as many torches as they could find, and set off to look for him in the cars. When they got near to where the beaters had flushed the prey from the woods, they left the cars with the headlights still ablaze and set out on foot, spreading out in twos and threes. The rain was coming down harder, pelting their heads.

Rob and Michael were in the woods now, brambles tearing at their clothes, but the trees gave some shelter from the rain.

'What's that?' asked Michael, pointing along the torch-light's wavering beam.

Rob looked. '*Shit!*' he said loudly.

It was blood.

140

'Over here!' shouted Rob, and they could hear the others coming, crashing through the undergrowth.

Rob and Michael crept forward. It *was* blood. A big thick smear of it, spread over the ground like a slug's trail, saved from dissolving in the rain by the overhanging trees. Rob directed the torch's beam on it, and followed it.

The two men moved forward, neither saying a word. The trail went on for twenty yards. Soon the others joined them, put their torch beams on it too. It glowed cherry-red, startling against the tired-looking greenery.

'Fuck!' said the gamekeeper, a robust, red-faced countryman who had kept them laughing all day. Now he looked as if he was about to cry with dismay.

The trail had ended.

There was a large man's body sprawled out on the ground. He had crawled a long way, weakened by blood loss, trying to get help until finally his strength had run out. His right leg was gone, shot away above the knee. All that remained of it was a powder-blackened jagged gaping wound. They could clearly see the stump of the bone in the torchlight, the pulverized crimson muscle surrounding it.

It was Cornelius.

The gamekeeper surged forward, fell to his knees beside the body. He put a hand to the big, bullish neck. 'He's alive,' he said, and took off his scarf. 'Somebody help me here.'

Rob went and helped the keeper tie the tourniquet on the leg. Cornelius groaned faintly.

'He'll die out here in the cold and wet, we have to get him back to the house,' said the keeper.

The men surged forward and hefted Cornelius upright. He was big, it was a hell of a job. Somehow, gasping and straining, they got him back to the Jeep and laid him out in the back. Then they all got in their cars, and sped back up to the house.

141

Ruby couldn't believe what she was seeing when they carried Cornelius into the hall. Pandemonium broke out. Vanessa collapsed in hysterics. Daisy looked like she was about to be sick. The men shoved past the women and heaved him on into the drawing room, leaving spatters of blood all over the marble flooring of the hall and wet globs of it on the drawing-room carpets. Someone was on the phone, summoning an ambulance.

Ruby stood silent and appalled as her ex-lover was carried past her. The hot metallic scent of blood filled her nostrils and she gagged, clapping a hand over her mouth. Vanessa's tortured shrieks seemed to scour her brain out like a knife. Daisy reached out for Vanessa and held her tight. All the other women were standing around the hall with shocked expressions. Their husbands and boyfriends were talking in hushed tones, explaining what had happened.

'It must have been an accident. He shot himself and then tried to crawl to get help.'

'*How* could it be an accident? He wasn't a fool. Cornelius knew how to carry a gun, keep it broken.'

'It was lucky we found him. Another hour out there, he'd have been a goner.'

'You're not suggesting someone *shot* him, for God's sake? That's ridiculous.'

Then there was a commotion from inside the drawing room.

'Shit!' yelled someone in there. 'His heart's stopped.'

Vanessa tore herself from Daisy's encircling arms. Ruby and Vi ran after her as she hared into the room. They stopped in the doorway, stricken with horror at what they were seeing. Rob was pounding Cornelius's chest with hands that were slippery with blood. Then he was bending, pinching the nose, breathing hard into his mouth. Then again the pounding, each thump reverberating in all their heads. Then the breathing. Then back to the chest. Then the breathing again.

Vanessa was silent now, standing feet away from her husband, unable to help him, tears rolling down her face.

Finally, Rob stopped what he was doing. He turned, looked at Michael, at Anthony.

'No good,' he said.

Vanessa sank to the floor in a dead faint.

142

The police found Cornelius's gun near the edge of the woods. It had been discharged, but then so had *all* the guns. A detective inspector arrived early next morning and everyone was interviewed after a miserable sleepless night, one at a time, to give their account of events. When Michael and Ruby had been questioned, they went out into the grounds for some air.

The weather was brighter now, and a robin was singing up near the house wall as they walked, wrapped up against the early-morning chill. Ruby felt sad and sickened. Once she'd loved Cornelius so much, but he had trampled on that love and ruined it. Hatred had taken its place. On her part and, more violently, on his.

But now she was truly free for the first time in her life. She wouldn't need to be frightened any more, wondering where the next assault would come from. Cornelius was dead. And with him, any threat he once posed.

'This is bad for Daisy, losing her dad like this,' said Michael as they walked, leaving tracks in the dew on the grass.

'I know.'

'The police seem to think it was accidental, though.'

Ruby stopped walking. 'Do they?'

'Yeah. So the DI said.'

Ruby looked at him. 'Cornelius has been shooting for years.'

'So he can't make a mistake? Come on, Ruby. Anyone can.'

'Is that what it was meant to look like? A mistake?'

Michael looked at her in consternation. 'What are you saying?'

'Michael, did you do it? Please tell me.' Ruby's eyes were suddenly filled with tears. This had been tormenting her ever since they'd carried Cornelius into the hall yesterday. 'I'm going mad here. You were so angry with him, at what he'd had done to me. I'm afraid you killed him. In that slow, horrible way. I think *you* shot his leg away and let him bleed to death.'

Michael eyed her thoughtfully.

'You know what?' he said at last. 'That's what he deserved. I really believe that. He was a callous, pompous bastard full of his own self-importance. But no, Ruby, I didn't kill him.'

'Do you swear?'

'Honey. On my life. On *yours*, if you like. I didn't kill Cornelius.'

Michael was telling the truth. He hadn't finished off Cornelius, much as he would have liked to. There were other things he couldn't, wouldn't ever, tell her. Like he was never going to tell her that her brother Charlie's 'accident' hadn't been an accident at all. Ruby was never going to know that. But maybe she deserved to know just a little more about this.

'I did see him after he was shot,' he admitted.

Her eyes widened in horror. 'Oh, Michael, you didn't.'

'I was on the next stand to him and I saw him go off into the woods – for a piss, I thought. He took his gun with him. I heard a shot – I heard *lots* of shots – but I thought one came from that direction. No one was near to us, so I went to have a look.'

'And you saw him?'

'Yeah. I did. Crawling along the ground, bleeding.'

'And you didn't help him.'

'*Help* him?' Michael let out a mirthless laugh. 'Ruby. I didn't kill him, OK? But you know what? I really wanted to whack that bastard, for all he's done to you. He knocked you up when you were young and stupid and sucked in by his charming ways. Then he dumped you and took Daisy off you. He never gave a *shit* about what happened to Kit because of the colour of his skin. And because you tried to befriend Daisy, he started waging war on you.' Fire flared in Michael's eyes. 'So no, Ruby. In answer to your question. I *didn't* help him.'

Ruby was silent, thinking of Cornelius alone and weakening, crying for help that never came. And Michael, watching him drag himself along through the woods. Not helping, as Cornelius's life slipped away.

'But there was something else,' said Michael.

Ruby snapped back to the present. 'What?'

'I saw someone moving away through the woods. He turned and stared me full in the face. He wasn't one of the beaters, he wasn't the gamekeeper or one of the guests.'

'What did he look like?'

'Young. Dark-haired. He looked straight at me, and then he walked away, out of the woods, and disappeared. If I saw him again, I'd recognize him.'

'Did you tell the police that?'

Michael shrugged. 'No. And I'm not going to.'

'Don't you think you should?' asked Ruby.

Michael stared at her face. He leaned forward, kissed her lips.

'No,' he said against her mouth. 'Justice has been done. That's good enough for me.'

143

Andrew Dorley was waiting at the station in Oxford for the train back to Leicester when he saw the papers on the newsstand announcing the shocking sudden death of the celebrated Tory peer Baron Bray. With shaking hands he picked one up, dropped the coins on the counter. Found a seat and slumped down upon it. Read the front-page news.

Cornelius Bray had died of gunshot wounds on a shooting weekend. The police were making their enquiries, but at the moment the cause of death appeared to be accidental. Andrew folded up the paper and sat there, patiently waiting for his train, ignoring the crowds, the booming noise of the tannoy.

'Oh – *Christ*,' he muttered, then he put a hand to his mouth, stifling a sudden, almost unstoppable laugh. He thought of his little brother Sebastian, and hoped that he would one day see him again. He didn't hold out much hope, though.

He thought of his mother, on pills for severe depression ever since Sebby left home, the awfulness of her failed suicide attempt. And his father, who had tried so hard to find Sebby. Dad had come back from London with a broken jaw and cracked ribs; black and blue all over from a savage beating administered by someone who said he wasn't to pester Lord Bray any more. Dad had never been the same, not since the day he'd walked back through the door. His kidneys had been damaged beyond repair and finally, just a few months ago, Dad had died.

After that, Andrew had been on a mission of vengeance, tracking Bray's movements. Sebby seemed to have vanished from the face of the earth and he *knew* that somehow Bray was involved in that. So he'd watched him, and followed him. Maybe he had Sebby locked away somewhere, who knew?

He'd followed Cornelius Bray to the shooting party in Oxfordshire. Approached him in the woods. There had been a scuffle when Andrew had demanded answers. Bray had dropped his gun.

'You don't know what you're dealing with, boy,' Bray had snapped at him when he had asked about Sebby. But he had seen the guilty panic in Bray's eyes as he bent to retrieve his weapon.

There had been a moment when Andrew could, *should*, have snatched up the gun. But he didn't. 'You *bastard*,' he burst out. 'You know something, don't you? Just tell me where he is. Tell me what's happened to him.'

But Bray was back in control. He lifted the gun, pointed it at Andrew.

'Fuck off,' said Cornelius flatly.

Something in the imperious way Bray said that made the red rage envelop Andrew's brain. Instead of backing away, he'd charged forward, grabbing the gun, forcing it down. Bray shouted something, but Andrew was deaf and blind with fury.

The gun went off.

Andrew stumbled back, shocked.

He heard Bray's gurgling groan of agony and he saw . . . oh Jesus, he saw . . .

Even now his mind flinched away from the blood, the

hideousness of it all. He wasn't a violent man. He could never hurt anyone, but now . . .

He'd backed away, then he'd seen the other man coming into the woods. All that was in his mind then was escape. He'd run away, out of the woods, down the hill, out onto the road. Shaking and sick, he'd gone back to the bed and breakfast and spent a sleepless, wretched night there. In the morning, in a frenzy of panic, he'd packed up his clothes, paid his bill. Then he'd gone to the train station, bought his ticket home.

And now here it was, in the newspaper.

Bray was *dead*.

Soon, his train was announced over the tannoy. Andrew stood up, stretching. Felt the weight of it all suddenly drop from his shoulders, leaving him lighter, cleaner. He dumped the paper in a waste bin, and went to catch his train home.

144

Cornelius Bray was buried on a breezy October day in the family plot beside his mother and his father, Sir Hilary. Many people attended the ceremony. His son Kit didn't, but Daisy did, feeling it was only fair that she should be there to support Vanessa.

'I can't believe he's gone,' Daisy said to Vanessa when the ceremony was finished.

'Neither can I,' said Vanessa, looking frail, bewildered and washed-out in funereal black.

'Shall I come back to the house with you?' asked Daisy. She couldn't take it in. Her father, that huge presence, was gone, never to return.

'No, darling,' said Vanessa with a faint smile. She took Daisy's hand in hers, hesitated, then said: 'I always tried to be a good mother to you, Daisy. I tried so hard. But I just couldn't deal with the fact that you weren't my child. I thought I would be able to, but I couldn't. And that was very unfair on you.'

Daisy felt horribly choked all of a sudden. 'I know you did your best.'

'I did. I hope I did. Even though you were never truly mine. You were Ruby's,' said Vanessa.

Daisy felt the tears spill over. She'd been crying buckets

over her father. She *knew* he'd been a bastard. She knew he'd lied to her. But he was the only father she'd had and she'd loved him. And now, he was gone.

'Shh, don't cry,' said Vanessa, and wiped a tear away from Daisy's cheek. 'It's never very comfortable, is it, living a lie? Now the truth's out, it will all get easier. Goodbye then, darling.'

Daisy kissed Vanessa's cheek lightly.

Vanessa turned and walked away.

'Wait,' Daisy called after her.

Vanessa halted, turned.

'Can I come to see you at the house sometime? Would you mind that?'

Vanessa gave a faint smile. 'No. I'd like that very much.'

'I'll phone you.'

'Yes. All right,' said Vanessa, and walked on.

When Vanessa got home to Brayfield, she had a cup of tea and then changed out of her funeral clothes and into jeans, a T-shirt and her old Barbour. She stepped out of the boot room at the back of the house, and went out into the pale autumn sunshine to join Ivan. He was working down in the orchard, gathering up the fallen apples to try out the cider press she'd purchased back in the spring.

Ivan saw her coming, and smiled. She was such a great lady, and married to such a bastard. But not any more. Now she was free of all that, and he was glad.

'Hello, Ivan,' said Vanessa with a faint ghost of her usual smile. Lovely Ivan, with his bushy beard and his whip-like strength; she felt so comfortable, so happy, when she was with him in the garden.

'How'd it go?' he asked.

'Awful,' she said.

A silence fell.

Then Ivan said gently: 'I've set the press up. Come and see.'

Vanessa nodded, and followed Ivan down to the barn.

145

'The coroner's returned a verdict of accidental death,' said Michael. 'I phoned Kit this morning, he told me.'

Ruby turned and stared at him. They were strolling along the wide sandy beach on St Brelade's Bay in Jersey. Michael had a house here and they had spent the weekend together there. It was a cold, starkly bright November day, and they were wrapped up in quilted coats against the gusting wind and the salty tang of the surf.

'Right,' she said.

Ruby didn't believe Cornelius's death had been accidental, but it was a relief that the law thought it was. She'd feared that Michael might be dragged into it all. Now she could breathe again.

'Early flight tomorrow,' said Michael.

Ruby kissed his cheek. 'Back to work,' she sighed.

'It's been a great weekend,' said Michael.

It had. They had made love last night, sweetly, gently; and had slept easy the whole night long.

'I love you, Michael,' she said.

He put his arm around her shoulder. 'Love you too, babe,' he said, and kissed her.

The following day Michael was back at his desk behind the restaurant, sorting out paperwork, writing a few letters, phoning his old mate Reg, his former number one man, who had shown Kit the ropes when he was a wet-behind-the-ears scruffy little bugger with a big mouth and no sense. The contract he'd had in partnership with Tito on the Albert Docks was completed now, all the units sold. Thank God *that* was finished.

Ruby popped in at lunchtime. They had a light lunch together in the restaurant. Then Kit came in, and Ruby seemed to freeze in her chair.

Michael beckoned him over, but to Ruby's dismay Kit took one look at her sitting there, turned on his heel and went out again.

'Jesus, that boy,' said Michael, shaking his head.

'It's OK,' said Ruby, though it killed her inside. 'He's got every right to feel the way he does.'

Michael gazed at her. 'D'you think he'll forgive you? Someday?'

Ruby gave a wan smile. 'Honestly? No. I don't.'

That afternoon, Michael paid a long-overdue visit to Tito. His younger brothers were there too, Fabio and Vittore – handsome thugs with dead eyes and big attitudes.

'My friend,' gushed Tito, throwing his arms wide.

'You're not my friend, Tito,' said Michael with a cool smile. 'And I'm not yours. We've done business together, but that's at an end now.'

Tito's arms fell to his side. His ice-blue eyes were watchful. 'And now . . . ?' he prompted.

'Now I have to tell you that I know you've been hounding Ruby Darke as a favour to that shit Cornelius Bray.'

'Oh yes?' Tito didn't deny it. 'But then . . . my poor old friend Cornelius is dead now. So sad.' It *was* sad for Tito. He'd cultivated Cornelius for so many years, holding those incriminating photos over his head like an axe to ensure his cooperation. Lord Bray had been *so* useful. So influential. Such a pity he was gone.

'That's true.' Michael's eyes were hard. 'You've been pushing your luck over this, abusing my good nature because of our connection. But it stops now. If you or any of your boys go near her ever again, then you'll force me to do what I really don't want to and I'll have to slit your fucking throat *personally*, do you understand?'

Tito held up his hands. 'Michael, believe me . . .'

'That's the point, right there: I *don't* believe you. But you'd better believe me. I mean it. All bets are off now. Clear?'

Tito nodded, very slowly.

Michael left, leaving Tito staring at the closed door.

Tito knew that Michael Ward was a man of honour. That he'd been forced to hold back out of respect, putting old values before personal gratification. But Tito wasn't a man of honour. He was a man of *action*.

Fabio stirred. 'He's got some fucking front, talking to you like that.'

'Yeah,' said Tito. He glanced at Fabio. At Vittore. His younger brothers were watching him, hungry as jackals. They weren't honourable men, either. One sign of weakness, and they would go for the jugular, to hell with family. Push him aside, take over.

'So what are you gonna do about it?' demanded Vittore.

Tito said nothing. His tilted his head towards the door, and slowly drew his hand across his throat.

His brothers smiled.

Then they followed Michael.

Ruby went back to work after lunch. There was always stuff to attend to. Jane had scheduled meetings for her with catering consultants this afternoon. The plan was to open coffee bars in five of the stores as a test; if it was successful, then the bars would be run out all through the chain.

'You have a nice weekend with that man of yours?' asked Jane, handing Ruby letters to sign.

'Just wonderful,' said Ruby.

She didn't hear the devastating news until the next day.

146

It was Rob who had broken the news to her. He'd got a call from Kit.

She would never forget it.

She had sat there, frozen in shock, while Rob with tears in his eyes said that Michael had been found dead in an alley with a bullet through his brain.

'No,' Ruby had shaken her head. '*No.*'

But it was true. Michael was dead.

'My God, all I seem to do lately is attend funerals,' said Vi with a shudder. 'My poor Ruby. How terrible this is. Still got the gorilla in tow, I see.'

Ruby glanced back at Rob, who was standing close by.

They were huddling out of the sleety rain in the shelter of the lychgate at the church. There were huge crowds here today – bigger than those who had attended the burial of Cornelius, Ruby noticed. Not that she cared. Not that she cared about *anything*, any more.

Michael's funeral was over. It had been a simple affair, with the coffin covered in white hothouse roses. All his boys had attended. Rob. Kit. All the rest of them. Even Reg, who had retired from the game long ago. And all Michael's business contacts and friends.

Vi was hugging Ruby, enveloping her in a cloud of Devon Violets.

'Ruby?' It was Daisy, rushing up. Vi stepped aside. Daisy hugged Ruby hard. 'It's just so terrible. I loved Michael,' she said, sobbing, smudging her mascara.

Kit had been one of the pall-bearers. Ruby watched him throughout; her beautiful son. He looked awful, almost grey with strain. Her heart had gone out to him. But his eyes had passed over her like she was not there.

'I'm glad I left the twins at home with Jody,' Daisy was saying. 'I couldn't bring them to this, it's too sad.'

Joe was there to pay his respects, with Betsy, Nadine and Billy. Betsy had said a tense hello, and Joe had given her a brotherly hug. Apart from that, they hadn't spoken.

The crowds jostled them. Kit was standing just over there – so close, yet a million miles away.

Kit was watching Tito. The fat sadistic fuck was here, and when he caught sight of Kit he gave him a big toothy grin. Kit's fists clenched. *That bastard.* A sickening vision of Gilda swam into Kit's head. He didn't know who had pulled the trigger on Michael, but he knew how Tito had been terrorizing Ruby, and he knew how furious Michael had been over that. He knew from Reg that Michael had visited Tito the day before his death, to give the wop one last warning over the Ruby situation, in case it should drift on even though Bray was out of the picture now.

He was drawing his own conclusions, and none of them were good.

For God's sake, Michael, why didn't you let me do it? he wondered furiously. Tito had become a ticking time bomb, they had both known that. So *why* hadn't Michael let him defuse the bastard, once and for all? He would never understand it. *Never.*

The moving crowds had jostled Daisy away from Ruby so that she was standing by Rob.

'Your mascara's all over your face,' he said, giving her a handkerchief.

'Is it . . . ?' asked Daisy vaguely. She rubbed at her sore eyes.

'You missed a bit,' said Rob. 'It's . . . oh fuck it, keep still,' he said, and wet his finger and tidied her up.

'This is so sad,' cried Daisy. Rob noted that the buttons on her black cardigan were undone and it was falling off one shoulder, almost exposing a breast. He didn't stare: he didn't want to embarrass her. 'Poor Ruby . . .'

'I know it's fucking awful. But at least it was quick,' said Rob, his voice breaking.

Daisy looked up at him curiously. She'd thought he was just another mound of muscle like the others that had surrounded Michael, but it was clear he had feelings too. He had nice straight dark-blond hair, and those sexy khaki-green eyes, and actually his mouth was rather nice . . .

'What?' asked Rob. She was utterly gorgeous, and endearingly dippy. He couldn't keep his eyes off her.

'Nothing,' said Daisy, starting to blush.

Seeing Rob was occupied with Daisy, Ruby moved over to where Kit was standing alone.

'Kit?' she said. 'Are you all right?'

Kit turned and stared at her. 'What?' he asked, his face like granite.

'This must be horrible for you,' she said. 'Michael and you were so close.'

'You think I want your sympathy?' he said coldly. He was in agony here over Michael. He wished so much that Michael had let *him* sort Tito. Then this wouldn't have happened.

Ruby swallowed hard. 'Kit . . . I just wanted to say something to you.'

'What?'

'That whoever did this . . .' She gulped again, hardly able to get the words out. '*Whoever* it was, I want them to pay. Do you understand?'

Kit stared at her. 'They'll pay,' he said at last.

'I just think—' started Ruby.

'No. That's enough. I don't care what else you *just think*,' he snapped. 'I don't want to hear a damned *thing* from you.'

And he walked away, into the crowds.

Ruby stood there, bereft, remembering Michael's words to her on the beach where they had been so happy.

Do you think he'll ever forgive you?

And her answer: *No. I don't.*

147

It was after Christmas, in the grey January doldrums, when
Kit was summoned to Michael's solicitor's office.

'What for?' he asked in surprise when he took the call.

'For the reading of Mr Ward's will,' said the receptionist.
'How does Tuesday suit you, Mr Miller? Two o'clock?'

The reading of the *will*? Kit agreed the appointment and
put the phone down and looked around his flat, not seeing
a thing. He had thought all that was over and done with.
He had *thought* Michael would leave everything he owned
to Ruby Darke. Of course she would be there on Tuesday
to scoop the jackpot. He felt himself bristle at the thought
of it, being closeted in an office with her, forced to be polite
when all he wanted was to throttle her.

But what the hell. He'd be there. And he'd try to resist
the urge, he really would. But only for Michael's sake.

Ruby wasn't there. No one else was, apart from him and
the young chubby solicitor, who smiled a lot and kept pushing
his glasses back up his nose when they slipped down. The
man read out the will, and twenty minutes later Kit reeled
out of the solicitor's office clutching a letter that Michael
had requested be delivered into his hands today.

Michael had left him everything. His businesses. His properties. ╱

Everything.

He went home to the flat and sat there on the couch with the letter in his hands. He was in a state of shock. He had never expected any of this.

He looked down at the letter. Then with slightly unsteady hands he slit the top, pulled it out. Unfolded it. It said:

Kit,

Everything I have, it's yours. But there are three conditions.

One, you've got to look after your sister Daisy. She's a sweet girl but she's a fruitcake, you know that. She'll need some guidance from you. Keep an eye on her. Make sure she's OK.

The second condition is harder. I know you've been hurt by all that's happened to you. But Ruby was in a mess, she couldn't help how everything panned out. She's a good woman, kind and strong. So it's my dearest wish that you should stop being an arsehole and give your mother a chance. You got that?

And finally on to the third. If I'm dead and that small matter we discussed hasn't been handled, I owe you at least an explanation. My wife Sheila knew how I felt about Tito; I always hated him. But he was her kin. Tito's mother Bella was Sheila's mother's sister – Sheila's aunt. I swore to Sheila I'd never cause pain to Bella over Tito, and I've held to that – even though the bastard hasn't returned the favour. He's been cashing in on the family connection for years, and so what I'm saying is this: I can't sort it. Can't bring myself to do it. How could I do that, break my word, kill Bella's son, inflict that kind of pain on her?

But Kit – if you want to, it's up to you. You can handle it.

Your decision.

OK, boy?

Be happy.

Love

Michael

Kit let the letter fall into his lap. His eyes were wet. He leaned his head back on the sofa and thought about it all. Daisy. Ruby. And him – the nameless abandoned boy who'd fought his way up from nothing. He was boss of the manor now. Now he understood why Michael had held him back for so long. But now the decision was his to make. Michael could rest easy.

''Bye, boss,' he murmured into the silence of the flat. He let the tears come then. His real father, that bastard Bray, went unmourned, but his *true* father, Michael Ward, would never ever be forgotten. 'I love you, boss,' he said.

Maybe somewhere Michael heard him.

Maybe not.

But he hoped so.

148

The launch of the select docklands development was going with a bang. At eight in the evening, nearly five hundred people were crammed into the marquee out on the square. There was a model of the whole thing, set out in the entrance lobby of the refurbished cotton warehouse, and VIPs were cooing over it, then going up and down in the lifts to marvel at the apartments with their stunning river views.

It was planned that later there would be designer shops, restaurants, a docklands railway – all the things needed to live the 'café society' life. There were drinks, nibbles and hostesses shimmying around among the jostling crowds, handing out smiles and nourishment. The noise and laughter both inside the building and out was deafening.

All Kit had to do was wait in the shadows, and watch.

He was watching Tito. Tito was surrounded by his heavies. Kit recognized some of them. Particularly the black-haired one, too bulky to move very fast, who had been there on the night Gilda died and Tito burned him.

All Kit had to do was wait. Drink would be taken. This was a social occasion, after all. No danger here.

By eleven thirty things were getting sloppy. People falling around the worse for drink. That was good.

Kit waited.

Now the crowds were dispersing, everyone heading home.

Giggling and stumbling on the cobbles, they were making for their cars, for taxis, for the Tube.

Twelve fifteen.

No Tito.

Twelve twenty.

Ah. There he was.

Kit, dressed in a black tracksuit with the hood pulled up, adjusted the black scarf over the lower half of his face. His heartbeat picked up as he moved forward, on a straight line of interception with Tito.

Tito's minders – three of them – were moving ahead. Tito himself, fat and prosperous-looking, was following yards behind, smoking a cigar and pulling on his coat. Kit saw the bright glint of Tito's grey beard and his crew-cut hair in the dim sodium glare of the overhead lights, then Tito passed into heavy shadow. The minders were chatting, unheeding, up ahead.

Now.

Kit moved in fast. Tito was confronted suddenly by a black figure, standing right in front of him. His eyes widened in shock. His mouth opened. Kit struck, driving the thin stiletto blade straight up between the third and fourth ribs, right into Tito's heart. Tito's mouth fell open further, his eyes stretching wide in his head.

'*Not smiling now, are you, Tito?*' whispered Kit, then he yanked the knife free.

Before Tito even hit the ground, Kit was gone, running flat-out, away.

Behind him, he heard Tito's boys start to shout.

Too late, boys. About a lifetime too late.

He ran all the way back to his car, parked over a mile away. Got in. Started the engine.

Job *done.*

EPILOGUE

Spring was coming. Birds were singing, the trees were in bud, the bright yellow daffodils were flowering in the garden. But in Ruby's heart, it was winter. She missed Michael so much. Even work, the thing that had sustained and absorbed her for so many years, seemed to give her no solace any more.

As usual, she went to the cemetery on Sunday to lay flowers on his grave. Daisy went with her. After she had come to Ruby's when Simon had attacked her, Daisy had never left. Rob had driven them to the cemetery. Jody was at home, with the twins.

'Come on,' said Ruby, taking Daisy's hand. 'I've got something to show you.'

While Rob waited at the gate, the two women walked over to a far corner of the graveyard. Ruby stopped in front of a moss-covered headstone.

'Look,' she said to Daisy.

Daisy read the wording on the stone. 'Alicia Darke?' she said aloud. 'Ted Darke?'

'Your grandmother and grandfather,' said Ruby.

She stared at the grave. All those years ago, it had been Ted's express wish that he be buried in the same grave as the wife who'd betrayed him. He *must* have loved her, somehow.

'Wow.'

'I never knew my mother. She died giving birth to me.'

'That's awful.'

Ruby looked at her daughter. *So* pretty, and so precious to her. She squeezed Daisy's hand.

'You look so like her.'

Ruby stared at the gravestone. Poor Ted. Cheated on by his young, flighty wife. Doomed to look a fool. Doomed to *act* like one, too. But Ruby couldn't feel angry about her sad upbringing any more. It had, after all, given her something to kick against, and look where that had taken her. Now she was Ruby Darke, head of an empire of her own making. And she had a wonderful daughter who might one day want to become involved in the business – maybe even take it over.

No Michael though.

And no Kit.

She had been in love just three times in her entire life. Once with Cornelius, then with her babies – and she had Daisy back, it was a miracle, but she had lost Kit and would never have another chance with him – and finally, blissfully, with Michael Ward.

Oh, Michael, I'll never forget you.

She had been cursed, but also very blessed. Kit's absence from her life was a constant nagging pain. But there was nothing to be done about that. His mind was made up.

Ruby let out a sigh. 'Come on,' she said. 'Let's go home.'

Rob had gone over to his flat above the garage block, and Jody had settled the twins down for their afternoon nap upstairs. Daisy and Ruby were in the small sitting room at the front of the house, watching an old Stewart Granger film and drinking tea. When they heard the car engine and the wheels crunching on the gravel outside, it was Daisy who stood up, stretching and yawning. She went to the window to see who it was.

'Oh,' she said, staring.

'What? Who is it?'

But Daisy just glanced at her and said nothing.

'Come on, don't keep me in suspense,' said Ruby, standing up and joining her at the window.

Ruby's breath caught in her throat as she saw the Bentley parked there. And then the driver got out and locked the car up.

Daisy was grinning now. Ruby felt as though all the breath had left her body.

'Well, aren't you going to open the door?' demanded Daisy.

Somehow Ruby got the use of her legs back. Her heart thudding in her chest, she crossed to the door, and went out into the hall. Sunlight was pouring through the stained-glass panels on either side of the front door, peppering the marble floor with blues, reds and golds. She was aware of Daisy following.

She took a deep, calming breath and opened the door.

Kit was striding up the path. As he saw her standing there, he paused. Yards apart, they stared at each other.

'I can't forgive you,' he said.

Ruby nodded. She didn't dare speak. She was terrified of breaking the spell, ruining the magic that had somehow – miraculously – brought him to her door.

'You gave me up. Abandoned me,' he said flatly.

'Yes,' she said, her heart hammering so violently that it was frightening.

'But Michael wanted me to give you a chance.'

Ruby swallowed hard. 'I see.'

'So I'm going to, OK? I'm going to try.'

'Right,' said Ruby. 'OK.'

They stared at each other. Daisy watched them, frozen, hardly able to draw breath.

Slowly, uncertainly, Ruby opened her arms wide.

Kit hesitated. Then he stepped forward and walked into his mother's embrace.

AUTHOR'S AFTERWORD

In 2006, I first read about mixed-race parents having twins of different colours and I was instantly fascinated. Although it's rare, this phenomenon of twins of radically different colour can – *has* – happened, when a parent is of mixed race. If a woman is of mixed race, her eggs will usually contain a mixture of genes coding for both black and white skin.

This got me thinking that such an accident of birth could be the subject for a book: then I imagined blonde, fair-skinned Daisy, and black-haired, dark-skinned Kit, separated at birth but meeting up later on. This book, *Nameless*, began to take shape from that.

Jessie Keane

extracts reading groups
competitions books new
discounts extracts extracts
competitions discounts
books new events
events books reading groups
extracts
new titles reading groups
interviews
events extracts
discounts
new books events
events new

www.panmacmillan.com

discounts extracts discounts
extracts events reading groups
competitions books extracts new